Purity

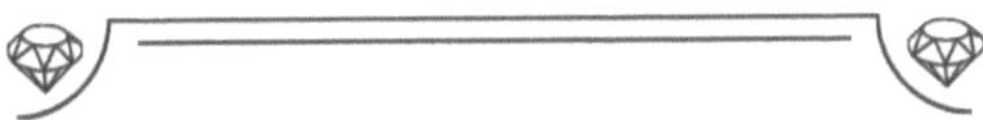

Diamonds of the First Water
Book Two

SYDNEY JANE BAILY

cat whisker press

Boston

Second Paperback Edition, 2024
ISBN 978-1-957421-54-4

Published by Cat Whisker Press

Cover: Dar Albert, Wicked Smart Designs
Book Design: Cat Whisker Studio
Editor: Chris Hall

DIAMONDS OF THE FIRST WATER

A Diamond for Christmas

Clarity

Purity

Adam

Radiance

Brilliance

OTHER WORKS

The RAKES ON THE RUN Series
Last Dance in London
Pursued in Paris
Banished to Brighton
Gretna Green by Sunset
The Lady Who Stole Christmas

The RARE CONFECTIONERY Series
The Duchess of Chocolate
The Toffee Heiress
My Lady Marzipan
The Gingerbread Lady

The DEFIANT HEARTS Series
An Improper Situation
An Irresistible Temptation
An Inescapable Attraction
An Inconceivable Deception
An Intriguing Proposition
An Impassioned Redemption

The BEASTLY LORDS Series
Lord Despair
Lord Anguish
Lord Vile
Lord Darkness
Lord Misery
Lord Wrath
Lord Corsair
Eleanor

PRESENTING LADY GUS

THE BLACK KNIGHT'S REWARD
with Marliss Melton

DEDICATION

To all those who are willing
to take a chance on love

I salute you, the risk takers!

INTRODUCTION TO
DIAMONDS OF THE FIRST WATER

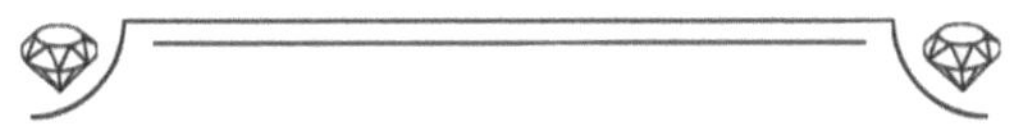

Once upon a time, an Irish family by the name of O'Diamáin emigrated to England from the north of Ireland, from County Doire to be specific. You may know the area as Derry or even Londonderry if you are thinking of it after King James I granted the city a royal charter.

Felim O'Diamáin, who was the youngest son, sailed across the Irish Sea to make his fortune, bringing his pretty wife and two young children with him. As the story goes, they stopped on the Isle of Man for a perfectly peaceful night before landing at Ravenglass the next day and traipsing through the Lake District.

Another version swears they took the shorter but far more dangerous route north across the sea to Portpatrick, finding themselves in the southernmost part of Scotland. From there, if they indeed came that way, they headed east toward Gretna Green. Not for any quick anvil marriage, mind you, but to traverse the border to England.

No one knows for sure the veracity of either tale, nor particularly cares. Once they arrived in England, Felim did very well for himself, as did his descendants.

At some point during the twelve-year reign of George I, another O'Diamáin by the name of Liam was made an earl for his devoted service to the Crown. During those years in the early eighteenth century, King George also created a few dukes, at least one marquess, some barons, a single viscount, and other earls. But we're not interested in any of them, although some may have helped to quell the riots that ensued when Hanoverian George outmaneuvered any pesky residual Stuarts hoping to claim the English throne.

Nevertheless, our interest lies with Liam. With his new earldom came much wealth and land, specifically in Derbyshire. And naturally, a title. However, George I, being of Germanic descent, didn't find the Celtic name of O'Diamáin tripped easily off his tongue. Neither did he master Gaelic or Manx, for that matter. In any case, with a little persuasion and an extra thousand acres, Liam became William, the Earl Diamond, as his male descendants have been known ever since.

Over the years, the earls have enlarged the original house to be an impressive manor, always named Oak Grove Hall, which is the translation of their long-ago home of County *Doire*.

Generations later, while inheriting the earldom and all its assets, Geoffrey, Lord Diamond and his beloved wife, Caroline, have wealth of a different nature as well—five healthy children: Clarity, Purity, Adam, Radiance, and Brilliance. They are known as the Diamonds of the First Water, at least by their parents.

This is Purity's story . . .

CHAPTER ONE

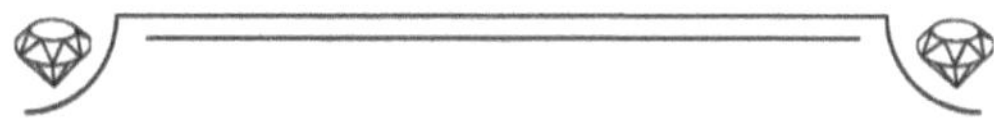

London, 1848

"You received my missive," came a smooth masculine voice behind Lady Purity Diamond, making a shiver race down her silk-clad spine.

Purity knew beyond a doubt she ought not to have strayed from the well-lit and crowded ballroom at the Marquess of Lansdowne's house on the south end of Berkeley Square. It was unlike her to do anything out of the acceptable and customary. Anyone who knew her would agree.

However, her entire day had been a little off-kilter, and she blamed her odd, restless mood upon its earlier events. She had slept poorly, awakened late, and lost a favorite glove by noon. When getting ready for the ball, she'd had a mishap with the hair curler.

Or rather, her maid, Alice, had the mishap, but it was Purity who suffered the disastrous effects of a too-hot papillote iron with a dreadfully singed curl that smelled of burned hair and pomade.

When someone else's rickety-wheeled carriage blocked passage along Berkeley Street, causing her and her mother to be later than was fashionable, she knew she would welcome the next day's dawn. Before that, however, she wanted to enjoy everything the evening offered.

Thus, it had been a great disappointment when her friend Harriet told her she'd missed the unveiling of a costly new painting in the marquess's drawing room.

Determined not to leave without seeing it since there would not be another ball at Lansdowne House that Season, Purity left her mother chatting with one of her fondest acquaintances. While knowing she ought to wait for Harriet, who was upon the dance floor, as it was the last dance and the ball would end along with the music, Purity went alone.

Despite having seen the drawing room once the year before, she paused in the entrance, admiring the robin's egg blue walls and the bold mauve band of color under the chair rail. Shining gilded accents were everywhere, amplifying the Etruscan design, right up to the patterns on the cream-and-pale pink ceiling, which, if studied long enough, would give one a neck ache.

The painting she sought was over the fireplace. Everyone that night was cheering it as a triumph. For a closer look, Purity crossed the polished floor onto the thick carpet, which muffled her steps as she approached the west wall and the marble mantle.

With two lamps still lit, she admired the masterpiece first from a few feet away and then moved closer to examine its detail. While glad she had managed to view the acquisition, she couldn't say she was particularly taken with it.

Another large work in a dark palette with very pale people reenacting some tragedy.

Maybe the painting would have seemed more interesting if Lord Lansdowne was presenting it.

And that's when it happened.

Interrupting her musing came the deep-timbered male voice and whomever it belonged to, speaking of a missive.

Taking a deep breath, standing as straight as possible to make herself a wee bit taller, Purity turned.

The attractiveness of the man observing her stole her breath as well as her senses. A rum duke if ever she saw one.

Who was he? How did she not know him?

"Good evening," she replied, keeping her tone calm, although in truth, she was a little afraid. This was the first time she'd ever been alone with a man who wasn't her father, brother, or one of their trusted family friends.

Although one of her brother's friends had kissed her, so perhaps he wasn't so trustworthy after all. Regardless, she'd never been on her own with an absolute stranger.

Impeccably dressed in black tails, slate gray trousers, and a vivid blue waistcoat, he approached her without responding, his eyes taking her in. He came to a stop beside her, turning his attention to the marquess's recent purchase.

Purity stared up at him, about to dart away now that he was no longer blocking her exit from the room. He was a head taller as most men were, since she and her older sister, Clarity, were both slightly below average. From the close proximity, she could tell his thick, coffee-colored hair was soft, and he had a little crimp in his earlobe. *How odd!*

Then he turned and looked down at her, and she nearly gasped aloud.

His eyes were amber, the color of golden toffee or a medium sherry. It might be a trick of the lighting, but their beauty mesmerized her, rendering her motionless. Moreover, the little shiver had become a sizable quiver.

"I was worried you would not receive my note in time to meet tonight or wouldn't be allowed entrance."

At these puzzling words from him, she shook her head. "I do not understand, my lord."

For the first time, he appeared uncertain, but he offered her a winsome smile. "You can read, can you not? Don't be ashamed if you can't. After all, I understand you do other things extraordinarily well."

With that, he reached out and lightly wrapped a gloved hand around each of her upper arms, drawing her closer.

Purity ought to be terrified, but he exuded charm and warmth, and was not the least bit threatening in manner. Moreover, the door was open, and his grip was loose. She could break away and be in the wide hallway in seconds.

So why wasn't she running?

"Of course I can read," she said, still captured by his amber gaze and wondering what else he thought she might do well.

He nodded. "How else would you know when to meet me?"

"I didn't—" she began.

He swooped down and claimed her mouth before she could finish. Firm, smooth lips pressed to hers, and all her senses narrowed down to what was directly before her.

The man tasted like brandy and smelled of a heady combination of orange blossom and something smoky and sensual, reminding her of the wooded vales near her family's country home in Derbyshire. She had never smelled the like.

More shocking, she'd never felt anything so sizzling as the sensations radiating from where his mouth and his fingers touched her. Scorching, simmering, sensual feelings.

When his kiss deepened, warming her and filling her head with his fragrance, Purity began to tremble. Her entire body seemed to be molten, especially low between her hips where she would vow she was turning to liquid.

His hands slid from her arms, where he'd undoubtedly crumpled the tops of her sleeves, to encircle her slender waist. Her belly tightened with a tingling sensation.

Then his strong fingers pressed into the small of her back, urging her against him. She tensed at this new impropriety, alarm bells clanging in her head like church chimes on a Sunday.

At her sudden stiffness, he raised his head, breaking the kiss and gazing down at her with a sultry smile.

Without thinking, she slapped him, wishing her soft satin evening glove hadn't slipped from his face without making any sort of resounding *thwack* that would make clear her indignation.

For despite having enjoyed his kiss—because obviously, he was experienced and the kiss itself was masterful—she knew it for a licentious liberty.

His golden eyes widened, and he released her, although he didn't step back.

"Now, now, kitten. That wasn't very nice. If you want to be my flogging-cully, you'll have to wait until I've stripped you bare. The most we can do here is enjoy a flyer, and if you can't wait until I take you home, then I will gladly oblige."

Looking around, he added, "Against that wall, I suppose, not against the Lansdowne's new prize painting."

Purity's mouth dropped as she understood he was suggesting an act of copulation.

"It'll have to be a flourish, my blue-eyed kitten," the stranger continued, "as quick as two goats for the ball is nearly over."

Ignoring the words she didn't understand, Purity locked on to the one she did.

"Kitten!" she exclaimed. "Did you truly call me kitten? Twice!"

He nodded, a wicked grin spreading over his ridiculously handsome face, displaying dimples. Pity she wanted to punch him in the nose if it were at all the ladylike thing to do. Perhaps a knee to his gut would suit better, if her gown allowed her such movement.

Or she would give him the cut direct next time they met. *That would teach him.*

"I shall have you know I am Lady Purity Diamond, and I—"

Before she could continue, he broke out in raucous laughter.

She clamped her mouth closed and crossed her arms, waiting for his amusement to reach its conclusion.

When it did, he shook his head. "Is that the name you're going by? That is a mouthful of deliciousness if ever I heard it."

Purity tilted her chin. "You are extremely impudent. There is nothing wrong with my name."

"Tell me, do you have a sister named Rare or Expensive?"

"That is not funny in the least. My sisters are Clarity—" She had to pause as he sniggered.

"And Brilliance—" She broke off again when he started to chuckle.

"And Radiance," she finished while he dissolved again into peals of laughter.

"No, stop please," he begged. "My sides are hurting. Is there, by any chance, a sister named Luster? For she will be the one for me. Lusty Diamond would be my ideal wench."

With those incorrigible words hanging in the air, Purity turned upon her heel and walked toward the door, the man's chortles still ringing in her ears.

In the doorway, another woman appeared, out of breath, wearing a gaudy scarlet satin gown and too much color upon her cheeks and lips. Knowing the frippery female to be a woman of easy virtue, Purity didn't acknowledge her, merely brushing past and out the open door.

Evidently, the scarlet woman was the one he'd intended to meet and to kiss. And what was the other thing he said? *Have a flyer?*

"Wretched rake!" Purity muttered under her breath, hurrying back to the ballroom.

MATTHEW WAS SORRY TO SEE the spitfire leave. Lady Purity was a passionate, gorgeous female without the savvy to know she ought not to have given him her name, not under any circumstances. She was lucky he was a gentleman. But what a dreadful mistake he'd made in thinking her a light-skirt.

When the actual high-flier with whom his friend had suggested an assignation sidled up, he sighed. She was a caricature of the desirable, petite woman he'd just kissed.

Just like that, he decided not to take what she was offering, not for any price. Instead, he apologized and strode out.

Perhaps he would catch Lady Purity still in the ballroom and . . . *and what?*

The last dance had concluded, and people were leaving. He could hardly go up to her without a formal introduction, nor was anyone likely to perform the necessary greeting when there were no more dances to enjoy.

Matthew would have to wait until the next event, glad he'd returned to London from two years on the Continent in time for the social Season. While he had put off finding a wife, for the first time, he had need of one. In his townhouse, tucked in bed in the makeshift nursery was a little girl for whom he now had sole responsibility.

A nanny was giving her all the necessary daily care, but a wife would be a proper mother to her, as long as he found the right one.

First, he had to win the heart of a decent lady who could see past his rather rakish reputation, and then he had to overcome any resistance she might have to raising someone else's child.

Matthew took another look around for Lady Purity but saw no lovely, dark-haired female wearing lapis-blue silk that matched her eyes. He shouldn't pin his hopes upon her. But despite having caught an unpleasant sulfuric aroma in her hair, the rest of her had smelled heavenly, like roses. She was as good a lady as any with whom to start his hunt. Not only had he felt an instant attraction, she had been interested in him, too, if her heated response was any indication.

The slap was a warning, a chastisement, but not an absolute sign of disinclination.

Humming to himself, Matthew went in search of a hackney to take him to his club. Usually assured of a friend most any time of the afternoon or evening at Boodle's, since it was after midnight, there would be only the bachelors.

"What, or rather who, has put that grin on your mug?" asked Lord Jasper Quinn, whom he'd known since his years at Cambridge.

Why not tell him? He was in such a good mood at having met a vision of a woman.

"Lady Purity," he began.

"The Diamond daughter?" His friend sounded incredulous.

When Matthew nodded, Quinn's shout of laughter elicited scowls from the less rambunctious gentlemen across the dining room.

"You have to be pulling my leg," he declared.

"Why?" Matthew asked. "You have eyes, don't you?"

"Yes, of course. She is a stunning wench, make no mistake. But you haven't been in London for nearly two years. She's our generation's answer to Mrs. Princum-Prancum, I dare say."

Not by their fiery kiss she wasn't, but Matthew would never disclose such a thing, except a few words to shut his friend's mouth.

"After all, you're the Fox, and you'll be hard put to gain any sport from her," Quinn continued.

Matthew did not care for that silly moniker.

"I found her to be an amusing female," he countered. "Not at all a prude."

Quinn's dark eyebrows shot up, and his eyes lit with interest. "Really? Do tell."

Now his friend was too curious.

"Mind your business. And I'll mind mine," he said.

His friend chuckled again. "I'll mind it, but I'll be on the watch for yours, too. And not only me, but *The Times* seems very interested in what the Bachelor Baron, recently returned from France, is up to."

"I noticed." It seemed someone was telling his every move. Before he had left for the Continent, he behaved similarly, enjoying willing widows and canary birds and occasionally an appealing married lady who begged for some companionship. Always discreet, he hadn't been written about any more than any other buck. Now however, he was in the paper every week.

"They will be even more interested if they hear you've set your scurrilous sights upon that Diamond girl," Quinn added. "Her elder sister snagged a viscount about a year ago. Just as pretty, but more given to laughter and merriment than the one currently circulating."

Matthew took a long sip of brandy. Purity Diamond's temperament had suited him fine, but he didn't want her name associated with his in *The Times. For her sake!* He didn't give a damn what they printed about him, especially since it was mostly true. He *was* a beard-splitter, and why not?

What else was a man to do before marriage?

However, seeing how her name was Purity, he thought it a great shame if she were smeared merely to sell papers. Sadly, he had no control—people tattled and whispered, and some even got paid for juicy stories.

"Don't say anything," he told Quinn, giving him a stern look.

Catching on instantly, his friend looked hurt. "As if I would. I shall leave it to you to keep me apprised of your fascinating love life."

They'd almost always seen eye-to-eye on which females were the gimcrack ewes. Once or twice, they'd even gone after the same one, without hard feelings no matter who walked away with the coveted prize.

Matthew downed his brandy and rose from the table. "I'm off. Can't stay out all night like the old days."

"Certainly not if you get hitched to an earl's prim daughter." Quinn saluted him with his glass.

Matthew ignored him, turning to leave. More and more, he liked to be home before dawn to look in on his daughter, as he thought of Diana.

How could he not think of her that way? He had slept with her mother, after all.

He'd taken only a few steps when he was nearly knocked on his arse.

CHAPTER TWO

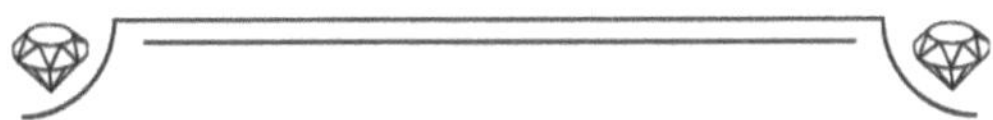

Lord Varley, also a Cambridge man, had shouldered him so hard while walking past, Matthew had almost been dinged to the floor. They'd never been true friends, having been at different colleges, but mild acquaintances. He knew the viscount had been close to marriage a couple years ago. Alas, Varley had been given the mitten by an angry fiancée who'd caught him tipping the velvet with another woman in a closet. Since said closet had been under the stairs of the fiancée's parents' home during a dinner party, the denouncement and penalty had been swift and final.

In any case, it was nothing to do with Matthew. Thus, he was surprised by the brusque way the man knocked into him and continued walking.

"Here now!" he exclaimed.

Varley slowed his walk slightly, gave Matthew his profile, and lifted a hand before continuing into the next room.

Not exactly an apology, but it would have to do. He'd never had any trouble with the viscount, and Boodle's was not the place to fight, even if he had been provoked.

"Blasted royster," he muttered and departed into the dark night and thick, sooty air of London.

AT THE FENWICKS' BI-ANNUAL dinner party for eligible unmarried persons, Matthew struck it lucky. In truth, luck had nothing to do with it.

Not happenstance, but snooping and questioning brought him to the same townhouse and the same drawing room as Lady Purity. He'd made it a point to ask about the Diamonds at Boodle's. And while her father, the earl, was not a member, men knew of him and his fine family of four daughters and a son.

When he learned Lady Purity's parents and even her father's parents were long-time friends of Matthew's neighbors, the elderly Lord and Lady Fenwick, he decided it was practically fate they be together. Consequently, when the Fenwicks held their twice-yearly dinner for single members of the *ton*, Matthew was confident she would be there. Naturally, he had secured his own invitation.

Who more eligible than him? Matthew asked his reflection as he passed the mirror in the Fenwicks' front hall. He could make fun of himself. Most would say, despite the man in the looking glass having a strong chin, straight teeth, and rather thick hair, that he was *not* the best match for any young lady since he was a bit of a scapegrace.

But he had a good income from his barony. Combine it with an appearance that was more than satisfactory to most females, and the baser parts of his nature were often overlooked.

Before him, standing in a small circle with other ladies and a few gentlemen, was Lady Purity, as expected. Her dark hair was threaded with pale-pink pearls to match her pink satin dress. And the sight of her, so petite and perfect, made his pulse quicken.

Tonight, he hoped to get her alone again, in the library or an empty bedroom, or even in the small back garden of the Fenwicks' Belgrave Square home.

Since the lady had been breaking all rules of good sense and decorum by being alone in Lansdowne's drawing room, despite Quinn's warning of her as a primster, Matthew assumed she was the adventurous sort, up for a lark. She hadn't fainted or had a fit when he'd kissed her. Rather, she'd handled herself as if she had some experience in such matters.

All in all, she seemed a likely target for a companionable wife. Hopefully untested in bed, yet passionate and ready to learn. And if he discovered she had wit and humor, then she would rise even further in his estimation. First thing was an introduction.

"There you are, Foxford," greeted Lord Fenwick, who never seemed to age but stayed eternally white-haired and sparkly eyed, like his wife who stood beside him.

Matthew had known them for his entire adulthood due to their house being on the same square as his own. Upon moving out of his family's home in Edinburgh, he had been beyond eager to return to London and was fortunate to have purchased a place in this plum neighborhood south of Hyde Park.

"Good evening, Fenwick," Matthew said before taking Lady Fenwick's offered hand. "Why haven't you run away with me yet, my lady?"

It was a game they had played from nearly the first time they'd been introduced, when her husband had cautioned Matthew against trying to steal the prettiest woman in the room.

"Are you still so devoted to this codger?" Matthew asked her.

"I am afraid I am," she replied. "Despite the fact that Fenwick and I were younger than you when we married, our love grows daily." She glanced at her husband, who returned her look with one of naked adoration.

Matthew swallowed away the lump in his throat. *How inspiring!*

"Coincidentally, on just such a subject," he ventured, "I am hoping you can assist me tonight. I am not here merely to look. I intend to take a wife this year. Will you introduce me to the single ladies you've gathered?"

Lady Fenwick smiled. "Gathered? You make it sound as though we collected them in a room like cheeses on a tray for you to sample."

Matthew laughed. "I don't know about sampling," he said wickedly, "but I would like to meet them, to learn their names and all that." He needed a proper introduction, not only to Lady Purity but also to the other polished, pretty females who were ready to marry.

"It may do you no good," Fenwick said. "You have been in the papers recently, more than once since you came back. Something about a lost earring turning up in your possession, and a husband finding you in his home when his wife was there alone."

Lady Fenwick gasped at the rudeness of making a guest feel uncomfortable, but her husband continued, undeterred.

"Or was it a lost wife in your possession?" He chuckled.

"Fenwick!" his wife admonished. "You know you cannot speak of such things, nor embarrass our guest. I do apologize, my lord." Then she narrowed her eyes. "But don't let any mischief, nor improprieties, happen at our home tonight. Everyone here is a friend or an offspring of a friend."

"Of course not, my lady," Matthew promised. He wasn't there to fence tongues with Lady Purity. But that was a lie! If the opportunity arose, that was precisely what he would do. But he didn't wish *only* to kiss her again. Getting her alone was something he thought important with each woman he wished to court. No one said anything interesting or intimate in public.

Then the introductions began. A pretty, fair-haired lady with a toothy smile reared back upon learning his name, practically disappearing behind a squelch-gutted female with lovely eyes but a dreadfully severe expression. Matthew removed them both instantly from his mental list of potential mates.

Also unsuitable was a brunette with a rail-thin figure. Something about her seemed sickly, as if a strong wind might take her away. He feared she wouldn't survive birthing an heir to his barony, never mind be strong enough to raise his existing daughter to maturity.

"I hope you find Lord and Lady Fenwick's dinner to your liking," he said after their introduction, thinking she ought to eat a double helping of everything.

Matthew didn't know if he was being overly fussy, but each lady he met seemed lacking compared to Lady Purity, to whom he was drawing closer.

At last, the Fenwicks brought him before her. She'd seen him coming. Of this, he was certain because her perfect smile had already faded. Regardless, she pretended not to know him.

"Lady Purity," Fenwick addressed her first. "This is Lord Foxford, known to me for many years."

She gave a shallow curtsy, not showing any sign they'd shared a passionate kiss, nor that she was shocked at learning his identity.

"Good evening, my lady," Matthew said, returning her curtsy with a slightly deeper bow.

Their host added, "She's on the marriage market now that her older sister has been recently snapped up."

Lady Purity winced and went from pale to puce.

"Fenwick!" his wife exclaimed.

"I hate to contradict our host," Lady Purity said, "but my sister has been married over a year, so not precisely *recent*. And I assure you, I am not on *any* market, marriage or otherwise."

"Just a figure of speech," Fenwick said, unbothered.

"It is my pleasure to meet you," Matthew said, hoping to allay any fears she might have that he would mention their first encounter. "What's more, Fenwick might as well be describing me, for I have of late put myself upon that very same market, looking for a wife."

Lady Purity's eyes grew wider.

"An unusual thing for a man to admit," Lady Fenwick pointed out.

"Indeed," Lady Purity agreed. "Why are you hoping to marry? I mean, at this time."

Why? Matthew considered her question. There was probably a correct answer that would win her over, but he didn't know it.

"I came home from the Continent after two years of traveling. My home is empty," he added, *except for Diana,* who filled it with her giggles, but he couldn't disclose that. Not yet.

"It lacks a woman's touch. I want a wife to fill it with warmth and her feminine quality. And naturally, I seek like-minded companionship, as I have witnessed with Lord and Lady Fenwick."

Instead of approval, Lady Purity's visage was downright dour.

"A woman isn't an object to be installed in your home to fill it with anything at all. It's not 1748, my lord! While I agree like-mindedness is essential, I also believe a joining of the hearts is crucial. Lord and Lady Fenwick have that beyond measure."

Before Matthew could respond, she made reference to his reputation, albeit in a less direct manner than Fenwick had.

"A man ought to be ready to devote himself *entirely* to his wife, forsaking all other females entirely. One cannot help wondering if you are prepared to do so. If a man is merely looking for companionship, that can be easily obtained from one's friends, one's horse, or even a well-mannered dog. Although, perhaps you would prefer a kitten, my lord."

Matthew couldn't stop the grin that spread across his face. He was entirely charmed.

"You are correct on all counts. We are past the time of arranged marriages, that is, unless one is of royal blood. And it is not as if I wish to snap up the first female I come across out of a sense of desperation. A wife is a special case, and I intend to find precisely the correct one for me. If I must get a kitten in the meantime for companionship, then I shall. It will make the wait for a wife that much more bearable.”

Her lips flattened in disapproval, and he wanted to laugh. He fully intended to give up mistresses and whores when he pledged his troth. After all, his young Diana was already the result of carelessness, and he’d seen the cost to the innocent.

“Wine?” Lady Fenwick offered, astutely reading the tension between two of her guests.

Soon, they were all drinking burgundy. A pallor of relaxation coated the room and its occupants, except Lady Purity, whose gaze followed him everywhere. He would give a gold sovereign to know her thoughts. He would give far more than that to be alone with her again.

PURITY WOULD GIVE UP A week’s allowance for the evening to end early. Instead, it grew worse when her dining companion turned out to be Lord Foxford. He looked so smug; she guessed he’d orchestrated the seating arrangement himself.

Why? She could only imagine it was to torment her because she’d let him kiss her.

Now that she knew his name, his behavior at Lansdowne House became understandable. He was a rake by all accounts. She’d seen his name in the papers linked with a married lady here or a widowed lady there. Indeed, he’d been busy for someone recently back on British soil.

His loose, irresponsible character vexed her the way a wealthy nip-cheese vexed a beggar.

Yet she’d not only been kissed by the Fox, she’d enjoyed it!

Now she had to sit through at least ten courses and two hours of discourse while around her were other single gentlemen with whom she was certain she had more in common.

“Did the lady-friend you intended to meet enjoy the painting?” she asked, thinking she would toss in something outrageous enough he might simply stop speaking to her completely.

It didn't work. "I hardly know," he said. "Come to think of it, I don't believe she had any actual appreciation for art."

He let that hang between them. Naturally, Purity imagined he had spent time kissing the prostitute and perhaps doing something wicked against the wall he had mentioned.

On the other hand, he must have paid the woman and was at least contributing to the economy of London.

She took a large swallow of wine and fought not to cough. When she turned to look at him again, his gaze went directly to her watering eyes.

"Your eyes are glistening like sapphires. They are the most beautiful blue I have ever seen."

He managed to make over-the-top flattery sound entirely sincere, which baffled her because she was not one to approve of fawning. Regardless, there could be only one response since she had been raised correctly.

"Thank you, my lord."

Through the delicate soup course and the turbot with lobster and Dutch sauces, followed by oyster and marrow pâtés with soft bread, she said very little, except to tell him not to use his knife to cut the bread.

"Always break it by hand," she advised, before allowing him to carry the conversation unless he asked her a direct question. Then she replied succinctly while asking him nothing in return, a grievous fault in a dining partner.

However, despite being brought up to make an enjoyable dining companion, Purity would not deign to show any interest in him, not even to ask him if he was enjoying the weather. The newspapers and her own experience had determined he would not make anyone a good husband unless he found a woman willing to put up with his famously scandalous behavior. Thus, she hoped her purposeful slight demonstrated her disapproval.

Still, as the meal wore on, she had the notion he was interested in her for that very position of wife. *Why else would he declare any such thing directly to her and in front of the Fenwicks?*

Needing to make it crystal clear she would never wish to be his baroness, no matter his compliments or his kissing ability, she intended to remain as cool as possible. Yet throughout the dinner, he never let the conversation lapse into an awkward silence. He regaled her with stories of his time abroad, making sure to ask if or where she had traveled. He asked about her siblings. He even asked if she would take more wine with him when her glass was empty. He did it all with perfect manners, and thus, it was hard to find fault.

Until he did two things so egregious, she could almost believe he did them on purpose to rile her. Over the dessert course of cream-topped sponge cake, *meringues a la crème,* and thick brandy custard with a sugar glaze, which as it was her favorite she was struggling to eat slowly, he shifted his fork to his right hand.

She nearly *tsk-tsked* to watch him holding it like a shovel. *Couldn't he see he was the only one handling his utensil in such a barbaric fashion?*

Purity was about to save him ridicule by instructing him when he leaned close—*too close!*—causing her to crane her head and look up at him.

Immediately, he smiled. "I was going to tell you something interesting, but now all I can say is you do look like a kitten after all."

Heat crept into her cheeks. She could smell his complex fragrance, reminding her as it had all through dinner, of their kiss. But she was no sweet little animal. Therefore, she was stunned when he raised his napkin and wiped the end of her nose.

Gasping could be heard from all the ladies and some of the gentlemen who witnessed it.

Purity felt her mouth drop open and had to snap it closed. *He had caused her complete and utter mortification!*

CHAPTER THREE

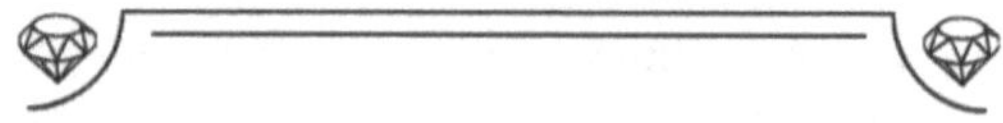

"Careful, Lord Foxford," Lady Fenwick chided while Purity sat in stunned silence, feeling all eyes upon her.

"She had a dob of custard upon her nose," her tormentor explained. "No gentleman would let that remain if he could do something about it."

"A gentleman ought to simply tell a lady and allow her to take care of the matter herself," Purity ended on a hiss, assuming her cheeks were now bright red. In a softer voice for only him to hear, she added, "You aren't supposed to draw attention to such a thing, nor should you touch me unasked."

"My apologies," he said, without appearing sorry. He leaned closer again and whispered, "Next time, I shall wait until you ask me to touch you."

Lord Fenwick, at the other end of the table, unaware of the quagmire of inappropriate behavior through which Purity found herself trudging, called out, "Well done, Foxford. I say it was the polite thing to do. You cannot leave a lady with cream upon her pretty face."

To Purity's amazement, a debate broke out over her dining companion's action. *Was he insolent or chivalrous?*

Sighing deeply to calm herself, she sent her gaze back to her dessert and tried her best to ignore the entire discussion.

Nothing like this had ever happened to her before, and such an occurrence was not covered in her favorite manners book, *The Gentleman and Lady's Book of Politeness and Propriety of Deportment*, although she would skim it when she returned home to make sure. How the custard got on the end of her nose, she couldn't imagine.

Then it dawned on her. There probably hadn't been any. *But why would Lord Foxford pretend?*

A possible answer came after dinner when the guests returned to the drawing room. The men had eschewed sitting alone with cigars and brandy since the evening was intended for spending time with the opposite sex. The Fenwicks had made a few successful matches already, it seemed, by the pairing up that was happening around the hearth.

Purity thought she might speak with a flaxen-haired man standing by himself. He had a pleasant visage.

"Since we are now firmly linked as the two most outlandish dining companions," Lord Foxford said softly at her elbow, "will you allow me to be your partner for charades or whatever entertainment comes next?"

Purity decided that had been his intent all along.

"I don't want to be considered outlandish, nor do I wish to be associated with anyone who is."

Regardless, since a brown-haired lady with a strand of rubies around her neck had taken the opportunity to attach herself to the blond man, Purity settled for one of two empty seats and let Lord Foxford sit beside her.

"I thought by your behavior at Lansdowne House—" he began.

"*Shh,*" she hissed, looking around to make sure no one was paying attention. "Whatever you thought, you were wrong. After all, I didn't go there to meet with anyone, merely to admire some art. Unlike yourself! In any case, why are you pestering me if you are seriously looking for a wife?"

He remained silent, which was a good thing, but he was fiddling with his gloves on his lap.

"Put your gloves in your pocket," she admonished him. "There is no need to have them out unless you intend to depart within minutes."

His eyes widened. "Are you schooling me in decorum?"

"Someone ought to," she muttered, noticing that Lady Fenwick was organizing guests for charades and other games with forfeits.

"Just as someone ought to instruct that young lady over there not to chew her lip," Purity pointed out. "She looks bovine yet probably fancies herself winsome. And that man with the mole on his forehead. Do you see him? He's doing all the talking while the lady beside him has the appearance of a trapped rabbit. Since she can't gnaw herself out of the situation, she must wait for him to take a breath and make an excuse to escape. What a tedious boor!"

"As I was over dinner," Lord Foxford surmised.

Purity had to be honest. "On the contrary, you were doing precisely the correct thing with a dining partner who was feeling surly and untalkative."

She was surprised when he laughed softly.

"You are brutally honest, even about yourself," he remarked. And he put his gloves away as she'd suggested.

"I suppose I am." Purity didn't like prevarication any more than she appreciated slovenliness, poor manners, or disorderly conduct. Life was much more pleasant when people adhered to expectations and behaved as politely as possible.

She sighed, not knowing how to explain herself, nor particularly caring to.

"Everyone!" called out Lord Fenwick while his wife gave a single swift clap of her hands to get their guests' attention. "Find a discreet corner to discuss your challenge."

While Purity had been wool-gathering, she had missed when Lord Foxford took the small square of paper from Lady Fenwick, confirming them as a team of two.

"It's a blindfolded game," he said, handing her their instructions.

"For two," she added upon reading it. "And something of a spectacle!" *Why couldn't people settle for cards or a pleasant piano recital when in the mixed company of strangers?*

At least it wasn't the romantic balcony scene from Romeo and Juliet, as her sister had once performed before a roomful of people, including their parents. Purity had been embarrassed for her.

"You don't know one another well enough for games of *Make Your Will,*" Lady Fenwick said, "or *Squeak, Piggy, Squeak.*"

"Thank God!" Purity whispered to Lord Foxford.

In her opinion, the former told too much to too many. As for the latter, squatting over someone's lap without touching them while squeaking was too awkward and primed for mishap.

Couple by couple, they went to the room's center where the furniture had been cleared away and did whatever their hostess had written on the slip of paper.

The first couple blew feathers in the air. When the lady's dropped first, her forfeit was to say a proverb backward. She was even allowed to choose it.

"I hope if I lose, I get such a forfeit," Purity confessed. There were so many embarrassing possibilities.

Next another couple played *The Messenger,* each getting half the room to whom they must tell the same message, starting with the first person in their line. When it reached the last person, he or she said the message out loud. The lady's message came through the line more accurately. Lady Fenwick cried a forfeit from the young man this time.

"You are to be a malleable Grecian statue," she told him.

Bravely, he stood in the center of the room and let the other men move his arms and legs and even twist his body, all the while trying not to laugh and never once complaining.

"More like a gargoyle than a Greek statue," Lord Foxford said when it was over, and Purity couldn't help giving him her first smile of the evening.

Soon, it was their turn to play *The Cordial Greeting*. Rising to his feet, he offered his hand, which she accepted.

"As they say in France," Lord Foxford remarked, "*Ce n'est que le premier pas qui coute.*"

While Purity was translating in her head—*it is only the first step that costs*—Lord Foxford drew her into the middle of the room.

"You go to that end, Foxford," said Lord Fenwick, gesturing one way.

"And you go the other," Lady Fenwick said to Purity.

Once they were at opposing ends of the spacious drawing room, Lord Fenwick blindfolded Lord Foxford. Purity watched it happen, his splendid, honeyed eyes gazing directly at her until they were covered, and then Lady Fenwick tied a kerchief around Purity's face, knotting it at the back.

She didn't like the feeling of cloth covering her eyes. Unable to see anything, she shivered.

"You know how this is played," Lady Fenwick said, her voice moving away. "Find each other and shake hands."

Hating the notion that everyone was staring at her, Purity began walking forward, or assumed she was. Keeping her hands up in front of her, she took small, shuffling steps in her butter-soft, gray kidskin shoes. *How hard could it be to walk in a straight path anyway?*

"That's it," someone said, encouragingly.

"Go left, Foxford," came Lord Fenwick's voice.

A few people chuckled, so Purity assumed he shouldn't do as instructed since the audience was allowed to attempt to misdirect them.

And then, everyone started to clap and some of the gentlemen stomped so she and Lord Foxford couldn't hear each other approaching. It was most disorienting.

Unseeing, she touched something warm, and she gasped. Belatedly, she realized it was a forehead and hair, both at her waist level.

A gentleman laughed, presumably the one seated whom she'd touched so familiarly. Someone else, hopefully a woman, spun her half a turn. She wished she knew whether she'd been sent the correct way.

And then, before she could acknowledge how unpleasant she found this game, large hands brushed across hers. For an instant, Purity thought she and Lord Foxford had passed by each other. But after flailing slightly, she touched him again. This time he grasped hold of her hands with his, and she was certain it was he by the scent of his cologne.

"A proper handshake," Lord Fenwick said.

"I know how to greet a lady properly," Lord Foxford replied.

Purity felt him lift her right hand, and then his warm lips dusted her knuckles.

The guests cheered as Purity experienced her second spine-tingling shiver of the evening. His firm lips reminded her of when he'd kissed her.

For a dreadful second, she imagined he would do it again with everyone watching.

Wrenching her hand free, she stripped off the blindfold and gasped for breath.

In front of her, Lord Foxford removed his. They locked gazes, and he frowned.

"Are you well?"

"Of course," she said. But her heart was racing for she'd had an uncomfortable sensation of suffocating.

"No forfeit from either of you," Lady Fenwick said.

Guests moaned, but Purity was relieved to return to her seat and take up a glass of sherry. Unfortunately, most of the charades, riddles, and pantomimes were short. And within the hour, they had to take another turn. However, with fortified wine and much laughter, Purity felt better about the next game.

This time their piece of paper said, "How? When? Where?"

"Out of the room," Lord Fenwick ordered, "while we choose an object. The first one of you who guesses what it is wins, and the other one pays the forfeit."

Purity could hardly listen because Lord Foxford, with a grin that spoke of wicked amusement, opened the drawing-room door and ushered her out into the empty hallway.

"Shut the door," Lord Fenwick ordered from inside. "And no listening at the keyhole."

"You heard our host," Lord Foxford said. "Come away from the door."

With that, Purity allowed him to draw her down the dimly lit passageway.

MATTHEW COULDN'T HAVE asked for a better game. Surely, protective mothers didn't know about this. Even better, there was no one to witness and whisper to *The Times*, which had been dogging his every step since his return.

Regardless, he wasn't going to waste a second of the perfect opportunity at an otherwise tepid dinner party for tame single people.

Taking her hand, he pulled her along behind him, down the Fenwicks' hallway toward the back of the house. In a few steps, he found an empty spot of wall with no painting or candle sconce. With his smoothest maneuver, he waltzed her in a half circle until he could press her back to the wall.

"My lord?" she asked.

"I have been desperate to kiss you again." Earlier in the evening, he wouldn't have said such an exaggeration, but by this time, having been beside her for hours and kissed the soft skin of her hand, he was not lying. He *was* desperate to have her mouth under his.

Without hesitation, he pressed close, feeling her soft curves meld to his firm chest. He couldn't help tilting his hips against hers, too, while he caged her with his hands on the striped wallpaper at either side of her head.

She said nothing, blinking her blue eyes at him as he lowered his head and claimed her mouth. He nearly groaned from the relief of tasting Lady Purity again and of drinking in the same delicate floral fragrance that clung to her skin and, this time, to her hair as well.

As before, her body relaxed as soon as their lips fused. Also as before, his desire flared like a fatty candle. He wanted to sweep her into his arms and take her away, anywhere they could be together.

After ravishing her mouth as quickly as he dared, he kissed his way along her sweet chin and down the column of her neck.

"My townhouse is on this square, just a few doors down," he said against the creamy soft skin of her collarbone.

She went rigid at his words. He ought to have expected it, but he'd been instantly caught up in the heady sensation of joining with her, able to imagine how good it would be if they made the two-backed beast. Obviously, his hasty invitation was impossible since the drawing-room door would open any second, but still, maybe they could arrange a tryst later.

Leaning back to see if she enjoyed it, too, he asked, "What are you thinking, kitten?"

He didn't see it coming this time since the hallway was dim on all sides. In fact, he heard it first before he felt it. *Slap!*

At the same time, the door opened, and he sprang back and away from her as one of the guest's heads popped out, followed by a lady's shoulders.

"We're ready for you."

Lady Purity was already strolling away from him, head high as if nothing had happened. Entering the room behind her, he couldn't find it in himself to regret the kiss, not to mention nibbling on her neck, although his cheek still stung. Without her gloves on, she'd delivered an impressive wallop.

Forgetting what they were doing, he was surprised when Lady Purity asked, "How do you like it?" followed by "When do you like it? Where do you like it?"

Asking all the correct questions within the confines of the game, she received equally informative answers and said, "A bow" before he could even consider them or formulate his own questions.

"A forfeit from Lord Foxford," Lady Fenwick said. "Lady Purity, you may be seated."

His dark-haired partner glanced at his cheek before smirking at him, which made him wonder if it was telltale red. Then she left him alone in the center of the drawing room.

His forfeit was to illustrate three of his best qualities in pantomime.

Matthew considered the roomful of people and what he could get away with. First, he pretended to mount his horse and ride. The other guests clapped. Then, since it would be difficult to mime making money, he pretended to draw back a bow and shoot an arrow, then lift his fist in triumph as if he'd hit the target dead center.

Lastly, after turning and looking directly at Lady Purity, he wrapped his arms around himself, closed his eyes, and tilted his head as if kissing.

The men fell silent, but the ladies clapped and laughed as he'd hoped. *Except for Lady Purity!*

When he opened his eyes, she appeared in a high tweague, with her arms crossed and her luscious lips pursed into a straight line. Moreover, if looks could kill, he would fall lifeless upon the thick Persian rug.

Instead, he grinned at her and winked.

CHAPTER FOUR

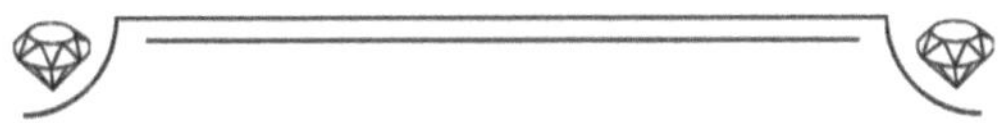

Matthew never doubted he would be granted entrance when he presented his calling card to the Diamonds' butler and asked if Lady Purity was accepting visitors.

Their home on Piccadilly was immaculate and impressive, but he wasn't the least daunted. A long-held family title, a good upbringing and a university education, plus a head for growing his fortune with investments gave him all the confidence he could ever need.

Not to mention the way women were attracted to him.

Thus, when Lady Purity agreed to a visit, he awaited her entrance in the elegant drawing room expecting a warm welcome.

Instead, as soon as she entered, she was hissing and spitting-angry like the kitten he'd named her—if said kitten had been dunked in a barrel of frigid rainwater.

"What on earth can you mean by coming to my home?" she demanded.

He glanced at the maid who had entered with her. She didn't make eye contact before going to the other end of the room and taking a seat.

"It is customary, isn't it?" Matthew asked. "When a gentleman meets a lady in whom he's interested, he visits her at her home."

"He asks the lady ahead of time. You should have asked me at the Fenwicks' party, and I would have told you a resounding no."

"Would you?" Matthew felt puzzled. "But we got along so well."

At her surprised visage, he asked, "Didn't we have a pleasant dinner and enjoy the entertainment after?" A smile spread across his face.

"Stop grinning," she snapped. Then she dropped her voice so her maid couldn't hear. "You have taken liberties each time I have been in your company."

"Didn't you enjoy my kiss? You seemed to like each one."

He watched her gorgeous blue eyes open wide before she closed them and shook her head. Clearly, he had infuriated her. When her eyes popped open, she took a step closer.

"That is not the point. You are not behaving like a true gentleman."

"I am trying. However, I'm glad I didn't ask permission to come visiting now that I know you would have forbidden me to do so."

"If I had forbidden your visit, you still could have had a footman drop off your card."

"For what reason?" Matthew had not actually visited a lady's home with the specific task of courting since he had never before been ready to take a wife. When he occasionally visited one of his friend's houses instead of seeing them at the club, he sometimes didn't even present a card. Their butlers knew him.

"You have your man-servant drop off your card so that I may *ignore* it," Lady Purity explained, "which would indicate even more clearly that I am not interested. At the most, I would send you a missive telling you not to try to visit me again."

"I see." *Could she really not wish to see him after they'd practically combusted in one another's arms?* There was only one reason she would turn down such pleasurable sensations.

"Are you already attached to another man?"

She pursed her lips. "That is an impertinent question. When you visit, you speak of the weather and some common reference from popular culture, such as a book you've read. You most certainly do not ask personal questions."

"Am I then visiting with you? For if I am, I should like to sit."

She sighed. "Very well. Since you are here and seem to be like a wild creature."

Matthew watched her take a seat before she gestured for him to take the one opposite. It struck him she was a particular young lady, perhaps even persnickety.

"You really were merely admiring the Marquess of Lansdowne's art, weren't you?"

"Indeed," she said.

Matthew had not really thought it possible, thinking it certain she had an arranged rendezvous, which he'd interrupted before using it to his own advantage.

"I believe I have misunderstood your nature."

"You have!" she declared. Then she narrowed her eyes. "How so?"

He cleared his throat, not about to tell her his view of her had changed from an adventurous rule-breaker to a stickling, prim Florence. That would only anger her. Regardless, he had an idea.

"It's not important but due solely to my own ignorance. I understand you are fluent in all the social customs and niceties, which I clearly am not. And as I told you, I am ready to take a wife."

"You shall not accomplish your task the way you are going about it."

"Agreed," he said. "Hence, will you help me?"

"Help you?"

"Yes. For instance, I don't even know how long this visit should last. Do I spend the day with you? Will you offer me tea now and later invite me to take lunch with you?"

"No," she said. "This visit should be a mere fifteen minutes in case I have other suitors coming."

"Do you?" he asked.

"Again, that is a private matter. You will find out if one shows up."

He sighed dramatically. "Then there is no tea?" He fully intended to drag out the visit as long as possible and see if some other man did, in fact, come sniffing around.

"There *can* be tea service," she said, "but usually, it has already been prepared and is waiting upon your arrival because you were expected. That way, you can drink it within the fifteen minutes of your visit. If served now, you would likely have to stay longer."

Matthew thought her the most delightful creature he'd ever met, getting flustered over tea service.

"How about if I agree to drink quickly while we discuss your assisting me in my quest?"

Her hesitation indicated he had her interest. He intended to have a great deal more of her by the end of their association—if there was an end. If there wasn't, then she would be his baroness. It all seemed monstrously simple.

"Very well," she said.

When she stood, he too rose to his feet, watching when she glanced at her maid. Lady Purity appeared to be warring within herself whether to ask the woman for tea, which would leave them alone, or ask another housemaid.

Matthew could practically see the machinery of her brain working. Then she went to the bell-pull by the door and tugged.

Her beautiful slender fingers caused him a visceral reaction he hadn't expected. This kitten had him all hot without even trying. He hoped his plan worked.

In a few minutes, they were once again seated, he'd removed his gloves, and they were drinking good strong tea.

"Thank you for bending the rules," he said. "As I understand it, the next time I meet a woman I fancy, I should ask her whether I may call upon her."

"Yes, exactly."

"And if she says no, then I can still drop off my calling card, but if there is no response, then I must accept my fate and move on."

"Again, yes, that's for the best."

"And if I do get my foot in the door, then I should stay no longer than a quarter hour and speak of nothing but the blandest topics."

"Let the lady guide the conversation, my lord."

Matthew tried to imagine being so mild. "Then I should be as a chair or a carpet."

That made her smile, which he liked.

"Well, perhaps not quite that passive, my lord, but do not ask anything personal." She sighed. "Now I shall break the rules of politeness and ask how it is that you don't know the common courtesies involved with visiting."

"I wasn't taught." That was only partly a lie. Of course, he knew most of the rules, not from his long-dead father, but explained by his mother and added to by his peers when they were all figuring out the treacherous terrain of behaving well in public.

He knew the correct forms of address, he knew how to dance without treading on toes, and he even knew the best manners to have when a duke was seated directly across from him. Dukes were such tricky animals.

However, Matthew never thought for a moment he couldn't break some of those rules at will. He was titled and wealthy, after all.

Whenever he had stretched the boundaries of the acceptable, it worked out for him, usually gleaning him a night with a lady of the *ton* who also eagerly wanted to break some rules. But this exacting task of "visiting" was an altogether different matter.

When Lady Purity appeared almost sorry for him, he added, "The only people I generally visit apart from my family, all of whom live in Scotland at present, are my friends from university or from my club. They are all gentlemen, none of whom I wish to woo."

She laughed softly at his words, and he was shocked at his loins stirring in response.

"I understand," she said before sipping her tea and looking as though she wanted to ask him something else.

"Go ahead with your question, my lady, for I can see you have one in mind. Since this is not a real visit, I believe we can speak frankly with one another."

"Thank you," she said. "I am merely wondering how you think it acceptable to kiss a lady whenever you wish. That is no way to get yourself a respectable wife."

"Aren't you respectable?" he asked.

"Yes," she shot back. "And that is why I can tell you it is not a good method. Moreover, the more outrageous your behavior and the more you appear in the newspapers, the less likely you will make a good match. Unless of course, you don't care about the quality of your wife."

She had a point. Matthew did care, and most definitely, he wanted an upstanding wife whom he didn't have to doubt or mistrust. The thought of being cuckolded was beyond abhorrent. It was also rage-inducing. Moreover, he wanted a good mother to his children. In fact, he would be extremely satisfied with Lady Purity, for while it was a silly name, he now understood it indicated her nature.

And best of all, her lips had responded to his, inflaming his passions in a way he thought would be delightful when they were enjoying a little rantum-scantum.

Yet here she was, telling him he'd already ruined any possibility with her. Thus, his spontaneous plan was the only way to stay near her, woo her, and win her over.

"I have a lot to learn, my lady." He gave a doleful shake of his head. "I hoped I could express my interest with a kiss."

"Correctly, you should have given me a compliment, not a kiss."

"A compliment?" That was easy. "Your eyes are the most beautiful blue, reminding me of the sky over the Mediterranean Sea. Your dark hair is like obsidian silk, through which I wish to run my fingers. Your lips are like rose petals, perfectly soft and plump. Your voice reminds me of a softly played flute."

Those petal lips of hers had parted during his sweet speech. She sighed again, and this time, she rolled her eyes.

"Not flattery, my lord. That is vulgar. A true compliment is what you should strive for. Remember the lady with the ruby necklace at Lord and Lady Fenwick's party?"

Matthew tried to recall, but he'd had eyes only for Lady Purity. He almost told her that but sensed such words were more of what she didn't wish to hear.

"I remember a lady with large teeth," he said. "Was she the one?"

"I don't believe so. In any case, if you do meet a lady with large teeth, you ought to tell her she has a nice smile and leave it at that."

"By a compliment, then, you mean a lie."

"In that case, yes. We should strive to make those around us at ease and happy. My older sister, Clarity, makes people happy simply by being in her presence. Most of us have to work a little harder."

"*You* make me happy," he said.

She paused and a little pink colored her cheeks.

"Thank you. That seemed a true compliment, albeit given the circumstances, perhaps inappropriate since we are *not* forming an attachment. Back to the lady with the rubies, she had perfectly styled hair, so you should pay her a true compliment by mentioning her becoming coiffure. Don't overdo, simply speak the bald truth without adding effusive adulation."

Matthew nodded. "I see. Nothing overblown."

"Exactly." She seemed to approve, which cheered him. He would love every kind of lesson she gave him and hoped to give a few in return.

She was spectacular. Strangely, Lady Purity didn't realize all the things he'd said about her were the truth, too. If he could get away with kissing her again right then and sliding his fingers into her shining hair, he would do it.

Not a word was flattery, but he hoped to have a chance to tell her all those things again when she was stretched out naked beneath him. Maybe then she would believe his compliments.

"I'VE FINISHED MY CUP of tea," Purity told Foxford, hoping he would understand her intent. He'd taken up enough of her time, and she had promised to visit with Clarity for lunch.

"Now I am supposed to leave. Is that right?" he asked.

She nodded, half-wishing she'd had another suitor pay a call, not to seem the least unpopular. Curtailing her vanity, Purity reminded herself she didn't give a fig what he thought.

"When shall I return?" Lord Foxford asked.

"Return?" She rose to her feet, watching him do the same. "Why would you return?"

She gasped, nearly slapping a hand across her own mouth. *What on earth had got into her?*

"My apologies. That was rude. My only excuse is that we've been speaking so forthrightly without the veneer of social graces that I momentarily forgot mine. What I meant was, why would you return?"

Luckily, the handsome man before her laughed at how she'd purposefully asked him again in the exact same manner.

"I need to come back for you to help me learn the proper ways to behave with a lady whom I wish to woo. Since grabbing her and kissing her soundly isn't correct, I am at a loss. How else will I get a wife if you won't help me?"

Lord Foxford sounded sincere, which struck her as improbable. On the one hand, he was a known libertine. As a thundering buck by all accounts, he obviously had no issues being around ladies. His name had been in the early morning paper—"Lord F__ had been seen acting in a forward manner at the Fenwicks' latest dinner party."

The reference was to him touching a woman's face at the dining table, but luckily, Purity's identity had not been mentioned or even hinted at.

Still, it could have been much worse if someone with loose lips had seen them kissing.

On the other hand, he probably had very little experience with innocent women, the kind one married. Purity hadn't seen him at any of the previous Season's events, so perhaps he truly had no idea how to behave.

If she had a third hand, she would add it in and wonder what any of his problems had to do with her.

"I mean no offense," she asked, "but why would I do any such thing? Why would I help you to ensnare a woman?"

Lord Foxford brushed down his coat despite not having been offered a biscuit or any cake, and then he drew back on his gloves.

"I sense you are a fastidious female. And from all you've said, you prefer things done properly. Therefore, I am offering myself as a challenge."

"A challenge?" She had to admit she was interested.

"More than that," he continued. "Not only am I a challenge to polish and prepare so I can win a wife, but I don't want to *ensnare* anyone. I want a woman to fall in love with me, and in turn, I with her."

Purity considered this. It was no small admission. Furthermore, she might enjoy helping him. She was going out in society, anyway.

"Coincidentally, a family friend needed a little polishing because he had not been much in society, and I tried to get my sister to do so, but she refused."

"Why?" Lord Foxford looked interested.

Purity declined to explain how Clarity didn't wish to help her now-husband spruce up enough to find a wife since she'd always been half in love with the man.

In Lord Foxford's case, Purity had no reservations about seeing this scandalous lord ankle-chained by year's end. It would be amusing to see who ended up with him.

"My sister's business is not yours," she answered, rising to her feet. "While I believe you have no excuse for your ignorance as you have not been absent from society, I shall consider your request."

Lord Foxford looked dissatisfied.

"When will I see you again?" he asked. "In order to receive your answer."

"I shall be at Rutherly's ball next week. If you attend, we can talk more then. If I've decided to help you, then we'll start that night."

"Thank you, my lady."

"Don't thank me yet," she reminded him. "I may decide you are more trouble than you are worth."

He grabbed his chest as if wounded, making her laugh again. And then he correctly and gentlemanly took the hand she offered, bowed over it, released her, and departed. It was almost a disappointment not to be grabbed and soundly kissed.

Smiling to herself, Purity couldn't wait to get to Clarity's home on Grosvenor Square and tell her everything. Well, *not* everything. Not about the two kisses. But she was eager to hear her sister's thoughts on whether she ought to involve herself with the love life of a rake by playing his etiquette tutor. She had no idea if she could mold the baron into an upstanding example of husband material.

If she accomplished it successfully, she would be doing some woman a good deed.

After speaking with Clarity, who thought it an amusing pastime, Purity was looking forward to the next ball.

CHAPTER FIVE

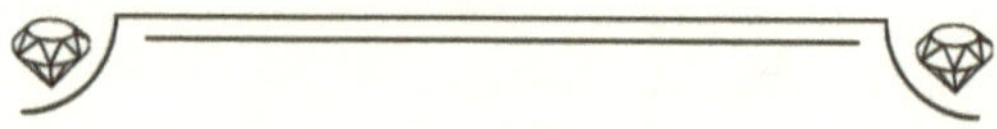

Suffering from a megrim all afternoon, Purity's mood was soured, and she would have preferred remaining home, resting on her bed. However, having decided to assist Foxford, as she now thought of him familiarly, she was unwilling not to show up as promised.

Thus, on the eve of Lord Rutherly's ball, she dressed in a new silver satin gown, had her hair dressed with a spray of small silver-painted leaves, and set out accompanied by her mother.

From the first moment Purity spotted her "challenge," she nearly called it off. His attire was all wrong for the occasion. *Strange!* She was sure he'd been appropriately dressed both at Lansdowne House and at the Fenwicks' party.

Now, however, not only was his hair mussed, but he also wore fawn-colored trousers as if out for a daytime jaunt rather than the desired black or, at the very least, a dark blue or gray check. Worse, his cravat was neither black nor white, nor did his waistcoat match anything. Instead, the former was pale blue, and the latter was a garish clashing vest in orange and black brocade. And no sign of a tailcoat but instead a frock coat.

Her poor eyes!

When he spotted her, he lifted a hand and waved before exclaiming loudly, "Lady Purity, well met."

She might have been imagining it, but it seemed a hush fell over the bustling, noisy ballroom, and all eyes turned toward him. Upon seeing where he was looking, the heads swiveled in her direction.

"Who is that?" her mother, Caroline Diamond, asked. "And why is he calling out your name like a farmer to his pigs?"

"He is Lord Foxford."

"The baron recently returned from France?" Clearly, her mother had read the papers.

"Yes, Mother. I was partnered with him at Lord and Lady Fenwick's dinner party."

"I see. We had best go in his direction before he starts hollering again. Perhaps he doesn't know anyone else."

"Perhaps he was raised in a forest by wolves," Purity muttered.

Her mother chuckled. Foxford met them halfway and stared rudely.

"Is this your sister you mentioned, the one who makes people happy?"

Purity sighed softly. *Hadn't she warned him about offering flummery?*

Such overt flattery worked only on the very young who didn't know it for a jest or on the extremely aged who understood it as a game. Since her mother, the countess, was neither, it was insulting.

Yet because Caroline Diamond was well-bred, she gave the merest disapproving shake of her head.

"Lord Foxford," Purity began, "may I present my mother, Lady Diamond?"

"The pleasure is all mine," he replied.

Without waiting for her mother to offer her hand, he reached out and snatched it, drawing it to him so swiftly, he yanked her a step closer. Then he kissed her gloved hand with a loud smacking of his lips.

Her mother glanced at Purity with her lovely green eyes wide.

"What a different apple each of you are and yet from the same tree," Foxford said. "A flaming redhead and a crow's wing of a daughter. One can almost wonder if she is really yours."

"Did you grow up in England?" Lady Diamond asked.

"Why, yes," Foxford replied, cocking his head curiously.

"Then I cannot imagine how a man of your standing could be so much of a spoony loggerhead. I wish you well, my lord."

With that, Lady Diamond strolled away to greet her friends. Purity would have to follow soon, but she would first take him to task.

"Have you forgotten all the bread-and-butter fashion for dress and for greeting?"

"Not forgotten, I fear, but never learned." He looked chagrined. "How will I get a wife to carry on the barony and bear me an heir?"

"You see," Purity declared. "That is an unacceptable topic."

"Not between us, surely. I feel as though I can say anything to you, kitten."

"But you may not," she informed him. "Moreover, I am not confident I can help. You appear not to know the basic harmony of fashion, such pleasant agreement being the soul of elegance. A lady of the *ton* will, at the very least, expect you to cut a bosh figure."

Looking alarmed, Foxford straightened. "I am a quick study. I promise I shall be teachable and malleable and entirely redeemable. Allow me to claim a dance or two. Or three," he added.

"Not three," she snapped. "By the way, can you dance?"

"Yes," he said. "In that, I shall not let you down."

"It won't be me who is disappointed at the end of the Season if you don't smarten up." Glancing at her empty card, she realized she had better make the rounds or she would be the one disappointed by a lack of partners.

"I am putting you down for the third dance as the first looks to be a march leading into a quadrille."

"And the one before dinner?" he prompted.

She paused. He knew that custom well enough, it seemed.

"We have already eaten a long meal together. Tonight, you ought to dine with a potential spouse. It's hard to guess at the outset, but I suggest you find a lady who interests you and secure the eleventh dance."

She wrote in his name with a tiny pencil from her reticule. "I shall, however, be your partner for the first dance *after* dinner so you can tell me how well you did."

He didn't look pleased. Perhaps Foxford was nervous about minding his manners.

"Remember to ask a lady for 'the honor of a dance' and don't tell any mother she might be the young lady's sister. That is absurdly fawning."

"Very well." He remained there, staring at her.

"And ask the young lady questions at dinner unless she's the quiet type, in which case amuse her as you did me at the Fenwicks' party. Whatever you do, do not touch her during the meal and guard against using vulgarisms."

"I shall do so and hope not to be a buffoon."

"Good," Purity said. "I must move along, or I shall have you as my only partner tonight."

He bowed. She nodded, and then she headed toward her mother.

"Don't forget the second dance," Foxford called after her, making her cringe although she didn't turn around. A few young ladies nearby giggled.

Sweet Mary! She had her work cut out for her.

MATTHEW THOUGHT THINGS were going well, and he didn't care what a grinagog he appeared to any of the other ladies present. His actions were a mere means to an end, and that end was Purity Diamond.

For the life of him, he couldn't discern why he'd fixed his sights upon her, beyond the fact that she was beautiful. Yet he had. It might be because their kisses were bloody outstanding. He was certain she hadn't let other rogues kiss her, at least not the way he had. Her high morals and adherence to propriety dictated otherwise.

Thus, despite slapping him *after* she'd melted against him like warm butter, Lady Purity must feel some attraction. He could almost believe their bodies recognized they were meant for one another before their brains and hearts.

Even if he was unable to win over the former until much later, he hoped to win over the latter soon. Once he had her heart, then he could convince her to marry him. Then he would introduce her to Diana.

Not that he was ashamed of the girl. However, her existence in his life and in his home might put off someone with Lady Purity's affinity for correctness. Therefore, better that he completely captivate her before she learned of the child's existence.

To that end, when the time came, he swept her into his arms for their first dance, and it was as memorable as he'd hoped. She was skilled at the waltz, easy to lead, and graceful as a butterfly. He couldn't bring himself to ruin the effortless flow, nor the enjoyment of being close to her, by making a purposeful misstep.

Besides, he'd told her he knew how to dance. This part of the evening he would allow her to think him as capable as he truly was.

After returning her to Lady Diamond, who wore a wary expression, the long evening ahead seemed interminable. He dallied a moment. Perhaps between dances he'd dazzle her with some stories.

Her mother excused herself to the retiring room with a sable feather that would not stay in place in her coppery-red coiffure. Or maybe she wanted to be away from him.

"Do you see someone here tonight with whom you might be interested?" Lady Purity asked him.

"Very much so," he said, giving her his best come-hither expression.

Instantly her cheeks pinkened. He loved doing that to her. The women he spent time with were not those who blushed easily, if at all.

"I meant a lady you might wish to offer a proposal of marriage," she clarified.

"Maybe. It's too early to tell," Matthew stalled. "Certainly not Lady Julia Jameson, a light-heeled wench if ever I saw one, and she was dancing with a man who might've been a decade her junior. I vow she must be nearing thirty. She's not unattractive, but her fortune isn't enough to make gentlemen forget she's known as a fustilugs when the ballgown attire is removed."

Lady Purity's brow furrowed. "I beg your pardon."

"It means she's rather a lusty beast between the sheets."

His lovely companion gasped, and her blush deepened.

"A man might want that in a mistress but not in a wife," he explained, in case she wondered why men weren't flocking to marry Lady Julia, who had been dancing all over London since he first moved back after university.

"I also spied Miss Westland, a bonny girl from all accounts at my club, but someone said she had a third . . . appendage." He nearly said the word "nipple." Having a polite conversation was harder than he had imagined. On the other hand, he wasn't trying to behave.

Lady Purity was shaking her head, wearing an expression of dismay.

Matthew continued, "How would any man at Boodle's know such an intimate fact unless she was a lewd bobtail, a game pullet, if you will?"

"My lord," she said as soon as he took a breath. "Gossip is a vulgarism I warned you about. Combine it with vicious slander, and you have entered into the lowest form of conversational offensiveness."

"Have I?" Matthew was mystified.

"Indeed, you have," she asserted.

"Then you also don't wish to know the amusing tale of Lord Varley's muck up when he gave a certain lady who was not his betrothed a green gown in a dark garden."

She stared silently. After a long, awkward moment, Lady Purity said, "I do not understand you, my lord."

Matthew cocked his head. She was clever. Most assuredly she *did* understand.

"This is another lesson, isn't it?" he asked.

Putting a delicate hand to her temple, she nodded.

"When presented with a double entendre, a lady has two choices. She can remain silent because she has *not* heard you, even if she has, or she may say 'I do not understand you.'" Her tone rose. "And then she can only pray you shut your vulgar potato trap!"

"Did I hear something about potatoes?" asked Lady Diamond, coming up behind. At the same time, the music for the next dance began, calling everyone to find their partners.

"My regards, Lady Purity, Lady Diamond. I will see you both later."

Matthew hurried off, wishing he could spend the entire evening with Purity. Dinner without her was far less satisfying than dinner with her. However, since it wasn't his companion's fault, he made sure to hold up his end of the conversation.

Yet when it was over, he all but skipped out of the dining room before halting and remembering to escort his partner and her mother, who had sat on either side of him, back to the ballroom. Bidding them good evening, he went in search of Lady Purity for their next dance.

To his astonishment and dismay, neither she nor Lady Diamond were still at the assembly. About to depart, Matthew recalled he'd allowed his name to be marked upon another seven ladies' cards.

Blast it all! He needed Lady Purity to see he was trying, even if he didn't give a fig about any one of his other partners. With her no longer there, Matthew would far rather be at his club drinking brandy with friends.

On the other hand, he was a gentleman. He might not have spent a great deal of time in London's ballrooms or on its dance floors, but he knew leaving a lady without a promised partner was unthinkable. It was practically a sacred duty, not to be shirked unless he dropped dead next to the refreshments.

Accordingly, he stayed, but his mind wandered to Lady Purity. She knew the rule as well as anyone and was more likely than most to follow it. *Was she taken ill?*

He hoped not, but he would use her sudden disappearance as an excuse to call upon her again.

He waited until three o'clock the following day. The minutes and hours between when he'd discovered her missing from the ball and handing his calling card to the Diamonds' butler seemed an eternity.

At least he was shown into the drawing room again—a good sign. He doubted that would be the case if Lady Purity was in a dire condition. However, the first person who entered was Lady Diamond.

For a moment, Matthew wondered if she would take him to task for his cloddish previous behavior. Right behind her, though, was Lady Purity, looking perfect. His relief must have shown upon his face, for immediately, the countess invited him to take a seat.

"After you," he said.

If it were a test, he had passed. When the two women, who looked as alike as chalk and cheese, were seated, he also sat.

"I admit I worried when you both disappeared last evening," he said after all greetings and pleasantries over the day's weather had been made.

Mother and daughter glanced at one another. He supposed that was another intimate matter he ought not to have mentioned. *What if Lady Purity had got her monthly flow unexpectedly?* He was a dolt to make reference to their leaving when they both appeared healthy.

Grinding his teeth at his own stupidity, he waited.

"I can tell you're working out how inappropriate was your last remark," Lady Diamond said. "Regardless, I shall answer because I believe you mean well. My daughter had a headache yesterday but elected to go to the ball. When it grew too painful, we came home."

"After apologizing to my upcoming dance partners," Lady Purity said.

"You didn't apologize to *me*," Matthew quipped, knowing he sounded childish, but he had been worried for nothing.

"Oh dear." Lady Purity frowned. "We asked the floor manager to contact everyone on the list with whom we didn't speak personally. I do hope there weren't others who were left wondering. If so, I shall be considered very rude."

Matthew reined in his irritation. All that mattered was she felt better.

"Are you fully recovered today?"

"I am. Thank you for coming and for asking."

Her smile seemed genuine, and earning it pleased him immensely.

"I confess I finished out the night having danced with so many ladies, I cannot remember their names. Is it the habit of the men to write down a list of their partners?"

This struck the two Diamond women as funny, for they both smiled, and then, despite their hair color, they looked very similar indeed.

"I believe the gentleman is only supposed to remember one lady in particular who strikes him, or at the most two," Lady Diamond said.

Lady Purity disagreed. "If you had more with whom you wished to visit, or even to whom you asked for a visit—as I instructed you—then when you got home, you ought to have written their names down directly while thinking of their faces."

This was news to Matthew. It seemed to be a novel idea for Lady Diamond, too, for she frowned at her daughter.

"Is that what you do?" her mother asked.

Lady Purity nodded emphatically. "Yes. It helps me recall people's names."

Matthew was charmed by this vignette, a conversation in which all three of them were on an even keel.

"Lady Diamond, may I ask how you kept all the names straight in your mind when you were your daughter's age attending assemblies?"

She considered. "I spent my youth in Bath with a much smaller social circle, so I knew everyone, and then when I came to London, I met Lord Diamond very quickly."

"Hence, you didn't have to be bothered by recalling other gentlemen *after* you met your intended?"

"Precisely," Lady Diamond said. "But I would heed my daughter's idea. She is far more organized than I ever could hope to be." She looked at Purity with admiration. "I shall try it when I go visiting and meet the Season's new crop of young ladies."

"Does the act of writing the names down secure them in one's memory?" Matthew asked.

"Somewhat," Lady Purity said. "Then in the morning, you must look over the names and think of their faces again. If you do that over a few more evenings and mornings, they should be firmly planted in the fertile soil of your brain."

"I promise to try it," he said, having no intention of keeping a journal of the insipid folks he met.

They fell silent. No tea was called for, and truly, Matthew didn't know what was supposed to occur. If he were courting her, he assumed he would be invited to dinner. As it was, he wondered if he could ensure himself more time with her, perhaps even alone, if he let her mother in on his dreadful failings.

"I confess I hate any whiff of subterfuge," Matthew began. "Thus, I must ask whether Lady Purity has made mention of my need for assistance in finding a wife."

The lady in question appeared surprised at his disclosure, and her mother even more so.

"She did not," the countess said, eyeing her offspring.

Lady Purity made her own defense. "Because I had not decided, my lord, although your initial greeting to us at last night's ball certainly pressed your case."

"I agree," Lady Diamond said. "This young man needs help if he is to succeed in London's society. You are fortunate to have met my daughter at Lord and Lady Fenwick's home."

"Very fortunate," Matthew agreed. They were going to keep their first interaction a secret. And keeping it gave them an intimate connection he hoped to exploit.

"However, I fear by the time I get to a ball or a dinner party, then it is too late. I make the errors beforehand while dressing and as soon as I open my mouth once I get to the assembly. What I need is prior tutoring."

The two ladies exchanged glances again.

"I suppose I can give you a few tips," Lady Purity allowed. "But you ought to take notes and—"

"Read them over in the evening and the morning," Matthew said.

She raised an eyebrow. "Lesson one, my lord. It is considered extremely rude to interrupt. Don't appear eager to hear your own voice or to show off your own knowledge. Listening is a particularly welcome and gracious skill."

Matthew felt duly chastised. He should not have interrupted, particularly a lady. While he'd made the other errors on purpose at the ball, that one was purely due to eagerness.

"And you are correct," Lady Purity concluded. "You ought to write everything down. Mother, shall we call for tea and get his lordship some paper and a pencil?"

"If you two don't mind," Lady Diamond said, "I do not wish nor do I need to take part in etiquette lessons, not from someone I've raised since she was in leading strings."

She rose, and Matthew jumped to his feet.

"The baron has *some* manners," the countess said, as if he couldn't hear her. "I'll send in tea, and I'm sure you can scrounge up writing implements in the library or perhaps in that chest of drawers."

She gestured to the other end of the room.

For Matthew's part, he was shocked she was going to leave them by themselves. That was not how he understood the quality folk to behave. Apparently, Lady Purity was also concerned.

"Will you send in Alice to sit with us?" she asked.

Her mother stopped by the open door. "What for?"

"Mother!"

Lady Diamond sighed. "I shall ask Lord Foxford what I asked Hollidge." She turned her piercing green eyes upon him. "Are you here to ruin my daughter?"

CHAPTER SIX

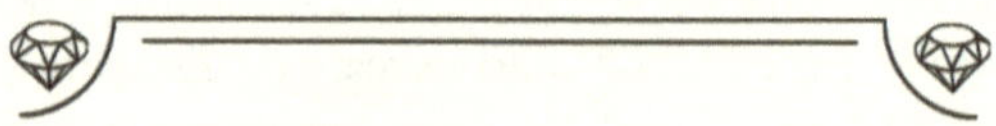

Matthew almost took a step back but managed to hold his ground. Never had a mother asked him anything like that. Her frankness nearly spoiled the fun of trying. Besides, he had two choices, lie to the woman whom he hoped would become his mother-in-law or tell the truth.

"I am not here *today* to do so, although Lady Purity is exceedingly tempting."

Some other day, in another place, yes, he might try to ruin her. He could make no promises to the contrary, and he hoped she didn't ask him to.

Lady Diamond frowned, and then she nodded.

"I see." She turned to her daughter. "I will send Mary in with tea and a few sheets of paper. And I shall find Alice to sit with you. Good day, Lord Foxford."

She was gone before either of them could say anything.

"I have never met anyone like Lady Diamond," Matthew said. "And who is Hollidge?"

"A long-time friend of the family who married my older sister."

Matthew sat in the space vacated by her mother on the sofa, no longer interested as long as the man wasn't a rival.

"Begin," he said. "Pretend I am your suitor. How would you wish me to behave? If I visited *after* you had given me permission, would I be allowed to sit close and take your hand?"

He shifted over until there was not an inch between their hips and thighs. Stripping off his gloves, he took hold of her hand. "Like this?"

Drawing her hand away, Lady Purity bristled. "No, you would not. You should sit where you were. Don't ever lean against a lady and only take her hand when it has been offered."

He didn't move. "Tell me more."

"Aren't you going to change seats?"

"We are only play-acting, so I see no necessity for moving. I have filed the knowledge away until I have a sheet of paper. What else can you think of, *ma chère?*"

"Don't speak with any affectation, including dropping in a smattering of French, no matter how perfect your accent. You did it the other night at the Fenwicks', too. All provincialism, foreign accents, mannerisms, exaggerations, and slang are likewise considered detestable. Above all, do not be flippant."

"Flippant?" Matthew asked. He might have to remain silent for his normal everyday parlance was ripe with flippancy.

"Gentlemen sometimes address ladies in a flippant manner," she pointed out, "such as calling me *kitten.*"

He winced. On the other hand, he had no intention of not calling her whatever he liked. It was too much fun.

"Most well-brought up ladies will feel obliged to ignore your deviations from the expected civility in conversation, appearing not to notice while inwardly rebelling against you."

"Are you rebelling?"

She sighed. "We are not talking about *me.* I only point out that an otherwise worthy man can cause himself irreparable harm when it comes to courting by creating a poor lasting impression without even realizing it. Flippancy denotes ill-breeding."

"Does it?" Matthew didn't like to think that was the case.

"It does," she insisted. "Even if it's not true but merely a personal failing. Add to that a man who keeps a vapid smile upon his face or has a wandering eye, a vacant stare, or as you did earlier, have your mouth half-open and ready to interrupt. These are all unwelcome traits in a suitor. Or a friend, for that matter."

"Duly noted." He was starting to wish he had written down her instructions when the maid entered with the tea service, followed by another maid, whom he took to be the aforementioned Alice.

The first placed a silver tray with a porcelain pot, two cups and saucers, and a plate of biscuits in front of them on the low table before the sofa, and then she withdrew a folded sheet of paper and a pencil from her pocket.

"Please give those to Lord Foxford," Lady Purity said. "That will be all." The girl curtsied and left. Then she addressed the other servant. "You may take a seat by the bookshelf."

The second maid nodded and went to the other end of the room.

"Now we are set to rights," Lady Purity said. "Everything is as it should be."

"Until I say how kind you are being, *comme un doux ange.*"

"You think you are being funny, but I will not waste my time," she vowed. "I won't be *a sweet angel,* as you say, if you don't take this seriously."

"I suppose you don't wish to hear my brogue, either, *sweet lass,*" he said, laying it on as thickly as a highlander.

She stared, stone-faced.

Matthew sighed. "I will take it seriously." And he made a little cross over his heart.

She was adorable when her dander was up. Then he tried to write with the single page resting on his pant leg and tore the paper.

"This won't do," she said. "We shall resume our tutelage in the library at the next mutually convenient time."

"What more is there?" he asked, half to himself, although pleased they would meet again, perhaps alone in the Diamonds' library.

"More?" her voice rose. "We have barely begun. You must learn to reflect before you speak, stop referring to any private matters in public, avoid all impertinent questions, make sure you never perform mimicry that embarrasses the other person, don't give advice unless asked, don't be ambiguous or whisper in front of others, never speak a classical quotation in mixed company—"

"Why not?"

"You just interrupted me, but the answer is because it makes you look like a snout-nose. That is, you are offering an ostentatious display, which no one appreciates. You must always take the woman by her left arm when on the street, keeping her against the building. If you cross the street, and continue in the same direction, then you must switch arms."

Matthew ran a hand through his hair. In truth, he had never been taught these things. Many of these rules came naturally through interacting politely with others and doing as they did in most cases. Except when he wanted to behave naturally with the men at Boodle's. Whenever he had been with a willing female, she didn't care if he whispered wicked French into her ear as he drove into her.

All these stodgy manners seemed to be for people forced together who didn't really wish to converse or learn anything about one another.

God, he hoped Purity would marry him because he couldn't imagine the tedium of watching his every word with ladies he was hoping to woo. Light-skirts and mistresses never gave a damn what he said. He nearly said that aloud, too.

Moreover, he would need something stronger than tea if he had to beat all this into his brain.

"Your mind has drifted. One of the very things I said was impolite. I am not going to waste my time any further today."

"It is simply so much to take in, and as you said, I need to write it down."

"Why don't you write down what you remember when you go home, and the next time you're here, we can review it and continue."

Was this getting him any closer to winning her?

"I am pleased you will allow me to come back."

A spark of triumph lit inside him. She must like him a little. Unfortunately, there was no way to steal a kiss today. Even he wouldn't humiliate her by doing so in front of her maid. More was the pity, too, because he had a notion he could win her better—or at least, easier—with pleasure than in any other way. Matthew didn't think it would take but a few caresses to have her helplessly willing.

Lady Purity shrugged. "I would help a needy urchin from Spitalfields or a stray dog that wandered in with matted fur."

She had doused his triumph quite handily. *Ouch!*

PURITY KNEW SHE WAS being hard on him, but Foxford was a slightly ridiculous, albeit mesmerizing man. She would have to be careful not to fall for him since so far, he made her tingle whenever she was in his presence.

To counter it, she had to embody the harshest teacher she recalled from her brief time at Ponder's End Boarding School for Young Ladies—namely the master of arithmetic who was as stern and strict as a sergeant—and view Lord Foxford as the densest of pupils. It wasn't easy. He made her want to laugh, but that would encourage him in his bad behavior.

And he made her want more than that.

When he sat beside her, she thought her body would erupt into flames. Moreover, the tingling along her skin where he rested against her arm and the length of her leg was entirely distracting. It was a wonder she could teach him any manners at all.

But she hadn't forgotten a moment of his inappropriate conduct outside of her home. Neither what she'd experienced for herself, nor what she'd read in the papers, no matter how loosely disguised *The Times* made their reports by using their coy language of a "foxy tod" or "a rakish reynard," or "a certain Lord F who might be better at the hunt than most of his counterparts."

To keep her mind off his handsome visage when she had to look at him, she focused on his left earlobe, the one with the crimp. As far as she'd seen, it was his only flaw.

"How did you get that imperfection on your ear?" she asked, immediately slapping a hand across her mouth. "Again, my apologies. I don't know what is it about you that makes me forget my years of upbringing."

His naughty grin didn't help. It made her stomach do flutter with excitement.

"My poor manners are affecting you, it seems, as much as yours are influencing me," Foxford mused. "I will let you wonder how it occurred, my lady. But I will give you a hint. Teeth were involved."

The blackguard! As she gasped, her insides danced again at the thought of a woman in the throes of passion biting his earlobe.

Glancing at Alice to see if she'd heard, Purity was relieved to see her enjoying an installment of *Sweeney Todd* or *Varney the Vampire*, either of which penny dreadful she usually kept rolled up in her apron pocket. Not only was she yards away, she was in a fictional world all to herself.

However, with Lord Foxford staring at her intensely, she absently reached out to snag a biscuit.

Was he taking any of this seriously?

She would test him at the next assembly.

A rap at the door captured her attention, and she was grateful for the interruption.

Their butler, Mr. Dunley, entered with a card on his silver tray. Purity took it and read, noticing Lord Foxford peering over.

"Lord Emberry," he scoffed. "That looby!"

Purity rose to her feet, and Foxford swiftly followed.

"Show him in, Mr. Dunley."

"You cannot be serious!" Foxford said, sounding bothered. "Is that even allowed? Having a visitor enter while another is still here."

Purity hid her smile at his outrage by looking down at the card again.

"It is allowed, my lord. It is also the moment at which you should politely take your leave."

"What? But we haven't finished!"

"I cannot tutor you in all facets in a single day." Before she could say more, Lord Emberry entered.

Purity would swear he was taken aback by the presence of the Fox. She wished there was a way to tell her handsome caller that the man already in her drawing room was no rival. She and Lord Emberry had enjoyed a delightful dance, and thus, she'd agreed to his request to visit.

Welcoming him warmly, she stretched out her hand to him, hearing Foxford make a sound of exasperation.

Stepping forward, Lord Emberry disregarded him, took her proffered hand, and bowed over it.

"I hope I have not interrupted anything," he said.

"You are," Foxford said rudely.

"Most definitely not," Purity insisted. "Lord Foxford was about to leave." She turned a severe glance toward him.

Luckily, he realized fighting now would be not only useless but dreadfully rude as well. For he nodded, looking resigned.

"Saw you in the papers again, old chap. Morning edition of *The Times*," Lord Emberry spoke up. "Quite the prattle about you and Lady Julia Jameson."

Purity caught her breath. She recalled the name. Foxford had said she was a lusty beast between the sheets!

"The devil!" he swore.

The improprieties were piling up. First, Lord Emberry should not have brought up any hint of an issue in mixed company, certainly not to embarrass her guest. And now Foxford's language was deteriorating.

What next? Was one of the men going to drop their trousers and start singing "Hasten back from the Crusades"?

As hostess, she had to get this under control.

"Lord Emberry, I would appreciate your not repeating gossip in my presence."

"My sincere apologies, my lady. I was merely surprised to see Foxford directly after having read about him with my midday meal and cup of coffee."

"Maybe you should have poured the cup of coffee over your head and warmed up your brains," Foxford quipped. "They seem to be frozen solid and therefore unusable."

"I say," Lord Emberry began.

"Do you?" Foxford responded, taking a step in his direction.

"Gentlemen, please." Purity wondered how it had got so quickly out of control. "This has devolved into an unpleasant scene. I must ask you both to vacate my home."

"I swear the paper printed a lie," Foxford vowed. "Utter rubbish. I never even danced with her."

"It is not my concern," Purity said, although she hoped he was telling the truth. She didn't like to think of him cheapening himself.

Doing everything wrong, he took her hand before she could offer it. Lingering over her knuckles, he feathered them with his warm breath before he kissed her skin, opening his mouth ever so slightly.

Shocked down to her toes, while a sizzle raced through her body, she could only stare until he raised his head.

"Thank you for your graciousness, my lady. I will see you anon."

She nodded, drawing her hand back slowly, able to feel the imprint of his kiss on her knuckles, along with a little hot dampness.

"Come along, Emberry," Foxford added, gesturing toward the drawing-room door with his head. "You heard the lady. Out. And don't come back."

"I didn't actually say that," Purity reminded them.

"You didn't need to. I'm sure Emberry here won't darken your door again after this egregious display of ill manners. Bringing up such lying tattle in front of a lady."

He nodded curtly to her would-be suitor.

Lord Emberry appeared confounded at how things had gone so wrong.

"Perhaps it best if I take my leave, then, my lady. May I visit another time?"

She considered Lord Emberry's question. "I think it best if you ask me when next we meet," she said.

Foxford waited until the man had bowed and headed for the door, ushering him ahead with a wave of his arm. Then he turned and winked at her, somehow taking all the energy and excitement with him.

At that instant, Alice finally rose to her feet. Apparently, she'd realized the room was empty of visitors or she'd finished reading her story. She'd missed all the conversation, an entire extra gentleman caller, and any matter of impropriety.

"Alice, you may take the tea service back to the kitchen."

It had undoubtedly grown cold, in the same way as she had lost the warmth that infused her in Foxford's dangerous presence.

Then Purity startled, recalling Lord Emberry's words, and hurried out of the room in search of the morning *Times*.

CHAPTER SEVEN

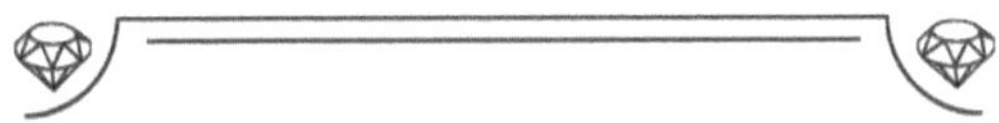

"May I make an introduction?" When the ball's hostess, Lady Tisendale, brought over a stranger, Purity tried to keep from looking past him. Foxford hadn't yet shown up, and she was trying desperately not to search for him.

She was *not* awaiting the sight of him. *Preposterous!*

Upon closer inspection, she thought she recognized the gentleman by her hostess's side, although she'd never danced with him.

"Lady Diamond, Lady Purity," said Lady Tisendale, "may I present Lord Pearson?"

Her mother inclined her head, while Purity curtsied. "Good evening, my lord."

"I am pleased to meet you. Enchanted, in fact. If your mother will allow, I hope you will do me the honor of a dance."

"Yes, my lord." She didn't ask her mother, as that was said as a formality. At her age, she could dance with whomever she wished. After examining her card, she penciled in his name and curtsied again as he bowed. Then he left with their hostess.

"He seemed an acceptable man," Purity said, looking after him. Lord Pearson was tall with a straight back and fair hair.

"I suppose," her mother said. "Perhaps a milksop."

"Mother! How can you judge the man upon so few words and such a brief interaction?" Strangely, she had the same impression yet didn't know why.

Lady Diamond shrugged. "Something about the set of his lips, or maybe it was in his eyes."

"It doesn't matter," Purity reminded her. "I shall merely dance with him. It's not—" she interrupted herself. "There he is!"

"Who?" her mother asked.

Foxford was already approaching, so Lady Diamond had her answer. As usual, he took her mother's hand before she offered. Purity was so used to him, it didn't bother her at all. Then again, she would be remiss if she didn't remind him.

Thus, after he'd greeted her mother, when Purity's glance met his over her gloved knuckles, she said, "You ought to have allowed us the option of presenting you with our hand. We might not have wished contact."

"Don't you?" he asked, still holding her hand and looking at her, his face inches away.

"Don't I?" she whispered, forgetting the thread of their conversation as her head filled with his delectable cologne.

Then her mother cleared her throat, and Purity recalled where she was and who had hold of her. She snatched back her hand so quickly, she well-nigh left her glove in his grasp.

"May I have the honor of a dance?" he asked.

"Nicely requested," her mother said.

"You may," Purity agreed. And examined her card.

"Is the dance before dinner still free?" Foxford was practically cross-eyed trying to read her card upside down.

"There is no dinner tonight," she informed him. "Only dancing and light refreshment."

His face soured.

"In any case," Purity said, "as I told you before, you ought to be dining with a lady whom you wish to court."

He sighed. "Very well, but will you allow me to bring you a glass of their nasty warm lemonade or watery wine, at the very least?"

"So graciously put," Lady Diamond quipped.

"If we see you during the interlude, then we would appreciate a glass of whatever you can procure," Purity told him. "I've put you down for the seventh dance."

"And?" he asked.

"And what?"

"A second dance is permissible. You told me that, I believe."

She glanced at her lovely, redheaded mother who raised a perfect eyebrow and, as usual, left the decision up to Purity.

"Later in the evening, then," she said, penciling in another dance and showing him.

"I will see you soon," he promised, bowing smartly and leaving them.

Sadly, the other gentlemen who filled in her card seemed tepid in comparison. Not mollycoddles, precisely, but without the Fox's dash-fire. She found herself looking forward to their dance instead of enjoying her partners and hoping to find a match. Moreover, she couldn't help watching to see with whom Foxford was dancing. To her surprise, she never saw him on the floor.

By the fourth dance, she started to fret that he was engaging in a light dalliance in the dimly lit garden. By the sixth dance, she wondered if he was having a tryst in one of the private rooms. When she stood with her mother before the seventh dance, she was in high dudgeon.

"Are you ready?" Foxford asked, startling her when he appeared from the side while she'd been scouting the crowded room.

She hesitated a moment too long, examining him for signs of indecorous behavior.

"For our dance," he reminded her, snagging the card dangling from her wrist. "It's time for the seventh."

"Yes," she hissed, snatching it back. "I am aware."

He bowed to her mother, then held out his hand, which Purity took. As they strolled to the dance floor, he asked, "Are you well? You seem out of sorts. Not another megrim, I hope."

"You shouldn't remark on a lady's health if you think it might not be at its pinnacle. But I am fine. My head does not ache in the least."

Her feet, however, were starting to throb a little, and she was glad she'd had the foresight not to assign another partner until after the interlude.

Then, against all her upbringing and besides knowing better, she asked, "Where have you been thus far?"

He didn't falter in his step. "Why, I have been here all night."

She nearly spat out the word *liar*, glad she still had the composure to bite her tongue. A moment later, Purity tried again.

"I haven't seen you upon the dance floor, not once."

"That's because I haven't danced. I ran into a friend—"

He had probably run right into some blowsabella.

"Lord Quinn," he continued. "I confess, he had a flask of cognac we were sharing over in that alcove with another chum."

Purity gazed where he gestured with his head, and there was a gentleman leaning against the wall, speaking with another man.

"I see," she said, her ire deflating. She had been looking in the wrong place, and those infernally large flower arrangements everyone was so keen on creating in oversized vases had been hiding him. "Then I, too, must confess. My imagination got the better of me. I assumed you were living up to your reputation."

"As a reprobate?" he asked, understanding immediately.

She shrugged slightly, then nodded.

Instead of being annoyed or insulted, he grinned down at her, turning her knees weak.

"Why are you looking like that?" she asked, wishing he would turn off his compelling charm.

"Because, kitten, I am thrilled you were looking for me at all. And here I thought you didn't like me. By the by, did I tell you how lovely you are in that burgundy satin? It's fierce but very feminine."

The heat crept up her neck.

"And now you're blushing so prettily, I want to sweep you out of here and kiss those rosy cheeks."

"Cease your nonsense," she said. "You are teasing me, which is not very kind."

"Isn't it?" He tightened his hold upon her. "I never said I was a kind man."

"I suppose you didn't."

"Why, then?" he asked.

"Why what?"

Foxford cocked his head. "Why were you looking for me?"

Purity was caught off guard. She plucked from her brain the first answer that came to mind.

"We are not supposed to carry on such a serious conversation lest it mar the enjoyment of the dance."

"My enjoyment isn't marred in the least," he assured her. To prove it, he gave her an energetic twirl at the end of the room.

"I'm glad you chose a waltz, but it would be easier to converse if we were alone somewhere quiet. Shall we take a walk in the garden when the music ends?"

"And there is the Fox I was expecting," Purity said, bewildered to find herself pleased that he'd asked her.

"Merely to talk," he promised, yet the glint in his eyes intimated more exciting, unspeakable actions.

She shivered. For a moment—a long, wistful moment— she considered how much she longed to cooperate with his wicked intentions. Then she cast such impossible thoughts aside with a sigh.

"Of course," Purity agreed. "We shall simply tell my mother we are heading out into the darkness. She will have no problem with that."

His grin reappeared. "Isn't there some warning about the use of sarcasm in your manners book?"

"Probably," she said. "Accordingly, if you behave, I will curb my tongue."

"Without access to your tongue, I suppose I shall have to behave."

Making sense of his words, she fell silent, a little shocked by him as usual.

MATTHEW HOPED HE HADN'T said something so crude his sweet kitten would stop speaking to him. Moreover, he didn't want to be banished from her side as soon as the dance concluded.

Therefore, after escorting her to her mother, he requested permission to bring over his good friend to meet them both.

Soon, Purity and her mother had made the acquaintance of Lord Quinn, who was a jovial sort to have at any party.

"Neither of you gentlemen have danced much," Lady Diamond remarked.

"To be frank," Quinn said, "I am not much for dancing, but I do enjoy the merriment of a ball."

"If there are ladies who wish to dance," Lady Purity said, "I hope you will put yourself to the trouble of being agreeable and offering them a partner. Otherwise, you are attending the wrong venue and ought to have gone to the theatre where you are permitted only to watch without participating."

Quinn sent Matthew a quick, side-eye glance. His friend thought Purity a stickling, prim, goody two-shoes. That much was clear. Matthew wanted him to like her for he intended to have her in his life permanently.

"I believe the lady has a point," he said. "If a wallflower sees you lounging, she will not know you don't wish to dance. She will naturally think you don't want to dance with her."

"Exactly, Lord Foxford," Lady Purity said, giving him a genuine smile.

Matthew's heart warmed at having won her approval. Then she leaned closer, allowing him to catch the delicate aroma of her rose perfume, an instantly arousing scent.

"But it is best not to call any lady a *wallflower*, any more than you would wish to be known as a *wall-prop* simply because you and Lord Quinn chose to stand and chat."

She was correct of course, except no one in their right mind would look at him or Quinn and think any such thing, not with their obvious good looks. Whereas, it was painfully clear why a shy female hugged the wall, fearful of any man's notice.

However, Matthew wouldn't point that out. Instead, he nodded sagely.

Purity included Quinn in her next pronouncement. "It would be perfectly proper for you two gentlemen to escort my mother and me to the refreshment area in the other room."

Matthew nearly laughed at the expression on Quinn's face. His friend didn't know he'd asked for such instruction. Before Quinn judged her insufferable, Matthew had to explain.

"Lady Purity has graciously agreed to *my* request of tutelage in the social graces. Since I was remiss in bringing a refreshment to them, which I previously offered, I appreciate her reminder."

"The social graces," Quinn repeated, and Matthew could tell he was a hairsbreadth away from laughing.

Quickly, he offered Lady Purity his arm, confident Quinn would escort Lady Diamond.

They hadn't gone two steps when Varley appeared, letting his gaze go between Matthew and Purity. He looked as if he might say something, but after a shallow bow to Purity, he moved on.

"Do you know that man, my lord?" Purity asked. "Since he was directly in our path and made eye contact, I wonder why he didn't make an introduction."

"An acquaintance from university and from my club, but not a friend."

Matthew was glad Varley hadn't shouldered him aside rudely as he had before. Following the viscount's path, he saw Varley meet up with a blond-haired lady whom Matthew knew too well. While her first name, which he'd rarely used, escaped him, he was sure it was Lady Tupmoure, with whom he'd had a torrid affair, lasting all of a fortnight.

Her surname had struck Matthew funny in a most juvenile way when he'd first learned it, and she had well lived up to the moniker. But apart from her singular skill, Matthew had found her to be unamusing, petty, and worst of all, a clinging vine. Seeing her again, he wished Varley joy of her, certain at least in bed he would experience that and more.

Refreshments were unfortunately more like the meager fare provided by Almack's outdated assembly rooms than a sumptuous repast. Yet the bread wasn't stale, at least, and was offered with creamy butter and fish paste. There were also cubes of aged cheddar and decanters of claret that was surprisingly full bodied.

"Not the worst," Quinn said, as they all put bread and cheese upon their plates and wandered the hall into the dining room where some had taken seats.

"Would you ladies like to sit?" Matthew asked.

In a few moments, the countess and her daughter were seated with a place to put their wine glasses and plates. Matthew and Quinn likewise had a place to rest their glasses while standing behind the ladies' chairs.

Quinn made himself sound respectable with stories of his large family and his success at university. Naturally, he let it slip he was a viscount in case the Diamonds were unaware. Matthew didn't mind his friend's boasting, so long as he kept himself polite.

Associating with Quinn could only increase Matthew's own respectability. It seemed to work, for both the countess and her daughter relaxed. If the ladies only knew that Quinn's name was not on everyone's tongues for the simple reason his appetite was mainly for females who weren't members of the *ton*, and hence of no interest to anybody.

When the music began again, Purity was whisked away from him onto the dance floor. To please her, he made the effort to find a lady who had not yet been asked for the next dance. At least Matthew could be on the parquet at the same time, even if he didn't care to see his kitten gazing at some other swell.

After what seemed an interminable time, it was his turn again with the only true diamond at the ball. The moment he claimed Purity, looking like a luscious satin rose petal, he enjoyed a sensation of rightness and satisfaction, not to mention a roaring wave of desire, which washed over him as they got into position.

"Did you notice how I danced with every wallfl— That is, every young lady who needed a partner?"

He hoped he'd scored a few more points on the dart board of their burgeoning association.

"I didn't notice, my lord. I was correctly giving my attention to each of my partners."

Had he danced with all those chits for nothing?

"But I think it is extremely gentlemanly of you to do so. I imagine after tonight, we won't need to do any further instruction. From what I've seen, I must conclude you knew everything all along and was merely in want of a little pressing to remind you."

The only thing he wanted to press was her body against the wall while covering her mouth with his own. Since voicing that inappropriate thought would earn him the loss of his dance partner for good, he didn't say it. Then he had another idea.

"I suppose you are correct, my lady. Although I was hoping we could go riding, and you would ensure I didn't say or do anything vulgar while upon horseback. Perhaps I shouldn't even suggest anything apart from a carriage ride in case the lady cannot sit a horse."

She gazed up at him. "Why would you say or do anything untoward while riding that you wouldn't do with your feet upon the ground?"

He shrugged. "There is the obvious sensual nature of riding a horse, in some ways mimicking the movement of a good tupping once you get up to a gallop."

Lady Purity gasped.

"No, it's true," he vowed, as if she were going to disavow his words. "Apart from that, following a woman on horseback is a veritable feast for the male eyes, watching the swaying of both the horse and the feminine form in harmony."

He knew he was getting to her by the way she missed a step.

"With a carriage ride on the other hand, one can enjoy the close quarters. Delightful! Even better if the lady's chaperone rides far behind."

"My lord," she said softly.

"Yes?" He hoped his face was the picture of innocence.

"Gentlemen do not say *any* of those things aloud."

"Don't they?" He whirled her along the length of the floor. "Yet my friends and I speak this way all the time. Did I mention I have never courted a woman before?"

"Yes, you did, nor had a female friend, apparently."

"Is it that obvious?" he asked.

"Sadly, it is."

That made him smile, which he quickly tried to quash and turn into a frown.

"I guess there are still some things for me to learn. Polite discourse being one."

She tilted her head, taking his measure. For a second, he thought she'd seen through his ruse. Sure of it when she parted her lips to speak.

"Purity," he jumped in, "will you ride in the park with me and give me some tips on appropriate topics of conversation?"

"My lord!" she said again, with agitation.

"What now, did I step on your foot?"

"You used my given name."

He grinned at her. "It slipped out. Do you prefer *kitten* after all?"

"I prefer neither. Is this dance exceedingly long?"

"I don't think so. Shall I call out to the manager and ask how much longer? I hope you're not eager to get away from me. I could hold you all night in my arms, preferably off the dance floor."

She shook her head. "You have gone too far. Now I know you are testing me with your impudence."

"Or is it im*pru*dence?" Matthew asked, hoping she wouldn't abandon him.

When she looked down at the floor, however, and back at him, he could see the laughter shining in her eyes. *Gorgeous, breathtaking eyes.* He thanked God he'd come across her at Lansdowne House. All at once, it dawned on him.

"*You* broke the rules!"

"I beg your pardon?" she asked.

"At Lansdowne House. If you hadn't flaunted propriety and gone by yourself to the drawing room, we never would have met. Thus, you came into my uncultivated sphere of your own volition. How wonderful, don't you think?"

"I don't understand what you are so pleased about."

"Only that we met because you behaved more like me. It was fortuitous, maybe even fate. And I am asking you to bring me into your world by teaching me to be more like you."

He hoped she would think their meeting romantic and fall into his arms, or in the current situation, offer him some hope of doing so in the future.

Instead, her expression became alarmed.

"Stop," she ordered quietly but firmly.

CHAPTER EIGHT

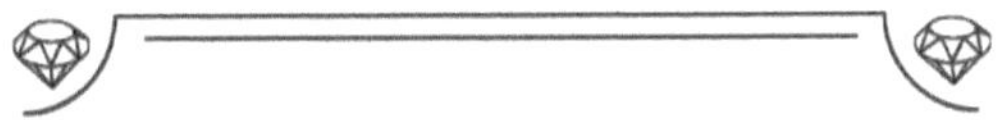

Matthew loved the way Purity's eyes flashed, catching the lights from around the room and looking like true sapphires.

"Why?" he asked, leaning down to catch her fragrance.

"The music, my lord," she said, glancing around, her voice sounding choked. She even had put a hand up to his chest. "It has stopped, yet you are still holding on to me."

Matthew sighed heavily. "Another mistake."

She was tugging to free herself, and they were in danger of making a spectacle. Quickly releasing his hold, he stepped back before calmly offering her his arm. Purity took it despite looking around to make sure no one had witnessed their lagging behind the other dancers.

In truth, he hadn't noticed the song had ended, too enchanted by everything about her.

Strangely, Varley of all people was watching them, although he turned away as soon as Matthew spied him. That man had a bee in his bonnet to be sure. Perhaps nothing more than blatant male interest in the most exquisite female in the room.

Maybe others were envious of how he'd scooped up the Season's diamond in both nature and name—for by his reckoning, he was the only gentleman to be granted two dances.

The rest of the evening he had to continue partnering with other ladies in case Purity was watching. But he stopped before the last dance so he could speak with her mother.

"I hope you've had a pleasurable evening, Lady Diamond."

"I have, thank you. Seeing my daughter happy gives me great happiness in return."

"May I collect Lady Purity for a ride in Hyde Park in two days? Weather permitting, naturally."

"It would be best if you ask her directly, my lord, for unlike my eldest daughter and my son, riding is not Lady Purity's favorite pastime."

"And what is?" he asked.

The countess narrowed her eyes. "If my daughter wishes you to know more about her, she will tell you herself. However, as far as the park goes, she would enjoy an open-air carriage more than horses, as long as we send a chaperone on horseback to accompany you."

"A splendid idea." Matthew decided not to wait and ask Purity. He would turn up and say the countess had given him permission.

They didn't call him the Fox for nothing.

MORE EXCITED THAN HE ought to be for a simple park outing in broad daylight, Matthew practically hopped out of his curricle. He enjoyed driving his jaunty two-wheeled contraption, sometimes a little too swiftly if the park wasn't crowded.

With his heart thumping at the prospect of seeing Purity again and his step light—*was this what it felt like to really admire a female?*—he rapped on the Diamonds' door.

Their butler, to whom he was now an accustomed visitor, gave Matthew entrance, allowing him to wait in the drawing room. The Piccadilly home was starting to feel familiar and comfortable.

For this reason, when a man he'd never seen before came in behind him, Matthew's hackles immediately rose at the notion of a rival suitor. That was until he noticed the distinct family resemblance.

"Mr. Dunley tells me you are Lord Foxford," said the dark-haired stranger with eyes as blue as his sister's. "I am the only Diamond brother."

"Well met," Matthew said, shaking the proffered hand and thinking him jovial at the onset. "As I understand it, you have no title different from your rather unique family name, thus you are Lord Diamond, just as your father."

"Indeed, I am. Sometimes confusing, but usually we muddle through. If there is a bill to pay for a horse or the tailor, I refer those to the senior Lord Diamond. If a pretty lady comes calling, then naturally, I am the Lord Diamond she seeks."

Matthew smiled, liking him on the spot. "I am here to take your sister for a ride."

"As am I," Diamond said. "I shall be your shadow on horseback."

"Ah, I see. Our chaperone." Matthew's happiness dimmed a little. He wasn't going to be able to pull anything over with this snappy young lord on the watch.

"Don't worry," young Diamond said. "I'm not a frig pig. Just behave with common decency and none of us shall end up in the gossip rags."

"Good day, Brother, Lord Foxford," Purity greeted them as she entered. "Apparently, I am being taken out in a carriage without being properly asked, as if I am a child or a dimwit. Either way, I do not appreciate it."

Her brother smiled as if used to such protests. However, since her expression was pleasant and she was dressed for the occasion in a ruddy-hued paisley dress and shawl with a matching bonnet, Matthew assumed she was game for the outing and merely needed her feathers smoothed.

"Lady Purity, my intent was to show you and your family the utmost respect, going above and beyond by asking your mother for the honor of taking you to the park. Alas, afterward, I didn't see you again at the ball. I was unaware I ought to have sent a formal invitation to your home after getting one of your parents' permission. Obviously, I am still greatly in need of your tutelage, and I hope you are not offended."

Diamond's mouth had dropped as if he'd never heard such deference to his sister. Purity, on the other hand, narrowed her eyes, recognizing drivel when she heard it.

"All you had to do was ask," she said softly, holding his gaze and utterly mesmerizing him until she blinked. "I am ready," she added.

Turning on her booted heel, she led the way from the room.

Diamond gave him a pitying look, as if Matthew were in for a trying time with his arse on a bandbox and no more hope of overcoming her iron barrier of politeness than of breaking down a brick wall with a teaspoon.

But Matthew knew her weakness—*his kiss!* Unfortunately, it was a useless weapon if he couldn't get the fair damsel alone.

On the other hand, he was granted the pleasure of close confines, feeling the heat of her pressed against his side, while she held her hat with one hand against the mild zephyr barely blowing through the leaves.

"Not enough pins, my lady?" he asked, giving her a sideways glance.

"I fear not. A little gusty out but blissfully sunny." With that, she directed her face toward the sunshine, closed her eyes, and seemed to drink it in.

What an odd kitten! She most assuredly wouldn't forgive herself if she blemished her skin, yet she was being almost devil-may-care about it.

With a start, he realized he ought to put up the hood to protect her. But that would shield them somewhat from her brother's watchful eye. *What a conundrum!*

After a minute of his wondering what to do, his companion said, "My lord, you appear to be on the horns of a dilemma, furrowing your brow when you ought to be relaxed and enjoying the day."

"I confess I don't know the correct course of action."

"Tell me," she said, placing her gloved hand upon his arm.

Such a simple gesture, trusting, genteel—and arousing as anything short of her dragging his head down to kiss her! He was momentarily tongue-tied.

Him, the Fox!

More than that, his shaft sprang to life, throbbing with longing. Not a particularly prudent time for scorching lust, so he took a deep breath and focused on the Hyde Park Corner entrance, turning right to go along the carriage path running parallel to Park Lane.

Then he cleared his throat. "I merely wondered whether, given the sunshine, I should put up the hood."

She laughed lightly. "Why all that fretting for such a trivial matter, my lord?"

"I wouldn't want your brother to think I'm trying to hide you from him."

"I see. How considerate of you. Extremely un-Foxlike, I would go so far as to say. Anyway, we'll be in the shade of the chestnut and lime trees soon enough. Thank you for worrying."

He'd been called a considerate lover before, but a compliment of simply being thoughtful was novel. He liked it, despite how parts of him desperately wanted to show her the other ways he could be considerate, too.

In fact, his length was not diminishing but pressing against his trousers, and he began to recite Shakespeare in his head to help it subside.

As soon as they entered the park, Matthew could see it was too full with other Londoners enjoying the warm day to show off any fancy driving, nothing to make her squeal with excitement or terror while she clutched him closely, pressing her breasts to his arm.

And there was his arousal again, as if he were a green youth and keeping company with his first milkmaid.

"*The Times* got it wrong yesterday. Did you read it?" she asked.

"I did not," he confessed. *That damned paper!* He had started to go out of his way *not* to read any but the most serious of the business pages, hoping not to happen upon any society gossip.

"A small mention was all," she told him, "reporting how badly you behaved on Lady Tisendale's dance floor, practically assaulting some horribly offended lady before abandoning her and leaving early. I attended the entire ball, and when you weren't dancing with me, you hardly danced. The few you did partake of seemed perfectly executed, not that I was watching you all evening, of course."

"I wouldn't have minded if you had been," he said, pleased to learn she'd been spying on him the way he had been on her. However, used to the truth being twisted, the answer was obvious. "The horribly offended lady was you."

"Me?" She paused. "*Oh!* When the music stopped," she recalled. Then she shook her head. "But you didn't assault me, and I wasn't offended, only a little embarrassed in case people were looking."

Matthew shrugged. "For the most part, some witness gives them a kernel of a story, and they make an entire meal out of it."

Diamond came alongside, interrupting their discussion.

"You can't get up to anything untoward in such a throng," he said. "I see a chum up ahead. I'll circle back in a few minutes."

With that, he urged his spirited mount forward.

"Adam," Purity called after him, but he disappeared between other riders and carriages. "Oh, what a nuisance. Unreliable half-wit of a brother."

"He is correct, isn't he?" Matthew asked. "I can't do anything wicked like kiss you, no matter how much I desperately wish to do so."

She blinked, lips slightly parted as her gaze dropped to his mouth. He could see the flutter of her pulse at the base of her neck.

"Incorrigible," she said finally.

Matthew could tell if they'd been alone, a kiss would certainly have been allowed, and it would have been spectacular. Her breasts were rising and falling more quickly with the pace of her breathing.

He would need more than the cover of a carriage hood to be able to follow his wish.

"Besides, it's not our behavior that is in question," she said, her cheeks pink.

Matthew attributed their high color more to her sensual thoughts than from the sun.

"It is the distinct inappropriateness of my being seated beside you," she continued, "with no chaperone in sight. Mother will tan his hide when we return."

"I say we should enjoy ourselves while we can."

"That does seem to be your philosophy," she agreed.

If he wasn't mistaken, she rolled her eyes.

Then she added, "Furthermore, I am enjoying myself."

"Then stop worrying over what other people will think. Just this once."

She took in a sharp breath and sent it out in an exasperated puff.

"Very well. I shall try."

"After all," he said, "you are a young woman with your life ahead of you, born into wealth and comfort, assured because of your beauty and sweetness to make a good marriage match. And yet, you do not always seem happy."

He hoped he hadn't said too much, but he added, "I have only been blessed to hear your laughter once, maybe twice."

"What you say is true," she agreed. "My eldest sister is nearly always happy and laughing and making others do the same. The comparison between us has ever been stark and to my detriment. I am not serious by nature, but I tend to want everything to be just so *before* I can relax."

"Really?" he quipped. "I hadn't noticed."

As intended, his words elicited a smile.

"When you find everything is not up to your standards," he observed, "you wish to make them perfect ahead of any enjoyment."

"Precisely," she said. "Ever since childhood. If my parents held a party, I felt it was my duty to make certain the guests were happy."

"There are things you cannot control, my lady," he reminded her, thinking of his father's untimely death. But he wouldn't mention that early, dreadful lesson when they were trying to have an entertaining ride. Yet, perhaps he could give her a new perspective.

"If people around us wish to have unkind thoughts, there is little you can do. What's more, even amongst the things you can influence, you might find a sense of relief if you don't worry about them, either. Occasionally, let someone else be concerned over all the trivialities of the day."

"The trivialities?" she asked.

He nodded. "Most of them are decidedly small issues, which will be forgotten when the sun sets, so why bother yourself?"

After a moment, she nodded, too. "I shall attempt a respite from trying to bring to order that which is insignificant." She tapped her chin. "I should make a list of things with which I am overly troubled. I can consult it to make sure I do not—"

When Matthew began to laugh, she broke off.

Raising her dark eyebrows, she asked, "What have I said that is amusing you?"

"You are going to make a list," he began, but fell to laughing again.

She crossed her arms over her shapely bosom.

"Please," he said between chortles. "Don't take offense. You must see how funny that is. An orderly, *careful* list of things you are trying not to care about."

He could imagine her diligently going to her writing desk, marking down what she ought not to worry over, and then worrying over whether she had included everything. Matthew laughed even harder.

"Cease braying like a donkey," she said without rancor, cracking a smile. "You are correct. I shall endeavor to be more like you in some matters."

He gasped for air. "I wouldn't suggest being so drastic in changing your nature."

She ignored him. "I should go somewhere fun where one needn't worry."

"And where is that, my lady?"

"Vauxhall," she pronounced, looking pleased with her suggestion.

He winced.

"Is there a problem?"

Shrugging, he tried to put it delicately. "I haven't been there for about three years, but my impression was the gardens had lost their sheen of respectability even then."

This time, she chuckled. "Did you just hear yourself, my lord? That sounds like something I would say."

"True enough." He was enjoying their companionable chatter. Not as much as he would enjoy tupping her, but he would take what was given, like a starving man with crumbs. "But I wouldn't want you to be shocked by the vulgar guests."

The whores who lingered upon the Dark Walk at Vauxhall were not the caliber of whom he ever partook, even as a randy youth. The food, too, was considered to lack the quality of its heyday. As for the entertainment, he simply wasn't sure. It had gone from being theatre-level to something one might witness at a country fair.

"My parents have a warm place in their hearts for Vauxhall since they went there when they were young and falling in love. They don't care how the Pleasure Gardens have changed. They still enjoy the fireworks and sometimes stroll around the less seedy sections at the front. Maybe tomorrow night, they will take me and my brother, too."

She cocked her head, looking more knowing than he'd previously believed. "*He* has an interest in looking at some of those vulgar guests you mentioned."

Matthew was shocked she was teasing him over hedge whores where young Diamond was concerned. But he thought she was also asking him a question.

"I have no interest in looking," he promised.

She frowned.

"Or touching," he amended. "What I am hoping to convey is that I do not go to the seedier parts of Vauxhall for any reason."

She smiled. "Good. You have enough trouble not causing a scandal in a ballroom or the theatre. I cannot imagine what you might get up to in a dark garden." Then she laughed heartily at her own words.

The sound was like water bubbling from a spring, enchanting him. She became more appealing the more he knew of her.

"Perhaps I shall see you and your family at Vauxhall tomorrow night."

"Perhaps," she agreed.

CHAPTER NINE

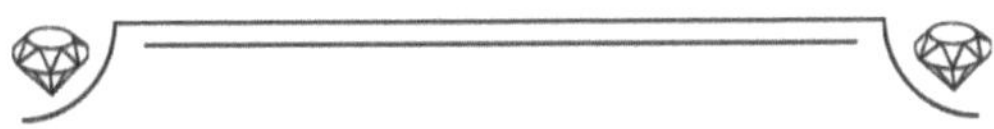

It was late, Vauxhall was growing chilly, and Purity had been denied the excitement of Foxford's presence all evening. It was vexing. When she'd mentioned attending, he'd expressed an interest in the place since he hadn't been in years.

Stupidly, she had pinned her hopes upon seeing him. Moreover, she'd been vain enough to think he might go merely to spend time with her.

The excursion hadn't been for nothing. She and her friend Harriet thought the music to be fine and the fireworks great fun, despite how fewer people of quality attended ever since the Pleasure Gardens had declared bankruptcy in 1840.

As Foxford had mentioned, some considered it a shabby shadow of its former glory. Regardless, her parents and brother had readily agreed to her suggestion to go, and Clarity had come with her husband, Hollidge, simply for a lark.

Purity had tried—and failed—to keep from looking for Foxford from the moment she'd arrived. Hours later, having eaten the less than palatable food, seen all the various amusements, including the well-known Cascade with its mechanical carriage and waterfall, and a wondrous show by a fire-eater, they were ready to leave.

When they turned from the Grand Walk and headed toward the gate leading to the ferry, she caught her breath. There *he* was, directly to her right, standing before one of the supper boxes. For a moment, she stopped to gawk.

Foxford was laughing with his friend, Lord Quinn, and with three females! He had probably been at Vauxhall all evening, and she simply hadn't encountered him. Since he was with women of obviously low repute, given their state of disgraceful undress, and since Purity had not been anywhere near the infamous Dark Walk, the reason for not running into him was clear.

He had lied to her about his interest in the vulgar, scantily clad women of the night.

Embarrassed for him to be with such low company, she hoped he didn't notice her, nor did she want her parents to see him either. Yet as she hurried to catch up to her family, who had continued walking, Foxford spied her.

His laughter halted, and from the corner of her eye, she watched him say something to his companions before rushing to intercept her.

"Lady Purity, well met," he said jovially.

"Hardly," she quipped, having to stop for politeness' sake, seeing her family halt up ahead and wait for her.

"Hardly?" he repeated. "Have you not enjoyed yourself? I know the food is mediocre, but you were correct that the entertainment is still worth the shilling admittance."

She could not tell him it was he who had displeased her and not Vauxhall.

"I am leaving, my lord. I bid you good evening."

He frowned. "Are you angry with me? I know we had mentioned meeting, but I was held up on personal business. When I arrived, I sought you out."

"I assure you I was not with that group of *ladies*," she said the word with exaggeration. "Besides, it matters to me not a whit whether we encounter one another. I mustn't keep my family waiting."

Before she left, Purity couldn't help a last remark.

"At least I know why you don't have time to write down names in the evening. You most likely never retire alone. Besides, why take note of a new acquaintance when she is still with you when you awaken in the morning."

Turning on her heel, she strode away, aghast at her own audacity. She had all but accused Foxford of spending the night with a slovenly lady of the night—as if there was anything unusual in that!

As if her disappointment mattered to him anyway.

Purity wished she hadn't seen him at all. Naively, she'd begun to create a fantasy in her mind that the so-called Fox was becoming a tame, upstanding citizen.

Thus, she was surprised upon receiving a letter from him the next morning. Two pages of writing disclosed everything he had done the day before and names with descriptions of every person whom he'd met.

Everyone except the ladies of the evening! There was no mention of rouge-cheeked women with red-painted lips and low-cut necklines. But at the end of it, he'd signed off by saying he was sipping brandy at midnight and going directly to bed.

Purity couldn't help but smile. At least he'd turned in early. What's more, even his penmanship was unexpectedly tidy.

Just when she'd condemned him as an unabashed rake, the man tried to convince her he was more of a monk.

However, over her breakfast an hour later, *The Times* had a different tale, and since she'd seen him with her own eyes, she couldn't discount it.

Lords F__ and Q__ were seen making a depraved display with the lowest company at Vauxhall. The type of pleasure they sought was easy to guess. The latter of the pair would do well to stay clear of the former unless he wishes to mire in the Fox's den of inequity. The former used his wily charm to particularly ill use in the Pleasure Gardens and was last seen escorting two of the 'ladies' into his carriage, while Lord Q settled for one.

Purity felt ill. Even more so when Foxford presented his calling card later that day and entered for a visit. He was impeccably dressed and smelled like Pears soap. The fresh scent, mildly spicy with a hint of thyme, was almost as alluring as his cologne. But it reminded her of why he might need a morning bath—attempting to wash away the dreadful debauchery of the night before.

"I didn't expect to see you today," she said.

"Will there be tea?" Foxford asked, his eyes dancing with amusement. "That's the polite thing to do, I've learned. Offer your guest a cup of tea."

"Not to the uninvited guest, if you recall." She left it at that.

After Alice took a seat at the other end of the room, Purity sat upon the edge of a wingback chair, not relaxing for an instant nor giving in to the usual thrilling tingle caused by his presence.

"To what do I owe this visit?" she asked, doing her best to maintain a disinterested tone. After all, it was not her place to chastise a grown man for his actions, no matter how disenchanted she was by them and consequently, by him.

And Purity did feel extremely let down, having hoped he would curtail his wilder side.

"I'm merely continuing in the fashion we have begun," he said simply. "To further my quest."

She could barely look at him. "You won't find a respectable wife among the women with whom you kept company at Vauxhall."

He laughed. "Absolutely not. I wholeheartedly agree."

"Then why waste your time?" she snapped, instantly wishing she hadn't. Her detachment had lasted less than a minute. What's more, she was all too aware if he'd taken two of them in his carriage, it had not been a waste of time at all. Instead, they were rather good value for his coin.

"I didn't waste my time," he said, confirming her fears.

The man was too entrenched in his ways. Another wave of disappointment rolled through her, as he was all but confessing to enjoying himself with those prostitutes.

"I see," she said. He was an unrepentant libertine.

"Good," he continued, as if the matter were closed.

Since it was his private business, Purity supposed it was.

"What did you think of my writing assignment?" he asked.

She had forgotten the two pages entirely. Now she considered them.

"It was detailed, especially for such a busy man." *Busy carousing and entertaining not one but two females,* she added silently.

His grin was almost boyish, squeezing her heart with a pang of longing. If only he weren't such a thundering buck.

"The account of my day didn't take too long. I cobbled it together, by which I mean I dictated it to my valet over a glass of brandy before heading to my bedroom for a more important matter."

Purity gasped and rose to her feet.

"You have gone too far, my lord."

Foxford jumped up. "I intended no offense," he said, frowning. "In truth, it was a bit of a rude jest, but I meant only that I was ready for a good night's sleep. Am I not allowed to mention a bedroom in a lady's presence, either?"

"You are not to bring up your nighttime antics at all," she said, ready to throw him out.

He ran a hand over his jaw as if contemplating. "I am starting to think there are too many barred words and topics, making it impossible for members of the opposite sex to carry on a conversation without stumbling into some of them."

"It is my nature to hope and wish you could behave like an honorable gentleman," Purity said, clasping her hands together to keep from wringing them like an anxious ninny. "However, since you cannot comport yourself, I shall no longer keep company with you. I want you to leave and not return."

His astounded expression gave her pause.

"My Lord Foxford, can you really think I would wish to spend time with you when you come from your bed having dallied with not one but two loose women? Even if you have attempted to scrub off your debauchery."

"Scrub off my debauchery?" he repeated, appearing entirely confounded. "What in blue blazes are you talking about?"

"You and those women I saw you with last night at Vauxhall," she reminded him. "Did you not leave with two of them?"

His mouth dropped open. "How could you know that? You had already departed the gardens."

"And yet I know," she said, her voice soft, wishing it didn't sound as sad as she felt. "All of London knows."

"I see. If you will give me a chance to tell you what transpired, I will," he said, "although since we have no arrangement between us, I don't owe you any explanation."

She narrowed her eyes at his peevish tone.

"It's true, you owe me nothing," she agreed.

They stood staring at one another like adversaries.

Then he cleared his throat. "Since I thought we were becoming friends, I wish to tell you anyway," he added. "For I do not welcome your thinking the worst of me."

He still sounded annoyed, but she'd caught him in his wicked ways with her own eyes.

"I did indeed leave with two of the women."

"Ah-ha" nearly burst from her lips, but she restrained herself. He was still a guest in her home. But she could remind him of the sordid truth.

"You took them in your carriage with the shades drawn."

Foxford shook his head. "No, I don't believe they were drawn."

Purity realized she'd added that detail, thinking he would have wanted utter privacy in order to do whatever hedonistic things they could get up to in a rocking carriage.

She shrugged. "Go on." *Would he confess to taking them to his home?*

"The two women live at a… a rooming house on the other side of the Haymarket, and I took them there."

Her stomach churned. Some brothels might be plush, housing the elite of Mayfair's courtesans, but not that far east. It would be a low, murky place with desperate, possibly diseased women.

Thinking of Foxford going indoors with them amongst the tattered bed-hangings, the filthy sheets with bedbugs, perhaps even lice, and the worn canvas curtains, not to mention the worn women, Purity shuddered and took a step back.

"I let them out of my carriage, and they went inside," he continued. "My driver took me home to write my assignment before I had a well-earned glass of brandy. And I dispatched the pages to you first thing."

Wanting to trust him, Purity almost allowed herself, except . . . It didn't beg believing. He was Foxy, the Fox, the Bachelor Baron, and all that. Even then, he was ridiculously attractive despite being a base and shameless libertine.

"You must excuse me if I find it difficult to accept a version in which you allow your fine carriage to be used as a hackney for London's light-skirts and then drop them off without enjoying their charms."

"That's because they hadn't any."

"You seemed amused by them when I walked by," she shot back.

After a hesitation, he said, "You are jealous." And then his annoyingly smug grin returned to his handsome face.

"Do not be absurd." She fisted her hands at her sides, wishing he wasn't correct. She was seethingly jealous of those blasted blowsabellas, but she was determined to fight her feelings for him tooth and nail until he was nothing more to her than a worn-out shoe.

"I don't have any personal interest in you beyond a sense of pity for the woman whom you take as your wife, for she shall have to put up with your philandering." Purity detested the tenor of their confrontation, and her queasiness grew. "I have already asked you to leave."

His expression darkened. "I haven't lied to you." Then he caught himself and his gaze slipped sideways before returning to hers. She wondered which lie he was recalling.

"At least, not about this," Foxford hedged.

"Oh!" she tossed up her hands in frustration while expelling a breath of utter exasperation. "You are impossible!"

"I am telling you the truth. Why would I take common Drury Lane vestals when I can afford a flash mollisher any day of the year—or *every day* for that matter?"

His anger had returned, and he stepped nearer, causing Purity to glance down the far end of the room where Alice dozed like an old dog.

"*You* are the one who is impossible," he insisted, closing the distance to stand toe-to-toe with her. "I have done everything you've instructed me to do, as if you are my sergeant. I haven't stepped a hairsbreadth out of line, not even when I desperately wanted to do this."

With those menacing words, he grasped her around her waist so swiftly she didn't have time to pull away or to shout. And then he claimed her mouth.

She melted. It was the only word she could think of with a brain turned quickly to mush. Purity would swear he had the touch of a necromancer, putting a mystical spell over her. For whenever he was close, she was not herself. Heat spread within. Flames licked through her body, making her breasts feel heavy and her nipples grow taut. Even more maddening was the throbbing pulse at her core.

Leaning into him, she tilted her head and returned his kiss with vigor. Somehow, her hands were already behind his head, and her fingers were threading into his hair. *So soft.*

Foxford groaned before demanding entrance to her mouth and sliding his tongue inside when she granted it. At the same time, his hands left her waist to cup her buttocks and grind her against his hips.

The room fell away. Her very existence as Lady Purity Diamond seemed to disintegrate. She was pure sensation instead. Breathing raggedly, her heart pounding, her body hot and drenched with pleasure. She wanted what men and women had been doing throughout time.

And she wanted that with Foxford! She could feel his arousal against her stomach and knew it meant he wanted her just as badly.

How long they kissed, fused by eager mouths with their bodies pressed so close her breasts were flattened against his chest, she had no idea. But all the while, his strong fingers flexed over her backside, making her long to experience his practiced touch all over her sizzling skin.

And then, he drew back. No longer did the baron look smug or angry. She would vow he appeared as stunned as she was.

"Why would I waste my time with any other woman?" he repeated.

She put her hand to her lips. They still felt warm and, if she could credit the sensation, a little swollen.

"In case you still think I am frequenting the lowliest brothels in London, I tell you in all earnestness and swear upon my father's soul that I did nothing more than offer those women a ride home. A small part of me thought you would be proud of my chivalry." He tugged upon the sleeve of his frock coat.

"And when I do take a wife, she shall have no need to worry about other women—whores or not—for I shall be entirely devoted to her. Good day."

Then he took his leave. After the sound of his footsteps died out, she still stood frozen, thinking herself every inch a dunce. She'd taken *The Times* small kernel, as he'd called it before, and made a twelve-course meal of it, adding in details that were not even written.

If only he hadn't been so vulgar as to use the word *whore*.

A loud snort came from beside the bookcase as Alice awakened herself and swiftly rose to her feet.

"Oh, my lady, I must have drifted off. Has your young man left already? I hope I didn't miss anything." Then she laughed and added, "Not that any of us ever have to worry about you, Lady Purity."

CHAPTER TEN

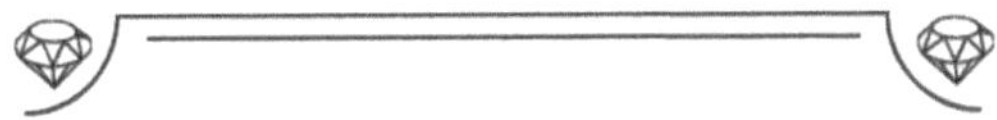

Matthew realized he was striding down Piccadilly without any destination in mind when his driver, following along beside, called down to him.

"Shall I take the horses home, my lord?"

"Yes, I shall walk the rest of the way." Although he was presently going in the opposite direction.

After watching Griffin disappear down the road, he turned left onto Old Bond Street and kept wandering farther than he meant to go.

Yet still, his thoughts were with Lady Purity.

Infuriating woman!

Spouting off her societal rules and then so easily breaking them as soon as he kissed her. Not only did she relax her morals, her entire body had softened against him. He, too, had felt molten desire. *It was the oddest thing!*

Not that desire was a strange phenomenon when he was kissing a lovely female, but the overwhelming intensity of it most assuredly was. He had been rendered helpless and even docile. If she'd put her finger to his chin, she could have led him anywhere.

"*Pah!*" And he'd sworn the truth on his father's soul. *How belittling!* As if he had to prove himself and his honor to Lady Purity Diamond. He was bending over backward to live up to expectations and got nothing for it but a scolding.

And a kiss that had swept him into a private world where only the two of them existed. *Miraculous!* If he'd had any doubt he was pursuing the correct woman, it had vanished when their lips touched again.

"Dolls!" he exclaimed, seeing a display of toys.

Coming out of his musings, he realized he'd reached the ever-intriguing Pantheon Bazaar on Oxford Street. Moreover, he had decided to purchase a doll for Diana, after seeing her curl up with a cushion in her small arms, and had nearly forgotten.

These were all porcelain with pale hair and blue eyes. The eyes were right, but he wanted the beauty of a dark-haired doll as rare as his Diamond.

"Her age, my lord?" asked the clerk when Matthew went in and inquired about the display.

"She's in her early twenties," he answered, still glancing around the shop.

"Then you want a collectible, my lord."

"A collectible?" Suddenly, Matthew laughed. "You wish to know the age of the child. Naturally. My mistake, madam. She's four, and a little rough on her toys, so not in need of a collectible."

"Then not porcelain, my lord. You can browse these fine wax-head dolls."

Matthew looked them over. "Why do they all have the same pale hair, not exactly blond yet not brown either?"

"It is mohair," the toy seller said. "Manufactured here in London and supplied to doll makers not only in Britain, my lord, but also in France and Germany."

Matthew picked one up.

"The body is cotton and sawdust," the woman continued. "Quite durable."

"They are cleverly done," he agreed, lifting up the little arm, which felt like stuffed cotton until the elbow.

"The lower part is kid leather."

Each hand had four sewn fingers. He glanced at the clerk. She smiled and shrugged.

"The children don't mind," she insisted.

Matthew wasn't sure it did the children of England any great service to let them grow up thinking some babies had eight fingers, but that was neither here nor there.

"Do you have any dark-haired dolls?"

"I shall have to look in the back. They are more costly since dark hair is actual human hair, and we only ever have one or two."

She disappeared for a few minutes while Matthew picked up another doll and then another. He gave a furtive glance into the bazaar's main thoroughfare, dreading the notion of any of his friends seeing him examining the wee outfits while wondering which one Diana might like best.

But when the toy-seller returned, he knew he'd found the one.

"TELL HER NURSE TO BRING Diana to my study," Matthew said when he returned home, more excited than he ought to be about presenting his gifts. He'd also bought a cradle and a little chair for the doll, and with embarrassment that had caused his face to turn scarlet, he had picked out a change of clothes, too.

"I shall be drummed out of Boodle's," he muttered to himself, but he was joyful all the same.

"Never mind," he said, changing his mind. "I shall go to the nursery."

He hardly ever went up to that floor, as his butler's expression showed.

"Don't worry, Mr. Jacobs," Matthew assured him. "Chaos shall not descend upon us."

Taking the stairs two at a time, Matthew found the nursery door open, the curtains pulled to let in the light, and a tidy room with a little girl sitting on a sofa. Diana was singing to herself despite how Mrs. Caldwell sat nearby reading her a book.

"Daddy," Diana yelled, jumping down and almost knocking everything out of his arms. Quickly, he set the packages down and lifted her to his hip.

"How is my little bug today?"

"Good."

"Has she been good?" he asked Mrs. Caldwell, whose face reminded him of freshly baked bread, although he couldn't say why. Something about her puffy cheeks, he supposed. In any case, he'd been lucky to find her on short notice.

"Miss Diana is always good, aren't you, poppet?"

"Do you mind when she sings while you read?" he asked.

"Not at all," the nurse said. "She's smart as a whip. She knows the story even if she's doing something else. When I ask her about it, I know she's been listening."

He smiled down at the wriggling creature in his arms, looking up at him with soft brown eyes.

"Is it your birthday?" he wondered.

"I don't think so," Diana said.

"Is it Christmas?"

"No," she said more assuredly.

"*Hm*. Shall I return what I've bought you then?" he teased.

"No, Papa!" She pushed at him and squirmed, trying to look down at the packages now she knew they were for her.

"Very well." He set her down. "This one first," he said.

She pulled the lid off the box with her sweet pudgy fingers and then ripped at the tissue paper, making him doubly glad he hadn't bought anything porcelain or breakable. In the next instant, she gasped as she saw the doll's head. Then she drew it out more carefully.

"A baby!" she exclaimed. "A pretty baby!"

Dark-haired and blue-eyed, the doll came wearing a light-blue cotton dress and matching hat, but Matthew bent down and handed Diana the next bundle of tissue paper.

She dropped the baby on her lap to rip it open. A pink dress appeared, not the usual color for a girl, but he thought it lovely anyway, having seen the like on Purity.

"Ooh," Diana cooed and hugged the dress to her as firmly as she'd hugged the doll. It was so easy to make a little girl happy. He needed to learn to do better with an adult female.

The next box was explored in short order, and he helped Diana lift out the painted wooden cradle. She clapped her hands with glee.

"Set it there," she ordered. "Please," she added, the *l* coming out more like a *w*, which he adored.

When they had the doll's bed in the place she wished, Diana laid her in.

"Time to go night-night, Clara," Diana said, having quickly chosen a name.

They opened the last box, and he drew out the little, upholstered chair.

Again, she clapped her hands and yanked the doll out of her slumber to settle her in the chair.

"A short nap," he quipped to Mrs. Caldwell.

"I brush her hair," Diana declared, jumping up to grab her own brush off the dresser before returning to start tearing at the doll's soft, dark hair.

"Easy, poppet," said the nursemaid.

Matthew smiled, glad Diana was happy, but the doll was going to be bald by bedtime, so he needn't have worried much over the hair color.

"I shall see you later," he said, but the little girl didn't even look up, happily scalping her baby.

"I will be your mama," she was telling the doll. "I don't have one, Clara, but now you do."

His heart lurched. He should have bought her a doll three months ago and probably a lot more.

"Mrs. Caldwell. Please tell me if I am remiss in providing anything Diana needs. And not merely needs but wants," he added.

"She's a very happy child," the nanny said. "You've done very well, my lord, if I may say."

Mrs. Caldwell had never asked but seemed to believe him a widower or a man who'd taken in an abandoned babe.

"If you think of anything," he persisted, bending down to drop a kiss on Diana's tawny-haired head before he went to the door.

"She likes to draw, always using a stick in the dirt outside."

He was surprised. The daughter of a baron was drawing in the dirt.

"I shall procure her a slate and a supply of chalk at once," he promised. "And paper, too, with some pencils. Might as well be more permanent than a slate."

"That would be perfect, my lord. I will use the slate to go over her letters with her."

He departed the happy scene. Matthew had taken on the little girl's care without much thought or planning. Luckily, Mrs. Caldwell would sort things out and make sure Diana didn't end up a wildling, not knowing how to read or write.

But the little girl's comment about a mother nagged at him. His usual thoughts would be solely for a wife to fulfill his own needs and desires and to satisfy his longing for pleasures of the female form. Yet Diana made him also wish for a woman who could make her a good mother, one who would guide her and hopefully love her even after having children of her own.

He avidly hoped Purity would be that woman.

PURITY WAS UNABLE TO STOP thinking about Foxford's visit. She wanted to apologize for believing the worst. On the other hand, he had displayed further bad behavior by kissing her.

But it was the very best of bad behavior. She smiled to herself.

In truth, she could heat herself up from tip to toe by simply recollecting it, especially his hands upon her body.

Given Foxford's reputation, no one could blame her for imagining him having a dalliance with one or both of those unfortunate women. Privately, while she thought them dreadfully vulgar, she knew she was being uncharitable. After all, it was unlikely they relished their low state and tawdry profession but had been driven to it by desperate circumstances.

On the other hand, she experienced the thinnest slice of envy at how easily they were able to interact with Foxford in public, even touch him, laugh, and press up against him. If he had been willing, they would have experienced all the mysteries still awaiting her on her wedding night.

She shook her head, wondering how her thoughts had strayed so far, especially when the only man she could picture in the marital bed was the Fox.

Because she insulted him, Purity knew she ought to find a way to apologize. While it wasn't entirely out of the question for her to pay him a visit if her mother was with her, a more appropriate response would be a note. Yet she wished that didn't seem inadequate.

She tapped her chin. Another possibility would be to host a small dinner party and invite Foxford, although having a gathering at her parents' home might lend his invitation too much import. Tongues would wag.

She paced the garden.

Unless other eligible men were invited, along with other single young ladies.

While she had been introduced at court, enjoying the pageantry of meeting the Queen, her parents hadn't provided a coming out party at their home. Purity had specifically requested they did not, loathing the spectacle of an assembly to spotlight herself. Despite her skill upon the piano, she thought it pretentious to invite a bevy of gentlemen and force them to listen.

She shuddered, imagining their eyes studying every inch of her upon meeting, watching how she ate, hanging on her every word, judging her piano recital.

Egad! Why did ladies put themselves through such an ordeal?

Nevertheless, a party of eligible single people, all with one goal in mind—to enjoy an evening with good company and mild flirtation—would be acceptable. She could stomach that. It would be like one of the Fenwicks' parties except without anyone being sent into the hallway.

Warming to the idea, Purity went in search of her father. Fortunately, he was home and in his study. Knowing she could have simply asked her mother, who loved a party and would instantly agree, Purity wished to give the earl the respect he deserved as head of the household.

Tapping upon the door, she heard scrambling noises and a thump. Finally, her father said, "Enter."

Both her parents were in the room. Her father was behind his desk, tugging at his cravat as if it were too tight, and her mother was in the opposite corner, smoothing her hair.

With a breathless appearance as if distraught, Lady Diamond gave her a salutatory wave.

"Is anything amiss?" Purity asked, hoping they hadn't received dire news in a letter from Adam.

"Not at all," her mother said.

"The idea!" her father chimed in.

"What idea?" Purity asked, wondering why they were behaving so strangely.

"Your mother and I were discussing…" he trailed off.

"Getting a dog," Lady Diamond finished after a pause.

Purity frowned. "We have dogs," she said, a pack of them at their country house in Derbyshire.

"Not hunting dogs," her mother said. "A companion dog. A small one, suitable for London, such as the Queen has."

Mention of a dog made Purity think of foxes, which in turn made her think of Foxford, which reminded her why she'd gone to find her father. However, she had to be polite.

"What did you decide?"

"About what?" her father asked, looking at the state of his desk.

Purity noticed it was messier than usual and stepped forward to retrieve some papers that had spilled to the floor.

"About the dog," she said, handing her father the loose sheets. Her parents were usually sharp as tacks.

"We'll be discussing it more later," her father said, grinning at Lady Diamond.

If Purity didn't know better, she would say her mother blushed. *What on earth?*

"Did you wish to speak with me?" the earl asked, finally bringing his full attention to his second eldest daughter.

"I was wondering about a party."

"Let's have one," her mother said at once, making her father smile fondly at his wife.

"I haven't even told you why or what for," Purity protested.

"Who needs a reason?" the countess asked. "It's the social season, and there are plenty of people looking for a place to be festive. Shall we, Diamond?"

"Whatever you want, my love," he returned. "You ladies figure it all out in that magnificent way you have, send me the bills, and tell me when to show up."

CHAPTER ELEVEN

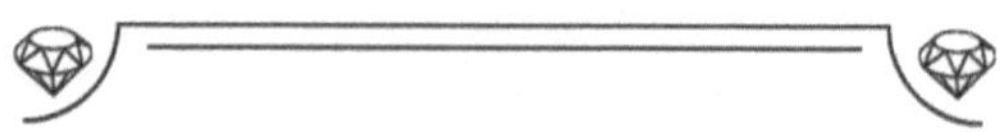

Matthew tried to shake off the shimmers, as he called the case of nerves. He hadn't felt the like in . . . actually, never. Usually, he strolled into an assembly with the confidence of a single man about town who needed nothing and no one. And he often left with the female of his choice or at least with her agreement to meet discreetly later.

While somewhat surprised, he had been beyond pleased to receive an invitation to a party at the Diamonds' residence. The earl and his countess were known as excellent hosts. Naturally, he concluded he was there at Purity's behest. And thus, with his pleasure came a little nervousness. More than he'd ever felt in his life, he wanted her to like him.

If Purity believed him up to snuff in terms of his manners to be in her parents' home and at their table, that was one thing, a rather good thing, at that. However, if she also wished to partner with him while dining, then he would know he was making slow but sure headway, like a ship sailing into the wind.

Unfortunately, on the appointed night, once Matthew arrived, he did not feel singled out despite having kissed her recently in the very room in which he now stood. Upon entering, he soon realized he was one of many unmarried men, including that oaf Emberry and even Quinn.

"Well met," he said, shaking hands with the latter and helping himself to a glass of claret. "This is an unexpected gathering."

"How so?" Quinn asked.

"I didn't see upon the invitation any mention that this was an assembly of the desperately single."

Quinn laughed. "You must not have looked closely enough, old chap. Besides, why else did *you* come?"

Foxford shrugged. "Curiosity, I suppose." He wasn't going to mention how he would go to the ends of the earth if Purity asked him.

"There's Pearson," he added as the viscount strolled in. "I suppose he had to be invited, given his title and fortune, but I swear the man could send a chattering monkey into a stupor of somnambulance within seconds. I can hardly keep my eyes open merely looking at him."

"You're in fine form tonight. Irritated that you won't have the Diamond daughter all to yourself?"

Foxford made a face. "And how did you get on the guest list?"

"I have you to thank, don't you think?" Quinn said. "I must have made such a good impression on your lady when you introduced me at the Tisendale ball."

"You must have. It certainly wasn't your behavior at Vauxhall." Foxford was a little sore at Quinn for that debacle, as his friend had brought the three doxies over while Matthew was hunting down Purity with no luck.

Quinn winced. "I forgot she witnessed that."

"What she didn't witness, *The Times* thoughtfully filled in."

Quinn lifted his glass in a toast. "Ah, yes. I made out slightly less debauched by going home with only one game pullet."

"I didn't go home with any of them," Matthew insisted, but he could see even his friend didn't believe him. "In any case, I explained—"

He interrupted himself when the double doors to the drawing room opened and a bouquet of young ladies entered at once.

What a silly, fantastical, wonderful idea, he thought, to have all the ladies enter as a group. Yet it did none of the other females any good. His glance fell upon Purity and stayed there. Clad in a plum satin with silver trim, she was every inch a shining jewel.

"Breathtaking," he murmured.

"Which one?" Quinn asked. "Or all of them?"

Matthew didn't answer nor did he move. Most of the men took a step in the ladies' direction toward one or the other, but he wasn't most men. He watched the majority close in upon Purity, yet she waved them aside, nodding politely but parting them like tall grass. To his delight, she came over to where he and Quinn stood.

"Good evening, fair lady," Quinn said first.

"Good evening, my lord. So glad you could come."

And then she was all his. Matthew waited for the moment she held out her hand to him, the only man to whom she had given the favor.

He took it, squeezed it gently in acknowledgment, and bowed.

"Good evening, my lady. I am honored to have been invited."

Her eyes sparkled up at him. "I especially wanted to make up for my misjudgment and hoped this dinner party will serve as a satisfactory apology."

Stunned by her frankness, especially in front of Quinn, who didn't have the grace to bugger off and leave them in private.

"It was unnecessary," Matthew returned. "Anyone would think what you thought, and the fault for your opinion of me rests entirely upon my shoulders."

She smiled sweetly at his words. And they were back to being upon solid footing. Now, he could only hope there was no mucking around with giving him another dining companion.

Her parents entered the room at that moment, making sure everyone had a drink so they could toast to one another's health. After about twenty minutes of idle prattle, in which Purity and all the other ladies made a point to greet and speak with each of the bachelors, they went in to dinner.

As Matthew had hoped, Purity let him take her arm and his name card was next to hers.

Did this signify what he hoped? Fervently, he wanted to give up the ruse of finding a wife when the woman he most desired was beside him.

At the very least, it sent a message to the other bachelors that he was being singled out with honor. Moreover, he would acknowledge such by being on his best behavior. He would be a saint, not even looking down her décolletage.

Whoops! That was precisely what he was doing, and he quickly averted his eyes, not peeking even once again.

Strangely, Matthew enjoyed the evening anyway, despite the impossibility of getting her into an upstairs room for the most hurried of trysts. Purity's company throughout dinner was exactly like her eyes, sparkling, entirely different from the quiet, disapproving female beside whom he'd sat at the Fenwicks' table. And even though conversation darted across and around the table, he still felt connected to her by her glances and short discussions with him alone.

After the fine meal, as expected from an earl's household, they all retired to a large salon at the back of the house overlooking the garden. None of the gentlemen were invited to remain in the dining room for brandy, since they could do that any time.

Instead, port, pale sherry, and Indian Madeira were offered while the ladies wishing to sing or play the piano told Lady Diamond, who quickly arranged the order. After stretching their legs and sipping their drinks for a few minutes, the guests settled onto arranged chairs for the evening's performances.

At the tail end, Purity's mother nodded in her direction.

Since Matthew was seated beside her, he felt her sigh.

"My turn to display my talents," she whispered.

He chuckled, not caring a fig whether she could sing or play. He'd listened politely to the other ladies but hadn't been particularly moved, even by a good voice singing "Love Always" or a bad one taking on the positively endless "Tragical Ballad of the Lady who Fell in Love with Her Serving Man."

By the final stanzas of the latter, Matthew was ready to hang himself by the curtain scarf if he thought the rod would stand his weight.

After it came an adequate rendition of one of John Field's "Nocturnes," and Matthew had thought the evening's entertainment was improving. Regardless, it seemed silly to think any young lady ought to be of an amateur standard high enough to entertain a roomful of critical *ton*, especially for the purpose of obtaining a husband.

After all, Matthew wasn't about to whip out a dueling pistol and demonstrate what a good shot he was.

However, when the first notes of Beethoven's "Für Elise" flowed from under Purity's fingers, Matthew could tell she had undertaken her piano instruction as she did everything in life, with determination to do it correctly and well.

In her case, that meant being far beyond capable. She must have practiced many hours to make the playing appear effortless. What's more, he could understand why their hostess had saved her daughter for last. It would not have been fair to the other ladies to follow such an astonishing performance.

Along with everyone in the room, he remained hushed and enraptured, leaning slightly forward in his seat, breathing as quietly as possible until the end. When the final soulful, heartbreaking notes died out, they all clapped enthusiastically. Purity stood and curtsied to her audience.

Rising spontaneously to his feet, Matthew clapped harder than anyone and roared his approval.

"Brava!" he called out.

At his reaction, the room fell silent again. Purity stared at him, cheeks blooming with color, and gave a barely discernible shake of her head. The other guests looked from her, to him, and then away with awkward glances.

Chastised, Matthew took his seat once more. He really did need lessons in etiquette. If he'd done that at a concert hall, he would have been joined by the multitude of listeners. Apparently in a private salon, his response was supposed to be restrained.

Purity didn't return to her seat. Instead, Lord Diamond announced they were returning to the drawing room where there was a treat to top off the evening.

Trays of syllabub met the guests' eyes when they entered, but Matthew wasn't interested. Although he very much enjoyed the traditional English concoction, having missed it while in France, he didn't take a serving. Even knowing this had been freshly made while they listened to the music, for the cream and white wine had not separated from the fruit juice in the glass dishes, his only interest was Purity, who was keeping her distance.

She hadn't allowed him to walk near her on the way back from the salon, and now she hovered between her parents.

"You made a muck of that," Quinn said as he came up beside him, holding his dessert. "This is heaven by the way."

Heaven had been listening to Purity. Heaven had been in her good graces all evening. Heaven was not frothy syllabub, but with nothing better to do, he turned and snatched one from the tray.

"Delicious," he muttered, attacking it ruthlessly, all the while staring at Purity who was deliberately not looking in his direction.

Half an hour later when the party ended, Matthew had managed to get no closer to her. Yet as he approached Lord and Lady Diamond, Purity did not shy away. After thanking his hosts, he glanced at her, and as she had done at the evening's onset, she offered him her hand.

"Good evening, Lady Purity." He wouldn't apologize, as that might only embarrass her again. But with her intense blue gaze fixed upon him, he mouthed the words, "I'm sorry" before he turned away.

PURITY LOOKED AT THE squirming sack her father carried into the drawing room where she and her sisters were reading and jumped to her feet. When he set it on the low table before the sofa, she peered inside and anger bloomed inside her.

"Kittens!" she exclaimed. "Did Lord Foxford send these?" The question was out before she could reconsider.

It had been two days since his breach of decorum at the party, naturally making every person in the room believe they had some sort of arrangement or understanding.

However, she knew her mortification had been inadvertent upon his part, and she didn't hold a grudge. After all, it was not as if they had been caught alone together and had their names linked in the newspapers.

Yet instead of a written note of apology, he was sending kittens. *How would she explain this to her family?*

"Foxford?" her father repeated while Ray and Bri squealed their excitement, each reaching in to pick up one of the wiggly balls of fluff. "Of course not," he said. "I found these little rascals at Tattersall's. The mama cat had birthed them in the clean hay, and the stable manager was making a fuss. He had put them all in the sack and was ready to toss them into the Thames."

"How dreadful," Ray said. "But their eyes are closed. They are too young to survive without their mother."

"Which is why I brought her home, too." He looked behind him. "Where is that footman?"

A moment later, the young man entered, holding a struggling, spitting cat by the scruff of its neck.

"Apologies, my lord. I all but lost it in the mews." With that, the cat made another desperate twist and escaped the footman's hold, dropping to the floor and instantly running under the sofa.

"I suggest we close the door," Purity said, which the man did on his way out. Then she lifted the canvas sack from the table and put it beside the hearth, rolling down the edges until it was evenly low all around and they could see the remaining helpless kittens.

"Put the babies back," she instructed her sisters, who did as they were told. Then she stood with her father and watched as the loud mewling of the kittens brought the frightened mama cat out from hiding.

In a flash of her tail, she jumped into the bag, too, protecting her babies while trying to settle beside them so they could nurse.

"She needs a larger bed," her father said. "And a more permanent place to live than this room. Somewhere out of the way until the kittens are weaned."

Purity smiled at her sisters. They were blessed with a considerate, gentle father in Geoffrey Diamond.

"May I keep them in my room?" Bri asked.

"I don't see why not," the earl said.

And that settled the excitement of the morning. Undoubtedly, their mother would approve of taking in a whole family of stray felines because of her soft heart.

"I guess we don't need a small companion dog now," Purity reminded him, having heard no more about it since the encounter in his study.

Her father cleared his throat. "No, it shall be lively enough for the time being. You two, go ask Mrs. Cumby for something larger for this brood, maybe a picnic basket," their father said, and her younger sisters scurried off, seeming to be children again instead of in their teens.

"And you," Lord Diamond said when they were alone, "why don't you tell me what's going on between you and Foxford."

CHAPTER TWELVE

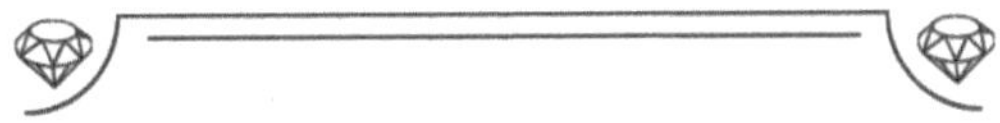

"Father!" Purity exclaimed, crouching down beside the crowded, ever-moving sack. "It is a litter, not a brood," she said.

"You are stalling, dear daughter. But I am a patient man. I have to be, what with five children."

She glanced up at him while absently reaching in to stroke the top of the mama cat's head. The creature must have felt more secure, for it purred and leaned against her fingers.

"There is nothing between Lord Foxford and me besides a burgeoning friendship. And even that is impossible because of our sexes. Soon, he will choose a wife from among the eligible young ladies, and that will be that."

She hadn't expected her father to laugh, but he did.

"My practical Purity. You can't fool me. At dinner, the man was your shadow, and then he nearly declared his devotion right there next to your pianoforte." He shook his head. "I behaved like a dunderhead whenever I was around your mother, too. From what your mother tells me, Foxford has been worse on more than one occasion."

"Not *because* of me," Purity insisted. "He was already lacking certain niceties when I met him. In fact, that's why I spend time with him, to help him."

"Is it now?" Her father's tone was one of disbelief, and his Diamond blue eyes danced.

"Father, don't ask me in such a fashion." She looked down at the kittens, all sucking with vigor while the mama cat curled around them, her eyes closed contentedly. "I was tutoring the man. That's all."

"It sounds a little stretched on the loom, my girl. That Foxford would seek help from you, a lovely earl's daughter, without any ulterior intention, and that you are no more interested in his lordship than assisting him to find a wife."

She shrugged. In truth, she had grown increasingly fond of the baron, nor could she deny to herself how his kisses inflamed her, constantly making her yearn for more.

"I suppose I think him interesting." That was all she would allow herself to confess.

Her father nodded. "I'm honored you are comfortable speaking to me. While I may never think any man good enough for you, I can see where he might have some charms. After all, he is a titled gentleman with a fortune, and he belongs to a good club, although not the same as my own. I don't know much about his family, but I also haven't heard anything bad about them either. His father died when he was young."

"I did not know," she said softly.

"Apart from his wealth," the earl continued, "I also have eyes. Foxford is not unattractive."

"No," she agreed, starting to squirm like one of the kittens.

"And he seems to be smitten with you."

She wrinkled her nose. "If you say so, Father."

"Then there is the matter of his reputation."

Her eyes flared open. "Yes, there is that."

"Many a young man of high birth and comfortable wealth find themselves spoken about in the papers, the topic of all kinds of nasty gossip."

"I don't care for gossip," she said.

He nodded. "I know, and you are a sensible girl. Sometimes, gossip is an outright lie. Sometimes, it is merely an embellishment of the unflattering truth. Who knows what is the case with the Fox?"

"You've heard him called that, have you?"

"I have," Lord Diamond said. "And a few other devilish monikers."

"What do you think?" she asked, rising to her feet.

This time, her father smiled broadly. "I think I am the luckiest of men to have children who want my opinion and listen to it."

"Of course, I do. After all, you and Mother have already gone through all this in the distant past."

His smile died. "Not that distant. I'm not as old as Methuselah."

"No, Father." She hid her smile at his touch of vanity. "I didn't mean that, but I am eager to hear your estimation of Lord Foxford."

"If I didn't think him redeemable based on your mother's opinion, then he wouldn't have been allowed in our home a second time, nor found himself at my dining room table seated next to my gem of a daughter."

"What if he is a libertine through and through?" Purity couldn't help asking, realizing she was wringing her hands and immediately ceased the awful habit.

Her father looked surprised. "I don't think you believe that of the man. You are known for your fastidiousness since you were very young. Remember when you hated to get your new boots soiled and insisted I carry you everywhere for a week so they would never touch the ground? Good thing you were a little sprite!"

She threw her arms around him. "I remember that. How I loved those boots!"

"I thought you were going to say, 'How I love my father.'"

"How I love my father," she repeated and kissed his cheek. "I am careful, to be sure. Fastidious, as you say, about most things."

He cocked his head and waited.

"I confess, I am also demanding of those around me, simply because I believe it makes life more pleasant when everyone is behaving as civilly as they can."

She took a deep breath. "In my opinion, Lord Foxford has been honest when saying he is seriously looking for a wife and will be a devoted husband once he marries. If I didn't believe that, then I would no longer be helping him to improve himself and to find the correct lady."

"And if you turn out to be the correct lady, then what?" her father asked.

"If I were to become his wife, I . . . I would be happy," she admitted.

Her father shrugged. "That's all you can hope for, as long as you follow your heart."

"You make it sound easy."

He laughed. "Oh, no, daughter. Take it from me, your ancient papa. It wasn't an easy path for your mother and me, and I don't think it was particularly smooth for Clarity and her Hollidge, either. No reason yours should be any different, but it will be worth it if you get your heart's fondest desire in the end."

MATTHEW WAS THRILLED when Purity accepted his invitation to an outdoor gala at Syon House. A sumptuous picnic would be presented along the river's edge, along with sporting activities, such as bowls, pall-mall, and archery.

Not a public event, only those with a ticket could attend. Still, it was a large enough gathering they might keep close company without their every word being overheard. Perhaps, they would promenade amongst the two hundred acres of parkland, forty of which were gardens. And into these, a determined man and woman could vanish for privacy.

However, Matthew had not been granted permission to collect Lady Purity and her chaperone. He had to settle for meeting her there, since her entire family had decided to attend, and they were naturally riding in the family's coach.

Instead for company, Quinn was hunkered down, eyes closed, on the other side of Matthew's brougham, looking abysmal. His friend procured a ticket because he had his eye on some lady from the Diamonds' dinner party, although Matthew couldn't remember which one. Quinn had expressed his gladness Matthew hadn't collected him in his open-air curricle, curled up, and fallen asleep.

Matthew only wished he could have brought Diana. But even if he was ready to present his daughter to his future wife, the gala was for adults only.

Luckily, the day dawned brightly, but the clouds blowing across the sun momentarily caused a chill before they floated away, threatening as usual. Any sunny day in England might be also a very wet one before bedtime.

At one o'clock, they arrived at the grounds of the Duke of Northumberland's Syon House. Matthew kicked Quinn's boot, and his friend roused himself, still looking the worse for wear. Why the man was rarely denounced in *The Times* when he was carousing most nights till dawn, Matthew couldn't fathom. Maybe after the rags discussed his own bad behavior, there was neither ink nor space for Quinn's.

"My head aches, but my spirit is strong to enjoy the day," his friend announced as they descended to the lawn. Quinn stretched, yawned, and set off at a jaunty pace that would let no one know Matthew had pounded upon his door and waited half an hour for him to get out of bed and dress.

Spying the Diamonds, Matthew stopped to stare at the vision that was Lady Purity in a stunning saffron-colored gown with the bluest ribbon trim. She was an exotic flower amongst the English roses, as every other lady seemed to be in pale pastel.

When he realized he was gawking, he set his feet in motion and joined their group, which was larger than he had anticipated.

"Greetings and good day," he said to one and all.

In quick succession, he was introduced to her younger sisters, one of whom was of similar appearance to Purity and her father, while the other was the image of her mother with flaming red hair.

Before they could head toward the festivities, her eldest sister, Viscountess Hollidge arrived with her husband. Another round of greetings ensued, and then finally, Matthew could fall into step with the object of his desire while the others led the way.

"You came with an entire entourage," he quipped.

"I suppose it seems that way," she agreed, appearing relaxed and joyful. She was mirroring Matthew's heart that day. "To me," she continued, "it is normal, even a little lacking when my brother isn't with us."

"And do you hope for a large family of your own, if I may ask?"

"You may, and I do," she answered when he had fully expected a reprimand for the personal question. "And you, my lord?" she asked.

"I will accept whatever offspring are given to me," he answered, thinking he ought to mention Diana. But then a conversation regarding her mother would ensue, and he didn't feel like going into that entire tale. Not at the start of a light-hearted occasion.

First thing, though, he wanted to clear the air, no matter how impossible that was in London proper. There, ten miles to the west in Brentford, where it was literally cleaner air, he could clear it in the figurative sense, too.

"I apologize for my overly exuberant display after your performance at the party. I was wrapped up in my admiration for you, not realizing I would cause embarrassment."

"I knew you meant no harm," she said. "I only kept my distance the remainder of the evening to tamp down any whispers that might immediately begin."

"That was prudently done of you," he agreed, although he was starting not to give a damn about who whispered what.

"To that point," he said, daring to broach the subject, "as I mentioned in the past, I have been seeking a wife. And while I appreciate all your attempts to civilize me, I think I would like to bring our lessons to an end."

"Is that so?" she asked a little stiffly. "And yet your exuberance, as you called it, plainly demonstrated your need for further etiquette instruction."

He laughed. "I fear all the tutoring in the world won't make me anywhere near as perfect as you, a most proper person who knows the correct response in every situation."

"That makes me sound insufferable," she said quietly. "Or fastidious, as my father rightly thinks me."

"No, not at all." He stopped and made her stop, too. He couldn't abide by her doubting her appeal. "You are wonderful, kitten."

She gave a strange gasping laugh, her blue eyes flashing. "I thank you, Lord Foxford." She grinned at him and put her hand up to shield her eyes, for the sun was directly over his shoulder. "Then why do you wish to stop our lessons?"

He grinned back. His heart was experiencing a strange ache, which he attributed to standing in the open air with a beautiful woman of whom he had grown immeasurably fond. It was so much more satisfying than even tupping a skilled courtesan, whom he knew nothing about nor wished to know.

"Because I would far rather court you, and I hope if you stop seeing me as your hopeless student, you might consider me as a suitor."

Purity didn't dismiss him out of hand. She blinked, and then—wonder of wonders—she nodded ever so slightly.

"Is that a *yes*?"

"I am considering your request," she said seriously.

Matthew nearly put his hands upon her waist so he could lift her in the air and twirl her around. Of course, she read something of his wild thoughts on his face and took a step back. Then she glanced to see where her family was.

"We ought to catch up with the rest of my group," she told him.

Matthew didn't mind. She had all but said she would marry him.

Perhaps not. Yet it was a far cry from the first time he went to her home when she flatly denied him any possibility of ever courting her. In fact, he was proud of how far he'd come.

And with that victory, he settled down to enjoy the afternoon. They participated in the games set out for invited guests. With her family, they played pall-mall. Lady Hollidge and her husband outscored the rest of them. There were rowboats for those so inclined, including Lord and Lady Diamond, and Matthew beat Purity and her younger sisters at bowls.

The weather held, despite clouds gathering down river toward the Channel. When it was time for the picnic, brought in wagons from the kitchens of Syon House by a veritable army of staff, they had all worked up an appetite.

Feasting on sandwiches of roast chicken and sliced tongue, along with meat pies of every variety, it was easy to believe themselves at a club or an inn. Salad, cold vegetables, and pickled eggs rounded out the offerings with loaf after loaf of bread and light, creamy butter. Along with sweet cider and lemonade, it was the ideal outdoor luncheon.

Matthew was seated between Purity and her redheaded sister at one of the many tables set out, and he had no need to speak a word through the whole meal since the Diamond family never stopped chattering. From their father, he learned about the house's Georgian renovations, using the same Lansdowne House architect, Robert Adam.

Making eye contact with the other quiet male figure, Lord Hollidge, they shared a moment's understanding of being on the outside. Matthew thought he would be a good man to get to know in the future.

And then to everyone's delight, wandering musicians came down to the picnic site from the house, a flutist, a violinist, and a mandolin player.

"Like a medieval banquet," the youngest sister, Miss Brilliance, declared.

Dessert was offered. Small cakes, lemon biscuits, custard tarts, and more, until Matthew wondered how any of them would ever stand again.

As if knowing his thoughts, Purity set down her empty lemonade glass, picked her gloves off her lap, and rose to her feet.

"I need to walk," she announced as the men scrambled to get up. Then she glanced at him. "It is good for one's digestion."

Turning her back, she politely tugged on her gloves out of his view before looking again at him with a questioning glance.

"I wholeheartedly agree," he said and offered her his arm, hoping it was the correct thing to do. For a moment, their glances locked. And then, under the watchful eyes of her parents, she wrapped her arm under his.

CHAPTER THIRTEEN

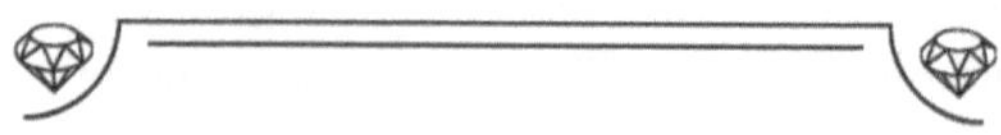

Matthew intended to get Purity away from the rest of her family as swiftly as possible before they decided to join in. He liked them, but he hadn't had a moment alone with her all day.

To his dismay, Quinn intercepted them after they were only a few yards away from those still seated. Matthew had just leaned down to tell her about his modest country manor in Surrey when his friend bounded up like a puppy with a young lady in tow.

"There you are, old sport, and the lovely Lady Purity. May I introduce Miss Moffett lately from Derwentwater in Keswick, who is here with her aunt and uncle? They are sponsoring her for the Season."

And with that, Purity took Miss blasted Moffett under her wing and walked ahead, leaving Matthew and Quinn to stroll behind.

"You meddlesome toad," Matthew said quietly.

Quinn laughed. "Come along, now, Foxy. You can't walk off with a Diamond under her parents' nose. With four of us, especially if the ladies stroll together, I don't think anyone will look at us twice."

"I *could* walk away with her, and I *did*. We have been stuck like a flock of birds all day, and I was looking forward to some private conversation. As long as we are within sight, no one minded a bit."

"Sorry, old chap. My mistake. I thought I was keeping you from another dreadful misstep. In any case, as soon as we get around the grove, then Miss Moffett and I shall part company with you and your lady."

"I don't recognize her at all from the Diamonds' dinner party."

"Because she wasn't at the party. I couldn't find the lady I was looking for," he added.

Quinn appeared unbothered by losing one woman, having quickly gained another.

"I just learned at the picnic that these gardens were designed by Capability Brown to create serene pleasure," Quinn said. "Hence, what else should one do here but pleasure each other? Miss Moffet and I are heading toward the hedges with the fountain in the middle."

"How wonderful for you," Matthew snapped. "So, you weren't looking to keep me from committing a scandalous slip but simply getting your latest prey away from her keepers."

"Something like that," Quinn said. "And your lady has done a capital job of helping me, too."

They passed by a thicket, and then Quinn sprinted ahead. "Ladies, this isn't a footrace, is it? You are walking too quickly for me. Regardless, I should now like to reclaim my hold upon Miss Moffett for the remainder of our promenade."

With that, he took hold of Miss Moffett's arm and strode away toward the hedges, leaving Purity frowning after them.

"I hope her aunt and uncle know she is alone with Lord Quinn. I feel responsible, as if I ought to continue to provide some sort of protection."

Glancing back the way they had come, she sighed. "What can her relations be thinking, letting a country girl go off with a stranger?"

Matthew was glad she didn't put their relationship on the same footing. After a moment, Purity shrugged.

"Some would say I am worrying overmuch about things that are plainly not my concern, nor in my control."

She tapped her chin, looking fetching, and he wanted to take her in his arms and ask to hear her deepest thoughts. He didn't have to. With her next words, he knew.

"Yet it is in my power to protect this young lady from ruin. Come along, Foxford."

She strode after the pair who had already disappeared.

Shaking his head, Matthew followed. Instead of a moment alone with her, they were going to play chaperone to his idiot friend, who most certainly wouldn't welcome the interference.

Soon, they were in the hedgerows, too. Quinn being his usual reckless self was moving at a fast clip into the densest part, making it hard to catch up. But Purity was equally determined to save Miss Moffett. She was like winged Nike, hurrying through the shrubberies until they reached the fountain.

"There you are," she declared, stopping so sharply that Matthew plummeted into the back of her, sending her sprawling with a cry of alarm.

She caught herself on the edge of the marble fountain's base, which hit her shins an instant before she planted her palms on its broad ledge and rose. Directly in front of her, in the middle of a small moat was the ten-foot statue of a naked warrior with long, muscular legs, a curved, long shield indicating his Roman nationality, and a long, thick—

"Oh, my!" Purity exclaimed as she stared at the appendage.

Perhaps the sculptor intended to frighten young ladies into behaving themselves, for even with a mostly flaccid lobcock, this soldier's member was impressive.

"I . . . ," she began. "That is. Well!" And she turned her back on it with her cheeks flaming.

"Are you unharmed?" Matthew asked, rushing forward. "A good thing you had your gloves on."

She looked down at them. "Yes, indeed, although they are not as fresh as they were when I left home." She brushed them together before realizing she'd lost her quarry as Quinn and Miss Moffett had vanished like morning mist.

"Your friend is incorrigible," she declared.

"You did your best by rooting them from this spot where they were trying to hide."

"Not *they*! I doubt Miss Moffett had any clue what he was about."

Matthew smiled at her starched tone. "And what do you think he was about, my lady?"

Her blue eyes narrowed upon him. "We both know he wanted to kiss her."

Matthew feared Quinn wanted to do a great deal more, but he could hope Purity was correct.

"Not the worst thing to happen to a young lady from the country," he said.

Her gaze was still locked on his when he saw her eyes widen slightly. In the next, her glance fell to his lips, and hot lust jolted through him. His smile died completely.

"Not the worst thing to happen to a young lady from Town, either," he said quietly.

She swallowed, and he followed the movement of her throat, a beautiful column he wanted to kiss more than he wanted his next breath.

"I suppose they might be simply looking at the flowers and at the river beyond," she said, her voice a little breathless.

Alarm bells rang loudly in Matthew's head as if half of London was burning and all brigades had been called. His desire was certainly as scorching as any fire!

Perhaps it was the look on his face, desperate and ravenous, that caused her to spin away from him. Purity circled to the far side of the fountain where, if desired, she could enjoy the soldier's equally impressive naked rump, but she didn't. Instead, she craned her neck, looking up at the sky.

"We shall not see any stars come nightfall. The clouds are moving in thickly now. Don't you think?"

He didn't bother to look. He knew there was a breeze, growing stronger by the soft curls moving across her delicate shoulders.

She looked like a summer goddess, and even a ten-foot statue of her would not be enough to show off her beauty.

At his silence, she glanced at him again, and he moved helplessly toward her. When was the last time they'd kissed? *Too blasted long!*

He knew he ought to behave like a gentleman, which meant escorting her immediately to an area where there were other people. For the briefest moment, he nearly gave in to his nobler instincts, but his baser ones took over when she tilted her head.

She might not mean it as a come-hither look, but when her lips parted, he could feel the blood pulsing in his veins.

At least, he certainly felt it in one place.

Still, she said nothing.

He believed she knew how much he wanted her, and perhaps she wanted him as desperately.

"Foxford," she began and took a step toward him.

That was a mistake. She ought to have moved away.

Matthew didn't remember giving his feet the command to close the distance between them, but in an instant, she was in his arms as he had dreamt of all day.

Without hesitation, he kissed her like a thirsty man drank water. To stop himself from sinking his hands into her hair and destroying any semblance of a tidy coiffure, he grabbed her buttocks. As soon as her warm globes were in his hands, he couldn't help kneading them with his fingers and drawing her up against him.

Slanting his mouth sideways, he sought to devour her, and she let him. Their tongues were already stroking before he'd even realized he'd gained access between her sweet lips.

How long they kissed, he couldn't say. He knew only relief that she was giving as much as he was. Moreover, they were taking from one another with equal vigor.

When he drew back, he waited for her blue eyes to open. *Would he see outrage creep over her face like the sun's fingers over the sill at dawn?*

She sucked in a deep, shuddering breath.

"We ought to return to the other guests," she said, her voice barely above a whisper.

He grinned at this novel experience. "You forgot to slap me."

Her eyes widened. When she raised both her hands that had remained hanging on to his jacket, he flinched. Yet she merely slid them up his chest before lacing her fingers behind his neck.

"Kiss me again," she invited. "Maybe I'll remember to slap you this time."

Matthew bent his head and did so, tugging at her lower lip, making her moan. The sound was the most sensual thing he'd ever heard. Releasing her rear end with a firm squeeze, he put his hands to her trim waist and lifted her high against him.

To his delight, she laughed softly. He wanted to make her laugh every day for the rest of their lives.

Victory was sweet. He had done it at last. He had won her over. Matthew was sure of it. If she freely allowed his kiss and even asked for another, then she was all but accepting they would get engaged. For that was how Purity's brain worked. Her dear, wonderful, fastidious brain!

Letting her slide down the front of him, his arousal throbbing, he could imagine their wedding night already. And they would wait until that night. He was determined to honor her as a husband who wouldn't deflower his innocent bride ahead of time. Although he would be sorely tested, even by the shortest of engagements.

Tilting his head, he leaned in for another soul-searing kiss.

"What have we here?" came a male voice. "Lovers about to have a flyer?"

"Or perhaps they just had one," said a female. "Did you hear her laughing as he groped her?"

Purity froze in his arms. It was too late for jumping apart, but they separated anyway. Matthew's heart was pounding so hard, he could hear it. By the look upon her stricken face, hers was also beating an erratic tattoo.

Slowly facing their discoverers, he recognized Varley and the blonde-haired Lady Tupmoure with whom he'd dallied in the month before he went to France. He'd seen them together before at Lady Tisendale's ball. All at once her given name—Emilia—came to him along with her excessive ire when he had left her bed for the final time, after announcing he was leaving the country by week's end.

Taking a step forward, he hoped to shield Purity, who remained deathly silent. She was undoubtedly terrified of the repercussions. He could only hope they didn't know her name.

"Varley," Matthew said. "What are you and her ladyship doing out here?" Turning the tables was the best way to disarm the issue. "Being out here together, if you're discovered, people will talk."

A moment of silence followed, and then the two intruders started to laugh.

"Foxford, that is rich! I say, have you met my wife?"

Varley's wife! Met her? She'd ridden rantipole atop him more than once. And worse, Lord and Lady Varley could be outside for as long as they wished and do everything except strip off and dance in the fountain. No one would care. Only he and Purity were at risk.

"I have been out of the country. I didn't realize you two had married." He was making normal, polite conversation, hoping Purity would understand he was trying to smooth over the situation.

However, with the pair's interested expressions, particularly the cunning set to Emilia's mouth, Matthew could think of only one way to make this any better.

"Have you and Lady Varley met my fiancée?" He was careful not to give Purity's name, just in case they were unaware of it. If so, then escaping unscathed was still a possibility.

To her credit, Purity didn't gasp or gainsay him, and he fervently hoped they could manage the calamity.

"Your *fiancée?*" Emilia asked, sounding incredulous. "Lady Purity Diamond has captured a thundering buck of the first head. Can it be true?"

Dammit all! Lady Varley knew who Purity was. Worse than that, she was annoyed. Matthew could tell by her tone. Her pride was pricked that he hadn't offered his hand in marriage after they'd danced the blanket hornpipe over the space of a fortnight.

Taking a breath, he turned and reached for Purity's hand, drawing her forward as the clouds finally opened and the showers began. She kept her glance averted from all three of them.

"How could I not ask Lady Purity to be my wife? I might have once been a buck of the first head, as you say, but she is clearly a diamond of the first water."

Matthew felt her cringe under his touch, but he continued, "The lady has well and truly tamed me. If our display of genuine affection bothered you, you must excuse us. In any case, I must get my lady out of the rain."

With that, he pushed between the two gawkers, bringing Purity with him.

"Let's get you back to your family."

She nodded. He had a feeling she was in shock. Matthew had been caught *in flagrante delicto* before, but never with anyone who wasn't prepared for such a fate, certainly not with anyone he cared about, and *never* with a virginal earl's daughter.

At the copse of trees, they came across another couple, their bodies turned away, the man shielding his lover against the tree to keep her dry and unidentified.

Instead of titillating, Matthew found it sordid for the first time and wondered why they didn't all go get rooms at an inn. *Himself included!* He should be shot for what had occurred. And with the memories of other times on the grounds of other estates, doing far more lascivious things for a lark to satisfy a salacious whim, the shame and regret rose to mock him.

He glanced at Purity to determine if she'd seen the couple, but her head remained down, gazing at nothing but the grass ahead of her. She seemed smaller and shrunken as if she might vanish entirely into her misery. Her distraught manner sliced at his heart.

Faced with the trembling woman beside him, he decided to swear off gardens altogether.

CHAPTER FOURTEEN

Purity couldn't clear the haze of stupefaction from her brain. What had occurred simply could *not* have happened. *Not to her!* A ridiculous thought, but it was the only one that kept circling.

She did *not* kiss a man while letting her bottom be squeezed like a ripe peach. She did *not* have a tryst next to a massive statue with a giant phallus. And she most certainly did *not* get caught sliding down the front of the Fox at a gala. *It was inconceivable!*

Thus, while her mind tried to make sense of the unthinkable, she remained silent, even when she and Foxford reached the picnic area and found it nearly deserted.

"Everyone has gone to the conservatory, my lady, to wait while the carriages are brought around," explained one of the staff, clearing plates into a basket.

Turning, they headed up the bank away from the river. Finally yanking her arm out of his grasp, Purity directed her gaze straight ahead. She could not look at him, although from the side of her eye, she saw Foxford sending her curious glances. If they made eye contact, she would turn to salt like Lot's wife and then melt into nothingness in the rain.

She wished he wouldn't speak, but quietly he said, "You had best perk up a bit before we see Lord and Lady Diamond."

Foolishly, he imagined she would be able to hide her ruin from those who knew her best.

Upon cresting the hill, they found other stragglers who had not yet made it under cover, and they joined the last of the guests to find shelter in the duke's spacious conservatory where he grew an array of exotic plants, as well as fruit trees.

Her family was easy to spot gathered around an orange tree. While her oldest sister had left with her husband, for they were nowhere to be seen, her younger sisters were mischievously touching the ripe fruit while her father gave them a stern eye.

"Do not pluck anything," he warned as Purity approached.

She made the mistake of looking directly at her mother. At once, Purity felt as though the countess read every moment of her disgrace. Almost imperceptibly, her mother's expression changed. As it did, the blood drained from Purity's head, as well.

"You missed all the excitement," Bri declared.

If she had any more excitement, Purity thought she would combust, but her sister jabbered on.

"The news spread as we were leaving the picnic area. A couple has been caught in a compromising situation."

Sweet Mary! At that moment, Purity wished she could faint, dropping like a handkerchief the way some women did. She'd seen it happen in rooms that were too warm, both at balls and at the theatre, and in the hot sun of a summer day. Yet she'd never seen one simply escape her disgrace by falling into unconsciousness.

All her family were staring at her and at Foxford, who stood grimly by her side. Too close in fact. The shame of her own sister bringing up the dreadful loss of her reputation and the ruin of her family name was crushing.

"Hush, Bri," her mother said, still gazing only at Purity. "We don't gossip, not about that poor country girl."

Miss Moffett! Purity briefly squeezed her eyes closed, with guilty relief and with regret surging through her. She had known better, and yet, she hadn't saved either of them from ignominy.

When she opened her eyes again, her mother was closer, reaching out her hand.

"Another megrim?" the countess asked, her gaze darting to the baron and seeming to judge and condemn him all at once.

Offering Purity her arm, her mother led her away. She heard her father bid Foxford good day and his stilted reply. And then she hurried through the rain to their awaiting carriage without a backward glance.

DESPITE PURITY BEING certain her mother knew the truth, Caroline Diamond remained her gracious and loving self. In the carriage, she didn't bombard her with questions. Instead, she allowed Purity the dignity of huddling in the corner, staring unseeingly out the window into the gray light of the rain showers that were already beginning to let up.

And while her younger sisters chattered about the day and her father put his head back and closed his eyes, her mother offered her comfort without even knowing precisely what the issue was. She'd taken the seat next to Purity, where normally Bri or Ray would sit, and calmly grasped her daughter's hand between both of hers, holding it lightly upon her skirt.

When her mother did that, Purity could almost believe everything was going to be fine. She would know in the morning whether the baron would do the honorable thing and make true what he'd told the awful prying couple by the fountain.

It would mean telling her parents something ahead of time, perhaps only that Foxford had asked for her hand and that she'd said yes. They didn't need to know any of the details, only that the upstanding Lord and Lady Diamond were going to have a licentious libertine as a son-in-law.

That thought nearly made her tears flow. But Purity didn't allow herself the self-pitying spectacle. Not until she reached the sanctuary of her bedchamber. Upon reaching their home, she excused herself, claiming the headache her mother had suggested.

"I'll send you up some tea. If you don't feel well enough to come down for supper, I'll send you up a tray then, too," her mother said, still not asking for an explanation. Although she added firmly, "We'll talk in the morning."

Purity nodded and disappeared, glad her mother was being understanding, and equally grateful she didn't have to face her father until she was ready. Not that he was a harsh man or even particularly judgmental, but she loved him beyond anything and didn't relish the look of disappointment she would inevitably see upon his face.

After accepting a tea tray and sending her maid away for the evening, Purity sat on the end of her bed and considered her culpability in the afternoon's events and how the past weeks had led her to her current predicament.

If she hadn't been so affected by Foxford's magnetism, she wouldn't have let him kiss her once, never mind all the other times. If he'd been a troll of a man without a sense of humor, no wit, nor an ounce of sense, and no devastating smile, she could have tutored him in the graces and social manners and never been in the smallest whit of danger or trouble.

Instead, she was in a barrel full of suds.

All because she liked him. More than that, her heart swelled when they were together. She was excited each time he was near and anticipated every meeting with gladness. She didn't have to be a soothsayer to know she had developed a *tendre* for the man.

Then she recalled the night of a late-July country party at her family's Derbyshire estate, two years earlier. To entertain their guests, her mother had invited a fortune-teller. Purity had long since put it out of her mind, but now, she considered what the woman had told her.

"Your heart will be much affected. You will be surprised. But don't let your rigid notions blind you."

Was she rigid? Her heart was definitely affected, and she *was* surprised by who was affecting it. Those were both true. But as for being blind to something, she didn't know what.

She ought to be grateful he had done the honorable thing by declaring them engaged. And she was. In fact, she ought to think of him as a man of honor since he hadn't betrayed her. He could as easily have left her with her shredded reputation on the grounds of Syon Park.

Regardless, it was impossible to put a renowned rake in the same class of honorable gentleman as her father, brother, or even her sister's husband.

Her eyes welled with tears. If she allowed her affection for Foxford to continue, if she opened her heart to him entirely and acknowledged the sentiment to be love, then she would be vulnerable. It was all too easy to imagine him taking up with a mistress after their marriage, and she would be devastated.

Purity had never thought she would have to worry about her husband's fidelity because her choice was always going to be a safe one.

Foxford wasn't safe! He was decidedly dangerous.

Finally, the tears spilled over. She'd been playing with fire, as they said, swimming out of her depth in an ocean with a shark as her companion. This behavior and the consequences were all usual and quite normal for him.

Wiping her face, she let the tea the maid brought in grow cold, despite a twinge of guilt at wasting it. *Was she ever going to feel good again?*

After undressing down to her shift, she brushed out her hair before plaiting it. Then she performed her evening ritual of washing her face and brushing her teeth before climbing into bed despite the early hour.

Lying on her back, she stared at the canopy above her. It was a pretty room she'd had since childhood. If she became the Baroness Foxford, what would her new room be like?

Turning on her side, she wondered what the man who would become her husband was doing at that moment. Mostly likely, he had gone from Syon Park to his club. *And then what?*

Having seen the fiery passion in his eyes when they'd been locked in an embrace, Purity could picture him slaking his lust on some woman of pleasure later that night.

She shuddered. Her mind was going down dark paths, and she needed to rein in the despondent thoughts. Tomorrow, hopefully, everything would seem less dire.

MATTHEW WAS TOO WORKED up to go home. Thus, he did what any right-thinking man would do when needing the company of his supportive peers. He went to his club.

After the doorman gave him entrance, he found a seat in the Boodle's reading room where soon he was brought a glass of soothingly expensive brandy.

And then he contemplated the events and, more importantly, the results of the day. He could hardly credit that, after all the dalliances he'd enjoyed, he had finally been caught unawares because of how blind his passion for Purity made him. Hearing nothing apart from her breathing and his own heartbeat, he'd allowed the Varleys to sneak upon them.

If only it had been Quinn who had come upon them.

Quinn! For the first time, he recalled the young Miss Brilliance's words about a couple caught. Lady Diamond had mentioned a country girl. *Had the blasted Varleys been rooting out men and women right and left?*

Knowing his friend, unless Quinn had fled London, he would arrive at any moment. Indeed, after a mere five-minute wait, Quinn showed his face. Strangely, he didn't look any worse for his experience and wore his usual affable smile.

"Well met," Quinn said. "Brandy," he requested from the server, and then he settled into a comfortable leather chair. "Enjoyable gala, was it not, except for the rain? That and you abandoning me at Syon so I had to make my own way home."

Matthew had entirely forgotten about that, too.

"My apologies. I had a situation on my hands that distracted me, but I believe you did, too."

"A situation?" Quinn asked. Then his frown cleared. "Oh, you mean the inconvenient discovery of myself and Miss Moffett having a proper smack." He shrugged. "It happens, as I am sure you know."

Matthew was taken aback by his friend's aplomb. "Who came upon you? Was it Varley and his lady?"

"Varley? No. It was a couple who were also alone together. We all surprised one another. Unfortunately, they made it back to tattle before we could, throwing us under the carriage wheel while they danced a merry jig."

"And what has come of it?" Matthew asked him. Not an engagement or Quinn wouldn't be so devil-may-care.

"Nothing has come of it, as I will not allow anything to." For the first time, his friend's tone was sharp. "Miss Moffett came with me of her own free will and enjoyed a little pully hawly. She should be grateful her skirt was down by the time we were discovered."

Matthew felt a slim shard of disgust. *Grateful!* He couldn't imagine dishonoring Purity in such a fashion. A kiss was one thing. But it had been broad daylight with very little cover.

"You knew she was a country girl, did you not?" Matthew asked, unable to stay a tone of disapproval.

Quinn sighed. "Country or Town, a muff is a tuzzy-muzzy is a quim all the same. Even if she'd been back in Derwentwater, if I recall from where she hails correctly, she could not have been unaware of the perils of taking a little delight."

"You won't ask for her hand, then?" Matthew already knew the answer.

Quinn laughed for a few moments, then answered, "No." He sipped his brandy. "I barely know the chit, but what I did realize rather quickly was that she was not suited to be my future viscountess. Eventually I will get around to choosing, but not because of sampling wares at a picnic."

Matthew fell silent. He didn't like the way his friend put it, but he supposed if he'd been caught with anyone besides Purity, he would feel the same way.

"Imagine putting the parson's noose around your neck," Quinn continued, "because of a single flourish in the bushes. I would rather step my foot in a rat-catcher's trap and chew my own leg off."

Matthew chuckled, glad he was not of a similar mind. In fact, he was looking forward, albeit nervously, to meeting with Lord Diamond in the morning.

"I intend to marry Lady Purity," he said steadily, wanting to say it aloud.

"What?" Quinn roared, but he spoke with mirth. "That's wonderful. A damn fine match. I didn't think you had it in you to win that particular lady."

Matthew declined to mention being discovered or how that was influencing the timing of his proposal.

"We have come to know and admire one another."

"Then I regret any remark I made about her being a Mrs. Princum-Prancum. Firstly, I would never disparage my good friend's wife, and secondly, if you are set on marrying her, then she must be a rum mort and no mistake."

"She is." Matthew was glad to know Quinn was genuinely pleased. His friend even raised his glass to toast Lady Purity's health. And then he went further.

"I propose we have supper at—"

"Not Dolly's Chop House," Matthew interrupted. "The food is all right, but you only go for the waitresses."

"And what's wrong with that?" his friend demanded.

Matthew stared him down

"As you like," Quinn said at last. "A finer meal to celebrate the end of the Bachelor Baron. The Café de l'Europe, perhaps? Or the Albion? I'll round up a few others. Franklin, for one, and Pearson and Dyer. Yes?"

Matthew nodded. "I look forward to it."

CHAPTER FIFTEEN

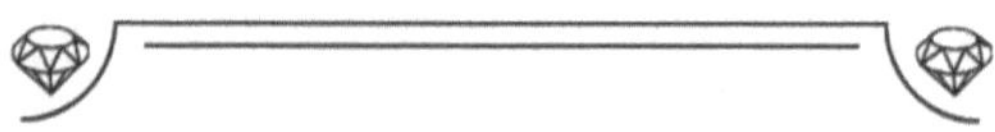

When barely sunrise, Purity climbed out of bed feeling raw, having scarcely slept through the longest night of her life. Her stomach grumbled since no supper tray had arrived the night before, probably because she hadn't responded to the timid knocking of the kitchen maid.

Unable to bring herself to drink the stale, stone-cold tea, Purity dressed hurriedly and carried the tray down with her all the way to the kitchen in the cellar.

"I'm sorry I wasted the tea," she told their staff upon entering.

Both their cook and their kitchen maid wore the same expressions of surprise and then worry.

"I know I am up dreadfully early, but if you could make me a pot of chocolate and a slice of toast, I'll wait in the breakfast room."

The two women glanced at one another, and Purity knew they thought her off her rocker for not simply tugging on the bell-pull upstairs. After all, she understood how routine and schedule made the house run like a top. She was throwing off both.

A few minutes later, in the intimate green-and-cream-colored salon where they always took their breakfast, she drank the soothing chocolate and felt better. Cook had made her a stack of toasted bread slathered with butter and provided raspberry jam, too.

After being much fortified, she made an attempt to read the prior afternoon's papers, yet when her father appeared an hour later, he caught her dozing on the only small divan in the room.

Ruminating upon what they must discuss, Purity wished she could disappear like the slices of toast.

He leaned over and kissed her forehead before tugging the bell-pull.

"Are you the only one who receives special early service, or do you think Cook will give me breakfast, too?"

Purity couldn't speak.

"Your mother seems to believe you had an unpleasant incident during the picnic. Do you want to tell me about it? Is there someone I need to shoot?" he added.

That made her smile slightly as he took a seat. And then it came tumbling out of her. Not all of it, of course, but enough so her father understood she had been caught alone with Foxford and was now presumed engaged.

"*Hm,*" Lord Diamond said. "A sticky predicament, indeed. One thing seems heartening. Foxford immediately spoke up for you."

"Yes, Father."

"However, if you don't like the fellow, then that doesn't make a bit of difference. If you are absolutely against becoming Lady Foxford, then we shall sort this out in some other manner. I know you were helping him as a lark at the outset, but perhaps you have grown a sincere attachment. If not, then you shouldn't have to be tied to the man for the rest of your life."

Purity knew her father to be the best, kindest man in the world. Therefore, she decided to tell him the truth.

"I do have feelings for him as you guessed before. But I am unsure as to his in return. Even less sure about his character."

"It is unlikely he can ever find anyone of your quality, dear daughter. He probably counts himself lucky the two of you were caught in the same snare."

Purity hadn't thought of that. It seemed there were many lovely ladies in London. He might fancy any or all of them.

"I hope he comes to speak with me today," the earl continued. "If he doesn't, then I will call him out as a blackguard. If he does come, then I will take his measure. If he seems the least bit slippery, I will forbid the marriage."

That would not help her reputation, but she couldn't bring herself to mention such to her father. Her mortification would be too great.

They stopped talking about the prior evening while he read the paper, and she remained with her eyes closed nearby, feeling comforted by his strong presence. When her mother entered not long after, they went over the whole thing again.

"All my fault," Lady Diamond said. "I let the wolf into the sheep's fold, as it were."

"I am hardly a sheep," Purity defended herself. "It wasn't as if Foxford tried to get me into a risky situation. We were simply in the wrong place at the wrong time."

On the other hand, he had steered her away from the rest of the guests even before Lord Quinn and Miss Moffett caught up to them.

"I suppose if he wishes to marry you, then I can forgive his trespasses," her mother said.

While both her parents were eating, Purity realized she was waiting on tenterhooks. If Foxford didn't show up at the earliest polite minute, then—

Through the open salon door, they heard the noise of their butler admitting a visitor. And a male one, by the timbre of his voice.

Purity sat up straighter, her mother glanced at her with an air of speculation, and her father rose from his chair.

"You ladies wait here," he ordered. "I will deal with Foxford, one way or the other."

Lord Diamond was no longer merely her father. The way he strode out of the room, he was every inch the head of the household.

Her mother sighed. "I love that man."

Her father and Foxford must have gone to the earl's study, for Purity heard their feet upon the stairs. For the next five minutes, she was on pins and needles. Her breathing was irregular, her heart was racing, and she felt all over cold.

"Stop twisting that napkin," her mother said. "I would suggest a walk outside, but I assume you want to be here when the men finish talking."

"I do. Besides, what if Bri or Ray come in for breakfast and I am not present?"

"What of it?" Lady Diamond asked. "I doubt Lord Foxford will mistake one of them for you."

Her mother had a peculiar wit at times, but she was correct. Purity could go wherever she pleased in the house. And at that moment, the music room called to her.

"I'll go play the piano. That will help calm me."

She wandered down the hall to the salon and seated herself at the instrument of torture, as she used to think of it until she became proficient. Now, she cherished her elegant grand pianoforte with its mahogany case and was happy her mother hadn't let her quit. More than once, Purity had found an hour at the piano soothed her.

Thus, after lifting the fallboard to reveal the decorative gold leaf inlay and the words "John Broadwood and Sons," also in gold, she let herself get lost in a piece she used for practice, Bach's "The Well-Tempered Clavier." In the past, she'd let it challenge her for hours, taking her through twenty-four pairs of preludes and fugues. Certainly, Foxford would complete his meeting with her father long before that.

THIS WASN'T MATTHEW'S first encounter with Lord Diamond. And while the previous ones had gone well, considering he'd compromised one of the man's daughters less than twenty-four hours earlier, the outcome of this meeting was dodgy at best.

After scanning the morning newspapers and being both surprised and immensely relieved not to find any mention of himself or Purity, he had headed directly to Piccadilly.

On the doorstep, after presenting his card and asking to see his lordship, Matthew was unsure of his reception with no idea whether Purity's father knew anything of the ill-advised incident by the statue.

If the Earl Diamond brought it up, then Matthew would apologize and confess how the fault was entirely his. He would explain how overwhelmed he'd been with the depth of his feelings for Purity. Accordingly, he had embraced her *before* declaring his resolve to marry her. A mere error of order, not of intention.

On the other hand, if the earl said nothing, then Matthew would simply ask for her hand as if this was planned. He was probably no more nervous than any other man asking permission to wed, except most other men didn't have the burden of an inglorious reputation hanging like the sword of Damocles, ready to destroy his happiness.

Sure enough, when Lord Diamond appeared in the front hall, he told rather than invited Matthew to follow him to his study. It was as impressive as an earl's study should be and clearly not a place merely to drink good brandy. Books, papers, and ledgers were strewn across a massive desk behind which Lord Diamond took a seat before gesturing for Matthew to sit across from him.

Then Purity's father looked him squarely in the eyes to take his measure. After a long moment, he nodded.

"I hope ninety percent of what I have heard or read is either false or blatant exaggeration," Lord Diamond began. "I experienced a little of such infamy myself," he added.

Matthew relaxed a moment. Here was a man who understood how difficult it was to be titled and wealthy and not be the object of everyone's scrutiny.

"As for the other ten percent, however, I would advise you to rein in your questionable tendencies and cease them immediately."

With that statement, he fixed Matthew with a blue-eyed stare that looked so much like Purity's, it was uncanny. Moreover, the earl sounded like his daughter, who was forever urging Matthew to change his rakish ways.

How could he convince the man he had already done so, particularly in light of why he was there?

"I would like to marry your daughter, my lord, and I assure you I will not dishonor her in any way for as long as I live."

Lord Diamond raised a dark eyebrow. "You may live a long time," he pointed out. "That's many years of being faithful. I believe there is only one way to ensure such fidelity, and that's with a loyal, loving heart. If your heart is not engaged, then neither shall you be, not to my daughter."

Matthew caught his breath. He hadn't expected to go to Piccadilly and have the depths of his emotions plumbed or dissected. He nodded but remained silent, not wishing to speak with the earl about his devotion instead of with Purity.

The Earl Diamond leaned forward. "Despite whatever occurred yesterday, and I don't wish to know as you two are adults, I don't want my daughter to become your wife unless I am assured of her future happiness, in so far as I can be."

Again, Matthew nodded.

"Are you fully prepared to be her husband?" Lord Diamond asked. "Elsewise, I suggest you walk out my door and never lay eyes upon her again."

Matthew flinched. The despair engendered by the earl's ultimatum was instant and overwhelming, like having his head plunged under water and held there. At school, it had happened once, and he had never forgotten the dread.

Until that moment, he had not truly examined his own feelings beyond knowing he admired Purity, thought her the most desirable woman he'd ever met, and believed they could be happy together.

Imagining such a finality of never being in her company again, the same helpless dread washed over him. His heart ached dully, the very heart of which her father had spoken, and which Matthew knew Purity had long-since claimed.

He could only describe it to himself as her having taken up all the space in that famed and mythical seat of the emotions. The realization rattled him as much as the newfound knowledge that his affections were truly and irrevocably engaged.

He was pleased and yet the smallest whit frightened, too.

"Your face is an expressive one," her father said into the prolonged silence.

Matthew had practically forgotten the man was there. Still, he wasn't going to mention *love* to anyone apart from Purity.

"I am prepared to marry your daughter," he said carefully, trying not to trip over his tongue, "by caring for her in all the ways in which you would deem necessary for her happiness, now and in the future."

The earl gave him another long look, pondering the words. Finally, he nodded. Then he made a face of exasperation.

"You know her mother and I eloped, and I don't regret it for an instant."

While Matthew's mouth was open, stunned by the notion of a carefree, outrageous Lord and Lady Diamond, the earl asked him briefly about his financial well-being, which was healthy indeed. And then a dowry was proposed, to which Matthew agreed immediately.

Satisfied, Lord Diamond rose to his feet and even put out his hand.

"I like this custom of shaking upon an agreement," he said. "Touching the flesh that I will rip limb from limb if you hurt my daughter makes it more tangible and permanent, don't you think?"

Matthew hesitated, again taken off guard by the earl, but he shook his hand with vigor.

"Yes, my lord," he said. "And I shall never give you cause for regret, nor for ripping my limbs."

He hadn't exactly been hat-in-hand, but Matthew had certainly been doubtful of his reception. Moreover, he'd been thoroughly put in his place and told where he had better stand by the formidable Lord Diamond. He could do nothing but admire his future father-in-law, wondering momentarily what his own father would have said in the same circumstances.

Dismissed, Matthew wandered along the hallway and down the stairs where luckily, he encountered Lady Diamond in the drawing room.

After a brief but polite conversation in which he informed the countess that his suit had been accepted, he followed her suggestion to seek out the source of the music.

Recognizing Purity's adept talent, he went directly to the salon. For a full minute, Matthew stood in the doorway and listened, watching the quick sure movements of her hands and enjoying the graceful bend to her neck where soft, dark spirals lay.

He wanted to drop kisses along that slender column, wrap his hands around her from behind, and grab hold of her luscious curves.

Now they were officially engaged, that dream was closer to reality. He hoped she wasn't as distraught as she'd seemed the afternoon before. Probably the shock had worn off. And since he'd followed through with asking her father for her hand, her mind should be at ease as soon as he told her the marriage had been arranged.

Not wishing to startle her, he gave a small cough. She straightened and lifted her fingers from the keys as he approached.

Uninvited, he sat beside her on the hard bench.

"Good day, Lord Foxford," she said.

Her greeting—classic, formal, and proper—made him smile.

"Good day, Lady Purity. My given name, by the way, is Matthew, and I invite you to use it whenever you wish."

She nodded somberly, and he wished she looked happier. There must be worse men she could marry. He noted she hadn't given him permission to call her anything. Therefore, he would continue with the name that suited her best.

"I am no music expert, kitten, but you play well in my estimation."

"Thank you. I have practiced for many hours. It's a good thing, too, for I have no voice for singing unlike my younger sisters."

Clearly, she was stalling from discussing anything important, either still embarrassed or perhaps worried for what came next.

"You are as good as any player in a—" he stopped himself. He nearly mentioned the only place he had heard a piano for the past few years, a bordello, both in London and in Paris.

"In an orchestra," he finished.

She frowned. "Highly unlikely. Remember we talked about flattery before."

"Of course." He ran a hand through his hair. "We ought to discuss our future."

Surprisingly, she gave a single harsh laugh.

"Is something funny?"

"Don't you think so?" she asked. "Maybe ironic is a better term. I always intended to marry a devoted, loyal gentleman, someone like my father."

"I see." He was about to be insulted.

"I never truly saw *you* as a potential suitor. I believe I told you that from the beginning. You and your ilk—"

"My ilk?" he repeated.

"There you go, interrupting again like you did before I started trying to civilize you. I guess I failed dreadfully." She shook her head. "Your ilk—the rakish swells of London's noblemen. You are the opposite to anyone who would attract me."

"I think you're lying," he said, feeling defensive. "You and I have an attraction as powerful as any I've ever felt."

She waved it away with a gesture of her hand.

"I wanted a husband such as my sister married. Staid, mannered, calm. A rum duke of a man in manner as well as in appearances."

"And I am none of those things?" He couldn't deny he was hurt by her low opinion. But he waited for her answer.

CHAPTER SIXTEEN

"Well?" Purity asked, staring at the piano keys and not at him. "Are you?"

Matthew hated this conversation and her disappointed, saddened tone.

"I can be loyal and well-mannered," he insisted.

"You have had many associations with other women, have you not?"

Matthew had a flash of dozens of mouths and naked bodies, but they were all as one and the same— inconsequential and unimportant.

"I don't like to speak about other women with you," he said, "but I have, yes. What import to that?"

"You didn't offer for any one of them. Were you never caught before?"

Purity ought not to compare herself to any of the females with whom he'd ever been associated. How could he make her understand the chasm of difference between all those women and her? And how could he make her believe him?

"They were not the type of women expecting an offer of marriage." Apart from the angry one who was now Varley's wife. She had wanted too much from Matthew. With Purity, however, it didn't seem too much at all.

As if reading his mind, she asked, "What about Lady Varley, before she was married?"

The devil take him if Purity wasn't the most perceptive lady he'd ever met.

"How did you know?" he asked.

"I didn't," she said softly. "Now, I do."

She was also tricky! He must remember that.

"In any case," she continued, "I guessed by the way she looked at me when they discovered us. He appeared gleeful, but she wore an expression of abject jealousy."

"Nonsense," Matthew said, hoping she was wrong. A jealous woman was a dangerous one. "They are practically newly wedded."

"Her husband is no Foxford, I suspect," Purity added.

The intimation shamed him, as if she believed he had such sexual prowess any female would prefer him. Not that he would dispute such a claim, but to have her thinking him capable of cuckoldry on a grand scale gave him a nauseous sensation.

"It doesn't matter what she feels or any of the others," he insisted. "They were all purely for sport."

"You are the Fox, after all," she muttered.

At that instant, he would gladly shed the moniker to have her look at him with respect. All he could do was remind her why he was there and hope she thought better of him for doing the honorable thing.

"Your father was amenable to my suit. We have agreed to all terms, and if you are likewise willing, then we can marry at your convenience. Two months from today, if you wish."

She cringed slightly. It was a good thing he had a secure sense of self-worth. Perhaps it was merely the way she had been forced without any say in the matter. Yet despite there being no real choice, given how they'd been discovered, he would be remiss if he didn't give her the semblance of being asked.

To that end, Matthew picked up one of her hands from the piano, making her turn to him. When he kissed its soft back, she sighed.

"Lady Purity, would you do me the tremendous honor of accepting my proposal of marriage?"

Her expression was sadly one of resignation.

"It is not as if I can turn you down," she said.

That hurt. But he'd just been thinking the same thing, so he added, "I hope you wouldn't want to do so, even if you could."

She snatched her hand back without giving him an answer.

"Why?" she snapped. "Because you are desperately in love with me, vowing to forsake all others?"

Surprised at her vehemence, Matthew wondered whether to disclose that he had, in fact, more than fondness for her. He could explain how from the beginning, he had lusted for her, and no mistake, since the first time he'd seen her in the marquess's drawing room. Over the weeks, however, base attraction had become genuine partiality to her above all others, and then he'd developed a tenderness for her such as he'd never known.

Was he ready to declare himself in love? Not while she was swinging like a pendulum between melancholy, ire, and taking out her bitterness upon him. She might say something he wouldn't be able to forget.

"My feelings for you are different and deeper than I've ever felt for any other female. I assume they will continue to grow and deepen."

"What about the women you enjoy for sport?" she asked, tapping a black key, letting the sharp sound underlie her words. "Will you still want them after we marry?" Purity spoke as if the words were dragged from her lips. She wanted to know even if it pained her.

"The papers have entertained London readers with your escapades," she continued, "but I would not find it entertaining, not one bit, if I were 'Lady F' and had to read about 'the Fox' sneaking into some other woman's boudoir."

Poor Purity. No wonder her feathers were ruffled. She thought the worst of him. Matthew was glad he could reassure her.

"I will remain faithful to you and to our marriage bed."

At the mention of their bed, she sucked in a breath, flaring her nostrils. Her awareness of what they would do sent desire flooding his veins.

"That eases my mind," she said softly. Then after another quiet moment, she added, "I apologize for being short with you."

Matthew didn't want her polite apology.

"You haven't given me your answer," he reminded her.

She nodded, then her glance met his again. Emotions fluttered in the cerulean depths.

How her eyes could be so deep a blue, sometimes like the sky before the sun went down, sometimes like the stormy sea, was unfathomable. He knew only that he was content to look into them forever.

"I will do you the honor," she said, her voice wavering, "and I honestly hope I do not live to regret it."

Like a punch to his gut, she had said it plainly. Matthew would make sure she didn't regret accepting him. In that moment, he vowed silently to become the man Purity Diamond deserved.

At least he could already measure up in one way. Releasing her hand, he took her face between his palms and held it still, watching her eyes grow as big as saucers. She swallowed and parted her lips.

Matthew doubted she knew how tantalizing she appeared. Lowering his mouth to hers, he breathed in her rose scent as their lips touched. The familiar yet entirely extraordinary sensations sizzled through him.

Tilting his head, he slid his hands back into her silken hair and anchored her in place.

They should take their time. This was the first kiss of what he prayed was a short engagement, hopefully leading to a long and happy marriage. He intended to make it perfect.

After brushing the tip of his tongue along her bottom lip, he slid it slowly into her mouth. He didn't explore or fence, merely stroking her tongue with his. Her hands found his shoulders, her fingers digging in. After sucking gently, he withdrew.

Leaning his forehead against hers, breathing hard, he heard her doing the same.

"Whenever we touch," he confessed, "it is as if I am on fire within."

Purity didn't speak, merely nodding, which he took to mean she had a similar reaction. A long moment later, he sat back, releasing her and getting his ring, which had been his father's, tangled in her hair.

What a buffoon!

"My apologies," he said, freeing himself. "I've made a mess of your coiffure."

"I'll go upstairs and tidy myself after you leave."

They continued to sit, staring at one another. Something was different. He frowned.

"Is aught the matter?" she asked.

"I just realized," he confessed. "Again, you forgot to slap me."

A small smile appeared on her lovely face. "I shall not slap you anymore now that we are engaged. Besides, I didn't slap you at Syon House when Lord and Lady Varley discovered us."

The mere mention of them soured his mood. While the twosome had aided him in his goal of securing her hand, he'd wanted to win Purity by himself, not have her forced to wed him while he was still trying to earn her admiration.

"You didn't have a chance to slap me then, but I'm sure you would have."

She nodded. "In all probability, when I regained my senses, yes, I would have."

Her little quip infused him with jollity. He still thought they suited like a dog and a bone.

"I shall endeavor to make you as happy as you make me," he vowed spontaneously.

When her smile grew, he felt elated. And her next words made him feel even better.

"I am responsible for my own happiness, my lord, as you are for yours. However, we can do our best to bring joy to each other's lives and at the very least, not make one another miserable."

"You are a wise young lady," he said, "and that is not flattery."

Her cheeks pinkened. "You should go now. We are unchaperoned, and even as an engaged couple, this is not allowed."

Another proper rule he despised, for he would be happy to sit all day beside her. Instead, Matthew rose to his feet, took her hand, and kissed it.

"I am both honored and grateful you accepted my proposal. And now, I bid you good day, Lady Purity." He hoped he'd been formal enough considering they had just been fused at the lips.

"I am grateful you proposed, my lord. Good day."

Not the warmest of sentiments, he thought. He didn't want her gratitude, but for today, he would accept it as better than nothing.

With a last wink he couldn't resist since it made her smile again, he departed the Diamond residence and considered it a morning well spent. Just like that, he had a fiancée.

PURITY WATCHED FOXFORD leave as her emotions wavered between anxiety and relief. When her mother suggested they visit Clarity and tell her the news, she agreed hesitatingly. She couldn't easily explain to anyone, not even her mother, how she felt irrationally unclothed. Yet Lord and Lady Varley having witnessed her in an intimate moment had stripped her daily costume of unblemished integrity.

A part of her thought she should remain indoors until the engagement was announced or maybe until after the marriage had occurred, at which time she hoped to reclaim her status of honor and respectability.

It was a foolish thought. She could not hide indoors for however long her parents decided was a suitable engagement. Moreover, if nothing appeared in the newspapers, then no one thought any less of her than they had two days earlier.

Her older sister welcomed the unexpected visit, having left Syon Park before the scene of Purity's inglorious entrance into the greenhouse and thus was blissfully ignorant. Clarity thought it a simple social call for tea and biscuits.

Not waiting for the tea service to arrive, their mother made the abrupt announcement.

"Your sister is now engaged to Lord Foxford."

Clarity's eyes grew as big as shillings, staring at Purity who remained silent. The proclamation didn't seem possible, not about her, not with Foxford. Surely, she would awaken from a dream to find her mother was talking about someone else entirely.

"Then that is why you took a stroll along the river at Syon Park," Clarity surmised, "so the baron could ask for your hand. How romantic."

Purity bit her lip. Would everyone who'd been at the picnic think similarly once her father put word of the engagement in the paper? That would be a welcome misinterpretation of the events.

"He declared his intent for our engagement at that time," she said, glad she didn't have to lie.

Clarity gave a clap of joy. "What wonderful news! He is dash-fire handsome, is he not?"

"He is," Purity agreed, wishing she was as pleased as her sister. His handsome appearance was not in question, but how he had made use of his good looks could not be immediately forgotten.

"Foxford has charm to spare," their mother agreed evenly.

But Purity shook her head. He had charmed his way under the skirts of many females if the tales were true.

"I sense something didn't go quite as properly as it ought to for my dear sister's liking," Clarity said, finally toning down her jubilance since she was the only one expressing such happiness.

Purity waved the words away with her hand. "I'm simply being overly particular, as usual." *If one could classify being caught by another couple in the throes of a passionate embrace as being overly particular.*

Regardless, Clarity put her arm around her. "It will all work out."

Her words made Purity want to scream. While Clarity wasn't buffle-headed, she had an outlook that always expected the best and the happiest for everyone around her.

But things didn't simply *work out*, not unless one managed and arranged and kept everyone in order, including herself.

And then she'd broken all her own rules!

Jumping to her feet she began to pace.

"Me! Marrying a rake. My reputation ruined. Me!" she repeated.

"What has happened?" Clarity asked, looking bewildered. "I have heard nothing about you or your reputation being ruined.

The maid entered with the tray carrying the tea service, so they fell silent until she'd set it down and left.

"What happened," Purity said, "is that I was led away from the rest of the guests at the picnic."

Clarity laughed. "Is that all? But you know how it is when one is outside of London proper. Certain rules are relaxed, whether at Syon Park or at a country estate. I witnessed a few other people going for a walk. You mustn't be so hard on yourself," she continued. "It's not as though you were caught embracing one another while making noisy horse smacks." And she laughed.

Purity caught her breath, her glance darting from her quiet mother to her amused sister. Finally, realizing the severity of the situation, Clarity stopped herself in a last hiccup of laughter.

"Oh, dear," she said. "You *were* caught."

Purity nodded. Now her sister and her mother knew the truth. Not only had she been kissing Foxford, but she had also been discovered.

"Of all of us sisters," Clarity said, her tone disbelieving, "I must admit you are the last one I would think to end up in such a predicament."

Their mother was sipping her tea, watching her eldest daughters.

"Your sister may very well be correct," Lady Diamond said, looking at Purity. "Sometimes these situations do work out exactly as hoped and very well to boot. Your Grandmother Diamond, for instance, was," she coughed and cleared her throat, "shall we say, compromised by your grandfather."

"What?" both girls exclaimed at once.

"Grandmother Marianne?" Clarity asked.

"With Grandfather James?" Purity added. "Are you sure?"

Their mother laughed. "Without a shade of a doubt."

"How is it neither of us knew about this?" Purity asked, retaking her seat on the sofa.

The countess gave a gentle shrug. "No one thinks of it now, which is the point of my telling you."

Clarity smiled. "Are you saying by the time Purity is a grandmother, the rumors will have died down entirely?"

Purity wanted to stick her tongue out at her older sister.

"Long before then," said their mother. "When I was marrying your father, he was the one who told me of the rumors of his parents' past. I promise, any unpleasantness dissipates quickly, especially if the couple is in love and has a strong marriage."

Purity's stomach twinged with worry. She was about to mention her doubts regarding both those points when her mother spoke again.

"Besides, a little scandal is practically a family tradition. Your father and I married at Gretna Green."

Purity turned open-mouthed to look at Clarity, seeing her expression mirrored. *Utter speechless shock!*

Their mother laughed. "I am delighted to be able still to surprise my daughters." Picking up her cup again, she leaned back and sipped with a satisfied smile.

"Mother!" Purity said at last. "Are you saying you and Father slipped over the border to Scotland for a hasty wedding?"

Her mother nodded. "If anyone ought to be shrouded in a blanket of appalled whispers, it should be us. Yet no one ever makes mention of it or even remembers."

"But why?" Clarity asked.

"Because we are the Earl and Countess Diamond," their mother said. "Most who recall, wouldn't dare bring it up in case we cut them. And the rest simply don't care."

Clarity shook her head. "No, I mean why did you elope? Did Father compromise you? Do you think our brother will behave in a similar fashion?"

"Compromise me!" their mother repeated, sounding rattled, but she didn't gainsay her daughter. Moreover, her cheeks went a pretty shade of rose. "Your brother will find his own way. And if Adam must abscond with his future lady-love, then I shall wish them well, as long as they make each other happy."

"Were Grandmother and Grandfather Chimes displeased by your elopement?" Purity asked.

"My parents were at the wedding, as were your father's. All four of them traveled to Scotland. But that's a story for another day."

"Are there any other surprises?" Clarity asked.

"I don't believe so," Lady Diamond said. "If there are, I shall save them for it is great fun not to be all out of new tales for my beloved girls. The point is that your father and I were not shunned by society, nor did anyone think any the less of us. Or if they did, it made no matter. Haven't you girls always been allowed access to the finest families?"

Purity considered. "To be honest, what you've told us does make me feel better."

"It's not that I recommend such a path, mind you," their mother continued. "In the case of your father, we loved one another, and I knew he was a good man. Hence, we took matters into our own hands. However, Clarity's wedding ceremony was truly perfect, and I would like you to have the same, just as you deserve. And so you shall!"

Purity might not become a social outcast after all. Even if she and Foxford married with no one bearing witness to any true courtship prior to their engagement—since there had, in fact, not been any.

Sniffing, she felt tears prick her eyes. Either from relief or the stressful feelings she had bottled up, Purity didn't know. Yet she did resent having strictly adhered to the rules all her life, only to have it all possibly have been for naught.

"Don't sink into a fit of blue devils," her mother said as Clarity refilled all their teacups. "Lord Foxford has done the honorable thing so far."

So far. Up until the wedding day and through the wedding night, Purity believed he would continue on the path. *Especially on the wedding night.* He'd made clear he wouldn't miss that.

But afterward? She had no way of knowing whether he would stay faithful or return to his wicked ways. Unlike her father, Foxford might *not* be a good man.

CHAPTER SEVENTEEN

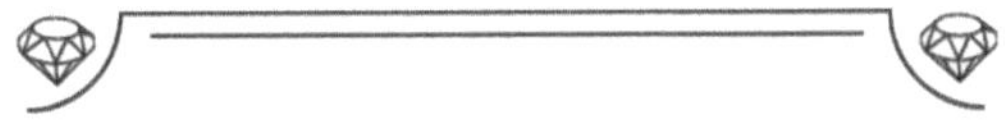

"I didn't want to say anything more in front of Clarity," Purity confided as she and her mother rode home, "because she wants to believe everyone is good and can be as happy as she is. But my relationship with Foxford is not like yours and father's or hers with Hollidge."

"No one's is like anyone else's," her mother said. "But how do you mean?"

"I'm not *certain* about him," Purity confessed, her voice falling to a whisper.

Her mother sighed. "And yet you love him anyway."

"Love him?" Purity's heart started to race.

"Well, don't you? You often seem glad in his company. You looked especially so when dancing with him." Her mother tossed her head and considered. "Besides, I don't think you would let yourself be caught by a man you didn't love."

Her mother was a mystery sometimes. "How was I caught by him?"

Lady Diamond smiled. "All that poppycock about him needing lessons in etiquette."

"Mother! I promise you he did."

"He made you think he did. I've seen him behave perfectly well when you weren't around."

Purity considered that he might have bamboozled her from the start.

"Now why do you suppose he wanted you to spend time with him?" her mother asked. "I say it was to win you over. And I believe he succeeded."

"I suppose he did. I confess I enjoy his company more than any other man I've ever met."

"And?" Lady Diamond persisted.

"And what?"

"It should be more than that, my dear daughter. There should be sparks."

Purity felt her cheeks warm and pressed her gloved hands to her cheeks.

"Then there are sparks," her mother declared, sounding confident. "I would hate for you to miss out on them."

Having experienced the sizzle, Purity would hate to have missed out, too. But her heart was at stake.

"What if he doesn't feel an equal ardor?" Purity asked, wondering aloud. Wanting a respectable wife and falling in love were two separate issues.

"If he doesn't love you in return, then your heart is in grave danger," her mother said. "Thus, if you truly think him a scoundrel, then perhaps your father had best have another word with him beyond dowries and wedding contracts."

"To compare methods of compromising?" Purity snapped.

The notion of her father and Foxford discussing her future husband's fidelity was mortifying. It ought not to be necessary, not if she were engaged to the correct man.

"Perhaps Grandfather Diamond should be consulted, too!" she added, her tone waspish.

"Purity! You've never said anything so disrespectful in all your years, so I shall forgive you. You are in a state of mental anguish, and there is little we can do."

"Precisely. There is nothing we can do. I am at Foxford's mercy. And Father cannot mold the man's character, so having him speak to my fiancé is as useless as sweeping sand at the shore."

"Diamond and I have had a fine marriage," her mother said, sounding hurt. "As have your grandparents."

Purity threw her arms around her. "I apologize. Truly, I do. I will ask you or Father if I need help, but I would rather deal with Foxford on my own terms. I should start the marriage the way I intend to go on with it."

They stayed hugging a moment longer. Then her mother nodded.

"That's my girl. I raised you to be able to handle even the wiliest of foxes. Besides, if you love him, then I believe he must be a good man."

Purity cocked her head at her mother's assumption.

"Deep down," Lady Diamond added.

Purity raised her eyebrows.

"Very deep down," her mother persisted.

Purity sighed. "Please stop. Any deeper and it will be only his marrow that is good."

They both laughed.

"Now, Mother, tell me all about the ceremony at Gretna Green."

FINISHING HIS CORRESPONDENCE, Matthew rose from his desk ready to go for a ride in the park, exercising both himself and his horse. Before he could stretch and grab his coat, his butler knocked and brought in an unexpected calling card.

Lady Varley's card was crisp with perfectly printed letters and drenched in patchouli leaf perfume. All at once, upon sniffing the scent, their entire brief, intense affair came to mind.

He'd met Emilia at a dinner party, thrown by Quinn's aunt, and noticed the lovely fair-haired female as soon as he'd entered because of the immodest cut of her gown. She was lively and pretty in a made-up, fashionable way, using the latest tools of artifice to great effect on her lips, cheeks, and eyes. Although the other bucks were circling her, it was Matthew who had the good fortune to be seated beside her at dinner.

As was his usual manner, he had set himself to charming her. In return, she was all over him before the pudding course, with her hand finding its way to his lap. About three years older than he, she clearly knew her way around the bedroom and was ready for a romp.

Emilia was his favorite kind of lover—he didn't have to pay her to pretend a great hour of passion, nor was she a simpering virgin who would cry the loss of her innocence when she understood he was not going to proffer his name in marriage after the deed was done.

When the dinner party ended and he strolled out into the night, Emilia's carriage awaited him a few houses farther along Cavendish Square with the shades down. Upon climbing in, they had a decision to make, his home or hers. Back at her townhouse, she practically raced him upstairs and declared she had no expectations beyond that night.

She had lied.

The earthy fragrance wafting from her calling card also brought her naked body to mind. After a fortnight of fornication, he had found out she wanted the respectability of marriage, a goal denied her previously due to some sad story he hadn't listened to. He should have been more attentive. Suddenly, she wanted him to fill another man's shoes in the church when all he'd wanted was to fill her with his stiff arousal before moving on.

Realizing what she was about, he'd told her they were finished. They were ill-suited because of her mean-spirited outlook and her often small-minded remarks—neither of which he mentioned. Instead, he reminded her he was going to France and might be away for years. *Hadn't she remembered him telling her?*

Her rage was neither glorious nor beautiful. It was ugly and unnerving. She accused him of tricking her and stealing her innocence, neither of which was true. Besides, he'd never told her how her perfume sometimes brought to mind overly ripe apples, the musty smell of a used wine cork, or even mildew.

And then, while he was on the Continent, she'd hooked Varley somehow. *Thank God!* No wonder the man had shouldered him aside at their club. He probably wished Matthew had married her, so he hadn't.

What did the chit want now?

There was only one way to find out, although he wondered at his own utter disinterest. Still, he owed it to her not to turn her away without hearing her out. After all, a gentleman ought to show some respect to a former lover.

Striding into his drawing room where his butler had allowed her to wait, Emilia's intentions were already clear. Without invitation, she had not only taken a seat but was reclining upon his sofa with her feet up at one end.

When he came to a halt in the middle of the room, she leaned back comfortably and unpinned her hat before tossing it to the floor.

And then, ever so slowly, eyeing him the entire time, Emilia peeled off her gloves.

He swallowed, staring silently at her bare hands.

Matthew waited for the usual arousal to send him winging to her side, yet it never came. Instead of an insatiable hunger and the flash-fire of desire, he felt only annoyance. She might as well have been a sack of potatoes lounging upon his divan.

Moreover, if he examined the moment carefully, he would concede it was Purity who had made the difference in him. Countless encounters with females like Emilia had not made a dent in his loneliness, nor filled up the empty space inside him for longer than it took to get dressed afterward.

With Purity, from a mere few kisses and furtive encounters that hadn't even entailed him removing his trousers, Matthew felt more satisfied than he had in years. Knowing she was his fiancée—his intended who would be beside him the rest of his days—having but to wait until his wedding night, the bubbling spring of constant yearning had been capped with contentment.

He was ready to wait for his kitten to curl upon his lap when she was ready. In truth, the anticipation was exhilarating.

Taking the chair opposite, he stretched out his long legs, crossing his ankles. Despite the distance of a few feet, he could smell Emilia's cloying perfume.

"What do you want?" he asked, not caring how rude he sounded.

She was obviously up to no good. Besides being married, she knew he was engaged and yet hadn't brought a companion to keep things remotely respectable.

"Aren't you going to sit over here?" she asked.

"No."

She pouted her red-stained lips, which didn't do a damn thing to entice him. "Won't you offer me a glass of sherry or wine?"

"It's too early for either," he pointed out, "and I won't bother ringing for tea service since you'll be gone before the tea has time to steep. An uninvited visit should last no longer than ten minutes." Purity would be proud of him. Moreso since he'd shaved five minutes off the polite time.

Emilia's brown eyes widened. "You are not being nice to me, which is a mistake. Do you recall how passionate we were the first night we met? Wouldn't you like to experience that again?" She glanced toward the door.

"We could go upstairs right now," she proposed. "I remember the way. Just once, perhaps for old-time's sake."

"No," he said again. Whatever game she was playing was tedious. For one thing, they'd never swived at his home, so she most certainly didn't know the way. Secondly, she might be with child and wishing to blame him. Thirdly, she might be seeking revenge upon Varley. Or she might simply be bored. Regardless, he didn't care.

Wishing he hadn't sat down as that indicated he wished to chat and draw out the visit, he rose again to his feet.

"If you came only for refreshments, then I must ask you to leave. I have business to attend to directly."

She didn't sit up or even remove her feet from the end of the sofa.

"Foxy, Foxy, Foxy," she began.

He cringed.

"That sweet little Diamond is not what you need. She's barely a bland morsel, and you will devour her in a single bite. Then what? When you're still hungry, what will you do?"

"I won't discuss my fiancée with you."

"Do you expect me to believe that upstanding earl's daughter is really engaged to be your wife? Come now. We both know you played the chivalrous gentleman to protect her, but you are as ready to gallivant as any man I know."

"You don't know me," he said.

"I do. And you are just like me, too wild to be tamed. Let's take up where we left off."

"But you have already been tamed, Lady *Varley*," he said, reminding her she was no longer Lady Tupmoure. "Or at least you made a vow. In other words, you are married, and I am not interested."

She was starting to believe him. He could see it in the set of her jaw and the way her eyes narrowed slightly. At last, she swung her feet to the floor. They both could see the dirty mark on the velvet from her boots.

"*Oops,*" she said without contrition. "How careless of me. Leaving a trace of my being here. I hope it doesn't get you into trouble. But you're used to trouble, aren't you? I hope Lady Purity is, too. She'll need to be if she's going to hitch herself to your horse."

"I don't intend to get into any trouble, with you or anyone else." He still didn't want to talk about Purity with her. It felt disloyal. Besides, he would toss out the sofa and start his married life with a new one. Not just street filth, but the scent of her perfume was probably all over it.

"Tell me," Lady Varley demanded, "is your cruel disinterest because I up and married after you left? Is that why you are pretending not to fancy me anymore?"

She seemed to have forgotten he'd broken it off in a decisive manner *before* he departed for the Continent.

"Even if I had remained in England, we would not be together. Frankly, whether you are married or not means nothing to me." He didn't add "because you mean nothing to me," but he hoped she received the message.

Her nostrils flared. "I gave you a chance. Don't ever claim otherwise." With that, she rose to her feet, snatched up her hat, and swept from the room.

Now he remembered what had most annoyed him about her—the high drama. Every time they swived, she would demand he spend the night and sulk when he didn't. She would literally cling to his arm and try to lure him back to bed. The one time she succeeded, he'd arisen before dawn and still she had pouted, asking when she would see him again.

When he parted from her, he had thought he had been kind but firm, setting her free to find a permanent solution to her loneliness. And it seemed she had, with Varley.

Apparently, their marriage was a sham.

CHAPTER EIGHTEEN

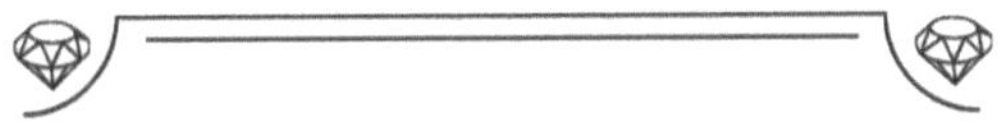

Two evenings later, Matthew assisted Purity and her mother into his carriage and climbed in behind them before his footman shut the door. He had insisted upon collecting them for a concert at the Hanover Square Rooms. Having the ladies come to his home and offer him a ride in the earl's conveyance would have been emasculating.

Besides, Matthew's brougham was plush and comfortable. As his baroness, Purity would soon be sharing it regularly. He wanted her to like everything about her new life.

Lady Diamond had agreed to play the chaperone. Although the three of them didn't address anything to do with the hurried engagement, the countess's presence helped to alleviate any lingering awkwardness.

"I have never heard of Monsieur Hector Berlioz," Lady Diamond admitted. "But I am grateful to have this opportunity to attend his concert with you."

Purity's mother was grace personified, making it seem as if he were doing her a great favor by bringing her when, in fact, she was being dragged along to offer the semblance of propriety. Matthew already knew Lord Diamond had been called out of town by his land manager. Elsewise, both parents would be watching his every move.

"I shall be pleased to have your knowledgeable presence, my lady, since I have not been a steady concertgoer in the past. However, while in Paris, I was introduced to Berlioz as both a composer and conductor. I thought his music to be sublime, and I hope you enjoy it."

Then he turned to Purity. "I will be most interested to know your opinion of the pianist."

Mother and daughter looked at one another. Then Purity said, "I am sure the concert pianist can play far better than I, my lord."

He shrugged. "I cannot imagine anyone playing better. I would like to give you a piano as my wedding gift, but I might need help in choosing a good instrument."

He was gratified by Lady Diamond's nod of approval.

"That is generous of you, my lord," Purity said. "However, I believe my parents will let me keep the piano I have since my father purchased it especially for me."

Two perfectly proper "my lords" in a row from his fiancée, as well as entirely neutral conversation, all the while with her gaze upon her gloved hands folded in her lap. If this were the young lady he'd first met, he would think her shy, demure, and boring.

Luckily, he knew she was none of those things. Purity was holding herself up to the highest standard of feminine decorous and modest behavior to counteract what had occurred before. And if she didn't stop by evening's end, Matthew would be forced to drag her behind the stage and kiss her soundly.

At the Hanover Square Rooms, also known as the Queen's Concert Rooms by those who liked to stay in that regal lady's good graces, Lady Diamond did two things—she started to introduce them to any friends or acquaintances they came across as an engaged couple, engendering many congratulations and well wishes.

Secondly, she gave them space to speak by themselves.

While the countess got into a deeper conversation about the merits of the mineral waters of Bath, where he understood she'd been raised, Matthew was able to take Purity's arm and stroll the lobby.

"Stop looking over your shoulder," he said. "Your mother is within shouting distance, other people are all around us, and I intend nothing untoward."

She nodded and stared at her slippered feet.

He wanted to shake her. "Honestly, kitten, I thought once we were engaged you would relax a little and let down your guard."

Purity visibly stiffened. "Relax?" she repeated. "Are you referring to my morals? I suppose you think I should hang all over you and rub your shoulder in public now that we are engaged."

Matthew couldn't help laughing. "I have never considered either of those things. Is that how you believe betrothed people behave?"

A couple stopped them and congratulated them upon their engagement. As soon as they'd moved on, she continued, "If you relaxed your morals any further, my lord, you would be a male light-skirt."

"A light-skirt," he said, ready to laugh again.

"A light-pants, then," she suggested, still looking far too solemn for the happy occasion of being out for the first time as a couple.

While he knew he'd been an out and outer for years, often enjoying himself too much, he was not a whore's bird. Plainly, Purity was still angry over the flirtatious females at Vauxhall. However, he no longer had any interest in women with their tendencies. He liked his kitten and her strait-laced manner, at least in public.

As long as she kept her fiery passion only for him, he would be satisfied.

"I promise I have no wish for you to behave any differently than the kind, genteel lady I have come to know."

"Well! I . . . I . . ." She closed her mouth and then sighed. "I cannot argue with you if you are going to be magnanimous."

"Why do you wish to argue with me?"

This time, her gaze rose to meet his and well-nigh knocked him back a step with the dazzling shimmering depths of her eyes.

"Because," she said softly, "I want—no, I *need* for us to keep our distance until the wedding. I nearly shamed my family, and whenever you are too close—"

Lady Diamond approached. "Everyone is going in."

Matthew escorted the ladies into the auditorium, decidedly frustrated at not hearing from Purity's own lips what she felt when he was close.

PURITY KNEW SHE WAS being the worst primsy-pate ever. Yet she'd never experienced anything like the surges of longing that assaulted her with Foxford's presence. Not only did her stomach flutter unbearably when he was near, but parts of her throbbed and pulsed, yearning for his touch.

She'd lain awake reliving their kisses and imagining his hands upon her most private parts many nights. Thus, the concert was torture. Seated beside him, breathing his familiar citrus and woodsy scent, she recalled how his mouth felt upon hers and how his hands had kneaded her flesh and caressed her back and hips.

With their joining as man and wife being imminent, the physical act had become all she could think about.

At that moment, she was unable to concentrate on anything except the sizzling of her body that had her squirming in the velvet seat. Relieved when the last notes died out, she rose, only to hear, "Encore."

The cry for more was caught up and repeated throughout the audience, and she regained her seat.

Her mother was clapping joyfully on one side of her, while Foxford leaned close on the other.

"You seem ready to leave. Are you not enjoying the performance?"

"I am," she promised, unable to tell him the truth. Their heads were practically touching. If she moved an inch and turned her head, their lips would meet.

Quickly, she swiveled in the other direction.

"The musicians are very good, are they not?" her mother asked. "And Monsieur Berlioz is an excellent conductor, even for the pieces that he did not compose."

"Indeed." Then Purity fell silent until the extra movement finished, and once again the clapping began. Finally, they rose to their feet and started the ambling movement out to the lobby.

"The answer to your earlier question," Lady Diamond told Foxford, "is no. I don't believe my daughter could have played any better. It was stirring, was it not?"

"It was," he agreed.

Purity knew she'd felt stirred for the entire performance and would love at that moment to be alone with her fiancé. She ached to press herself against him, to mold her curves to his planes, to sink her fingers into his hair, and to kiss him soundly.

With tongues.

"Mm," she sighed, humming with desire as they shuffled up the aisle. It was like a madness. *Did it ease off after one consummated?* She only half hoped that was the case.

"I was taken by the—" Foxford began but trailed off as something or someone caught his eye.

Purity followed his gaze. *Lady Varley!* She was standing by herself, one hand on her hip staring directly at the two of them.

"By the timing," he concluded. "A conductor is like a puppeteer, able to command each musician to start and stop precisely upon a flick of his hand."

Purity heard her mother agree, yet she couldn't help returning the lady's frank regard. Lady Varley was an attractive woman, no doubt, but her expression, one of unadulterated dislike, spoiled her good looks.

Not to mention causing a shiver to snake down Purity's spine.

Having last seen Lady Varley at Syon Park, exclaiming over Foxford being a "thundering buck," it wasn't a far cry to imagine the lady was jealous. After all, Lord Varley had little reputation for anything except losing a fiancée once to another man.

"Before we leave," her mother said, "I must speak with Lady Frances. She's waving me down. I think she just heard about the engagement. I shall return anon."

Before her mother had gone a few yards, Lady Varley approached from the other direction.

"What do you want?" Foxford asked, surprising Purity by his impoliteness.

While she disliked the way Lord and Lady Varley had come upon them and made insinuations, there was no need to have an adversarial relationship after the damage had been done.

Purity took a step forward, practically blocking Foxford.

"Did you enjoy the concert, my lady?" she asked in order to bring them back into the realm of civility.

"I did," Lady Varley said, then she fell silent, taking Purity's measure. Like a rival!

"Surely, you are not alone," Purity continued when nothing more was said into the awkward pause.

"Varley is roundabout somewhere," she said, dismissing any concern with a shrug. "All the evening's chatter is of your engagement. You two make quite the pair."

Purity glanced back at Foxford, whose expression was unsmiling and unusually severe.

"Why, thank you," Purity said for both of them.

"Just as Foxford and I did at one time," Lady Varley continued. "I think he even brought me here once."

"Emilia," Foxford warned, his tone like a low growl.

Emilia! Purity was doubly shocked, both by Lady Varley's bold statement and by Foxford's unforgiveable use of the lady's given name. *In public! And not even of his own family member!*

Her next thought—that the two were well matched—flitted unbidden through her brain. But Lady Varley was in his past, and Purity was not so naïve as to misunderstand the woman's motives. She still wanted Foxford! He had come back from the Continent, and Lady Varley was miffed she could no longer have an association with him now that she was married.

"I hope you don't make such statements in front of your husband," Purity chastised. "Unless you don't mind hurting the man to whom you owe your utmost loyalty."

Probably expecting more of a reaction, Lady Varley simply rolled her eyes, made a noise of disgust, and walked away.

"She is a bit of a nuisance, isn't she?" Purity remarked.

Foxford let out a bark of laughter. "Thank God, kitten. I thought you might take her seriously, which wouldn't do at all. She was trying to throw you decidedly off-kilter."

"She did not succeed. I feel sorry for her," she said.

"Feel sorry for whom?" her mother asked, returning in time to hear her last remark.

"No one important," Purity said, hoping that was the case.

"Not at all," Foxford agreed.

CHAPTER NINETEEN

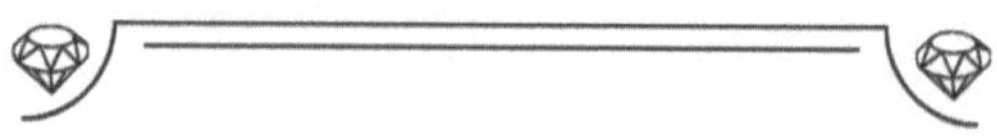

"Dammit!" Matthew slammed the late-afternoon edition of *The Times* onto his dining room table with such force his teacup clattered sideways in its saucer, spilling the contents. Throwing his napkin atop the mess to blot the worst of it, he rose to his feet and was halfway to the door when he stopped.

What could he do about the vicious slander? It was printed. The damage was done! Thrashing Varley within an inch of his life or confronting his shrew of a wife would do no good.

He was supposed to meet Quinn and their friends at Café de l'Europe next to the Haymarket Theatre later that evening. When he did, he would face a group of men who had all read an exaggerated tale of what Lord and Lady Varley happened upon at Syon Park. In the interim of a week, they had embellished it beyond all recognition. One would think he and Purity had been discovered naked as needles writhing on the grass. Their engagement would be tainted.

Worse, it would distress Purity no end. Matthew's fury was growing by the minute.

He couldn't simply sit still and stew for hours. Changing swiftly, he headed to the pugilist's club and worked his body and his anger out upon a few hapless sparring partners. No facers were allowed, but each time he planted a punch to the other man's gut, he imagined Varley was the recipient.

Finally, aching and sweaty, he went home to soak in a tub and get ready for his celebratory engagement dinner. And if any of the other gentlemen brought up *The Times*, he would smile and tell them to go to hell.

But he wanted to speak with Quinn alone first. Across Mayfair at his friend's residence on Cavendish Square, he rapped on the door impatiently.

"Lord Quinn will be with you shortly, my lord," the butler said.

Luckily, it was not too early to start drinking. No one would have blamed him for adopting the standards of a dedicated debauchee and drinking directly after reading the tattle hours ago, and not stopping.

Matthew wasn't one of those. Nonetheless, his reputation, careless actions, and poor judgment had got him deep in the suds. And even though he and Purity had been partaking of a relatively tame act compared to some things he'd done in a garden, his fiancée was going to pay for his previous behavior. She would be held up as yet another in a long line, which simply wasn't the case.

"A glass of your employer's claret, please," he asked Quinn's butler before the man disappeared to tell him he was waiting.

Ten minutes later, glass in hand, Matthew was still brooding over having made an enemy of Lady Varley, while wondering what he'd ever done to harm her husband.

"Here I am," Quinn announced unnecessarily as he entered, already holding his own glass of wine in one hand and a full decanter in the other. "Sorry to keep you waiting. I assume I look presentable for having hurried with my toilette."

Matthew rolled his eyes. "I could not give a fig how you look. Did you see the paper today?"

"I did, which is why I'll forgive you for coming over uninvited and demanding my best claret."

Matthew wasn't in the mood for his friend's teasing, but since he was about to be in a group, he would need to change his disposition.

"Do you know, I think nothing would have ever shown up in *The Times* if I hadn't rebuffed Lady Varley. She paid me a visit recently."

"Do tell," Quinn said. "The former Lady Tupmoure sought you out at home, did she?"

Matthew nodded. "I told her I wasn't interested in taking up with her."

Quinn winced. "Why would you be? Purity is a true diamond, and Lady Varley is more like a colorful paste gem. Regardless, women don't like to hear the truth. If I were you, I would have mixed giblets with her, clothing on if you were in a hurry, and sent her on her way with a smile."

"I didn't want her, clothing on or off."

"You *cannot* be the Fox," Quinn said.

"I am no longer the Fox," Matthew agreed. "I am an engaged man, and damn lucky to boot having made an agreement with Lord Diamond. This type of public cackle could certainly sour a father on giving away his daughter. I can only hope it hasn't sconced the engagement."

"Lord Diamond knew whom he was accepting as his son-in-law. He doesn't seem the type to get ruffled."

Matthew hoped Quinn was correct, but his anger still swirled inside.

"The next time I see Varley, I am going to call him out."

"No," Quinn said, pouring them both another glass, "you're not. I imagine you'd name me as your second, and I hate the sight of blood. Besides, you could be killed or kill the man. How will either help? You cannot leave your lady alone to face any scorn that may come from the titillating column while you go to meet your maker or to languish at Newgate."

Quinn was right, but that didn't stop Matthew from imagining what he might do the next time he spotted his sandy-haired nemesis. Surely, no one would blame him for landing a nosegay or even a full floorer.

"Didn't you have something to do with Varley's engagement splintering so fabulously a week before he was to wed the fortune of his dreams?"

Quinn's words filtered into Matthew's savage thoughts.

"I did not! As I understand it, the fortune-in-question caught him enjoying himself more than any man should in a cupboard. What has that to do with me?"

"I am not friends with Varley, you understand," Quinn said, "but when you went to the Continent, he was at the club telling everyone how you had caused his ruin. He was drunk as David's sow, sucking the monkey for a fortnight straight before he sobered up. Most of us assumed you'd done your usual prank and taken the fun out of his wedding night before he could get the bride to bed."

Matthew heard this with growing horror. "None of that is right. I did no such thing. I can barely recall Varley's blasted fiancée."

"Lady Penelope Cadmium. My sister knows her."

"Well, bully for your sister, but I've never laid eyes on this Cadmium woman. Why would Varley blame me?"

Drinking the wine too quickly, he choked and swore loudly. *Again, Varley's fault!*

"Without your biting off my head," Quinn said, "I must remind you that you can't blame anyone for believing Varley and thinking you had something to do with it. After all, you do have a way of mucking up other men's happiness, including mine."

The anger fizzled out of Matthew like a doused candle.

"Not you, too." But he had an inkling he knew what his friend was talking about. They'd celebrated leaving Cambridge with a rather boisterous carousing. It might have lasted a week. Quinn had introduced him to the lady he was favoring at the time, and somehow, by week's end, Matthew ended up in her boudoir, exhilarated by liquor, by life, and by living in the greatest city in the world. His celebration entailed a feather bed jig with his friend's love interest.

Quinn had shrugged it off with a quip about not seeing her again as he didn't fancy *a buttered bun.*

"Dammit, man," Matthew said. "I barely remember her, and I didn't think you cared that much."

Quinn's eyes darkened as he held up his glass of wine and stared into its ruby depths.

"I don't now, but back then, I did. And strangely, I still remember her. She had a sweet smile and a dusting of freckles. She married a soldier and lives in Birmingham."

Then he shook his head. "If I had cared greatly, if you had broken me, then what? You couldn't undo what you did."

Matthew stared. Lately, more than once, he was starting to think he'd taken his happy bachelor life to unwise extremes.

"Any woman who would pick me over you was a terrible judge of character and not worth your sparing her another thought, sweet smile or not. She simply wasn't worthy of you. In fact, you might be thankful I sussed out her true nature since she was more than willing to let me tup her."

Quinn didn't appear appeased. "Is that how you justify it? Or is that your apology?"

"Neither. *This* is my apology." Matthew rose to his feet. "I'm sorry I wapped her. I was stupid and selfish. You are my friend, and I let my prick get in the way of honor."

He reached out his hand across the space between them, willing Quinn to take it. After a moment, he did. They shook, and Matthew regained his chair, feeling better about the day.

Then Quinn smiled.

"It must be a pretty big prick because it has gotten in your way a lot."

"If I have to go around and apologize to every man I've cuckolded, then I won't have time for anything else." Matthew shook his head. "That was a joke and a gross overstatement. I swear, most of the females in my life have been unattached."

"If you say so."

Matthew thought it was true. Hoped it was true.

"Do you think Varley told that tawdry tale to *The Times*?" Quinn asked.

"It makes sense if he holds a grudge over the loss of his fiancée, although I cannot imagine why he holds me in any way accountable."

Quinn drained his glass. "Maybe Lady Varley tattled to the newspaper."

Matthew shrugged. "Maybe." Suddenly he felt weary. "I hope I haven't left it too late to become respectable."

"I thought it would be the reign of Queen Dick before you made yourself all plummy."

Matthew grinned at his friend's sarcasm, then rose to his feet. His stomach was grumbling, and he was glad they were going for a good meal.

"You made me see things a little differently, and for that, I am grateful. Tomorrow, I had best go to that daunting Diamond residence and talk to my fiancée. I hope things are still plummy there, too."

"I say you might still want to think about appeasing Lady Varley," Quinn said. "She might have some more wicked tricks down her décolletage if you don't."

That erased the smile from Matthew's face.

"I am glad I came over and disturbed your toilette, although your cravat could use another try." Knowing his friend liked a level of perfection in his appearance, it was the best way to annoy him.

As expected, Quinn went to the round mirror behind a wall sconce and tried to examine his neckcloth, while Matthew strode to the door.

"Come along, I was speaking in jest. But perhaps your valet is in need of spectacles. I won't even make mention of the rat's nest he made of your hair until we're in the carriage."

PURITY WAS GOING FOR A walk. She imagined it would feel good to go into one of London's boxing clubs and use her fists on someone. She'd never had that inclination before, but *The Times* had barely concealed her identity in the paper the day before.

A 'Pure' sparkling gem of a lady was getting her lips polished by a certain Foxy gent of late at the river's edge. This editor has been told the lady in question used a Syon Park gala to get herself a green gown when before it was a pretty yellow. Mayhap to protect it from further damage, she tossed it upon a nearby hedge. Mayhap to protect her, the banns will soon be read.

Ugh! It was disgusting. And at no time had her day dress left her person and, most assuredly, had never been tossed onto any shrubbery.

With her gloved hands fisted at her sides, she hurried out, not bothering with bringing Alice as she intended neither to see nor speak to anyone. Besides, she had no reputation left to guard.

Wearing her best walking boots, she took up a good pace.

Ten feet from her own front door, she spied Foxford's carriage pull to the side of the road. Turning her face, she hurried toward the river. She hoped he hadn't even seen her.

"Lady Purity," he called to her.

Blast the man!

At that moment, instead of the usual anticipatory butterflies at the thought of seeing him, she had rocks in her stomach, weighing her down with humiliation and anger.

Skirting the east side of Green Park, she ignored him still calling after her, but by the time she reached St. James's Park, crowded as usual with beautifully dressed nobility of both sexes, Purity could no longer pretend he wasn't dogging her steps.

Slightly out of breath, she turned her head.

"What do you want?" Her tone came out uncharacteristically sharp, but it matched the emotions churning inside her.

"To talk to you, of course," he said, being his usual unconcerned self as far as she could tell. After all, he was used to the infamy even as those around them started to notice the pair. "Where are we going?"

"*We* are going nowhere," she told him, as more heads turned. "*I* am going to Westminster Bridge where I shall refrain from throwing myself into the Thames only by the thin thread of self-preservation to which I still cling."

Determined to get away from the elite of society who were watching and being watched at the park, she kept walking, not even bothering with the tended stone path. Instead, she tramped upon the flowers and across the grass as she made her way to Bridge Street.

Foxford remained silent, but he didn't leave her. He continued following, much to her annoyance. Anyone who saw their silly parade and knew him would know her by association and be reminded of *The Times* paragraph in the social section. *How could he not realize he was making it worse?*

Finally, Purity strode onto the bridge, which was congested with carriages, riders, and pedestrians. Halfway across, she stopped and leaned upon the railing to stare at Waterloo Bridge in the distance, glad she'd had the sense to put on her full-brimmed bonnet, for she'd inadvertently left her parasol in the front hall.

Foxford settled beside her. She sighed. If he started to apologize again or to placate her with how this would all blow over like a spring zephyr, she would scream.

"Believe me, kitten, I am sorry," he said.

The knot in the back of her neck tightened.

"Luckily by tomorrow, some other nob's blunder will be on everyone's lips," he added.

She closed her eyes and pursed her lips to keep from screaming. She was Lady Purity Diamond. She didn't cause a scene in public. She certainly didn't raise her voice or cry or have a fit of red devils.

All those things would be disgraceful outside the confines of her own bedroom.

"Leave me in peace," she said quietly. "Turn around and go back to wherever you were going when you noticed me."

"I was coming to see you since I assumed you would be upset."

She still couldn't look at him. He had dragged her into his sordid world of scandal, and she found it difficult to forgive him.

"How would seeing me or my seeing you, for that matter, help in any way?"

"We can face this together," he offered.

She opened her eyes. Down below, a sailboat moved swiftly in the breeze. She wished she could float down like a feather and land on it, letting the boat take her out to sea.

Instead, she would have to hide in her home when the next ball or dinner party invitation came. The notion of facing her peers in a confined space where she couldn't flee was as unappealing as a cup of cold, stale tea. Colorful fans would be raised over whispering mouths, and all eyes would be upon her.

While she tried not to partake in the vulgar act of gossip, many others did. And what was a better topic than an earl's daughter caught with a renowned rake?

Unable to bear her own thoughts, Purity turned and started to walk again, but Foxford's hand snagged her arm.

Outrageous!

CHAPTER TWENTY

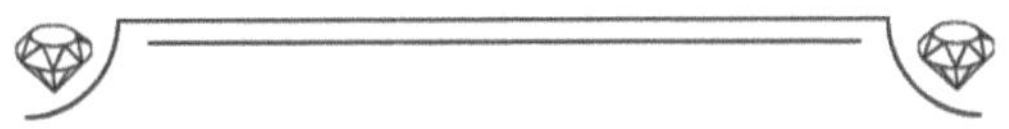

"You cannot do that," Purity insisted, already imagining every passerby was watching with interest.

Wrenching her arm free, she whirled away, getting only a few more steps before Foxford caught her again.

She turned on him, feeling feral. If she didn't have gloves on, she might do him an injury as her mother had taught her in a lesson on dealing with unwanted harassment. A well-placed scratch would buy her freedom. She could always bring her knee up to his manly parts, as her father had suggested to do in a dire emergency, but that seemed extreme.

Besides, this man was her fiancé, and if the marriage occurred, then she didn't want to unman him to the point they would be unable to have children.

Foxford stared down at her. "Tell me what I can do."

"You have done enough. Haven't you made it so we must marry?" she bit out. "Why? Why would you do this to me?"

A shadow crossed his face. He clenched his jaw. She even watched the muscles in his neck flex. None of that helped.

"*The Times* is not my fault," he insisted. "What precisely are you accusing me of?"

"Condemning me to be attached to you," she said, unable to rein in her intense feelings while trying desperately not to give in to histrionics. Her tone was strangely grating and accusatory. But after all, she was standing on a high bridge over quickly moving water with the Houses of Parliament overshadowing her and arguing with the notorious Bachelor Baron.

"You are opposite to the dream I had for a husband." *Was that clear enough for him?* "I want a man with all the social graces, as well as someone who can be loyal and loving."

"I am all those things," Foxford insisted, but his tone was more hesitant than adamant.

Purity shook her head. "People don't change their nature in the space of weeks," she hissed out the last word.

Foxford came a step closer as if they were in the intimate confines of a drawing room and not in the middle of Westminster Bridge.

"I didn't need to change, at least not my manners. I have always known which spoon or fork to use. I know how to comport myself in the company of the *ton* or even the royal family."

"Liar!" she said. "Then why did you need me to help you catch yourself a wife?"

"It was you!" he declared, throwing his hands in the air, then pointing at her. "It was always you."

"You are lying!" Purity said again, anguish bringing those tears to her eyes she vowed would not be spilled in public.

"I am not lying. I promise you. Didn't I behave well enough at the concert?"

She waved that away with a gesture of her hand. "One night listening to music. Even you couldn't blunder at the theatre."

"I do not blunder anywhere. Test me, put me through the trials."

"I don't need to. This very instant you are causing a scene, proving you don't understand the rules of polite society."

"Not fair," he said. "I tried to visit you at home."

Sighing, she glanced around her. In truth, no one seemed to care about two people having a row. But she did. "I will allow you to escort me home."

Without waiting, she began to walk the way she had come.

He fell into step beside her.

"Ask me some blasted questions about manners."

She pressed her lips tightly. This wasn't a game. This was her life and her future. And he was a rake, and an uncouth one at that.

"I have guarded against vulgarisms," he stated when she didn't speak. "I no longer fidget with my gloves, nor my pocket watch. I appear interested in everything those around me say even when I would rather stick my head in a barrel of pickled herring than listen to another insipid word. I don't interrupt, and I use no French affectations."

She continued to look ahead. "You have a good memory, and you mimic well, like a trained monkey."

"Argh!" he shouted over the side of the bridge, letting his yell of frustration blow out across the water.

This startled her, but in an instant, he was walking calmly alongside again.

"I never needed your help," he vowed. "It was simply a way to be close to you when you wouldn't let me near."

"Do you remember why I wouldn't let you near me, Lord Perfect Manners? Because of your reputation," she reminded him. "Are you saying you are not a libertine either?"

He hesitated, perhaps unwilling to accept the unflattering label.

"I suppose I was," Foxford allowed at last, "but I am no longer. I have had no association with any other female since the day we met."

"Another lie. What about the trio of women at the Vauxhall Pleasure Gardens?"

"Surely you are joking," he said. "I will speak of them one last time and then never again. Quinn came up to me, trailing those females who were hoping for some blunt from a willing gentleman."

"And?" she prompted.

"And I was not willing," he said flatly. "That covey of sad cattle was not remotely the class of women, not even of courtesans, with whom I would interact. Frankly, I'm insulted."

Was he serious?

"Moreover, I was only at Vauxhall hoping to see you. To that end, I looked all evening, but the place has gone downhill, as I told you it had. Even the harlots were the seediest. Frankly, I would recommend you no longer go to Vauxhall."

"I see," she said.

"Is that all you can say? We've filleted and exposed my doings as if I were a freshly caught codfish. And all you can say is, 'I see.'"

"Did you intend for us to be discovered at Syon Park?" she asked, dreading the answer.

For if he had truly wanted her from the beginning, he might have become tired of waiting. His goal had been accomplished with one wretchedly wonderful kiss.

He halted. Someone behind them knocked into him and then, after a few choice curses, moved around them.

"Hey, there! Mind your mouth around a lady," Foxford called after the stranger, who kept moving, perhaps more quickly at the baron's sharp tone. Then surprisingly, Foxford took her arm and began to walk again.

"I swear to you, I did not have any hand in getting us discovered. I would never do such a dastardly thing. I cannot, however, blame you for thinking the worst of me. It has come to my understanding recently that I have somewhat of a bad reputation."

It was Purity's turn to stop dead, yet she managed to keep moving. *Had he only just learned that?* It was laughable if he hadn't realized the extent of his notoriety. Her steps faltered, but she corrected herself and let him continue.

"My plan has been to woo and win you by fair means. Granted, it has gone more slowly than I would have liked, and now, it has charged ahead like a stallion. Still, I promise you, I would never have wished for your reputation to suffer. I know what it means to you."

Did he? she wondered. *Could any man, let alone a handsome, privileged cove of a man, understand?*

"Fine words but too late," she reminded him. "The newspaper and, I suppose, its readers think as you once did—that my name is a silly name and now an ironic one, too. I am considered impure and loose. It would seem we became engaged to no avail."

"If I could do anything to change what has occurred, I would. I believe our engagement, long enough to show that you are not . . . well, showing, if you understand my meaning, will help restore your good name. That, and your refusal to hide indoors."

"That was precisely what I intended to do," she confessed.

"I guessed as much, and it's exactly the wrong thing. You have never had to face anything like this, but I would urge you to go about your normal life. If you disappear, you will appear guilty."

"But I am," she said. "*We* are."

"We are not guilty of what they think. Not yet," he added, so softly she almost didn't hear him.

But she did, and it sent warmth winging through her. In the shake of a lamb's tail, her thoughts flew, as they constantly did, to their wedding night, to being naked before him, to having him touch her . . .

"Let me dance with you at the next ball," he continued. "Twice, in fact. By then, our engagement will have been announced more formally than your mother did the other night. I, for one, will not *play* the happy bridegroom. I shall truly be one. If you can manage to smile, we shall seem a happy couple indeed. Everyone will be jealous, and they can all go to—"

"Foxford," she stopped his blasphemy.

"Why, Lady Purity, you broke your own rule and interrupted me. I am aghast."

Against all odds, a glimmer of mirth danced through her. She smiled.

Somehow, he'd managed to put her in a better mood and even make her feel less distraught. She supposed he was correct, and she would do better to hold her head up and not give a fig about the opinion of anyone beyond her family, who loved her.

MATTHEW HAD SUCCEEDED beyond what he could have hoped. But then, after they had passed through the crowded St. James Park and were strolling along the edge of Green Park, nearly at the Diamonds' home, Purity asked him a difficult question.

"What about *your* family?"

His heart sped up.

"What would you like to know about them?"

"When shall you introduce me to them? Won't they be astonished to learn you have a fiancée and are engaged to someone they have never met?"

"My father is deceased," he told her.

She squeezed his arm.

"My father told me. I am sorry for that."

"He died seventeen years ago. I couldn't tell you exactly from what. Influenza, I believe. My mother remarried. Since her new husband is a Scot, they live in Edinburgh, as do my full sister and my two half-brothers. We can visit after we are married. I'm sure my mother will adore you."

"Very well."

He'd wrapped that up neatly, without having to go into how he and his stepfather had often been at loggerheads, or the relief he'd experienced when he went to English boarding school to escape Edinburgh.

After university, he had never gone back except for brief visits. He wanted to look at the future and starting his own family, not dwell upon the past.

To that end, he made Purity promise to attend a dinner and dance at the end of the week before taking his leave. Feeling a tad cowardly, he decided not to enter the Diamond home in case her parents still had the recent column in hand.

Instead, he was of two minds. One told him to go directly to Lady Varley and blast her hair back, for he was certain she was behind *The Times* rubbish. The other, though, directed his steps to his club, hoping Varley would be there. Maybe gloating.

Lady Fortuna smiled, and the man was already seated in the dining room. Even better, Quinn wasn't there to stop him from confronting the wretch.

Walking directly to the table at which Varley was scoffing down a plate of roast beef, minted peas, and Yorkshire puddings, Foxford wasted no time.

"You're a loathsome worm without a backbone, taking your spite out upon an innocent lady. Tell me, do you toss off while reading about other people in the paper?"

Instead of jumping to his feet with fisted outrage, which would have suited Matthew perfectly fine, Varley smiled.

"Good day, Foxford. What's all this bristling about? You've never minded *The Times* keeping us up-to-date on your adventures before."

"My adventures are my business. Why don't you mind your own?"

Varley shrugged. "I promise you, I do."

Matthew flexed his fingers. Gentlemen around them had stopped eating, pausing with silverware to their mouths. A few had newspapers on their tablecloths and eyed him with amusement. In a moment, someone was probably going to call out a wager on how many blows it would take him to level Varley to the carpet.

Matthew took a deep breath. He wished the red haze weren't before his eyes, but where Purity was concerned, it was difficult to take a placid view of her tormentor.

If fisticuffs weren't in his future, perhaps he could still get in a low blow. Towering over the seated Varley, he said the most disrespectful thing that came to mind.

"You need to tether your wife by a shorter lead. She's a vindictive hoyden."

This time Varley clenched his jaw, but still he didn't rise to the bait or rise from his chair for that matter.

"Insulting Lady Varley will do you no good. If she wishes to speak to a newspaper editor about what she saw with her own eyes, then she will. And I shall offer her applause for it. I suppose you won't need a tether for that prim mouse whom you intend to join in wedlock. She doesn't seem to have the spunk to roam very far."

Matthew sighed. Naturally, Varley would turn the tables and try to insult Purity, but the worst the man could come up with was how well-behaved she was. That was the type of woman Matthew wanted by his side, although he did not consider her mousy in the least.

Regardless, he might as well take this right to the gutter. For the first time, Matthew smiled back.

"I am not talking about whether your wife went to *The Times* with her long-tongued, chaff-cutter of a mouth. I am talking about her intruding upon my personal residence. Next time Emilia comes sniffing around my door," he said loud enough for the eavesdroppers to hear. "I will give my staff instructions not to allow her entrance. My butler only let her in because of our earlier association," he added to twist the knife that he'd swived with Varley's wife, "but I didn't appreciate her lounging in my drawing room uninvited earlier this week. After all, tongues might wag that I was *polishing* some part of her."

That did it.

Varley blanched as white as his well-tended cravat. Finally, he was horn mad.

Tossing his napkin onto the table, he rose to his feet and took a swing at Matthew, who had his arms up before his opponent landed the blow.

Attacked first, he was within his rights to plant a facer, which he did. It felt damn good, too, until Varley returned the favor and caught him on his right cheek bone before he could dodge the hit. They landed a few more punches, finally one each to the gut before the club manager came over and put a halt to it.

Sadly for Varley, Matthew managed to give him one more plump in the breadbasket, which doubled the man over and sent him back two steps into the chair at the next table.

Matthew straightened his jacket. "Mind me, Varley, keep your wife away from my house."

Turning, he walked out, knowing he'd just made an enemy.

CHAPTER TWENTY-ONE

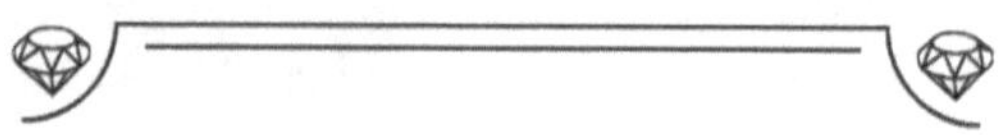

Purity was surprised to learn Lord Varley was in his carriage outside her family's home, having sent his footman to the door with a calling card. She couldn't help the tremor of trepidation upon telling their butler to grant him entrance to the drawing room. After all, the last time she'd seen his lordship, he seemed to be relishing her disgrace.

With Alice hurriedly installed at one end of the room, Purity greeted Lord Varley. It was evident instantly that he had been in an altercation, yet unforgivably rude for her to make mention of his appearance.

"Good day, my lord. Are you well?"

"Good day, Lady Purity. I come to offer my apologies for what has happened."

He could only mean one thing. She decided to be frank.

"Why would you be apologizing unless it was you who had a discussion with the editor of *The Times*?"

"Perish the thought," he said. "I assure you I will never tell anyone what I saw. You have my word as a gentleman." He went so far as to pat the area over his heart with his palm. "However, my wife can be flighty, and I cannot vouch for what she has done or might do."

"Are you saying it was Lady Varley who tattled?"

"Only that it is possible."

"And you came to apologize on her behalf?" she repeated. "Forgive me if I think a note would have sufficed."

"I wanted to warn you in the most stringent fashion so you would take me seriously. Do you see my face?"

She nodded.

"Your so-called fiancé did this to me."

Purity was unable to stifle a gasp.

"In public, at our club," Lord Varley added with obvious distaste. "Brawling like a common ruffian."

Ready to ask what was the provocation, she decided it had to be over the dastardly *Times* column. Thus, while she didn't condone fighting outside of a sporting club, she could hardly find fault with Foxford for protecting her honor.

"I cannot imagine why you thought it necessary to show me the results," she said stiffly.

"Has Foxford been here yet?" he asked.

She put a hand to her chest. Their conversation had gotten out of hand. He had no right to ask any such thing.

"State your business, please," Purity said firmly.

"As I said, I want you to heed my warning. A nice young lady such as yourself ought not to be anywhere near that rake." His voice caught on the last word, and she realized he was distraught.

"My lord?"

"Foxford ruined my first engagement, snatching away my happiness due to his own careless philandering. And my wife has been harmed by his insatiable hunger, too. He's a menace. After nearly destroying her with unfulfilled promises, he fled to the Continent. Now that he's back, I believe he is trying to renew their acquaintance."

He had started pacing but stopped abruptly as if realizing he was in someone else's home.

"If my wife spoke to the papers, and I'm not saying she did, mind you, it was only to shed light on the doings of London's infamous Bachelor Baron. True, she bears a grudge against Foxford as do half the ladies in Mayfair, I expect, and Paris, too, if he continued his outlandish indiscretions while away."

Purity wished her unwelcome visitor wasn't giving voice to all her worst fears about what an ardent seducer Foxford was. Finally, he took a deep breath.

"Perhaps with *The Times* story, my wife hoped your parents would sensibly put a stop to any association between you and that hell-born satyr."

"I see." Purity could think of nothing more to add. She'd never had such a bold, disturbing conversation with a stranger before.

"I once more find myself apologizing, this time for distressing you. I know at Syon House, Lady Varley and I should have turned immediately away upon discovering you."

Purity winced, wishing the maid wasn't seated where she could see and hear everything, but that was the point of a chaperone.

"However, I have come across him before in a similar situation."

"I do not understand," she said. *Although she feared she did.* While she hoped Lord Varley had the sense and manners not to mention Foxford with another woman, she suddenly had a notion why the man hated her fiancé so much.

"Are you referring to your former fiancée?" she asked, her voice soft due to the delicate subject. She knew only that the eldest daughter of an extraordinarily wealthy family, even by the *ton*'s standards, had given him the mitten.

Lord Varley responded with a sigh, leaving her none the wiser. But she assumed Foxford had enjoyed a tryst with the bride, causing her to break it off.

"*And* with your current wife," Purity said, this time without question. Foxford had already admitted such.

Lord Varley pressed his lips together, saying nothing. He rose higher in her esteem for not speaking of anything sordid. *The poor man!*

Was it possible Foxford had made a paramour of two of this man's lady loves?

"I shall take my leave. But heed me, Lady Purity. The Fox is no gentleman, nor can I imagine him making an honest husband of himself. While I confess I threw the first punch, it was only after Foxford taunted me that he'd been intimate with my wife. You may ask him whether I lie."

He bowed. Wordlessly, she gave a shallow curtsy, and he left.

Well, hell's bells! She certainly hadn't expected that.

PURITY HAD AGREED TO dance twice with Foxford at the next ball, which was the following evening at the Lowther Rooms on King William Street. She intended to hold her head high and let the rumors of her ruin swirl around her without effect, like water off a duck's back.

Lord Varley's visit had shaken her, and she'd considered writing to Foxford to tell him she would not attend. However, after reflection, the disclosure that her fiancé had tormented the other man, not once but twice, with acts of selfish passion didn't really change anything.

It was all in the past, she kept reminding herself. Foxford vowed he had been with no one else since meeting her, and after their discussion on the bridge, she had no reason to doubt him. He could have walked away if he had wanted to continue a life of debauchery.

On the other hand, she could and did blame him fully for the slander in *The Times*. If he hadn't angered Lord and Lady Varley, apparently each of them separately, then Purity wouldn't have ended up "getting her lips polished," as the paper had described it.

With a sigh, she descended from her father's coach. She had always known no good would come from a lifetime of such immoral behavior, and dreadful consequences could occur. But it was beyond aggravating to have been caught up in someone else's consequences.

With both her parents attending the ball, she was bolstered by the combined strength of the earl and countess. Moreover, Purity recalled Foxford's words about making everyone jealous with their happy engagement and entered the building with a stiff smile.

Strange advice, for she wouldn't envy anyone in her position, not for a moment.

Even stranger, upon seeing him waiting at the foot of the stairs, dressed impeccably in dark blue tails with a bright white shirt and gray waistcoat, the familiar sizzling heat winged through her.

How could she still want Foxford so much when he had hurt people by his careless assignations? If she allowed herself to think he might hurt her, then she would not be able to go through with it. And that would be an even bigger debacle since her father had already placed an announcement in the papers, leaving out *The Times*, as the earl now considered those publishers an enemy of his family.

As Foxford came closer, she saw the damage. Lord Varley had given as good as he got, it seemed.

The baron greeted her parents, not calling attention to the bruises on his cheek and around his eye, nor did they. Purity knew she was supposed to ignore the fact that her fiancé had been brawling.

When he offered his arm to her, she laid her hand atop it, letting him guide her into the ballroom, with Lord and Lady Diamond following.

"No flummery at all, kitten. You are without a doubt the most beautiful woman here."

Purity thought she must be wavering in her strict standards. Even though she could not believe his words to be true—*after all, her lovely mother stood close by*—still, she not only allowed him the flattery, she enjoyed it.

"Thank you. And you are looking very fine tonight, my lord, at least in your dress if not your face."

He grinned, and the butterflies took off in her stomach.

"Varley and I disagreed on a few things, like whether he ought to be allowed to sit smugly eating roast beef when he is a horse's arse."

"Foxford!" Purity exclaimed. "While I appreciate your defending me, as I believe you were doing, I cannot condone such actions. You were both injured."

He faltered in his steps and came to a stop where there was room for all of them by large, curtained windows.

"How do you know he was injured?" His manner was no longer congenial.

"Lord Varley paid me a visit." There was no reason to hide the fact.

"Why? What was his purpose?" Foxford's tone was clipped.

"He said he came to warn me away from you."

"That pompous toad!" he said loudly enough that her parents' conversation halted momentarily behind them before resuming.

"Calm yourself, my lord. Tonight, we are supposed to be happily enjoying our engagement, remember?"

He hesitated and then took a deep breath.

"I saw the announcement," he said, sounding more like himself. "We are now official."

"Indeed, we are." Glancing around, Purity saw plain evidence of interest.

Guests were staring, mouths were moving, and expressions held varying degrees of pity, amusement, or disdain. It didn't help that he was yelling about *pompous toads*.

She looked at her parents. They were already chatting with their long-time friends, Lord and Lady Trent. In the next moment, Lord and Lady Fenwick approached. It was wonderful to see the elderly couple attending a ball with no duty other than to dance and have fun.

"Good evening, my lord, my lady," Purity said, curtsying to both at once.

"I thought these two would make a match," Lord Fenwick said. "Didn't I say that, wife? Directly after our party for the young people?"

"Yes, Fenwick dear, you did." His wife nodded to them. "He did, you know."

"I shall always be grateful for your part in introducing me to my fiancée," Foxford said smoothly. "Your wedding invitation is being printed as we speak."

"Such a good man," Lady Fenwick said.

Purity watched Foxford's cheeks darken slightly. He was probably unused to anyone saying that in public or in private, for that matter.

"You had your chance while I was single, my lady," he quipped. "I promised to steal you away on more than one occasion, but now I have vowed my loyalty and fidelity to Lady Purity."

Lady Fenwick beamed at them while Lord Fenwick chuckled.

"Looks as though you had to fight for her. Good show, Foxford. You must have won since she's with you." He nodded to his wife. "I knew they would make a match, didn't I?" he repeated before they took a few steps toward her parents and joined that illustrious circle.

To her amazement, more established couples of rank and good standing came over to congratulate them before going to speak with her parents. It dawned on her they were offering public support to counteract the dreadful gossip column.

"You were correct," she told Foxford during their first dance, relaxing into the familiar movements of a quadrille. "Coming out into society was the best decision and will go a long way to putting the unpleasantness behind us."

"Unpleasantness," he murmured. "A good word for it. But then I imagine you could make the worst disaster sound like nothing more than spilled tea. Rather a useful skill, especially in a crisis."

She smiled at him. Now that the dancing had started, giving guests something to do besides whisper about her and the Fox, she was enjoying herself.

"Let us hope we don't have to test my skill tonight, my lord. I, for one, do not wish for any further crisis."

"Agreed."

When Lord and Lady Varley appeared by the third dance, Purity hoped her skills of smoothing things over were not about to become necessary. Lord Varley still sported a mark on his face and managed to glare menacingly at Foxford, who naturally returned the look and followed the man's movements across the room with a sharp gaze.

Lady Varley, on the other hand, seemed entirely oblivious to any underpinnings of discontent and took to the dance floor with another gentleman.

Since Purity could not remain by Foxford's side all night, nor promise him every dance, she felt a knot of concern tie itself tightly inside. When called away to dance, she fixed him with a hard stare.

"Please, my lord, do not *do* anything."

"I have no idea what you mean. If I find a willing lass, I shall dance. Otherwise, I will await your return here."

"Very well."

The next hour crept by in the same way. She danced again with Foxford and with a few other gentlemen, but the entire time, she was on tenterhooks.

Finally, they were called in for a buffet supper, which was adequate to stop any pangs of hunger or thirst, and then the rest of the night was before them.

Purity, along with her mother, excused themselves to the retiring room set aside for the ladies. Spacious, well lit, they could attend to their needs, fix their hair, address any stray threads, tears, or pulled hems that trailed with a danger of tripping them.

Purity's was the latter issue from one of her dance partners standing upon her hem before supper.

"Are you happy?" her mother asked, when they were seated on soft tufted stools before a mirror, blotting any shine off their faces with handkerchiefs from their reticules.

"I am," she said, staring back at Lady Diamond's reflection.

"You sound surprised, dear daughter."

Purity shrugged. "I suppose I am still getting used to the idea of being engaged. I must admit, once the dancing started and I realized I could dance for the fun of it, without having to consider each man as a potential husband, I saw the benefit to a fiancé."

Her mother smiled. "That is as good a reason as any. Do you wish to tell me about your intended's black-and-blue face?"

"Not really," Purity said.

The countess shook her head. "At least you didn't lie and try to tell me he's a clumsy walloping sort."

"Never, Mother. It's obvious he got into a brawl. It was over my honor and that awful *Times* column, so I cannot be too hard on him."

Just then, the bell sounded for the next dance. Her mother rose. "The Sauteuse is next. I must find your father. We never miss this dance. Will you be all right?"

"Yes, I'll be out in a minute. I'm going to put a few stitches in my hem, and I'll join you directly."

Her mother dashed off, called by fond memories of other balls when the same music spurred her and the earl's love. Or at least, that's what Purity imagined as she reached for the tray before her with all the accessories necessary to mend her dress. She could ask an attending maid, but it would be just as quick to do it herself.

From behind the partition, Lady Varley appeared, startling Purity.

"Greetings, Lady Purity."

CHAPTER TWENTY-TWO

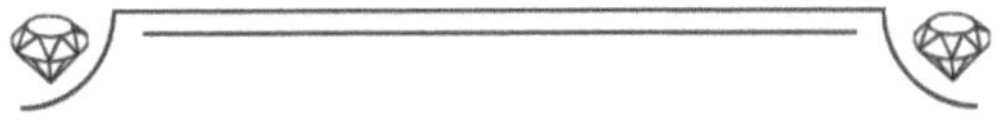

"It is rude to eavesdrop," Purity told her, knowing this woman was no friend. More than that, Lady Varley had purposefully waited until Lady Diamond left.

Regardless, she felt perfectly able to stand up for herself and deflect whatever Lady Varley would say. Therefore, Purity added, "I bid you good evening all the same."

"I read of your engagement. Congratulations."

"Thank you, but unnecessary, since you were one of the first to learn of it," Purity said. "I believe you have offered your sincere felicitations already." *Or utterly insincere, as the case might be.*

"Indeed, I did, but your engagement didn't seem true until I saw it in print."

Purity didn't know what to say to that, so she threaded the needle and hoped the woman would go away. Instead, Lady Varley took the stool vacated by the countess.

"I must apologize for the fighting that occurred," she said, watching Purity's profile.

"Why would you need to do that?" Purity asked, hurrying with her stitching so she could escape.

"I understand from what was overheard at the gentlemen's club, they came to blows over me." She batted her eyes as if it were a badge of honor.

"You?" Purity exclaimed.

"Why, yes. I had a private encounter with Foxy recently. I believe your fiancé was boasting about it to get my husband's dander up. He succeeded."

Purity considered this information, wondering if it could be true, while keeping her gaze on the work at hand.

"If you don't believe me, you can ask either one of them. Varley threw the first punch on my behalf, dear soul, and then Foxy gave it back to him. While you're at it, ask him about his drawing-room sofa and whether it needed to be cleaned recently. I'm afraid we got quite *heated* upon it a few days ago." Lady Varley trailed off, waiting for some indication her attempt to send Purity into a great tweague had succeeded.

Purity said nothing, not even when she carelessly pricked her finger. After years of practice, she would not let this baggage dressed like a lady make her lose her civility or behave like a sorry scrub. She didn't even pull her hand out from under the fabric in order to suck the sore spot.

Lady Varley sighed. "I told Foxy you were too much of a bland morsel to give him a run. Why, you can't even scrounge up the spark to gainsay me. It would be pointless, anyway. I was stretched out on his cream-colored divan as surely as you and I are here now, and he . . . well, never mind. If you aren't a complete simpleton, then you know what I'm saying. I imagine this won't be the last time a woman tells you she enjoyed herself tremendously with your fiancé, or in the future, with your husband."

Purity finished the last stitch, knotted the end of the thread, and snapped it off. Then she rose to her feet, refusing to give Lady Varley the satisfaction of seeing how her knees were trembling.

Smoothing her dress, she looked in the mirror, noticing how pale she'd grown and how bright her own eyes.

"There, that's better," she declared, lifting her chin.

Reaching for her gloves, Purity slowly, carefully donned each one before securing her reticule once more upon her wrist. Then she touched her hair, which was perfect. Finally, she turned.

Despite remaining composed, there must have been something in her countenance, for Lady Varley took a hurried step back.

Hardly knowing how she did it, Purity nodded to her as if they had just discussed the quality of the supper or the musicians.

"Good evening," Purity said politely, as that was how she had been raised.

Then she brushed past, leaving the woman to rot in her own base conduct of which Purity would never participate.

SOMETHING HAD HAPPENED. Matthew sensed it when Purity stiffened at his touch for their last dance of the evening.

"Is there anything wrong, kitten?" he asked.

Her blue eyes blazed at him, glittering with . . . contempt? The answer was clearly *yes*. Something had in fact happened, beyond the fighting at his club, beyond her being compromised at Syon Park, beyond *The Times* slimy paragraph.

"Do not call me thusly," she hissed. "It is demeaning and dismissive."

Surprised by her vehemence, he shook his head. "It is meant to be endearing."

"How many women?" she asked, her voice barely above a whisper.

"I beg your pardon." Matthew wondered if he ought to steer her off the dance floor. If she were going to question him on his number of sexual partners, he would need a glass of brandy, a pen, and a piece of paper.

"How many women have you called by the same nickname?"

He breathed a sigh of relief. *Was that all that was bothering her?*

"None. Only you."

She gave a quick roll of her eyes and glanced away.

"Truly." He spread his fingers upon her back, feeling the warmth of her body seeping through the thin rose silk of her gown.

"When you first looked up at me, I thought you were adorable but also sensual. What's more, you were somewhere you were not supposed to be and by yourself, so I assumed you were mischievous, too. The first word that popped into my head was *kitten.*"

He spun her around at the end of the dance floor and started up the other side.

"And I won't promise not to call you that," he added.

Her beautiful mouth turned down, looking displeased.

"I have never called anyone else by that name."

"What did you call them, then?" she asked flatly. "What about Lady Varley? Was it only *Emilia* you murmured to her when tupping her?"

Purity had shocked him down to his toes. *What the hell?*

He wanted the dance to end in order to speak without the infernal twirling and turning of their heads. However, when the music stopped, he wouldn't be able to speak privately with her, not at the ball. It wasn't as if they could find a secluded corner or stroll out into the garden.

Even if she was willing, it was the last thing they should risk before their marriage while trying to restore her reputation.

Helplessly, he looked down at her. "May I call upon you tomorrow?"

"No," she bit out.

"Purity," he said desperately.

"I have never given you permission," she pointed out, "to use my first name."

"I've had my tongue inside your mouth," he reminded her, making her eyes widen as she glanced around them. "I believe I may use your given name. Besides, if not kitten or Purity, what would you have your fiancé call you?"

"Perhaps I would rather you were not my fiancé at all."

And then Lady Purity did the unthinkable. She yanked her hand free from his grasp and walked away, blazing a path between the other dancing couples.

For a moment, Matthew stood motionless. When another pair of dancers nearly collided with him, however, he roused himself from his stupor and followed her. His delightful kitten had turned into a hell-cat, and he had no idea why.

HAVING DIRECTED HIS footman to the Diamonds' front door with his calling card, Matthew waited outside in his carriage, tapping his hand on his trouser leg. For two days, he had sent sweet notes and large bouquets of flowers, apologizing for he knew not what while asking Purity to give him a chance to explain, nonetheless.

After she'd abandoned him in the middle of a waltz, striding directly to her parents, the three Diamonds had left within minutes.

The earl had sent him a warning look, and Matthew kept his distance. But unlike Purity, he had stayed through the rest of the ball, explained his fiancée had a megrim, and continued to accept the bountiful congratulations.

His patience was now at an end. When his footman returned with a shake of his head, Matthew thought he might explode like gunpowder.

"I was told Lady Purity is not accepting visitors, my lord."

He was at the end of his rope. It was a long one, too. Some would say he'd had too long of a rope for too many years, swinging on it with wild abandon. But now, Purity had snipped it short.

Climbing down from his carriage, Matthew went to the door and rapped twice.

It swung open, and Mr. Dunley came into view.

"I am here to see my fiancée, Lady Purity."

The man opened his mouth, but Matthew spoke for him.

"I understand she is not seeing anyone. But I am not *anyone*. I am engaged to be her husband."

The butler did not wish to be in the middle of this lovers' spat. That much was clear.

"Unfortunately, my lord—"

"Then tell Lord or Lady Diamond I must speak with one of them. I don't care which one, but I refuse to be left standing on the doorstep like a beggar."

Matthew stared down the butler, daring him to shut the door in his face instead of allowing him entry.

After a brief hesitation, Mr. Dunley stood back, opening the door wide.

"If you will wait in the drawing room, my lord, I will fetch *someone*."

The man sounded exasperated.

For all Matthew could expect, Miss Brilliance or Miss Radiance might enter. Thankfully, ten long minutes later, it was Purity herself, rigid as a flagpole. She didn't smile or greet him politely. She entered the room silently, came to a standstill a few feet in front of him, and waited.

"Good day," he offered, suddenly nervous at her lack of greeting. Her expression couldn't have been any less formidable than Medusa's, and he almost didn't want to look into her deep-blue eyes for fear of being struck down.

"Are you well?" he asked.

She nodded, her lips pursed.

"Did you receive my flowers and my notes?"

Again, she nodded.

"Won't you speak?" he asked.

She paced away from him and back again.

"I don't like confrontation, nor impolite remarks," she said, "and thus, I do not wish to converse with you at present."

Matthew had already removed his hat, and now he scratched his head.

"I am only confronting you in person because I could see no other way to elicit a response. As for the other, I shall refrain from any remarks that might be indecorous or rude as best I can."

"I was speaking of myself," she said. "Since everything I want to say to you seems to be about your sordid actions, I think it better if I remain silent."

"Absurd," he said, scanning his mind over the past few days. "I have not become any more of a scoundrel now than I was a week ago. Therefore, whatever has changed is within you, and I want to know why. I believe I deserve an answer even if you must speak about indecorous topics."

"You deserve nothing but contempt," she said before closing her mouth tightly again as if regretting even having said that little.

Inside, Matthew felt a wave of panic. He had been downright happy as her future husband. He couldn't believe it might end so abruptly.

"You are judging and condemning me without even telling me why."

She nodded.

"That isn't being polite," he said. "That is cowardly."

Purity gasped. "It does not hold that one who is reserved and well-mannered is a coward," she said. "Simply because I lack boldness of speech and action."

"Then tell me," he demanded.

"Lady Varley," she said simply, her tone brittle.

He sighed. In truth, he was a little surprised this bee had got into Purity's bonnet again. He thought that was behind them.

"I told you she is in the past."

"But not the distant past," she insisted. "Much more recently, I understand. Were you or were you not alone with her in your home?" She tilted her head and observed his reaction.

The devil take him! Instantly, he realized he ought to have told her. Appearances were important in his world, and vastly more so to Purity. And this appeared bad indeed.

With Purity's gaze upon him, Matthew could not lie, but fortunately, he didn't need to.

"The incident was so inconsequential I did not bring it to your attention. Lady Varley came to my home with the intent of us taking up together."

Hadn't he told himself Purity was a smart, discerning woman? But she could not have guessed this. Emilia had to have told her. He wondered what else the witch had said.

Purity remained silent, still watching and waiting.

"I should have told you," he said, understanding dawning on him. "Because if we are a couple, then there ought not to be secrets between us."

She nodded.

"At least now I know why I have been banished. May we sit?"

Stiffly, she took a seat upon the sofa. Purposefully, he sat on a chair rather than beside her.

"I would not do anything to hurt you," he vowed. "When she showed up at my door, I told her in plain, uncertain terms I was not interested, and she left."

"Even after I told you Lord Varley had paid me a visit, you didn't return the confidence."

He considered his actions. "I knew it would bother you, but I can see *not* telling you has bothered you more."

"Especially because I had to hear it from *her*, as if you two shared a clandestine pact."

Her wounded tone broke his heart, and he couldn't help rising to his feet and going over to sit beside her.

If possible, she sat even straighter and stiffer. Not caring about the propriety, he reached for her hand, which was ungloved, soft and perfect, and held it between both of his.

"Please, kitten. That woman is not worth a disagreement of this proportion. I, for one, am only grateful she is not my wife. I even feel sorry for Varley."

She nodded, staring at their entwined hands. "I suppose I do, too."

"Please forgive me for not telling you." With the matter explained, Matthew thought she would agree to forgive him. He was wrong.

"I do not care for lies or half-truths," she said, "or being kept in the dark."

"Naturally," he agreed. "And I won't do it again. I promise."

"Is there anything else you wish to disclose?" she asked.

He swallowed, his mind casting around through all the years of misbehavior.

"Could you be more specific?" he asked. "If you wish me to tell you about every poor choice I've made, then we might need to order the tea tray."

She didn't even crack a smile.

CHAPTER TWENTY-THREE

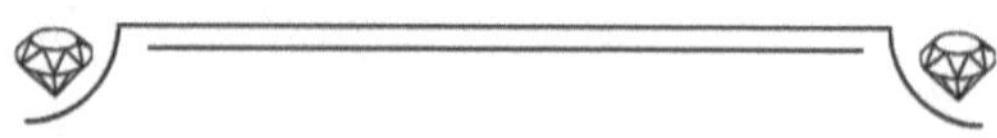

Purity knew Foxford was making light of her question in order to ease things between them, but she couldn't so easily let go of the raw pain she'd felt since being blindsided by Lady Varley. She had only Foxford's word that nothing had happened, and she was trying to cling to her belief in him despite the swirling doubts.

He sighed. "I am a gentleman, despite doing some churlish things, and I don't think it right of me to make a list of women with whom I've shared a kiss."

"Or done more," she said softly.

"Or more," he agreed. He ran a hand through his hair. "Honestly, I am not certain what I ought to say. I cannot go back and undo things I've done. And since that was all before I met you, my previous actions do not count for anything. The best I can offer is that at least you won't end up with an inexperienced dullard in your bed."

Purity didn't gasp only because she was used to his inappropriate remarks. Besides, she appreciated that he wouldn't speak of his former conquests. It elevated him, but that wasn't what she wanted to know.

"Why did you and Lord Varley exchange blows?" she asked.

"Because I knew he had spoken to *The Times*, or his wife had. I couldn't call her out or set my fists against her, nor could I buy up every paper in London, but I thought thumping Varley might make me feel better."

Purity decided to stomach the unpleasant task of confronting the other terrible things the woman had said.

"Lady Varley said you fought over her. She was telling the truth about going to your house. So why would I doubt her? Did you attack Lord Varley because of what was written about me, or did he throw the first blow because he thought there was something between you and his wife."

Matthew's momentary silence, rather than instantly contradicting the version, made her catch her breath.

"He hit me first, but only because I taunted him about Lady Varley, it's true," he said.

Wrenching her hand free, she covered her face.

"I cannot be with a man who uses his indiscretions to torture another. How cruel!"

"You don't understand," Foxford began. "He was smugly enjoying a meal while you were in pain over the filthy gossip. Nor would he behave with honor by standing and facing me so I could land a facer. I had to goad him to it by discussing his unfaithful choice of a life's mate."

It sounded credible, but also disdainful. Could she tolerate a life with this type of man and his unfamiliar world of rashness? On the other hand, she'd spent three days missing him, wanting his presence, feeling empty at the thought of no longer ending up as his wife.

"You cannot hold this against me," Foxford insisted. "You don't understand how men deal with such things. It was a matter of honor."

Her thoughts were spinning at his ridiculous statement.

"You think women do not understand honor?"

"I think you do not have to uphold it, fight for it, or worry over it in the same way that a man does. Varley thought he had bested me, first by sneaking upon us and hoping to shame you in order to harm me, and then by allowing his wife to tattle."

"So, you insulted his wife to be honorable," she concluded.

He shook his head. "I needed him to do the gentlemanly thing of using our fists. It is clean. It is not sneaky. It finishes the matter, or it ought to."

"You are right," she said. "I do not understand."

He surprised her by taking her face between his hands.

"Honor to a man is like reputation to a woman. Does that help to clarify it?"

For the first time, she recalled she'd entered the room merely to tell him to go away and leave her alone for another week. For that reason, she had not brought her maid, and yet they had been closeted together alone.

"It does," she said, hoping none of her family found them in such a situation.

Her hope turned to dread when he lowered his mouth to hers. This would be impossible to explain.

And then, as she knew would happen, all rational thought vanished. She had missed him so very much, his touch and his smell and his grin and his kiss.

She hadn't even had time to put her hands on him when he drew back.

"My apologies. We were in close contact for as long as I could manage without kissing you."

She wished it hadn't been so brief, but their luck had held considering the door was open.

He rose to his feet and reached for her hand to bring her up beside him.

"I don't suppose you have time to spend the day with me."

She smiled slightly. "The whole day would not be proper."

"I shall take as long as you will give me," Foxford declared. "Can you secure a maid or your mother as chaperone and come with me now?"

"Where are we going?"

"To The Pantechnicon. I am going to buy a new sofa for my drawing room. I want you to choose the fabric and the style. After all, it shall be your drawing room, too."

Purity heard only the word *sofa*, remembered Lady Varley's awful confession, and slapped Foxford hard across the cheek. His head snapped to the side, and a moment later, her tears began to fall.

"What the devil?" he asked, laying a glove to his red cheek.

"You are a liar," she said, choking on the despair rising in her throat. "If I cannot believe you now, how shall I ever trust you when I am your wife?"

She couldn't look at his face another instant. The man lied as easily as he breathed, and she had willingly believed him. *Again!*

Before another false word left his lips, she fled the room.

MATTHEW WANDERED OUT of the fine house on Piccadilly speculating how he could have made it worse.

He ought to return to his study and consult his schedule. He knew he had a ledger to look over, sent by his Surrey estate manager the day before. His Tangley Manor was a medieval monstrosity, but he loved it, despite its hunger for coin. And he had correspondence to answer. Moreover, his banker had requested to meet with him, and he had an appointment with a solicitor regarding the marriage documents.

He doubted he would need them now.

Yet instead of doing anything responsible, he headed to Boodle's to drown himself first with wine and then with brandy.

When Quinn entered the dining room hours later, Matthew was already in his cups and thinking of going to a tavern for gin. He wanted to obliterate the day from his mind, and gin could do that better than anything else he knew.

"You missed a clutter downstairs," Quinn said. "One of our senior members accused one of our junior members of cheating."

"At what?" Matthew asked, leaning his head on the cool white tablecloth.

Quinn frowned down at him. "What on earth are you doing?"

"Resting. The room is spinning. Who was cheating at what?"

"Sanders gave old Rosen a physicking at faro. I don't think he cheated at all. I think Rosen needs spectacles."

Matthew rummaged around in his pockets until he pulled out some coins. Picking out two pence, he pushed them across the table.

"Give these to Rosen so he can buy another pack of cards. That'll set him right."

Quinn laughed. "It's not the cards he has lost. It's a goodly chunk of his fortune. If I had known you were up here, I would have fetched you down to witness. You should have seen them both buttering their bets, higher and higher, with the rest of the chaps edging off wagers on the side."

"Then what?" Matthew asked, trying to care and failing.

"Sanders kept winning. The last hand, Sanders had swabbers while the only face Rosen had was his own." Quinn laughed and took a seat. "What has you half seas over? Nothing to do with your lovely lady, I hope."

"Why would you think that?"

"Because for weeks, every one of your moods has been caused by that gimcrack. She has you wrapped around her finger but good. It's like you're already married and living under the cat's foot."

Matthew started to laugh at the funny little phrase about a henpecked husband.

"More like a kitten's paw," he muttered. "I may as well enjoy it as a single man because I don't think the gimcrack, as you so crassly call her, is ever going to become my Lady Foxford."

"Why? What did you do?"

Matthew slapped the table, echoing the sound her hand had made. "That's the rub. I don't know. Not a clue. One minute we were kissing and going out to the shops, the next, she was calling me a liar."

Quinn poured himself a glass of brandy from the near-empty bottle.

"*Hm*. I've never thought of you as a liar."

"Thank you," Matthew said, drawing the bottle back to his side of the table and tipping the dregs into his mouth. "Another," he called out to the waiter.

"You're speaking to a floor lamp," Quinn said.

"Blast!" He looked again. No wonder the chap hadn't moved the last two times he'd demanded more liquor. "I don't think the lamp knows where the best brandy is stored."

He started to laugh and couldn't stop.

Quinn joined in, but soon they both fell into silence.

"What am I to do?" Matthew asked.

"About what exactly?"

Matthew groaned. "About Purity Diamond, of course? About my *kitten*?"

"Whoa, old boy," Quinn exclaimed. "Don't say too much now, will you? You'll regret it tomorrow."

"Probably."

"Do you love her?" his friend asked.

"Even drunk as an emperor, I'm not so spoony that I don't know the answer. Yes, I love her."

Quinn sighed. "I was afraid of that."

Matthew started to laugh again. "Why?" Everything seemed either amusing or tragic.

"Because it means I shall have to help you. I know you would help me in similar circumstances."

"She slapped me," he said. "Three times so far. Or was it four?"

"Then she must love you, too, or she wouldn't let you near her that many times to offend her."

"She doesn't trust me," Matthew said. "Not regarding other women."

"One can hardly blame her. You know what you need?"

"More brandy?" Matthew asked hopefully. "Weren't we going to get some gin?"

"No, the headache isn't worth it. You need to get in good with her family. What about her eldest sister, the one who got married while you were away?"

"Does she have gin?" Matthew wondered if he was going to die of thirst.

"No, old chum, but she probably has some sway. Convince her you love Lady Purity, and your troubles will be over."

Matthew rose to his feet and staggered. "I have sway a-plenty." And he roared with laughter again.

SOBER AND BATHED, Matthew handed his calling card to the butler at Lord and Lady Hollidge's home on Grosvenor Square the following day. Perhaps he should have brought Quinn with him in order to vouch for his character. After all, it was his friend's half-baked idea, which had sounded spectacular at the time.

However, not only did his success seem less certain while he was standing upon a stranger's doorstep, bringing his friend along would have been childish, even spineless.

The butler allowed him into the entrance hall and asked him to wait while he climbed the stairs. This gave his nerves time to prickle with doubt until he was pacing in a circle.

Purity was worth the discomfort of coming hat-in-hand to win over her sister.

The butler returned and escorted him into a serene and sunny drawing room. *Better than being shown the door,* Matthew thought.

It occurred to him that Lady Hollidge might not know he was on the outs unless Purity had come to see her between the slap and this morning.

Footsteps had him turning to see . . . Matthew startled. For a moment, he thought Purity had entered the room.

"I receive that expression quite a bit," her sister, Clarity, promised. "I am sure Lady Purity does, too. The impression only lasts an instant, and then you can easily see I am not she and vice versa."

While she spoke, she did a quick tour of the room, picking up each pillow, fluffing it with a solid thump, and setting it down again.

"If your eyes don't tell you, then our differing natures quickly will."

"Indeed, my lady. Your sister was on my mind, so naturally you reminded me of her."

Matthew had only met Lady Hollidge at the Syon House gala. She had been always in movement, whether playing the lawn games or chatting with other guests, laughing a great deal, and appearing genuinely happy. Her husband had been always by her side, not somber but decidedly less animated than his viscountess.

The only time Matthew remembered her being still had been during the picnic, but she and Lord Hollidge had not sat near Matthew, so he hadn't talked with her. They'd departed while he had been stupidly destroying Purity's reputation next to the ridiculously endowed statue.

"Would you care for tea?" she offered.

Her question reminded him of Purity. He ought to say no since he was uninvited and imposing, so he did, just as she'd instructed him.

"Thank you, no. I have no intention of taking up much of your time."

"Shall we sit?" she asked.

"Yes, thank you." Matthew waited for her to take a spot on the sofa before he sat in a chair opposite.

"I suppose you are here because my sister no longer wishes to marry you," she began before he could think how to start.

The devil. He'd hoped she hadn't been privy to an earful of his faults. On the other hand, he appreciated her direct manner. Apparently, she had no qualms about making her guest feel uncomfortable.

"You know about that, then," he said lamely.

"Frankly, I was surprised when I learned of her decision. You seem to make my sister happy, albeit a little nervous. I watched you two at the gala." She shook her head. "And you certainly shall never get a finer woman than her. So why did you cock it all up?"

"I honestly don't know what I did wrong."

"Engaging in certain amorous activities upon your sofa with Lady Varley might be top of the list," Lady Hollidge said, and her tone was no longer the least bit welcoming.

CHAPTER TWENTY-FOUR

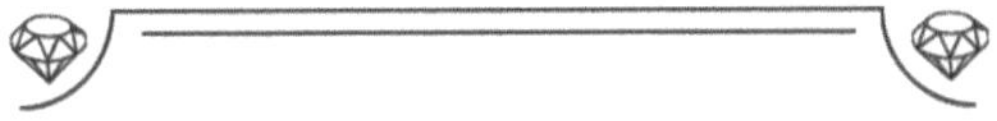

Lady Hollidge sounded downright fierce, and Matthew realized she had been playing at the part of kind hostess every bit as well as Purity. Her sister was, in fact, blazing angry. He would be lucky not to receive another stinging Diamond slap.

"I most emphatically vow I did not tup her on my sofa," he said, thinking too late how he ought to curb his vulgar language. In any case, he distinctly recalled always going to Emilia's townhouse. But that Lady Hollidge should even bring up the sofa was a mystery to ponder.

"You vow and yet you appear to still be considering," she said.

"It's not that. I admit I had an association with Lady Varley before she was married, but how on earth did *you* know she was on my sofa recently?"

"My sister told me. She also informed me you inexplicably wished to purchase a new one."

It was coming clear to him. "And hence Lady Purity assumed it was because that one was sullied."

"Indeed, she did," Lady Hollidge agreed, "because the female in question confessed to sullying it. With you! Moreover, you just admitted Lady Varley was on it."

"She came over uninvited, as I told your sister. I neglected to mention how I found her reclining like Lady Muck-Muck because I thought it would upset my fiancée."

At Lady Hollidge's doubtful countenance, he added, "I swear it. You need only use the brains God gave you. You said yourself I could not find a finer woman than your sister, and I wholeheartedly agree. So why would I ruin our engagement with a married woman who cannot hold a candle to her?"

Lady Hollidge tilted her head, again reminding him of Purity.

"Mayhap you did it because it was easy, because Lady Varley put herself before you, and because you thought you would get away with it."

"Ridiculous," he insisted. *But how to prove himself?* He didn't know the words to convince her.

"I don't agree with talking about another lady when she is not privy to it, but in this case, I must. I broke off my extremely brief entanglement with Lady Varley *before* I went to the Continent. Thus, it makes no sense that I would take up with her now when she is married, and when I . . ." He hesitated, unable to believe he was going to say these words to Lady Hollidge, but he tapped his chest in the vicinity of his heart, the area that had been aching since Purity had fled in tears, leaving him speechless in the Diamonds' drawing room.

"When I have finally found a woman I adore with every fiber of my being. When at last, I am happy," he finished.

Like sunshine streaming through a window, the viscountess's entire face lit up, and Matthew thought her nearly as breathtaking as Purity. When she smiled at him for the first time, transforming from lovely to spectacular, he knew everything was going to be fine. *What an absurd but wonderful gift the eldest sister had.*

"Well said," came a man's voice.

Matthew turned to see the viscount leaning against the door's casement, arms folded, having taken in the entire conversation.

When Matthew rose to his feet, the man came over and shook his hand.

"I couldn't help eavesdropping because, well, frankly, I wasn't going to leave my wife alone with an ill-famed rake."

Matthew shook his head. "That is all behind me."

"I am very good at understanding people," Lady Hollidge said. "Am I not, Alex?"

"You are," Lord Hollidge agreed.

Matthew thought them a charming couple.

"I can hear your earnestness," Lady Hollidge continued, "when you speak of my sister."

"I am entirely in earnest," Matthew assured her. "It is my greatest desire to marry Lady Purity and make her happy. I will follow all her rules of decorum and politeness and do so willingly."

Lady Hollidge gave a single clap. "Perfect. Then I shall speak with her. I assume that is why you came here, to plead your case."

"It is."

"Why do you wish to get rid of your sofa?" Lord Hollidge asked.

"Lady Varley's boots," Matthew explained. "She rudely rested them on the velvet. What's more, her perfume clings like ivy to bricks. I want to honor Lady Purity when she comes to live in my home and make it her own. That sofa could be cleaned, but it wouldn't be respectful to allow my beautiful bride to sit upon it."

He finished with a shrug.

"You really do understand and love her," Lady Hollidge said, glancing at her husband. "I couldn't be more relieved."

PURITY WAITED FOR THE reappearance of her fiancé, as she was allowing herself to think of him again. Both Clarity and her husband had made a point to come over and speak on Foxford's behalf.

Accordingly, from the upstairs window, when she saw his carriage draw up to the house, she raced down to wait in the drawing-room doorway.

Foxford had come back!

"My lord," she greeted when Mr. Dunley gave him entrance. "Please come this way."

She wished she had her older sister's lack of inhibition and could throw herself into his arms. Instead, she had only the proper words for the occasion.

"I offer my deepest apologies," she told him immediately. "I jumped to a conclusion without letting you explain. Lady Varley put lies in my ear at the King William Street ball. Then you seemed to confirm her poisonous words by mentioning the sofa."

He considered a moment.

"In the place of an apology," he said, "I would rather you let me kiss you."

"But you must accept my sincere regret," she insisted. *Didn't he know her heart would be heavy with guilt until he did?* "That's how these things are handled and overcome and then put behind us."

"Is that so?" He offered a smile that tugged at her heart.

"Don't you think?" she asked. He had a look on his face that said otherwise.

Instead of agreeing, Foxford moved closer.

Purity didn't back up. She'd been desperate to feel his arms around her and now stood her ground until they were toe-to-toe.

"Lady Purity Diamond, may I please have the honor of kissing you senseless?"

She laughed at his question, asked almost seriously. But he was waiting for an answer, for her permission. Since they were alone, she nodded.

Foxford rested a hand on either side of her waist and drew her close.

"You haven't yet said you forgive me," she reminded him.

He dropped a kiss on her lips, causing the first sizzle to snake through her.

"I struck you," she said, but he kissed her again.

"Rather hard," she added as he nibbled a path down her neck, making her shiver.

"Strange, the effect you have on me," Purity said, closing her eyes and leaning her head back against the paneled door. "For I am the least violent person you could hope to meet."

His lips were on the upper swell of her breast, but he paused and lifted his head. She opened her eyes to see his eyebrows raised.

"Truly, I am," she promised. "And I vow I shall never again slap you."

He grinned. "I forgive you, kitten. After all, if I hadn't been a scapegrace in the past, then you wouldn't have thought the worst of me."

"I will not jump to any more conclusions."

"I know it's hard to trust me, but I shall tell you what I told your sister since I ought to have told you first."

She bit her lower lip. *What was he confessing now?*

"I adore you."

Oh!

"I don't know how it happened. I wasn't expecting it when we met, not even after we kissed. I only knew I wanted to see you again. And again."

His hands were caressing her, roaming up and down her ribcage, and Purity fervently wished she didn't have on quite so many layers.

"And every time I encountered you, I admired you more until I didn't want a single day to go by without you in it."

She nodded, knowing exactly how he felt.

"I have come to the point," Foxford finished, "when your happiness is more important than my own, and I wish to have you naked in my bed every night and wake up beside you each dawn."

Despite being more than a little shocked by his words, she definitely wanted to be bare-skinned with Matthew Foxford. Yet hearing him say it aloud made her fight the urge to hush him.

He swooped in for another searing kiss.

In the span of a heartbeat, her body ignited into flames. Foxford pressed her against the door, caging her with his broad hands on either side. His long physique leaned into her softness, sparking every wicked fantasy she'd had of him.

"Hot," she murmured against his mouth as her body grew heavy with wanting.

"*Mm,*" he agreed. "That's why being in the buff like an Abram cove is so appealing. I cannot wait to strip you on our wedding night."

That freedom sounded blissful. When he lowered a hand to her skirts, she again closed her eyes.

"I want to draw up your gown like this," he said.

The whispering glide of her soft shift along with her stiff petticoat and brushed cotton day gown slid up her stocking-clad legs.

"And then I want to stroke your thighs."

Somehow, he was managing to do exactly that. His fingers slid into the opening of her drawers at her apex and skimmed across the skin of her upper thigh, making her knees wobble.

Deep inside, desire flooded her, and she tilted her hips toward him.

"I want to touch you," he whispered against her collar bone. "Everywhere."

She wanted that more than she wanted air. In fact, she couldn't catch her breath, alternately panting and holding a lungful.

Time stopped. She waited, her core throbbing.

Purity bit her lower lip. When the pad of Foxford's thumb stroked softly across her core, she gasped. When he did it again, a moan escaped her. As her heartbeat sped up from fluttering to galloping, the pulsing between her legs matched its pace.

Keenly aware of the hard door behind her buttocks and shoulders, she was grateful for its support as Foxford continued to caress her with a firmer sweep of his fingers.

Relishing each touch, she craved the next and the next, realizing there was a steady rhythm to his ministrations, like musical notes. Her body grew molten, her breasts heavy, and even her skin became prickly all over.

When tension built low between her hips, she moaned, desperate for release.

Mindless of anything except his hands and his mouth upon her, when he tugged at her décolletage with his teeth and his lips clasped her nipple, she hissed her pleasure and began to unravel.

Thrusting her hands into his hair, she kept his mouth in place. As he sucked harder, her core tightened, and shuddering pleasure rolled through her. She could do nothing but cling to his thick head of hair and bask in the cresting sensations as they peaked and finally ebbed.

As soon as her body began to relax, he removed his hand from under her skirts, and she felt them fall back into place. Still gulping air, eyes closed, Purity relished the moments of being so wildly wanton that she could not even stand straight. For surely, having been turned to jelly, she would collapse at his feet if she pushed away from the drawing-room door.

"Kitten," Foxford said softly, and she opened her eyes.

"Should I apologize?" he asked before offering her a wry, tilted smile. "At least I am fairly certain you are not going to slap me."

Having his golden amber gaze on her, realizing where she was and what he had done, her cheeks heated as much as her entire body had only seconds before.

"Now, now," he said. "Don't go hiding behind that blushing countenance. You are mine, remember? And I am yours. We are allowed to pleasure one another."

"*Before* the wedding?" she asked, knowing the correct answer. This was most definitely not in any etiquette book for engaged couples.

"I have reformed in all regards except where you are concerned," he said. "I restrained myself quite honorably."

She knew he was teasing. "I think perhaps you should allow me a few feet of air," she said.

He nodded, and to her mortification, he drew the neckline of her dress up to cover her nipple. *How had she not realized they were having a discussion while she was exposed?*

"Sweet Mary," she whispered when he moved away, and she took a weak step.

This made him chuckle. "You came so quickly, like a firecracker needing only the smallest spark."

"Stop, please," she begged, but she couldn't wipe the foolish smile from her face. Knowing the act of joining as man and wife was still to come, she could hardly fathom what that would feel like. But she would be counting the days.

"May we take up where we left off the other day?" he asked. "Can you come with me to choose furniture? Perhaps your mother would join us?"

"My parents have gone for the day and taken my younger sisters. And my brother is back at university this week."

His eyes lit up, and suddenly, she found herself once more in Foxford's embrace.

"You should have told me that at the start, and we could have done so much more. We still can."

"You are a rogue," she said without rancor. "I shall take my maid and be pleased to go with you."

In fifteen minutes, Purity, along with Alice, climbed into Foxford's carriage, her body having finally calmed and her heartbeat having slowed to normal. They went only as far as

Motcomb Street, passing close to the baron's home on Belgrave Square. With a fluttering feeling, Purity imagined going inside to see his private life, which would soon include her.

They alighted at The Pantechnicon, entering one of the two large buildings through the Greek-style Doric column façade.

"I purchased my curricle next door," Foxford said, pointing to the other building.

She had been to the "shop of shops" before, but it was always a monstrous thrill to see so many varied goods housed in one place. Purity thoroughly enjoyed choosing not only the style of sofa and its fabric, but at Foxford's insistence, new drawing-room chairs, too.

"It couldn't be any easier than to purchase here," he said, "and have everything delivered five minutes away to your new home. They have a special wagon just for the furniture deliveries. I see them going up and down the street nearly every day."

She was comfortable enough to tease him. "You aren't purchasing new chairs because Lady Varley lounged upon them, too, are you?"

He laughed out loud before answering, "Not at all."

Then she thought about his reputation. She wasn't sure what could be done on a wingback chair or a tufted ottoman, but after the way he'd touched her against a door, she supposed anything was possible.

"Or any other women?" she asked more seriously, half fearing the answer.

"Any other women, what, my sweet?" he asked, beaming at her.

She decided to drop the matter. She was in love with a former libertine, and she had better get used to it. There were bound to be a few bumps in the road to their happily ever after existence.

In a display of pianos, Purity played on three of them to try out their resonance and timbre. Other shoppers stopped to listen. Afterward, she told him quietly she preferred her own instrument, not wanting to insult the purveyors.

"And I prefer playing your body," he whispered in her ear. "I never knew how talented my fingers were until today."

Almost combusting on the spot, she had to draw out her fan and cool her face. They finished by strolling through the wine department.

Afterward, they went to the drapers to choose new curtains and the famed carpet dealer at the East India warehouse on Billiter Street.

"A better price and selection," Foxford had said, "than going to one of the Oxford shops."

And then they decided to go to Gunter's for a refreshing ice dessert.

At the shop's entrance, a child shouted out, "Papa."

Thinking nothing of it apart from the sweetness of the tone, Purity turned to see the giver and the receiver of such a loving address.

Foxford had turned, too.

Purity saw a little girl over his shoulder with light brown hair. Strangely, when the child called out the word again, she seemed to be speaking to *him*.

What's more, Foxford moved a few steps in the girl's direction.

CHAPTER TWENTY-FIVE

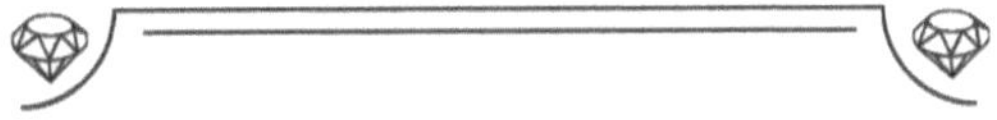

Matthew knew what would happen as soon as he saw Diana. Or more importantly, as soon as Diana saw him. The child's sweet face was lit with happiness, and she tore her hand from her nanny's grasp and ran toward him at the speed of a wild boar.

Right there, in the middle of the pavement, Matthew bent low and scooped up the little girl as soon as she was within arm's reach, *before* she managed to crash into his knees as she was wont to do. Her doll, which she always carried, was jammed into his chest. She clung to it like a best friend.

"Well, my lady," he asked her. "How are you today? Enjoying the sunshine?"

She nodded and gave her ever-ready smile. His heart pinched at her innocence.

Thinking of innocence, he was well-aware that Purity was taking this in with her cobalt-blue gaze.

"Spin me," Diana demanded with a regal tone.

Wanting to please her as usual, he spun in a circle, hearing her giggling. He knew he looked like a court jester, but when it came to his little girl, he didn't care if the queen herself was watching.

But he did care what Purity thought.

When he was still again, he glanced back at her. Standing amidst the hurly-burly passing on either side of her, she looked as beautiful as she did when dressed in her finest ball gown. Her gorgeous mouth was slightly open in surprise.

Come to think of it, better it *had* been the queen than his stunned fiancée!

Not sure what else to do, he nodded, and she unfroze, closing the yards between them, her head slightly tilted with an inquiring expression.

He sighed, giving Diana another squeezing hug. This would undoubtedly become sticky.

With the utmost formality and as if he weren't holding a squirming child, he said, "Lady Purity, may I introduce my d . . . Diana."

"Hello," said his bundle of joy, always willing to greet a stranger.

A single raised eyebrow indicated Purity noticed his hesitation. It was gutless of him. He would do better. He couldn't let himself be cowed by fear of losing all the good standing he had only just regained with her.

"She is my *daughter*," he added.

And there was the predicted reaction. Purity's eyes widened ever-so slightly. Then she looked again at the girl in his arms, probably trying to discern a likeness.

In the next moment, she spoke to Diana, "Good day to you, Miss Norland," before glancing at him again. "I am correct in that being your family name, am I not?"

"Indeed. I have not yet experienced you being incorrect. Well, maybe once," he teased, thinking of their recent encounter in the drawing room.

He'd hit the mark, and her cheeks pinkened. It was wicked of him. He only wanted her to recall that they were all fallible people, after all.

She rallied. "I was unaware you had off-spring, my lord. Or had been married?"

He noticed the hint of a question.

"I have never wed," he said, feeling less thrilled about the direction of their conversation. "I await that honor with you."

Was she once again going to back out?

"You look like Clara," Diana said, thrusting it forward.

Purity examined the well-loved wax and cotton doll. "Do you think so?" she asked.

Diana nodded. "Yes. She's a pretty baby."

"Then I thank you kindly."

"Papa," Diana said, pushing against him. "Put me down."

He did as instructed.

"Are you coming home with us?" Diana asked him.

At his daughter's mention of "us," Purity looked around until she spied the person who was attending the child, a middle-aged woman.

"No, sweetums. I'll see you later. Be good for Mrs. Caldwell."

Diana made her favorite exaggerated frowning face. "I always am."

Then she grinned, dashing off like the sprite she was, nearly trampling and being trampled in return, before she returned pell-mell to his side once again.

"Goodbye, pretty lady," she said. "Goodbye, Papa."

And then she ran back to her nanny.

"Four years of age?" Purity asked.

"Round about."

This earned him a scowl. "Don't you know?"

"Not precisely, no."

"I see," Purity said. Her saddened expression made his gut tighten. "And she lives with you?"

"You do not understand, I assure you." Matthew wanted to rail with righteous indignation that she was condemning him unfairly. Yet however much he branded his paternity with the stamp of magnanimity, he had fornicated with Diana's mother. There was no denying it. She could as easily be his if the timing were different.

Catching himself from offering a long explanation that had no place in front of Gunter's Café, instead he sighed.

"While I don't think this is the time or place, I owe you the full story."

"You owe me nothing," she said softly. "However, I must return home. I've been out longer than expected, and my family may have returned already. I wouldn't want them to become concerned."

"You no longer wish to have an ice or a cake?" He gestured toward the busy doorway behind her.

"No, thank you," she said, remaining perfectly calm and polite.

That worried him.

Then she added, "You may wish to call your daughter back and offer her a flavored ice."

He didn't respond, still staring into her eyes, trying to discern how much trouble he was in. He shouldn't have concealed Diana from her, but he had hoped they would become close enough he could tell her anything without it mattering. The engagement had happened too quickly, and now he was out of time for telling his secret since his secret had revealed herself.

Matthew should press the point of wishing to convey Purity home in his carriage, but her brittle demeanor spoke loudly. She needed to be away from him and to process what she'd learned. Maybe she simply didn't want to be a stepmother.

Nodding, he doffed his hat and bowed to her.

"At some date in the very near future, I hope you will allow me to enlighten you on Diana's situation. I would hate for you to jump to any conclusions."

Purity pursed her lips, and a spark of anger flared to life inside him. She was so bloody perfect that Matthew didn't know how anyone around her could possibly measure up.

Was he to feel unworthy the rest of his life for having enjoyed himself in his younger years? He wasn't sure he wanted a critical wife who was always going to look down her nose at him, deeming him inferior.

"You knew I was a rake," he reminded her, earning him a stony expression.

She raised a gloved hand at the unpleasant word.

"Good day, Lord Foxford." She started walking before he could respond in kind.

Clearly, she was eager to be away from him.

"Good day, Lady Purity," Matthew said quietly. It was better to let her go.

Obviously, he was out of her books at that moment. And while he was growing weary of being in the wrong and didn't intend to grovel, he would make sure she understood everything.

PURITY COULDN'T DENY being surprised to meet Foxford's by-blow. She seemed to be a dear little girl, not to mention fortunate. He had claimed her rather than allowing her to languish in an orphanage, if there was no mother involved.

Was there a mother involved? Perhaps Foxford was paying some woman's keep somewhere while raising their child.

Better he should have been more careful in the first place!

She ought to have been more careful, too. She'd allowed herself to be kissed in her own drawing room—more than kissed, but she couldn't put a name to what else had occurred. The moment Foxford had entered her home, her heart had started to beat faster and her body to tingle delightfully. His skillful touch had caused an overwhelming storm of sensations, which had ended with the most extraordinary release.

Purity could not dredge up an ounce of regret. Even knowing he'd kept from her the information of having a child, which was disturbing and begged the obvious question—*what else might he be hiding?*

Shaking her head, she looked around, realizing she was walking aimlessly along one side of Berkeley Square and that her maid was once again following. How kind of Alice to give Foxford and her privacy when they had started interacting with his daughter.

His daughter!

Purity could scarcely believe she was now thinking of him as a father.

Why wasn't she angry? True, she had experienced a moment of utter shock, but she was determined to live up to her promise not to pass judgment the way she had over the sofa.

Knowing Foxford had gone to the trouble to plead his case to her sister had further opened her heart to him. She smiled to herself. Despite how wrong she'd been about Lady Varley, he had thought no less of her for having misjudged him, and she'd concluded they would have a good marriage. Like her parents had.

Did his having a daughter change anything?

The little girl had been delightful, as most girls her age were. Purity could and would find no fault with her, nor place upon her any blame the way some people did. No guttersnipe wished to be poor, nor did any orphan wish to be such. They had no more choice in the matter than she did in loving Foxford.

But how could he not know her exact age?

That had been disappointing, making her doubt his responsibility. If he was so offhand about a child, how would he care for a wife? Her thoughts were spinning futilely.

"I think a new hat is in order, Alice," she said, deciding on the spot that she would feel better if she bought something pretty and unexpected. That's what Clarity would do. Naturally, her sister would have already made friends with Diana and probably insisted she join them for ices at Gunter's, whereas Purity had needed distance from the unexpected development. At least for the time being.

There was a shop on Oxford Street she favored, but Old Bond Street was closer, so she headed in that direction. An hour later with a hatbox in hand, she walked the rest of the way home, ready for a restorative cup of tea. It had been an extraordinarily long day with tasks and goals all over London.

And then Purity had what she hoped was a brilliant idea. Sitting at her writing desk, she began to write her betrothed a letter.

THREE DAYS LATER AFTER receiving Foxford's answer, Purity, accompanied by Alice, showed up at his Belgrave Square residence. She carried a special surprise for Diana.

The butler gave them immediate entrance into the drawing room and said both tea and Lord Foxford would arrive at once. Her maid was invited to meet the house staff and thus was whisked away after gaining Purity's nod of approval.

In any other house, with any other man, she knew this would be highly improper. But she was used to being highly improper with him.

As promised, Foxford entered less than a minute later, dressed impeccably, dash-fire handsome, and his face all but healed. Strangely, he looked wary.

"Lady Purity, welcome to my home." He started to move toward her, then stopped. She knew he was trying to behave and keep an appropriate distance.

When he put his hands behind his back and clasped them together, she was touched.

"Won't you have a seat?" he offered. "And put down your basket?"

"I shall do both. Thank you for letting me come today." Her heart was beginning to pound, hoping everything would go smoothly.

Setting the basket on the low table, she took a seat on one of the chairs. There was no sofa yet, and the room was a little short on seating.

She smiled, knowing he had removed the offensive item on her account.

"I allowed my maid to be stolen away by your butler."

"I'm glad you did," he said.

At her raised eyebrows, he added, "Because I was hoping we could speak privately. On the other hand, it worries me somewhat that you acquiesced. In fact, your contacting me and asking to visit gave me pause. I don't think I slept last night."

Before she could say anything more, the butler entered along with a housemaid, both carrying platters with the tea service. Besides the teapot and cups, there was also a plate of small sandwiches, another of assorted biscuits and slices of cake. There was even a bowl with apples and grapes.

"I asked for a variety," he explained, "not knowing what you would prefer. And I made sure it was ready at the appointed time of your visit."

She surveyed the selection, having never seen such an extensive offering for a simple visit in which the host or hostess ought to put out precisely enough to be eaten within fifteen minutes. He was trying so hard.

Purity bit her lip on saying anything apart from the kindest words.

"Everything looks perfect," she told him, expecting him to take the other chair, but he remained standing.

It was a more egregious error than putting out too much food, for remaining on his feet made her feel ill at ease, something the host should never do.

"I believe I know why you have come," he began.

She shook her head. "My lord—"

"I am interrupting you, which is a grievous fault. But once you stash and stow our engagement again, as I fear you are here to do, then I shall not come crawling as before. More current flaws along with the hauntings of previous missteps will undoubtedly emerge, and we shall be in the same circumstance. I have no evidence to prove my innocence for any number of things you think I have done because I am guilty of most of them."

He paced back and forth in front of her.

"The success I had hoped for has proven to be like milking a pigeon since I have failed to win and keep you. Nonetheless, I want you to know I have tried to be a man worthy of your deep affections, and I can do no more."

Then he came to a halt before her. "As for Diana, you have discovered her existence, and I will not apologize for her."

"Yes, I—"

"You have often thought the worst of me with good reason," he continued, "based upon my shady past. And no matter my efforts, I have been unable to prove to you I have changed my spots, like that fabled leopard. When word of our dissolved engagement gets around, my peers will think another one of my escapades, as you once called my ill-advised actions, has driven us apart. No blame shall fall upon you."

With such a tantalizing opening, Purity finally was given leave to speak, but from the basket came the smallest of sounds, followed by another, and then they continued without ceasing.

"What the devil!" Foxford exclaimed, belying all his fine words of improvement by swearing in front of her.

"They were sleeping," she said, "but apparently, they have awakened."

Purity opened the lid. Not one but two tiny, fluffy heads, poked up and over the rim.

"Kittens!" Foxford said, and he couldn't have sounded more surprised than if an elephant had appeared.

She laughed. "Indeed. We have been raising them, but my mother said they are ready to live independently from their mama. My younger sisters are keeping her and two of her babies. My sister, Lady Hollidge, is taking two, and I have brought these two to live with us. I thought Miss Norland would enjoy having them to cuddle and to raise."

"I am certain she would," Foxford agreed.

Rising, Purity lifted up a kitten and held it out to him.

"Oh, well, I . . . that is . . . ," he stammered.

"Come along, my lord. I thought your penchant for the word indicated a fondness for felines."

"No, my penchant for the word only indicates my fondness for you."

Nevertheless, he took hold of the small ball of fluff. "Are you certain it doesn't need its mother any longer?"

"Quite. Cook has been giving them all kitchen scraps, mostly chicken and beef, for a week, and bowls of milk, too, of course."

Purity picked up the other one, not an exact replica but the same gray and white coat.

"We have one with gray eyes, and this one"—she held it up so he could see—"has green eyes. Very pretty."

"I was up most of the night," he told her, "as I mentioned. Thus, I confess I am feeling a little bewattled. Did you say they are here to live with *us*, meaning with you and me?"

He was unable to breathe while he waited for her answer.

CHAPTER TWENTY-SIX

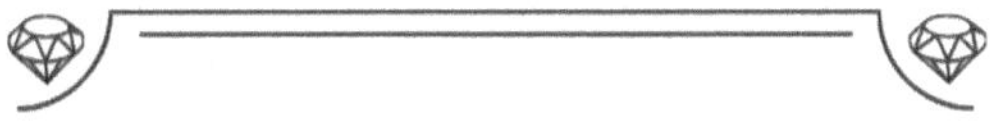

Purity answered quickly, putting him out of his misery. "Yes, I did. If you are agreeable to having them."

Matthew's face broke into a broad grin, and he put the kitten back into the basket before reaching for the one in her hands and restoring it to its sibling.

Then he drew her to standing and wrapped his arms around her, holding her close so she could feel the rapid tattoo of his heartbeat.

Then he looked down at her, his amber eyes glistening.

"I don't care if you bring a pride of lions with you, as long as you are still marrying me."

"That's good," she said, taking his face in her hands. "I left the lions on the doorstep."

He barked out a shaky laugh before bending low and claiming her mouth under his. As he tilted his head, she parted her lips to allow him entrance, relishing his tongue stroking hers. She didn't know how long they kissed, giving, taking, heating up and sizzling all over, but Purity would have been content to spend the day doing nothing more.

However, the kittens were mewling pitifully.

After Foxford had thoroughly ravished her mouth, he rested his forehead upon hers.

"I was certain I knew why you had come."

"And you were wrong."

"Thank God!" He sucked in a long breath. "May I explain about Diana?"

"If you wish. Shall we partake of the wonderful tea service? I would feel awful if the maid came to collect it and found a full pot as well as untouched platters. Imagine her showing your cook our ingratitude."

He tilted back his head and laughed. "Heaven forbid we insult my maid and cook."

After she sat, Foxford dragged the other chair next to hers.

"Now I wish we had the blasted sofa so we could sit close."

"You must stop swearing, at least in front of the child," she admonished to hide her own wish for a horizontal surface and some privacy with him.

Picking up her cup, she sipped while watching the kittens try to get out of the deep-sided basket.

"Diana will love them," he promised. Then he added, "You should have said something to stop me going on and on."

"You know how I feel about interrupting." Reaching for a biscuit, she added, "It is nearly as bad as vulgarisms."

After a pause, in which Purity hoped he didn't make her ask for the story, he said, "I shall get this all out at once. I knew Diana's mother *before* I left England."

And by the way he said "knew," it was clear to Purity what he meant.

"It was probably three years ago," he added. "She had fallen into the suds, finding no way to support herself except one. I didn't know she had a totiken already, hidden away. When I came back to England, her solicitor found me within a day. He'd been awaiting my return. Her mother had passed away, and Diana was living at the Infant Orphan Asylum in Wanstead."

"How terrible," Purity said, setting down her cup. "I am sure some of those places are comfortable, but I've read stories of dreadful conditions."

"Truthfully, I feared what I would find. Fortunately, it wasn't too bad, but it was crowded. The asylum isn't a very old place, and it was built of white stone with turrets topped by cupolas. Very uplifting, I thought. And I shall never forget the touching inscription over the door—*'A structure of hope built on the foundation of faith by the hand of charity.'* Her mother had secured Diana a place when she fell ill since I was nowhere to be found."

Foxford snapped a lemon biscuit in half but ate neither piece.

"It sounds as though Diana's mother did everything she could to give her daughter the best future," Purity said, considering the desperation of a woman who had to leave her child, not knowing for certain the outcome.

"Indeed," Foxford agreed. "Although you could have knocked me over with a feather when I learned she'd been left to my care." He winced. "A little like property, but her mother was hopeful I would take her in. She knew I had the means and the space, but she didn't realize I would be away when . . . when the cancerous disease took her."

Purity shivered. "How did she guess you would care for Diana?"

MATTHEW LOOKED DOWN a moment, then straight back into Purity's eyes.

"Miss Barnes, for that was her name, said in her letter to me that she knew from our brief acquaintance I was a kind man."

Matthew could not possibly explain how he'd felt upon receiving that letter or the solicitor's insistence that he was the one Miss Barnes wanted to raise her child. He'd read and re-read the words in her wavering handwriting. He had asked a dozen questions. He had paced his study and run his fingers through his hair until he looked decidedly unkempt, but he'd never thought of leaving the little girl in the orphanage.

"I consider it an honor for her mother to have left Diana to my care. Just as your trust in me gives me the redemption I seek."

Purity caught her breath. "Do not place me upon such a pedestal, my lord. We are all imperfect, and one day, I may slip up. I would hate for you to be disillusioned."

"Never," he promised.

The kittens were still mewing, and it seemed wrong to keep the little girl from them a moment longer. He went to the bell-pull.

"I hope she won't be rough with them," Purity said. "My sisters were mostly gentle at that age, but all children are different."

"She is gentle, from all I have witnessed. I've known her almost four months now."

"And she calls you 'Papa' already?" Purity sounded surprised.

He shrugged and took his seat once more. "She did that from the moment I picked her up at the orphanage. Diana said she had been waiting for me. In the carriage ride home, she said her mother told her not to worry, her papa would come for her."

"Gracious!" Purity looked to be choking back tears. "And do you have any knowledge of her true father?"

"I do not. In her profession, it is possible Miss Barnes didn't know, either. Frankly, at this point, it seems unimportant. I can give Diana a good life in which she'll want for nothing. She has already claimed my heart, so I gave her my last name."

He grinned. "And now I can give her the most upstanding, wonderful woman I know to help me raise her."

"Again, no pedestal, please," Purity said, blushing becomingly.

Matthew couldn't help leaning toward her to kiss her again.

But the door opened, and instead of a maid or his butler come to ask his wish, it was Diana herself, rushing ahead of her nanny.

"Come back, Miss Diana," the woman said, freezing in the doorway. "Apologies, my lord. She got it into her head that she knew your visitor, whom she spied from the nursery window."

"I do," Diana proclaimed, having already skipped over to Purity. "It's the pretty lady." She held up her doll. "Same as Clara."

"You may leave us, Mrs. Caldwell," Matthew told the nanny. "We were just sending for Miss Diana anyway to show her the—"

"Kittens!" the little girl cried out with glee.

He was glad to see she didn't simply drop Clara on the floor and snatch up one of the little cats. Rather, Diana placed her beloved doll carefully on the table and then looked to him for permission.

"May I touch?" she asked quietly.

His heart clenched at her sweetness. "Indeed, you may. Lady Purity brought them to live with us. Will you help take care of them?"

"I will, Papa."

Purity, still seated by the basket, reached in and plucked out one of the kittens. After showing her how to hold it, she handed it to Diana.

"That's well done of you, Miss Norland," Purity said.

"I am Diana," the little girl said, then asked, "What is its name?" She was unable to stroke the cat while carefully cradling it with both arms.

"That's for you to decide," Purity said. "Neither of them have names yet." But when her gaze found Matthew's, he knew she was fibbing. She was giving the child an extra gift.

"Maybe Miss Diana can spend a little time thinking about it," he said, imagining the names she might come up with in a hurry.

"Oh, no, Papa, they'll tell me."

"Will they?"

Diana laughed in her bubbly fashion.

He looked at Purity. "Did you know these cats can speak?"

"I did not," Purity said, "but maybe Miss Norland… I mean, Diana knows more about this type of thing than we do."

The little girl nodded emphatically and stared down at the kitten that was amazingly calm. Then she giggled.

Matthew looked at Purity, whose own face was filled with joy, and he wondered how he had become such a lucky man.

"That is a quiet puss," he said. "Is it talking to you?"

"Yes, Papa. She is Miss Soft," she said.

Matthew was glad the name wasn't worse.

Diana kissed its head before plopping it into the basket and hauling out the other one.

"They have very tiny bones and are fragile, like your papa's best dinnerware. Are you allowed to play with the fine porcelain dishes?" Purity asked.

His little girl shook her head.

"Because dishes might shatter," Purity explained. "The kittens won't shatter, but they can get hurt if they are dropped or squeezed too hard."

Diana nodded, her eyes large in her attentive face.

"I'm glad you understand," Purity said. "You're a sensible girl. What is this one's name?"

"*Hm,*" she said, rocking the green-eyed cat that was a little less docile than Miss Soft and trying to escape. "It is Miss Wriggles."

Before his little girl could return the kitten to the basket, it jumped from her arms, hit the table, knocked over one of the teacups, and trod though the platter of sweets, managing to get a little cream cake on all four paws. Like lightning, it jumped to the ground from the low table, leaving a mess behind as well as sticky footprints, before running to the far end of the room.

Diana was laughing so hard, he thought she might collapse.

"Miss Wriggles, indeed," Matthew said. "I suppose I should be glad the new sofa and chairs weren't in place, lest Miss Wriggles get her grubby paws on them."

But it didn't truly matter because Purity was laughing, too, while trying to sop up the spilled tea with a napkin after making sure the doll was lifted to safety.

"I've always heard it's a good thing to butter a cat's paws before it goes out in order to keep it from running away," she said, "but I've never heard of tea and cake being useful to keeping a cat."

"I'll find her," Diana said and dashed from the room.

"I don't believe Miss Wriggles left the room," Matthew said, astonished that the little girl would think so.

Then they saw the cat race through the door after her.

"Now Miss Wriggles is going to find her instead." He went to the door to make sure the nanny kept an eye on them both.

"I hate to tell you this," Purity said, and even those words said lightly made his stomach twinge. Matthew wouldn't truly relax until they were legally wed.

"What is it?" he asked, returning to take the soggy napkin from her and drop it upon the tray before drawing her up beside him.

"Tell me," he said, nuzzling her temple with a small kiss.

"That is actually *Mister* Wriggles."

They both started to laugh again, as Miss Soft tipped over the basket and made her escape, too.

"What have you done to my orderly household?" he demanded. "I thought you were going to bring your persnickety skills to organize me after we wed. Instead, we're not even married yet, and you've brought feline chaos."

Still, he tried to kiss her.

She squirmed like one of the kittens.

"I would be content if we could stay right here in one another's arms, no matter the impropriety. However, I believe we ought to find them, or at least tell your staff. If someone should leave a door open or if the kittens were to get access to the coal chute, then it might be a very sad ending."

"Agreed," he said. "I cannot credit that I'm going to put off kissing you to chase cats."

"That's the sacrifice we parents must make, I suppose," she said.

He blinked. "Are you saying you will help me raise her?"

"Yes," she said, offering an emphatic nod. "I shall."

THE WEDDING OF LORD Diamond's second oldest daughter to the baron, Matthew Norland, Lord Foxford, was hailed as a splendid if surprising event. Some went to watch because they couldn't believe the Fox was tying the marital knot. Others attended because they couldn't believe Lady Purity would attach herself to such a wild fellow.

Many witnessed the ceremony because St. James's Church was large enough that no one noticed them sneak in, but only their true friends and family would be at the wedding feast afterward.

"I shall tell everyone you are ready to go to the church," Lady Diamond said, pausing at the door to Purity's bedroom. "Another gorgeous bride in the family."

Humming to herself, she descended the staircase.

"It's funny, isn't it?" Purity said to Clarity as they stood side-by-side, taking a last look in the mirror. "I shall have a daughter who is older than yours."

Clarity sent her a happy smile. "And without having to wait, I shall have a niece old enough to play with. I shall be the most entertaining of aunts."

"Undoubtedly," Purity agreed.

"Then let us get you married, for I am certain it is the wedding night to which you are most looking forward."

"Clarity!" Purity exclaimed, turning away from her reflection after seeing her own cheeks become as red as August tomatoes.

Her sister chuckled. "You are marrying the renowned Fox, after all."

Thankfully, Clarity said nothing more. And Purity was able to gather her nerves into a wiry bundle and control them when her father took her arm and walked her up the aisle to give her away.

After he kissed her forehead, she was certain she heard him say, "Two to go," as he stepped to the side to join her mother.

Then her focus was purely on her husband-to-be, in a black tailcoat with a gray waistcoat and bright white shirt, finished with a black cravat. A more perfect bridegroom she could not imagine. As his amber eyes found hers, she let everything else fall away, wondering if she would even hear the words of the clergyman who officiated.

Naturally, Diana wore a new white dress to match Purity's, who had decided to follow the example set by their queen. Yet where Diana had a crown of flowers in her hair, Purity wore a tiara with a single diamond in the center and a row of sapphires stretching out along either side.

Throughout the eleven o'clock ceremony, Purity continued to keep any jitters at bay and was elated not to make a misstep. At the afternoon wedding "breakfast" in her parents' home, she managed to stave off any anxiousness over the events to come that night—or at least, she did during the first four courses of the relatively modest six-course meal.

Lord and Lady Diamond had foregone any vulgar display of ostentatious abundance, having no need to prove their wealth and standing. Therefore, Purity knew they would be finished in under two hours, from the soup through the final toast to their health accompanying a slice of the wedding cake.

Despite the tastefully inelaborate meal, when it came to the cake, Lady Diamond had decided on a large, lavish confection. It had a place of prominence on the sideboard and had held Diana's gaze for an hour.

The little girl, who Purity's family had immediately accepted, had been allowed to attend the grown-up wedding feast, but as most four-year-olds do, she grew tweaguey and tired and had to be led away by her nanny with the promise of cake when she awakened.

Looking around the table at all her family and friends, Purity felt blessed. The Season had the expected outcome of her finding a husband. However, the man who now sat beside her was the most unexpected of all. If someone had suggested after the first time she'd encountered Matthew—as she now gave herself permission to think of him and even to call him—that he would be her life's mate, she would have thought the notion outrageous. They seemed as different as chalk and cheese, or at least, their reputations were.

Yet from all the time they'd spent with one another, she knew they were surprisingly well-suited with a similar outlook on many things. And regarding passion, at that moment, they were both of a single mind entirely. She knew this for her husband's hand had slid over to touch her leg, causing her to quiver.

When he moved it higher, stroking the top of her thigh, she nearly choked on her morsel of roast chicken.

Her husband!

CHAPTER TWENTY-SEVEN

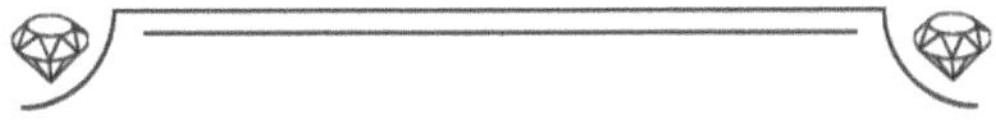

Matthew, although speaking with Lord Quinn, who had not tried to contain his amusement at seeing his friend and London's famed Bachelor Baron finally leg-shackled, seemed to sense her attention was upon him. He turned to face her with a wicked grin that had Purity's toes curling.

How could she not be focused on the man when his fingers rested practically in her lap? And directly below his hand, her body was throbbing at her core.

All at once, that tightly held bundle of nerves unraveled itself and joined a troop of butterflies in her stomach.

Pushing her half-eaten food away, she caught sight of the thick, gold band that Matthew had withdrawn from the left-hand corner of his right-hand waistcoat pocket during the service. The noise of him unwrapping it from a small sheaf of silver paper would stay in her memory forever as it sounded loud in the silent church. And then he'd slid it upon her finger.

She brought her glass of claret to her lips, hoping it would calm her.

Matthew leaned closer to whisper in her ear.

"Not too much, kitten. I want you fully alert when I tease you to begging and pleasure you all night."

"All night?" she spluttered.

He laughed. "We'll take naps in between."

"In between what?" she asked.

"Swiving, of course."

She closed her mouth to ponder how many times one could do *the act* in a single night, glad that her new husband was experienced enough for both of them.

Finally, they travelled home in their carriage, alone at last without need of a chaperone. They'd decided against an immediate wedding trip, thinking after they settled in as a family, they would go to Scotland for an extended visit with Matthew's relatives.

Finally at home, too early for bed, they sat in the drawing room on their new sofa.

"Well," Purity said, on tenterhooks for what was to come.

"We did it," Matthew commented, his leg jiggling and the fingers of one hand plucking distractedly at his trousers.

"Indeed," she agreed. Then she jumped up, causing him to do the same. Yet as she went to the bell-pull in her new home, she gestured for him to sit. "You don't have to do that every time now that we're married."

"Of course I do," he said, remaining standing. "As my wife, I shall show you even more respect, not less."

Nodding, she waited for the butler, a little surprised when the familiar Mr. Dunley didn't enter.

"Tea, please, Mr. Jacobs," she said. Yet as he bowed, she thought of the relaxing properties of wine. "And a glass of burgundy."

Then she turned to her husband but didn't ask him what he wanted. Instead, she added, "And brandy for his lordship, please."

On second thought, she might like to try that, too. She could do whatever she wanted as a married woman on her first night in the house of which she would be mistress.

"And a glass of brandy for me, as well."

"Yes, my lady." Mr. Jacobs disappeared swiftly. He was probably worried she was going to ask for more beverages.

"Come here, kitten," Matthew said, patting the sofa.

After she sat beside him, he put his arm around her shoulders and drew her close.

"You shall have to drink all that or risk offending my staff."

When she stiffened in dismay, he laughed.

"I'm speaking in jest. You are understandably nervous in a new place."

She nodded, glad he understood. "It shows, does it?"

"Just a little. But if you drink all that, you'll spend your night in the water-closet, so I might encourage you to restrict yourself to sharing a glass of brandy with me, and then we can retire early."

"We can?" she asked, deciding not to tell him he shouldn't mention the water-closet. She supposed as husband and wife, they could speak more freely.

He nodded. "Unless you need to write down the names of everyone with whom you spoke today."

She laughed. "No, I think I can remember every detail without doing that. But are we allowed?"

"Are we allowed what?" he asked, plainly perplexed.

Her cheeks heated, and she buried her face against his chest and mumbled into his coat.

"I cannot understand you, lady wife," he said.

Sighing, she tried again. "Can we retire to our bedroom while it is still light out? What will the staff think?"

For some reason, that struck him as exceedingly funny, and he laughed heartily, causing her head to jiggle on his chest until she sat up.

"You are Lady Foxford now, *not* Mrs. Princum-Prancum. And the longer we wait, the worse your nervousness shall grow. So, let us get to bed. We can always send for a late supper delivered to our room after."

"After," she murmured, letting him take her hand and draw her to the door. In the hallway, they met two maids, each carrying a tray with everything she'd ordered.

"I am terribly sorry," she began. She was starting her management of the household very poorly. To make it less wasteful, she handed Matthew a glass of brandy and took the other one.

"Please, enjoy the tea yourselves and give the cook this glass of wine with our thanks."

Then he tugged her away from the wide-eyed maids.

"They think I am ridiculous," she said on the stairs. "Look, I'm holding a glass and I still have my gloves on!"

"Nonsense, *they* think you are generous. *I* think you're ridiculous." And he escorted her into their bedroom.

"What about Diana?" she asked belatedly.

"She definitely thinks you're ridiculous, too."

"Foxford," she begged, "stop teasing me at every turn."

"You won't say that later," he promised mysteriously. Before she could ask, he added, "Mrs. Caldwell has strict instructions that we are not to be disturbed, not by a little girl or her kittens or even Clara, the all but bald doll."

Purity laughed.

"Our little girl will be put to bed after her dinner with a story and a hug," he promised. "But right now, it's your turn."

To be put to bed! That sobered her, and unthinkingly, Purity took a large drink from the brandy, imagining it to be smooth as fruity red wine.

"Sweet Mary!" she exclaimed around the coughing and the spluttering. It was a shocking heat, burning its way down her throat and somehow having got into her lungs, as well.

Her new husband patted her back until she waved him away.

"Foxford—"

"How about Matthew?" he said.

She nodded but didn't want to be deterred from her request. "Could we get directly to it, Matthew? To the swiving, I mean?"

He'd been untying his cravat but stopped and stared at her. Then he cocked his head.

"Are you saying you don't wish to follow proper bedroom etiquette?"

Purity had never heard of it. Instantly, she regretted not asking Clarity more questions.

With her fingers twisting in her skirts, she said, "Much as I believe in adhering to etiquette, as you know, I would as soon set everything aside and dive right in."

He shook his head. "Impossible," he said. "These things must be done correctly. You have taught me that. Or the whole thing will be ruined."

"Ruined?" she repeated. "Very well. What must we do before we get into bed?"

He sighed heavily. "There are a number of things. I should have made a list for you. That was badly done of me."

A list! "I have a decent memory," she said. "Why don't you tell me or simply begin?"

"First thing to do," he started, then paused and looked around the room, "is we turn down the bed so we can fall easily into it."

After drinking his brandy in one large swallow—which she found monstrously impressive—he set his glass down. Then he stalked to the four-poster bed and tugged at the counterpane, followed by the next layers of blanket and sheet. She joined in on the other side, neatening the mess he'd made.

"Then we plump the pillows," he said.

Purity stared in amazement as Matthew attacked the pillows with gusto, squeezing, kneading, and thumping each of the four pillows until their down innards had been duly rearranged.

"Next we make sure the curtains are drawn to avoid drafts when we are unclothed."

"Surely, your maid always does that when she lights the coals in the hearth and turns up the oil lamps."

"It's on the list," he said, tapping his temple, "in my head."

"I fail to see what any of this has to do with etiquette," she said. "It's more like housekeeping duties."

On the other hand, the mundane acts had succeeded in driving away her anxiousness.

"Now we must undress one another, a single piece of clothing at a time."

That seemed reasonable and fair. "But you have removed your coat and were already untying your cravat," she pointed out.

"True. However, my coat is considered outerwear, and my cravat is ornamental and hard to remove if you don't know the knots. In any case, the man gets to start."

He drew close, raised her arm by her wrist, and stripped off her glove, then her other.

Purity shivered, feeling immediately naked without her silken hand coverings. Moreover, the skin at her wrists tingled where his fingers touched her.

"Weren't they two items?" she asked, despite being happy they had begun the more intimate tasks at last. "Not that I am complaining." In case he said they had to beat the rug or look under the bed for dust before they continued.

"Gloves, stockings, and shoes count as one article each," he explained, "since they always come in pairs."

"You removed your gloves in the front hall," she said.

"That was remiss of me, wasn't it?" His gaze caught hers before lowering to her mouth. "Between my gloves, jacket, and undone cravat, you may remove two items from me."

Matthew stood before her, arms hanging at his sides, and waited.

Purity swallowed the lump in her throat. Since he'd untied his neckcloth, she captured one end and drew it from him. Realizing he'd tossed her gloves onto the chest of drawers, she put his blue silk cravat there, too.

Then she unbuttoned his cream-colored waistcoat, before pushing it down his arms. She went around the back of him to slide it off completely, taking a moment to enjoy the sight of his broad back. She even paused to lay her cheek against his back and breathe in the sensual fragrance that suited him perfectly.

Her womanly parts throbbed from the sensual act of being close, and she moved away to lay his waistcoat over the chair by the window.

"Sit," he ordered, gesturing to the same chair.

His commanding tone sent a shiver down her spine, and she did as he said. In an instant, he crouched at her feet, wrapped his fingers behind her ankle so he could lift her leg, before sliding off her soft shoe of the palest-pink kid leather.

Purity closed her eyes at the sight of his bent head and the feel of his fingers cradling her heel. Then he removed her other shoe and rose again, drawing her up beside him.

"Now yours," she said.

He shook his head. "I cannot allow you to put your hands on my boots. You are my wife, and thus I shall be pleased to do it."

In the shake of a lamb's tail, Matthew had tossed his ankle boots to the side of the room.

"Turn around," he said, an edge to his tone.

Far more swiftly than she could manage, he undid the buttons of her white satin dress purchased specifically for their wedding day.

When he whipped it over her head, she hoped it was undamaged and watched him drape it over his waistcoat. Their garments mingling made her stomach flutter again.

Purity stood in her finest satin corset, two horsehair stiffened petticoats, her best silk chemise, and her stockings.

With his gaze taking her in from top to bottom, her skin quickly came up with goosebumps as if she was cold.

She was anything but. In fact, as soon as he had pulled off her dress, she would swear her body became hotter.

"My turn," she said.

"I'm all yours," he said, his glance resting on the tops of her breasts.

She slid her fingers under his braces going over each of his broad shoulders.

"These are one item," she said.

"Yes," he agreed, then nothing more as she drew them down his arms until the braces hung at his sides.

Unfastening the buckles that were clipped at the waist of his trousers, she removed the suspenders with a sense of accomplishment at having handled the unfamiliar task. These she put on the top of his chest of drawers, returning to stand in front of him.

Purity reached out to finger the fabric of his white lawn shirt, even though it was his turn to remove something. Swiftly, he captured her hand under his, pressing it atop his chest. His strong heart pounded under her flattened palm.

Taking his other hand, she placed it over her bosom so he could feel her answering beat.

Their gazes locked, and her mouth went dry even as other parts of her dampened.

"Your petticoat," he said.

"Petticoat*s*," she corrected, emphasizing the plural. They usually were a little heavy, but all day, she'd been floating on air, not even noticing their bulk.

Matthew untied them at the back, and both layers fell from her hips. After helping her step out of the pile, he kicked it a little viciously to the side.

She chuckled. She'd often wanted to do the exact same thing.

"Your shirt," she murmured. "Oh, but the collar." She eyed the detachable garment with doubt.

"I'll do it," he said, "to be quick."

"Not if it ruins everything," she said, watching him take off the studs that held it in place.

"I was teasing." His voice was husky. "There is no etiquette, no list, no rules. Only myself torturing us with an idiotic game."

She laughed. "It was appreciated," she said. "Truly. When you said there were rules, I calmed a little."

He barked out a laugh. "I knew you would. But there are none except to pleasure one another."

"I see."

He tugged his fine lawn shirt out of his trousers, showing it to be longer than she thought. With his arm arched over his shoulder, he grabbed a handful of the cotton, shrugged his shoulders, and drew it over his head.

Her mouth dropped open as she watched the play of his shoulder muscles. He was spectacular.

"Your corset," he said, and the hoarse tenor of his voice made it obvious he was as affected by her as she was by him. He made quick work of the laces and hooks with practiced fingers until she was in her chemise, drawers, and stockings.

She resisted the urge to scratch her rib cage as she normally would. That didn't seem a particularly ladylike thing to do in mixed company, even in front of her husband.

And then he reached for her, feathering his fingers into her hair.

"Ow! My maid used extra pins and combs and an aigrette," she explained with an apologetic shrug, "to secure my coiffure. I shall need a minute."

Luckily, there was a small mirror atop his chest of drawers. If she was to share the room, she would have to replace it with a more generously sized looking glass. In any case, she drew out the many accessories and then unplaited her hair before running her fingers through it.

All the while, she was aware of him leaning against the bed, his long legs crossed at the ankles, as he watched her.

"Your maid was expecting a strong wind," he said wryly.

She nodded, feeling nervous again.

"Kitten," he said softly when she dithered with her back to him. "Come here."

Taking a last glance at herself in the mirror, she turned.

CHAPTER TWENTY-EIGHT

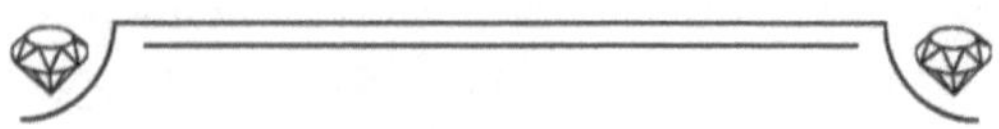

Matthew had never wanted any woman more than he wanted Purity at that moment. He'd been determined not to pounce like a wolf and overwhelm her, but the slow approach had become intolerable.

Holding out his hand, he was gratified when she came willingly toward him, and he could pull her against his body. At last! Spreading his legs, he nestled her close to his hips, caging her with his thighs.

It seemed a lifetime that he'd waited for her, and in truth, it had been. A lifetime of meaningless encounters.

Unfastening the tiny buttons of her chemise, he loosened the neckline enough to draw it down one of her exquisite shoulders and then the other before she shimmied out of it.

He wanted to give her all the pleasure he possibly could and not disappoint her in the least. At the same time, she was the most precious creature he had ever met, and he intended to be gentle.

"I confess, to me, you are like a fragile crystal figurine or a porcelain doll."

At once, she wrapped his fingers around her bare left breast, warm and soft, and held it there.

"I am flesh and blood."

"And the prettiest breast I have ever seen."

"How fortunate," she said, taking his other hand. "I have another just like it."

She surprised him with her boldness, and he could barely breathe for wanting her.

Cupping her breasts, he brushed his thumbs over her dusky nipples, making her gasp before he lowered his head to suck each one softly.

"Please," she said, sliding her hands up his bare chest.

With that small utterance, he put his hands to her waist and turned, so they'd exchanged places, then he lifted her and set her upon the bed. As quickly as he could, he shed his trousers and stockings, while she watched.

Matthew didn't think he had ever been scrutinized quite so closely. He was beginning to experience a flutter of nerves, the likes of which he hadn't felt since he was a green cub, an inexperienced, unsure looby. In truth, he thought his own cheeks might be reddening.

With a shake of his head at his own foolishness, he stood at the foot of the bed and slid each of her stockings down, enjoying the exploration of his wife's slender legs and noticing how she trembled under his touch.

And then he did what he had dreamt of doing for weeks. He kissed the fine bones on the inside of her right ankle before trailing gossamer kisses up her slender calf. All the while, she leaned upon her elbows, watching him with her intense blue eyes and with her lips slightly parted in anticipation of his next move.

When he reached Purity's thighs, he took off the last impediment, although it was easy enough to swive with her drawers still on as they had the usefully wicked opening at a lady's core. He had used and appreciated such convenience many times over the years, but he intended for his wife to be entirely bare.

First the ribbon at her waist, a quick tug, and then he drew the soft two-pieced drawers down her legs before settling between them.

"What are you doing?" she asked, the first words she'd spoken in many minutes.

He grinned and dropped a kiss just above her woman's mound, and then another on her upper thigh, and then the other.

"Oh!" she said on a long breath. And her hips lifted slightly.

With that invitation, Matthew put the tip of his tongue to her core to taste the very essence of Purity.

"Oh!" she exclaimed again, slipping her fingers into his hair. And then she fell silent as he slid his hands under her arse to position her, before rolling his tongue across her once again.

Over and over, he swirled and teased her bud until she began to thrash beneath him. As she'd done when he'd brought her to release in her drawing room, she came quickly. Her body stiffened while he continued to feast on her pink pearl, then her hands fell away from him to the bed as she moaned her release.

When he knew she had finished and was floating in that languid place after reaching the pinnacle of pleasure, he kissed his way up her smooth stomach. Resting on his forearms, he looked down at her beautiful face when her eyes fluttered open.

Her beaming smile made his heart ache with love. She was his, and for the first time in his life, he knew what it meant to belong completely to someone else. Every new moment was a revelation of how much he adored her.

Lowering his mouth to hers, he claimed her smile. When she sank her fingers into his hair again and held his head, he realized she was kissing him, and not the other way around. And while she tilted her head and sucked his tongue into her mouth, he felt her hips lifting against him.

Matthew was throbbing, his arousal as hard as he could ever recall it. With her body's invitation, he readily fit the head of his sex to her slick sheath. He wanted to bury his length deep inside her with a single satisfying stroke, but he eased in, an inch at a time.

Lifting his head to judge her acceptance, he smiled at the woman he loved beyond words. She appeared pensive, waiting, experiencing, allowing him the honor of taking her innocence.

When he hit the petal-thin barrier, he thrust forward watching her countenance.

She winced, and he stilled.

"Go on," she said. "There is no point in halting now. Would you silence the musicians when the guests are already in the midst of a dance?"

He tried not to laugh. He failed, glad when she smiled again.

"I would never be so rude," he said and thrust forward.

"Ah," she breathed out.

Again, he stopped, desperate to move but wanting to know whether she was fine.

"Are you waiting for something?" she asked. "Or am I to do the next thing on the list?"

Purity Norland, Lady Foxford was a saucy wench, jesting with him while he was deflowering her.

Slowly, he drew out before rocking forward again, filling her. After he set a rhythm, she arched back and closed her eyes once more. He closed his, too, becoming pure sensation until he was about to explode with unadulterated pleasure.

Sliding his hand between their bodies, he caressed the center of her desire. Within moments, she tensed, close to her second release. He couldn't halt the racing tide of passion that flooded his veins and erupted from him, only hoping she would join him as he spent.

Feeling her nails rake his back, he was assured she had.

In the aftermath, they lay quietly atop the rumpled sheet. Drawing up the coverings, Matthew was content to bask in satisfied fulfillment.

Then Purity's sleepy voice reached his ears.

"How long before we can swive again?"

As it turned out, they both fell asleep, and it was dawn before they awakened to start the dance of desire once more.

With his lady wife riding rantipole at the time of their release, she now looked down at him with a thoughtful expression.

"The crimp on your earlobe," she said while he played with her nipples. "Why did the woman bite you, pray tell?"

His eyes widened, then he burst out laughing, making her jiggle up and down atop him.

"I don't see why my question is funny. The notion of some female mindlessly sinking her teeth into your earlobe isn't amusing at all."

At that moment, Matthew had the seed of hope that she loved him, for if he wasn't mistaken, she was jealous—even though she was now the Baroness Foxford, a title no one in England could have ever expected Purity Diamond to have.

"There was *no* woman," he said at last.

"But you said a lady's teeth were involved."

"I never did." He wrapped his arms around her and pulled her down to splay across his satiated body. "You imagined that all by yourself. It *was* a female, but a dog. My nursemaid left me sitting on the ground while she dashed back indoors for my coat. I wasn't a baby, mind you. I was almost three years old. Nearby was one of Father's hunting dogs. When it came over to play with me, I stood up and grabbed its tail. The nipper took a bite of my ear."

Purity gasped. "How terrible!" She grasped the tender lobe between her fingers.

"I don't remember it," he said, "but as my mother tells it, she discovered me after I yelled, saw the blood, and fainted beside me on the grass."

"That wasn't very helpful of her," Purity said. "I can imagine the scene though."

"The nursemaid was sacked, I'm sorry to say, but the dog was still treated like a prince. And my father joked his beloved hunter mistook me for a young fox."

PURITY KNEW EVERYTHING was going as well as could be expected in a household of the newly married. She and Diana got along like two peas in a pod. It was a delight to take her on outings, and Bri and Ray were very good with her too, as if she were a younger sister.

The Foxford staff adjusted to their new mistress of the house. Purity easily slid into the role of baroness as if she'd been born and raised for it, which naturally, she had. After all, one of the first books she'd ever memorized was *Domestic Management*, which offered her much useful information on improving her staff's manners.

They had remembered everyone they held dear in their stacks of "at home" cards, invitations sent out by her sisters as one of their duties as bridesmaids. Consequently, beloved visitors came in twos and threes to call upon Lord and Lady Foxford in their new domestic arrangement.

And at night, she and Matthew lost themselves in one another. She had no complaints in that regard, nor in most others. Purity had his admiration and his professed devotion. She shared his name, his carriage, his house, and his bed.

So why did she worry that something was missing?

The nagging in the back of Purity's mind was starting to distract her. And any small thing that went amiss vexed her like a massive disaster. At that moment, she was trying to arrange flowers that Matthew had brought her when he'd come home for their evening meal.

After dinner, she'd spread them out on a piece of linen in her salon on the second floor and knelt beside them. Next to her was a household book open to the chapter on flower arranging. Yet still two vases stood empty, awaiting to be filled in an artful manner.

After a few minutes of cutting the stems too short and pricking herself on the roses, Purity sat back on her heels. She ought to have chosen something that held her attention better, such as playing the piano or reading.

Instead, her mind wandered like one of the kittens trying to make its way across the polished front hall. A funny sight to see, but her own helpless mental meandering wasn't the least amusing.

Her thoughts leapt from the flowers before her to the sensual pleasure they shared, which was beyond what she'd imagined. Her husband's kisses were as toe-tingling as before they'd married. However, they'd managed to get this far without once expressing that deepest of emotions. At least, not to one another.

Purity knew the longer time went on without either of them saying it, the more awkward it would become. *Yet how could she be the first to blurt it, and when?*

"Please pass the salt cellar and by the way, I love you."

Was Matthew *madly in love with her?*

Snapping the stem of the daisy still in her hands, Purity tossed it down. She wasn't naïve enough to mistake their nightly passion for anything but lust. He had been participating in precisely the same for his entire adult life and had told her with frankness that he had never loved any one of the women he'd bedded.

Sadly, he hadn't said he was making an exception for her.

Any day, she might discover she was carrying his child, yet instead of that making her joyful, it caused her to worry. *Once he had the necessary heir to the barony, then what?*

What if Matthew's infatuation with her cooled? If he was withholding his heart, then heartbreak would surely follow. She feared Lord and Lady Fenwick had something they did not. For that ancient couple could hardly be expected to tup every night, yet their love shone whenever they were near one another.

Moreover, they'd put off their wedding trip to Scotland because of a spate of exceedingly rainy weather followed by Diana being indisposed.

"She has merely caught a mild cold, my lady," said Mrs. Caldwell when Purity grew alarmed. "Don't fret."

Now their little girl was well, yet neither of them had mentioned the long trek to Edinburgh. *Didn't Matthew want to introduce her to his mother?*

Thus, when the demon of her agitated thoughts poked his head around the open doorway, dressed to go out, her stomach clenched.

After seeing what she was doing, he merely nodded and winked. "I shall be back anon."

"Where are you going?" Purity bit her tongue as soon as the words were out. She sounded possessive and jealous, especially when her voice caught in her throat.

"To my club. Quinn said he hasn't seen me in a donkey's age. I won't stay long."

"That's all right," she said, rising to her feet. "Stay out as long as you like. I plan to read a story to Diana and then take a bath."

At her tone, he cocked his head, frowning a little, then he entered the room.

"Careful," she warned. "Don't step on them."

He surveyed the flowers. "It appears you've already waltzed atop them and done enough damage without my help."

He was teasing but having him point out her failure nearly made her cry. She stared at the floor, unable to meet his gaze because of the foolish tears stinging her eyes.

"Kitten," he said, "look at me."

She shrugged and glanced at his waistcoat.

"Is something wrong?" he asked.

Everything! she thought. "No, nothing. What could be wrong?"

His gloved finger under her chin made her look at him.

"Kitten," he repeated when he looked into her eyes. "Tell me."

"Nothing, I assure you. Just . . . just . . . Clarity would have these flowers looking gorgeous by now. She has a talent for it."

"Don't worry about that." He drew her into his arms, which only served to make a tear spill out and down her cheek. "I'll buy you more, I promise. You can practice, just like you did when you were a youngster learning the piano. You'll soon surpass any other lady in London with your floral designs."

She shrugged again.

"I won't go out if you wish for me to stay home," he vowed. "I'll gladly listen to you read and be even happier to watch you bathe."

A small laugh escaped her lips. Everything was fine. He was attentive and caring. He wasn't going out to meet a woman. If he was, he wouldn't have offered to stay. He ought to go spend time with his friend. After all, he had no family. While she spent many a morning with her mother or one or more of her sisters, he had no one but her and Diana.

It was merely the stress of settling into her new life, that was all. She didn't want her husband to think her needy.

"Of course not. I am being silly. Go to your club and enjoy yourself. I insist. I shall be awake when you return."

He took her face between his palms. "I am looking forward to it." Then he claimed her mouth in a way she imagined only a lover could do—if only she didn't already know he'd done the same with many others.

She sighed. He probably thought it was due to the satisfying kiss that sent tremors of awareness throughout her body. Later, when she relaxed in their copper soaking tub, she would think of him touching her and remind herself what a lucky woman she was to have such a passionate husband. And then they would pleasure one another as soon as he came home.

"Please give Lord Quinn my regards. We should invite him to bring a lady friend to dinner some evening soon."

"Perhaps," he agreed, releasing her. "But Quinn has had many chances and can never seem to choose only one."

He was chuckling to himself when he left, while a stone settled in her stomach.

Could any man who had been used to variety settle for only one?

CHAPTER TWENTY-NINE

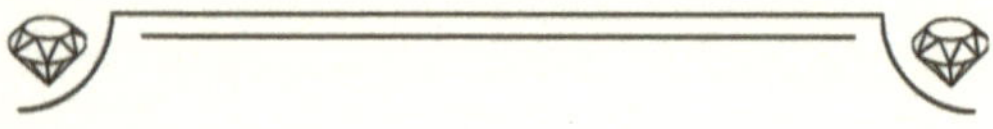

Days later, it was his turn to question her when, after dressing to the nines, she was heading out the front door precisely as he came down the stairs.

"Where are you off to today?"

Purity realized she didn't have a ready answer. And in her brief hesitation, his eyes flickered with doubt.

"I am going to visit Clarity and her little ones."

"But you're not taking Diana," he pointed out.

He had caught her in a lie too easily. And now she had to add to it.

"My sister's littlest has sniffles, and I didn't want to risk Diana catching anything again. I will be home in a couple of hours."

She turned, wincing at her string of lies.

"Purity," he called after her.

Freezing in place, she turned back to him as he closed the distance between them.

"You're not taking your maid with you," he asked.

"Being married has a few privileges, my lord. And one is I can at least leave my home when going to my sister's without need of a chaperone."

"And what else?" he asked.

"What else?" she repeated, examining the flecks of gold in his sherry-colored eyes.

"You said a *few* privileges," he reminded her, drawing her into an embrace.

She smiled up at him. "Then there is being able to kiss a handsome man whenever I wish," she added.

On tiptoe, she kissed him.

"We ought never to go anywhere without doing that," she said, glad he had caught her.

"Agreed," he said before letting her slip out the door.

Having picked up a newly framed painting with the help of their driver, she dropped it off at her sister's home for safe-keeping and away from Matthew's eyes. At least, she had gone to Clarity's in truth.

On the other hand, she could see how easy it was for a spouse to go anywhere and do anything with the other being none the wiser.

The following morning, when her husband disclosed his tasks—first joining Lord Quinn at Tattersall's to view horses before a meeting with his trader at the Stock Exchange at Capel Court, she experienced the same sense of misgiving, a twinge of doubt.

Completely irrational and, as far as she knew, unwarranted. *As far as she knew.*

But why was he being so particular in his details? He was either reassuring her or fooling her.

When Matthew leaned in to kiss her, her heart ached. The problem, she realized, was clearly etiquette. Somewhere in one of her beloved books on manners, she'd read about the danger of a lady expressing her love ahead of her suitor. However, she and Matthew were past that, and she was a married woman able to think for herself. That night, she would tell him plainly of her love and see what came of it, for she could not go on tormenting herself.

Meanwhile, she expected Clarity any minute with the painting.

However, before her sister arrived with the special surprise, Mr. Jacobs entered her salon with a note delivered by a stranger. Unfolding the page, she was puzzled by the brevity of the words as well as their intent.

Our little girl is unwell. Come to Fenton's Hotel at once. I know she will feel better when she sees you.
Foxford

"Is Miss Norland here?" she asked Mr. Jacobs, thinking her husband's note especially odd since he'd been out of the house for less than an hour.

"No, my lady. She went on an outing with Mrs. Caldwell to Green Park, about the same time as his lordship departed."

Purity supposed if they left at the same time, then Matthew must have bypassed Tattersall's, deciding to walk with Diana to the park, which was not far from the hotel on St. James's Street. If Diana had become ill, then he would have wanted to get her indoors out of the sun and onto a soft bed.

"Very well. Please hail a hackney and give the driver this address." She handed the butler the single sheet. "I shall be downstairs directly."

Feeling a sense of urgency, she hurried to her dressing room, deciding not to change but merely to don her hat and gloves before going downstairs to the waiting cab.

Despite the usual traffic, Purity thought the driver excelled in his duty of getting her across Mayfair. After alighting, she waved him on, knowing she would ride with Matthew on the way home. A quick glance up and down St James's Street, however, showed no sign of his curricle, and she hurried inside Fenton's.

Not the least bit lowly or in any way alarming, the inn was bright and smelled of furniture polish. The carpets were clean, and the establishment had been known to house foreign dignitaries, according to the newspapers.

"Lord Foxford, please," she said to the manager, "and he has a child with him."

"I didn't see a child," the man said, "but his lordship told us to expect you. Room thirty-six. Top of the stairs, end of the hall, upon the right."

"Gracious!" she said. "Do you have thirty-six rooms?"

"No, my lady, we have sixteen." And with that mystifying statement, he bowed and gestured for her to take the stairs.

Upon finding the indicated door, she tapped, and it swung open. Peering inside, she saw no one at all.

All at once, it occurred to her that Matthew was behind the door, and this was a game. Only the night before, they'd been discussing finally going on their wedding trip to Scotland. She had told him how she'd never stayed in a public inn and was looking forward to it.

With a smile on her face, she stepped inside onto a plush carpet. However, when the door closed with a solid thump, it was Lord Varley's hand on the wooden panel, not Matthew's.

"How good of you to come," he said, and his tone sent shivers up and down her spine. She stepped away from him, farther into the spacious chamber, sporting a four-poster bed, a wardrobe, and a writing desk.

"I came because my husband said young Miss Norland needed me." There was no sign of the little girl or the baron.

"Naturally. I knew you would come, regardless of the fact she is your husband's misbegotten brat. As I said, good of you because you are, by all accounts, a good person. Which is why I cannot understand your continued fascination with Foxford, a decidedly bad person."

Purity knew one thing with certainty—Diana wasn't Matthew's, and yet he was caring for her regardless, through the kindness of his nature.

He was no more a bad person than was her Grandfather Diamond, despite having been of a similar nature in his younger days. Thundering bucks were not necessarily bad men, a mistake it had taken her many misjudgments to learn.

None of this was Varley's business. "Where is Miss Norland?"

He cocked his head. "I assume she is with her whey-faced nanny with whom I saw her depart earlier."

"I don't think Mrs. Caldwell is particularly whey-faced at all. Random insults are beneath a gentleman," Purity reminded him, unsettled with the knowledge he had been watching their home.

Lord Varley shook his head. "You are truly a gem, an actual Diamond. I wish I hadn't stepped into the parson's mousetrap before we met, or I would have wooed you with the fervency of a hound having scented a fox."

He laughed softly. "I suppose I shouldn't use any fox metaphors where you are concerned. In any case. Here you are, misled and brought to ruin, and yet you are still chastising *me* for insulting someone's nursemaid."

Purity caught her breath. *How stupid of her!*

In her hurry to help the child, she hadn't considered the consequences of rushing headlong into an unknown situation.

"It's a wonder you were never kidnapped or sold to a brothel," Lord Varley continued.

"Stop such foul musings," Purity ordered, "and step out of my way."

"I suggest you make yourself comfortable. By the time I release you from this room, you will be Lady *Purity* no longer."

For a second, the blood seemed to rush from her head, but she took a deep breath and reminded herself of her parents' teachings, which calmed her. She had no intention of letting this man touch her.

To that end, she quickly removed her gloves, rolled them tightly, and tucked them into her reticule so she wouldn't lose them when she ran. After all, they were her favorite—pale pink and extremely soft leather.

"Oh, dear lady!" he said. "You've blanched. Do not fear for a moment. I shall not lay a hand upon you. I am no scoundrel. Time alone with me in this room will do damage enough, especially when my wife comes by later, accompanied by an impartial friend to bear witness. Along with the manager attesting to the time of your arrival—that's all I need to destroy your reputation beyond any hope."

Purity considered to what end such nefarious actions might produce when he added, "This is not about you. You are merely an unfortunate bystander. It will injure Foxford greatly. When my wife tells the newspapers that Foxy's own baroness, a newly wedded one at that, has met me here for a tryst, he will be rabidly enraged by your betrayal. That will knock him down a few pegs. Frankly, it is long past time."

Purity didn't worry about the latter, not for a second. Matthew would never believe she could play him false. However, having her name sullied—*again!*—was not to be tolerated. She needed to escape before his wife arrived.

Suddenly, he yanked his cravat until it came free and tossed it onto the bed.

"What are you doing?" she asked.

If he was going to undress, then she was reconsidering her first plan and would use her nails upon him to escape.

"This must look as real as possible. Thank you for removing your gloves. May I press you to take off your shoes as well and perhaps your hat?"

"Are you mad? I can think of no other explanation for these bizarre antics."

His expression darkened. "Do you know something, my lady? I might be a lunatic, driven there by Foxford."

Purity could no longer stand for his position as a victim. "You must take responsibility for your own actions. Were you not dallying with then Lady Tupmoure?"

He sighed. "I was, but that infernal Fox blunders through everything without ever paying the piper while the rest of us are left floundering in his wake. I, for one, intend to pay him back, shilling for shilling."

"By ruining me?"

That seemed to give him pause. But finally, he nodded.

"You seem to be the only person he cares about more than himself. If Foxford is capable of love, I would say he loves you, although I don't believe it will last. He'll have moved on with another female by the Twelfthtide."

Purity hoped not, although that was her constant fear.

"More reason for you to release me," she insisted. "While you are up to the boughs in jealousy and anger at this moment, I believe your conscience will regret taking out your vengeance upon me."

Before she could press her case, there was a pounding upon the door.

Purity's heart skipped a beat. It was too late. Lady Varley and her friend would come in, and she would be ruined far beyond a rumor of a kiss at the Syon Park fountain.

"She is early!" Lord Varley said, sounding annoyed.

To that point, he immediately ran his hands through his hair, mussing it beyond repair without the help of a valet or his comb.

"Must look real for her friend, Lady—"

The door burst open, sending Matthew rushing in shoulder first.

"ARE YOU HURT?" MATTHEW asked Purity, although he could see she appeared unharmed. Accordingly, his heart returned to his chest from where it had lodged in his throat the moment their butler had showed him the nefarious missive.

"I am not," she said, but she looked pleased to see him, nonetheless. "We thought you were Lady Varley," she added.

"Did you? What a strange thing to say. I don't look anything like her," Matthew quipped. "Nor does this man's wife have the might to do what I just did."

Rubbing his shoulder, he eyed Varley, who appeared in distress and in disarray. "Someone is going to have to pay good coin for that door lock."

"What are *you* doing here?" Varley demanded, sounding peeved.

"I'm sorry," Matthew replied, ready to start swinging his fists. "Was this a private party?"

"Obviously," Varley replied, gesturing to Purity and to the bed.

Purity stared at him as if she thought he might believe the arse. To reassure her, he winked before crossing his arms and addressing Varley again.

"You are certainly going about it slowly, old chap. If I had this goddess alone in a room, we would be in a tight clench as soon as the door closed and rolling on the bed a minute later."

"Foxford!" his delightful wife exclaimed, her pale cheeks staining pink.

He grinned but had to turn his attention again to the blackguard who began smoothing his hair as he spoke.

"How do you know we weren't so passionate *and* quick that we've already made the two-backed beast?" Then the man made a great show of swaggering to the bed and snatching up his cravat, which he jammed into his pocket.

"Varley, my good man, if you can make love to a woman without disturbing her hat, then you are a better man than I. Or far less energetic, at any rate. Now, why don't you tell me what this is about before I thrash you within an inch of your life."

Purity stepped forward. "I don't think that's necessary. Lord Varley simply wanted to speak with me. He's not a contented man, you see, and he went about trying to make himself feel better by hurting you. He never meant me any real harm."

Matthew noticed Varley was staring at Purity in shock. Apparently, he hadn't thought his defense would come from that quarter.

"He sought to hurt me through you," Matthew reminded her, "and if I'm not mistaken, he hoped to ruin your reputation beyond repair."

"Yes," she agreed, "but without actually *ruining* me if you understand my meaning."

He well-nigh rolled his eyes at his lady's precise way of speaking. Besides, Matthew had already *ruined* her in that regard thoroughly and enjoyably many times over. That was hardly the point.

"She is trying to cover for herself," Varley insisted. "Of course we swived, and she only just put her hat back on."

Matthew couldn't help it. He smiled, and then he started to laugh.

CHAPTER THIRTY

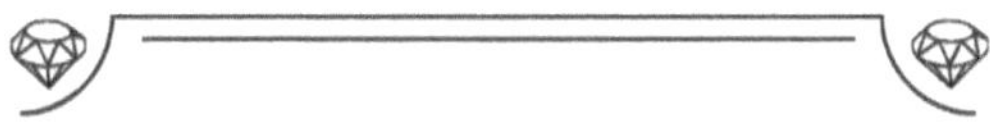

Matthew wanted to hate Varley, but he felt sorry for him, stuck with Emilia Tupmoure for a wife.

"No one will believe Lady Foxford chose you over me," Matthew said. "I am sorry to say, but it's the truth. I have a reputation for pleasing ladies to the point that they have taken some lunatic measures to keep me."

Varley looked at Purity. She nodded sagely.

"He is the Fox, after all," she said.

Varley winced.

"Do *you* have a nickname, my lord?" she asked him.

Varley's nostrils flared. "No."

"Well then," she said, shrugging slightly as if that was the end of it.

Matthew had to stop himself from laughing out loud at the man's confounded expression.

"I suggest you return to your wife and try to work it out with her," Matthew said. "You destroyed your own engagement by getting caught with Emilia. I had nothing to do with it. Why don't you set aside your anger with me and embrace the female you ended up with?"

Varley clenched his fists, maybe reliving the moment when he lost his fiancée and her massive fortune, caught with his head under Emilia's skirts.

"If *you* hadn't broken it off with Emilia," Varley reminded him, "she wouldn't have set her cap at *me*. Despite knowing I was already engaged, she enticed me like a Greek siren."

Matthew was sure his expression mirrored Purity's, one of utter surprise.

"I cannot be blamed for your weakness, nor for Emilia's actions. You ought to have remained faithful to your fiancée if you truly cared about her."

"What do you know about fidelity?" Varley demanded.

Matthew was done talking.

"Get out!"

However, Purity was still behaving like a hostess whose party was souring and which she hoped to remedy.

"You and Lady Varley chose to marry one another. Surely, there must be some attraction that didn't perish because she cost you a different wife."

Matthew nodded, crossing his arms over his chest to keep himself from throwing punches.

"Maybe there is more to unify the two of you than your hatred of my husband," she suggested.

Varley stared at Purity, then back at him.

"I think Lady Foxford has a valid point," Matthew said.

Most of all, he wanted this war to end today, no longer needing to look over his shoulder, nor worry what might be in the newspapers. Varley had been dogging his tracks for the past three months—reporting or embellishing at will. Of that, Matthew was now certain.

For that matter, he no longer wished to dodge a glancing blow when Varley passed him in the sanctuary of their club.

"This conversation would have been better done without a lady present," Matthew added, certain she'd never heard the like before.

Come to think of it, he had never had such an odd discussion, trying to convince a man to be satisfied with the wife he had, even though she was probably disloyal, both root and branch.

When Purity bit her lip and appeared about to speak again, Matthew prayed she didn't spout some rule regarding kidnapping a lady that might set Varley off to more threats.

For while it was the case that most would believe Purity's version of events if they came to light, the *ton* would always cling to a shadow of a doubt regarding her faithfulness after she seemingly went to meet privately with a married man.

She ought to have known better.

Finally, Varley snatched up his hat.

"You are not worth my effort," he said to Matthew. "This lady will come to her senses and see you for what you are."

Matthew fisted his hands again but was loath to come to blows in front of his wife.

In any case, perhaps recalling their last altercation, Varley moved quickly to the door. But then he took the time to nod courteously at Purity, who gave him a friendly little wave of dismissal before he turned and left.

In a heartbeat, Matthew was on her, grabbing her upper arms and hauling her close.

"You idiot!" he said without heat, too relieved at finding her unharmed to be angry any longer. "Why did you come here willy-nilly?"

"Don't be ridiculous," she snapped, before putting her arms around his neck. "I did no such thing. I was lured here by the dire tidings that Diana needed me and that you were waiting."

He squeezed her tightly. "You came at my bidding?"

"Yes," she answered, sounding a little breathless as she went on tiptoe gaining a few inches.

"But Lady Purity, meeting in the middle of the day in an inn is inappropriate, indecorous, improper—do all dreary words start with the letter *I*?"

"They might," she said. "I haven't bothered to investigate."

With that, she slid her fingers into his hair.

"Are you trying to compromise me?" he asked.

"Yes. Is it working?" Her saucy smile made desire roar through his body.

For answer, he kicked the door closed behind him and lowered his mouth to hers. He had been frightened for her beyond reason, and now, he had trouble holding back and being gentle. He wanted to dive into her lushness, to stroke her tongue with his, to lower her onto the bed, and pleasure her until they were both mindless and breathless.

He would settle for an outstanding kiss, and by *settle*, he meant relish, worship, and cherish her with his mouth until he could do so again with his entire body when they went home.

Delving between her lips, he thrust his tongue into her mouth, growling when she caressed it with her own. Releasing her upper arms in order to cup her soft, rounded buttocks, he drew her up against him.

She growled a little in response, the sound reverberating in his mouth, making him want to drop to his knees and declare his utter devotion to this woman.

"I love you," he whispered against her mouth.

Freezing, she drew back and looked him in the eyes with her brilliant-blue gaze. Her direct stare.

"I love you, Purity Diamond, with all that I am."

"You love me?" she asked, rocking him back on his heels with her question.

"Of course!" *Didn't she love him? Was this a new concept to her?* "Why would you question me?"

"You never said it before," she remarked, astounding him further.

"I did," he promised. "I have told you more than once how I adore you."

"Adore is not love," she said softly.

"Isn't it? Is there a list of proper words for couples that I need to study, too?"

"Stop teasing," she said, her voice sounding thick with emotion. And he grew serious.

"You have been laboring under the misapprehension that I married you and have been tupping you nightly *without* loving you, is that correct?"

"I wasn't sure."

"You weren't sure," he repeated, shaking his head. "I hope you won't let Diana or any of our other children, should we be so blessed, marry with such uncertainty."

She shrugged, swallowed, sniffed, and then offered him a watery smile.

She was a priceless treasure, and he ought to have done better by her.

"I should have said those words before. In my defense, I truly thought that adoring and cherishing you were the same thing as loving you. But I will keep repeating 'I love you' until you believe me."

After a second, she offered him a short nod.

He chuckled. "Truly? Is that your entire response? Isn't there some rule of etiquette that demands you say something?"

She tilted her head. "I don't think there is a rule, but from my heart, I will tell you I have been afraid. I have tried not to let my fear overwhelm my true feelings."

"Which are?" He knew it was wrong, but he squeezed her bottom while he asked.

"Ooh!" She made a little squeal of surprise.

Then she reached out and stroked his cheek.

"That I love you, my Lord Fox, with all my heart."

His body relaxed, all tension draining from him, and taking his bones with it. Again, he felt like dropping to his knees. *She loved him!* He had never pushed her to say it but had hoped in time she would.

Taking her with him, he took the few steps to the bed and sank onto it, dragging her down beside him. But he ran his hand over his eyes, feeling overcome.

"Are you well?" she asked.

"I am, indeed. I am truly happy. I don't think I have ever felt this way before."

"That's absurd," she said, but she was grinning with pleasure.

"Naturally, I've been pleased, but usually because I was getting something I wanted, like fine brandy or a plum horse or . . ." He trailed off.

"Or a woman."

He sighed. "Yes. If I set my sights and got her, it was like winning. But this is different. This is utter, bone-deep contentment from loving you and finally knowing I have earned your love in return. And I predict this happiness will be long-lasting, don't you?"

"I do." She blinked and offered what he could only think of as a sensual smile. "You told Varley if we were alone—that is, you and *the goddess*, as you called me—in this very room, then you would have me in a clench, which we did as soon as the door closed. But I believe we are meant to be rolling on the bed if I recall correctly."

"How remiss of me." He pressed her down upon the counterpane.

"My hat," she said.

"I'm good with removing hats," he promised and then froze. *What an asinine thing to say!* Her active mind would be reminded of other women whose hat he'd removed.

However, she merely sighed.

"That's all right, then, my lord. I shall let you remove it for me."

Quickly but gently, he did, dropping the pins to the floor and sending the pretty pink hat gliding across the room.

"And your hair?"

"I still have to go out in public," she said. "Let's risk leaving my hairpins. If one of us gets pricked, I shall be to blame."

"I assure you, lady wife, you shall be pricked, but the blame will be mine."

"A double entendre," she said. "I am supposed to say I do not understand, but all I can think of is how glad I am that you are good with buttons, too."

Deftly, he undid the buttons down the back of her pale blue-and-white striped day dress. Each layer, he removed until—at last—she was entirely bare.

"You *are* a goddess!"

She shrugged slightly, which made her bounteous bosom rise and fall while a pretty flush spread up her chest and neck to her cheeks.

While she climbed onto the bed and drew her knees up to her chest to shield herself, giving him a delightful view of Carvel's ring and her sweet buttocks, he shed his clothing with the greatest haste.

"I do admire your long powerful legs," she said.

"I have something else that is long and powerful," he pointed out, unable to keep his arousal from stiffening like an oar, ready to guide his boat to the dock.

She giggled, a strange, enchanting sound from his Purity Foxford.

"Another double entendre, my lord."

He shrugged, joining her upon the bed. Utterly joyful, he wanted to laugh while making the most serious, ardent love at the same time.

All he could think to do, however, was kiss her. Rolling on top, settling himself between her thighs, which parted naturally for him, he took her face between his palms.

Her indigo-blue eyes stared up at him fearlessly. "How did you know I was here?"

"I was at Tattersall's looking at prize horseflesh when it occurred to me that my wife seemed unhappy. And I have made it my number one task to make you happy, so I came home to see what I could do. Jacobs met me with the note."

She nodded. "I'm ever so glad we're together. Here. Now."

"You came here for Diana and for me," he said wonderingly. "I love you."

"Kiss me," she demanded.

"I wouldn't continue if we weren't married. It would be a devilishly scandalous tryst."

"How chivalric," Purity said, digging her fingers into his shoulders and wriggling her hips under him, urging him to get on with it.

"Although I ought to halt anyway," he added, teasing her mercilessly. "Propriety and decency demand I stop at once and take you home to our marital bed."

"Propriety and decency be damned," she said, sinking her fingers into his hair and dragging his head down to her. "Besides, that is an imaginary rule."

Matthew claimed her lips, tilting his head and devouring her. As his tongue slipped into her mouth, he felt the magical moment when she surrendered.

"Mm," she moaned as he stroked her tongue.

Tracing a line of open-mouthed kisses down the slender column of her neck, he plucked one of her rosy nipples between his lips, swirling the tip of his tongue against it.

"I like that," she said with frankness.

He was glad she spoke. Previously when they swived, he guessed her likes and dislikes. He'd been storing away in his memory each time she gasped or moaned, intent on mastering the art of pleasing her.

After attending to her other lovely peak, he feathered a path with his tongue down her stomach, laying a teasing trail over her hip bones to their cradle, halting only to nuzzle the short soft thatch between her legs.

Purity gasped and lifted her hips. This was one thing he already knew she enjoyed immensely. Continuing to scorch a path over her heated skin, he noted the gooseflesh left in his wake as she hummed with pleasure.

Each time he had her naked, every inch of her was a new horizon to explore, her slender ankle needed to be stroked, the back of her knee was ripe for a kiss, the inside of each thigh was perfect for his tongue to tease.

When she was writhing, he couldn't deny either of them any longer.

Settling over her heated body, Matthew nestled between her thighs, fitting the tip of his shaft to her moist core.

"Yes, please," she said, with her usual politeness.

Instead of making him laugh, however, it further inflamed him.

Yes, please, indeed!

Slowly, carefully, he entered her, glad that she felt slippery already from his ministrations. Yet as he penetrated deeper, he braced himself on one forearm and slid his other hand between their bodies. With his thumb, he found the apex of her passion, the little nubbin that made her gasp and arch back.

This, he circled and stroked while sliding his arousal all the way inside her until he was solidly sheathed.

Holding on to his control by the thinnest of threads, he kissed her, feasting on the sweetest lips he could ever imagine. Then he lifted his head and smiled at her.

"Now," she whispered.

He wanted to reach under her, take her buttocks in his hands, and cradle her hips up against him so he could thrust deeply. But her release had to come first.

Continuing to caress her pearl with his thumb, he rose and surged into her again. A steady, time-perfected rhythm that had her trembling beneath him while sweat broke out between his shoulder blades.

From his position, he watched her face, beautiful and beloved, until she tilted back with closed eyes and her dark lashes feathering her cheeks. He saw the moment when the force of her pleasure swept her over the edge.

He knew she was soaring.

With her body clenching around him, he could wait no longer, driving into her and drawing out, his hips rocking at a galloping pace that had him joining her in a heady, breathless peak within seconds.

Her womanly channel was still rippling up and down his shaft when he spent inside her.

A few moments later, he felt the tension seep from her body. As she relaxed, so did he. With her eyes still closed, her kissable lips formed a wide smile.

Not wanting to crush her, Matthew collapsed to the side. A moment later, he covered them both with the counterpane as their skin chilled while the heat of their desire ebbed and cooled.

And then the door flew open.

CHAPTER THIRTY-ONE

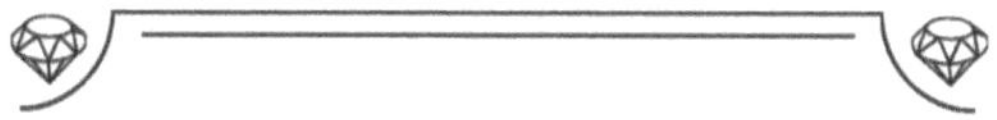

"*Ah-ha!* I have caught y—" The woman's voice broke off mid-triumph. "*Oh!*" Lady Varley added with surprise before stepping back and treading on the foot of another woman behind her, who exclaimed in pain.

Startled, Purity fervently wished her husband had taken the time to lock the door and not merely kick it closed. Regardless, she knew the best course of action was to remain calm. Before she could speak, Matthew was propped upon his elbow, talking to the woman as if they were meeting upon the street.

"Lady Varley, can my wife and I help you in some way? Otherwise, I must insist you turn around and take your maid with you."

Purity knew it wasn't a maid but the witness Lord Varley had mentioned.

"Where is my husband?" Lady Varley asked.

"I haven't the foggiest idea," Matthew said. "Perhaps he is at home, waiting for you. Have you tried looking for him there? For I assure you, he's not here. Why would you think he was?"

He didn't spare Purity a glance, trying to draw all the attention to himself, as if she wasn't truly there. Perhaps he hoped she would toss the counterpane over her head and hide, but it was too late for such modesty.

Lady Varley still looked shaken. Evidently, she had been expecting to find her husband. *Wanting* to find him, in fact, in their unhinged plan to punish Matthew.

Yet Lady Varley couldn't be driven to help her husband wreak vengeance because he'd lost his first fiancée. Thus, Purity decided her ladyship must be using Lord Varley to soothe her own jealous ire.

What a pair!

With a green-eyed gleam shining from her eyes, Lady Varley had recovered from her shock and swaggered into the room, hands on her hips. The truth dawned on Purity— the woman *still* wanted Matthew for her own.

"Foxy, Foxy, are you really going to settle for this insipid girl?" Lady Varley swished closer.

Behind her, her friend, whom Purity recognized as Lady Saunders, dithered in the doorway. Clearly, the scandal she was there to see had not materialized. Instead, she was merely intruding upon a newly married couple.

"I can see she has some appeal in a dewy, fresh way," Lady Varley continued, "but you're a man of experience and exotic tastes. In a fortnight, you'll be sniffing around some other bitch."

"I beg your pardon!" Purity said, sitting upright while clutching the bedclothes to her chest. "Such foul language is uncalled for. It is not only unladylike but demeans the speaker far more than the one of whom you speak. Yet it also offends the ears of anyone within hearing. Don't you agree, Lady Saunders?"

"Oh, well, I…" She trailed off and disappeared out of sight.

Purity directed her attention once more to Lady Varley. "Shame on you."

The woman gawked, clearly never having been ashamed of anything.

Even Matthew, who'd probably never been told to feel an ounce of shame either, turned his handsome head to stare at her.

Purity didn't care. Despite lying naked in bed, having recently been tricked by one man and being tupped by another, she believed deep down that proper manners and good behavior were the thread that held the cloth of society together.

Without such, all would be incomprehensible bedlam, a chaotic place in which she would rather not exist.

"As I understand the history between you and Lord Foxford," Purity continued, "you shared a fleeting affair, very brief, one which *you* didn't wish to end. But to your continued dissatisfaction, he broke it off. The fortnight before he went sniffing elsewhere was what happened to *you!*"

"I don't know that I was sniffing anywhere, my love," Matthew interjected.

Purity gave him a quelling stare and continued, "I shall not discuss my own history with my husband, but I think you ought to grow a spine of iron, face the facts plainly in front of you, and stop sniveling over Lord Foxford when you are married to Lord Varley. It is most unbecoming and, frankly, degrades the entire female sex. Have you considered that?"

Lady Varley's mouth opened once, then twice, before she snapped it closed.

Purity hoped she was reaching the woman's innate common sense.

"Why would you wish to debase yourself by chasing a man who doesn't want you? Or waste your energy hating him? Is he truly worth it?"

Again, Matthew made a small squawking sound of protest, but she elbowed him under the covers.

"You are an attractive woman, Lady Varley. You ought to be using your resources to build a good marriage. Don't you want children? They are a better legacy than bitterness, I would warrant."

While Purity half-feared Lady Varley would react badly, perhaps throw a fit of temper, instead, she remained silent.

In the next instant, she stared again at Matthew, seemingly studying him.

Luckily, he didn't utter a word.

Finally, Lady Varley shook her head and sighed.

"I wish you joy of him," she said to Purity, "although I am hard pressed to believe he will change from being a buck dangler to a rum husband overnight. But that will be your problem, not mine."

With that, she turned and swept from the room. Lady Saunders pulled the door closed before following her friend.

Matthew threw himself back onto the mattress. "My arse on a bandbox! I cannot believe what you just did."

"Lady Varley's friend had very nice manners, don't you think?" Purity mused. "I'm impressed how she stayed quiet throughout, didn't make eye contact to embarrass us, and courteously closed the door. What a gem!"

Matthew started to chuckle. Then he put his arm across his eyes and howled with laughter, his muscular body rocking.

"What is so amusing?" Purity began to feel the tug of annoyance. *Was he laughing at her?* She poked his shoulder.

Finally, he ceased braying like a donkey and reached for her. Wrapping his strong fingers around her arm, making her shiver at his touch, he pulled her down until she lay beside him again. Turning on his side, he rested on his elbow and looked down at her.

Foolishly, she felt a moment's embarrassment at what had occurred. She hadn't had even a second to contemplate having been caught in bed after swiving. Now, her cheeks bloomed with self-conscious warmth, and she made sure her breasts were covered—all under his mirthful gaze.

"Even at a time like this, you want everything done in a bread-and-butter fashion. You are priceless, my lady. Indeed, you are a—"

"Don't say it," she warned.

Matthew gasped. "You interrupted me," he pointed out. "How unspeakably rude!"

"And I would again," she said, "to stop you from calling me—"

"A Diamond of the first water," he finished.

She rolled her eyes but couldn't help smiling. The trite term sounded rather complimentary, not to mention downright sensual when Matthew said the words in his husky tone and then stroked her bare shoulder.

"Since you cannot be *un*compromised," he pointed out, leaning closer. That same finger now lightly trailed a path down her chest as far as he could before she tightened the counterpane and stopped its progress.

"And since the genie cannot be stuffed back inside the lamp, so to speak, meaning we are naked and alone, we might as well make use of this bed at least once more. After all, I imagine Varley has stuck me with the bill for the room."

Purity nearly denied him. Once could be forgiven as a passionate loss of one's better sense. But twice was premeditated and deliberate flaunting of what was considered all square.

Therefore, she put her hands up to ward him off. As soon as she touched his chest, however, instead of pushing him away, her fingers glided up and over his shoulders so she could draw him down to her.

He was right. Pandora's box was open. They had finally declared their love. They ran hotter than Hades for one another. There was no point in pretending otherwise.

SOMETHING HAD BEEN bothering Matthew from the moment he'd entered the room. And now, as his lovely wife tugged on her gloves after pinning her adorable hat, Matthew knew what it was.

"Why weren't you wearing your gloves when I came in? I have never seen you in that state of undress in public unless dining."

"I removed them just in case," she said, giving the front of her skirts a last smoothing stroke.

"In case of what?" he asked.

"In case I needed to defend myself."

"I know that your slap is more efficient without your glove's impediment, but it would hardly have stopped Varley if he'd intended you any real harm."

"I removed my gloves to uncover my fingernails," she said.

He smiled. "I was correct from the start. You *are* a kitten, and you unsheathed your claws. I am glad indeed you didn't have to defend yourself."

"I have other methods," she promised, then lifted one knee to demonstrate. "The skirt doesn't make it easy, but I would have managed if I'd had to."

His eyes widened. "I have no doubt you would have. A good thing Varley wasn't the violent type, but I shall be glad to know I have you to protect me should I ever need it."

He almost wished she'd unleashed her claws and her knee. After all, Varley had once said Purity was a prim mouse. After swiving on their wedding night, he'd already known she was a wildcat in bed. Now, he knew she was also a fierce lioness, ready to defend herself should the need arise.

More importantly, they had weathered a potential scandal together. With any luck, the Varleys would recede into the distance, never to bother them again.

When they walked through the front door, Diana was the first to greet them with an embrace. Then as usual, a string of questions came at them like a barrage of soldier's bullets.

"Where were you? Isn't it a pretty day? May we go to the park later? Did you bring me anything?"

"How are the kittens?" Matthew found any talk of them usually distracted her.

Sure enough, as he handed Mr. Jacobs his hat and gloves, Diana prattled on about every detail of Miss Soft and Miss

Wriggles, who had been forced to keep the incorrect designation because as she explained it, "Kitties are girls and dogs are boys, Papa."

Despite having some correspondence to get to, he found he didn't want to leave his family. Such a pleasant word—*family*. He was close to being ready to make the trip up north to introduce his two ladies, as he thought of them, to the rest of his relations.

Knowing he had Purity's heart made his own soar like a falcon, and he wanted everyone to meet the wife who thought him worthy of her love.

And then, he was struck speechless.

Over the fireplace, an unremarkable landscape painting he'd picked up at a Christie and Manson's auction had hung. Now, in its place was the portrait of his father, which he had last seen when he was a boy.

Wordlessly, he looked at Purity who took his arm and held it tightly. Diana was on his other side, staring at the strange man, so very familiar to Matthew.

"How?" he asked finally.

"Who is he?" Diana asked.

"That's your papa's father," Purity answered. "Your grandfather. A handsome man, indeed."

"And a dog," Diana added. "Can we have a dog?"

"No, dear one," Purity answered. "I believe Cook has a snack for you waiting. She was making currant rolls early this morning."

And Diana ran off as his wife knew she would, leaving them alone. Matthew had tears in his eyes and couldn't blink for fear they would spill.

"Are you pleased?" Purity asked, leaning her head on his upper arm and examining the painting alongside him.

Matthew sniffed. After a few moments, he said, "I hadn't forgotten what my father looked like, but the details had blurred over the years. Seeing this, I'm pleased to say he is how my memory informed me." He chuckled. "And that dog!"

Purity laughed. "Is that the one which bit your ear?"

"I believe so. Father said it was always underfoot, but he adored it. I thought it had the most doleful eyes and softest fur," he added. "Not to mention the sharpest teeth."

"Thank goodness it wasn't a sheepdog," she said. "You might have lost your entire ear."

What a gift Purity had given him! He turned to wrap her in his arms.

"I cannot believe the painting is here. The best gift I expected from my wife was my favorite French cologne. How did you manage this?"

She shrugged slightly, but he could tell she was bubbling to tell him.

"As a new bride should, I wrote to my mother-in-law after the wedding."

"I didn't know you had made contact," he said with a frown. "But I think I should have been the one to do that."

She shook her head. "For new circumstances, I consult an etiquette book, such as *A Guide to the Usages of Society*, or sometimes an earlier work. I've read *Il Libro del Cortegiano* for amusement only, of course. Many customs have changed since 1528."

"Have they?" he asked, thinking his wife a most remarkable woman. "I suppose you read it in its original Italian."

"Naturally," she said without the least pretension. "In all the modern guides, authors agree that a daughter-in-law should show respect to her new family by introducing herself, so I did. Your mother was welcoming in her letters and happy for both of us. She has invited us to go there and stay. I know you've put it off, but I hope you will consider it soon."

He spoke from his heart. "I cannot wait to show you off. But you didn't explain about the painting. Last I saw it, it was in our country home in Surrey, but my mother cleared it out and sold off everything she could to bring money to her new husband."

"After her first warm letter to me," Purity continued, "when you mentioned not having anything of your father's, I recalled the painting and wrote to her again. She had it stored in their attic in Edinburgh, and I asked her to send it at once."

Matthew shook his head and glanced at it again. "It is as though you have returned him to me."

"I wish I could. Your mother has other things put aside for you. A signet ring, a snuff box, some handkerchiefs, and more. We shall bring it all back here. Maybe we'll have a son one day to whom you shall pass your father's things."

He took her face in his palms. "If we do, I shall be grateful. Yet if we never have anything more than we have right now, I shall consider myself bountifully blessed. In a pragmatic way, I thought it was time to get a wife." He brushed his hand over her beautiful hair, still a little mussed from their tempestuous afternoon.

"I never knew in doing so, I would get back the decent part of me who is my father's son. You have done a monstrous good job of civilizing me, kitten."

Her cheeks pinkened.

Suddenly, Matthew startled. "We met in front of a painting."

"We first kissed in front of a painting, too," she agreed.

He grinned.

"Kiss me," she said.

And he did.

EPILOGUE

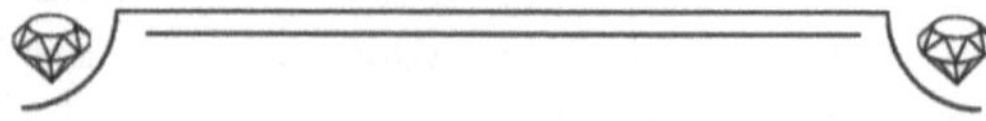

Scotland, 1848

"Are we there yet?" Diana asked for the hundredth time. Or it felt that way at any rate, ever since they'd passed under the grand columns of the Euston Arch nine hours earlier and strolled toward the train that would take them all the way to Edinburgh.

Inside London's Euston Station, Diana had held tightly to Purity's hand while looking up at the massive wrought-iron roof arching overhead. The little girl had been eager for the adventure.

As a family, with Nanny Caldwell, the four of them wandered along one of the two 420-foot-long platforms until a porter directed them to their first-class carriage compartment, which comfortably held six.

Purity couldn't have imagined how the thickly padded seats, clean carpet, and real glass windows with curtains would become a wretchedly detested jail cell after riding within the paneled interior for so long.

On top of the tedium, noise, and jerking motion of the train, it seemed no sooner had they left the city behind than Diana had started to ask that dreadful question, through Camden, Boxmoor, Aylesbury Junction, Rugby, Coventry, and Birmingham, where they got out and stretched their legs. At that point, they weren't even halfway there.

"Darling," Purity said, gritting her teeth because the incessant enquiry was driving her mad, "Papa told you it was 390 miles or thereabouts when we started. That's a very long way, isn't it?"

The little girl nodded. "Yes, Mama."

Purity still felt that word like a gentle squeeze to her heart every time Diana said it. It had been only a couple weeks ago that the little girl had come up to her and taken her hand while wearing a serious expression.

She had tugged Purity down so they could speak face-to-face.

"Pretty lady," as she had called her since they met, "Miss Soft and Miss Wriggles wonder if they can call you 'Mama.'" Her brown eyes had stared unblinkingly.

Purity recalled how her breath had hitched.

"Yes, darling one," she had said at once and wrapped Diana in an embrace.

With her voice muffled against Purity's shoulder, the girl had added, "I could call you that, too, if you wish."

"Yes!" Purity had answered. "All three of you, please."

And now they were on their way to Scotland to visit with Matthew's mother and stepfather, his full sister, who'd been a newborn at the time of Baron Foxford's untimely death, as well as his two half-brothers.

"Will we be there soon?" Diana asked.

Purity shot a wide-eyed glance at her husband seated facing backward across from them.

"At least she asked it differently," he quipped. Then he looked at his daughter, who despite asking questions, was staring out the window of the train carriage past Purity's shoulder. "Are you asking once a mile, do you suppose?"

Diana laughed. "Papa, how would I know?"

"I don't know either, but I believe you've asked about three-hundred and sixty times, so we shall be there in about another forty questions."

Diana giggled. Even Purity chuckled, although she had a few butterflies in her stomach, adding more as they grew closer. It was something important to meet a man's mother. *What female would ever measure up and not be found lacking?*

She knew her own mother was going to scrutinize Adam's fiancée if and when she got the chance. *What young lady would be good enough for the heir to the Diamond earldom?* Purity couldn't imagine, but she would be pleased to find out.

On the other hand, she was already Matthew's wife, so she wasn't seeking permission or even approval, so much as acceptance. If his mother's letters were any indication, they would mix like sugar into hot tea. Very well indeed!

"I hope the kittens aren't crying," Diana said, another remark she'd already made a dozen times.

"Miss Soft and Miss Wriggles will be fine until our return. They would want you to have a monstrous good time," Matthew said. "When I was a boy, this trip would have taken days by coach, and even earlier this year, we would have had to change trains and go by coach for part of the way. Or if we went up via Newcastle upon Tyne, we would have had to cross the River Tweed and the River Tyne. The ferry is crowded, and delays are inevitable."

Diana yawned.

Purity smiled. Diana might be unimpressed by the fact they could get to Edinburgh in a very long day on a single train, but she was astonished.

"I wonder what the world will be like when you are my age," Purity remarked.

"In another fifty years?" the little girl asked.

Fifty years! Purity frowned, causing Matthew to laugh.

"Mrs. Caldwell," he said, waking up the nanny who slept sitting up but leaning against the other side of the carriage. With a snort, she roused and blinked at them.

"Yes, my lord."

"Would you read with Diana, please? Or maybe you could point out some sights."

"Sights, my lord?"

"Anything out the window on *that* side of the compartment."

Diana complied, slipping off her shoes and standing on the plush seat in her stockinged feet so she could look outside.

"Well, done, Lord Fox," Purity said as he rose to his feet, stretched, and then took the seat beside her.

"I thought that was a good idea. Now I can sit by my beautiful wife and hold her hand while making money at the same time."

Purity let pass her husband's mild reference to his railroad investments. She didn't want to give him a big head since he already knew how proud she was of his business sense. He had helped fund the main line of the Caledonian the year before to massive success, and the section of rail they needed from Carstairs to Edinburgh had only opened in April.

Perfect timing as far as she was concerned. All in all, the share capital of the early investors was valued at about two million pounds, and Matthew had a healthy amount of it.

"They will let us disembark at Carstairs, won't they? To stretch and get some air."

"Yes," he said. "If they don't, we'll do so anyway and take a coach the rest of the way."

She shook her head. "That's even smaller and far more uncomfortable, not to mention slower."

"You are correct. We'll stay in this blasted carriage all the way to John O'Groats if we have to."

"Absolutely not! A minute longer than Edinburgh and I vow I shall scream. The infernal racquet is getting to me, and I do not mean Diana."

"Our ears shall rattle for hours afterward," he agreed.

She decided to change the subject since he'd become ever quieter the closer they got to Edinburgh.

"Are you excited to see your family?"

"*You* are my family," he said. "And that annoying little person over there, too."

"Yes, and you are mine, but I also love my parents and sisters and brother, too. And now I shall get to meet yours and see how much they look like you. It's most exciting."

"They will all love you, I'm sure."

"I don't know many Scots," she continued. "But I hear they can be a little rougher than us. I vow I shall not point out anything lacking in their manners. I only hope I can understand their accents."

"Be yourself, and if you get into any trouble, I shall translate."

A FEW HOURS LATER, PURITY was dozing when she heard Matthew softly say, "I didn't expect that."

Rousing herself, she looked around to get her bearings. Diana and Mrs. Caldwell slumbered together, but her husband wasn't looking at them. He was gazing out the window beside him.

She saw a family—*his* family—gathered in the lamplight upon the single platform at Lothian Road Station as the train pulled in.

"I honestly didn't think they would be so interested. And at this ungodly hour, I imagined they would merely send a wagon."

"You are the prodigal son returning," Purity reminded him.

His gaze shot to hers. "That makes me a little queasy. When I left, I didn't just amble, I ran, so eager was I to get away. With a stepfather I didn't want and my mother having her new children." He shrugged and added, "I didn't belong."

"They are your kin," she reminded him, touching his knee.

He captured it under his gloved hand.

"I was lonely until I met you, kitten, and I must confess I didn't behave particularly well." He paused as the steam engine pulling their carriage came to a halt.

"What I'm trying to say, wife, is thank you. I would not have come back here without you, not yet, maybe never. Because it was your gentle tutelage that turned 'the Fox' into the respectable Lord Foxford. I'm proud to see my family again and to let them know the man I have become. Even more so to introduce you and Diana. I simply could not be happier."

He leaned over and kissed her as Mrs. Caldwell and Diana stirred and stretched.

"Nor I, my lord," Purity vowed. Then she sighed and teased him. "After all, your name has not been mentioned even once in an entire month in any of the newspapers."

He grinned.

"Are we there yet?" Diana asked.

Purity looked at her husband before answering. "Yes, dear one, we have arrived."

London, December 1848

VAST CROWDS WERE GATHERED on The Mall. Matthew had insisted Purity brave the evening chill to join them and see a spectacle that promised to change the world. Unlike the rabble, however, standing on the cold gas-lit streets of St. James's, looking up with anticipation, they were seated in his cozy curricle.

A French inventor who had managed to light the rear of a train the month prior at Paddington Station wanted to do something special in the heart of London. All the more people could be impressed by his invention—electric light!

To that end, Monsieur Le Mott climbed one hundred feet above The Mall and stationed his electric lamp, running on batteries, upon a balcony that encircled the feet of the Grand Old Duke of York monument.

With the hood up, warming bricks all around their feet, Matthew and Purity snuggled under a thick Scottish wool blanket, a gift from his mother. Still, he worried he'd been selfish.

"For your comfort, we should have brought the brougham," he said.

Afterward, they were going to a dinner party at the Fenwicks', and his lovely wife was dressed to impress. Her midnight hair was only visible where the pearls threaded through it glowed like little moons in the lamplight, but her pale face was clear as were her soft, pink, kissable lips.

"Nonsense," she said. "Then we wouldn't have this unencumbered view and our poor driver would have to sit outside in the cold instead of us."

Matthew chuckled. "He's probably here, anyway. I heard Mr. Jacobs say most of the staff intended to come. At least, those who hadn't made the demonstration at the National Gallery."

Two weeks earlier, a rival inventor had set up his electric lamp on the steps of the gallery and set the recently opened Trafalgar Square ablaze in brilliant light. Matthew and Purity had attended that demonstration and taken Diana, although they'd had to awaken her at the correct time.

As fun as it was to be elbowed repeatedly by their little girl who barely recalled the awe-inspiring event a week later, Matthew had decided tonight would be a romantic moment for only the two of them. And then they nearly missed it.

"Kiss me," she said as she often did, and he happily obliged.

As their lips met, a roar went up from the crowd, but they didn't stop, delving into each other with a hunger that had not diminished since the first time they'd met.

Finally, he pulled back, and they both opened their eyes.

"Oh, my," she said. "Astounding."

"It is astounding," he agreed, hardly able to believe how clearly he could see her sable hair, clever brow, and even the deep blue of her sparkling eyes.

"I meant our kiss," she said, making him smile.

"So did I," he agreed.

Around them, people were still exclaiming. A bright halo shone from the top of the monument, making the area circling it as bright as daylight. Matthew could even see the colors of people's clothing yards away.

"The gas lamps are as nothing in comparison," Purity said.

"I cannot imagine these electric lamps everywhere," Matthew said. "It would be like harnessing small suns. Why, I can't even look at it for more than a few moments. I'm seeing spots."

"I as well, and you may be correct." She sighed. "Perhaps these electric lamps will never be popular. I, for one, should not wish to spend my evenings squinting to avoid being blinded. But it was worth seeing. Aren't people wonderful?" she added. "Always advancing their knowledge, even if it's not practical."

"You, in particular, are wonderful," Matthew said. "Shall we go?"

With a flick of the reins, they left the gawkers and the enthusiasts behind, but not the electric lamp. For it was all the talk—along with a debate over its brilliance versus the diffusive light of a gas lamp—at the Fenwicks' home for most of the evening.

Over breakfast the following morning, Matthew was delighted to see a description of the previous evening's event in *The Times*, which he no longer minded reading since mention of "the Fox" had all but vanished.

"Kitten, you have made it into the newspaper."

Purity dropped her fork with a clatter. "No!"

He nodded. "Let me read it to you. 'The potency and *purity* of the electric light may be inferred from the circumstance that—'"

Matthew didn't get to finish for a piece of buttered toast hit him squarely in the head, bouncing off onto the table. He could only stare at his wife in utter shock.

Diana, who'd been singing to herself while eating porridge, shrieked with glee.

"Mama!" she exclaimed.

His wife had been giving their little girl the earliest lessons on good behavior, so it was no surprise when Diana added, "That's not proper!"

Purity wiped her fingers upon her napkin and shrugged delicately.

"Sometimes, dear daughter, one must break the rules." And then she continued most fastidiously eating her coddled eggs.

Finis

ABOUT THE AUTHOR

USA Today bestselling author Sydney Jane Baily writes historical romance set in Victorian England, late 19th-century America, the Middle Ages, the Georgian era, and the Regency period. She believes in happily-ever-after stories with engaging characters and attention to period detail.

Born and raised in California, she has traveled the world, spending a lot of exceedingly happy time in the U.K. where her extended family resides, eating fish and chips, drinking shandy, and snacking on Maltesers and Cadbury bars. Sydney currently lives in New England with her family—human, canine, and feline.

At her website, SydneyJaneBaily.com, you can learn more about her books, sign up for her newsletter (and get a free book), and contact her. She loves to hear from her readers.

www.ingramcontent.com/pod-product-compliance
Lightning Source LLC
Chambersburg PA
CBHW060653190726
48289CB00002B/391